Wormwood

G. P. Taylor has spent his whole life searching for the hidden secrets of the universe. He lectures on the paranormal and folklore and lives in a secluded graveyard. He can be contacted at www.shadowmancer.com

Wormwood

G. P. Taylor

faber and faber

First published in 2004
by Faber and Faber Limited
3 Queen Square London WC1N 3AU

Typeset by Faber and Faber
Printed in England by Mackays of Chatham plc, Chatham, Kent

A CIP record for this book
is available from the British Library

ISBN 0–571–22150–5

2 4 6 8 10 9 7 5 3 1

*To JC & KST you have beaten back the Black Dog
and filled my life with your light.*

1 : Wormwood

From the top-floor window of his large four-storey house on Bloomsbury Square Dr Sabian Blake could see the farthest depths of space. He stared out into the night sky through the thick lens of his long brass telescope. He had watched the skies for the past week, and he was waiting – waiting for the sign that he knew would come that night. The strange glow to the north had grown stronger and brighter, causing the stars to fade and never allowing the night to be truly dark. The full moon had burned blood red, lighting the streets with a warm crimson glow as bright as the sun.

Blake was an astronomer, doctor, scientist and a master of the Cabala. Every hour of every day was spent working out the times of the rising of the sun and the waning of the stars. He measured the phases of the moon as it crossed the sky and when Betelgeuse set beyond the horizon. Blake turned the minute-glass as the sand timer spilled its soft white particles from one orb to the other, and on the fifty-ninth count he took great pride in waiting until the final grains of sand had trickled from the top chamber before carefully turning the large hour-glass. Its dark wood was decorated with serpent columns whose jewel eyes, gold teeth and carved scales shimmered in the moonlight. Blake checked each sand hour against the old brass clock that ticked and tocked laboriously next to the astrolabe on the ornate stone mantel of the empty fireplace.

Blake did Cabalistic calculations all night, every night, dusk till dawn, from the moon's rising till setting. From his computations he knew that somewhere in the Twelfth House of the universe a sign would be given. The Nemorensis said so. The Nemorensis never lied; it was the only book to be trusted. To touch the Nemorensis was to hold the secrets of the cosmos in your hands. No one knew where the book had come from, but many had died trying to find its secrets.

Now the Book of Nemorensis belonged to Blake. It was his by right, divine right as he often thought to himself. As he looked into deep space and nervously bit his lip, he thought of the morning of the Feast of St Quirtle when, shortly after dawn, he had opened the parcel that a coachman had delivered to his door.

From the outset Blake had been suspicious of the coachman, because he had never seen anyone who claimed such a low estate to be dressed so well. There was no hint of shabbiness. His neat black coat and clean boots spoke of Highgate, not of the Rotherhithe ruffians who usually plied their trade in London town. His pure white skin held no trace of hard labour, no trace of the London grime from horse muck and carriage grease. He had no discernible accent other than the powdered softness of a Lincoln's Inn dandy. What had intrigued Blake about the man was the gold ring he wore on the middle finger of his right hand. It had a large red stone set in a gold mount cut into the shape of the sun. From one side a flaming trail formed the thick gold band that encircled his finger. Messenger the man was, coachman he was not!

Blake didn't care. His eyes had immediately been enticed by the shape and contours of the gift he was being offered. This was an epiphany, a gift to a wise man – a wise man lured by a passion that he could feel rising from the soles of his feet and turning his stomach. It was an exquisite feeling, exciting and dangerous. Deep inside, Blake knew that the gift he was about to open would have life-changing possibilities. He almost choked with excitement as he tried to contain the sudden rush that swept over his body like a spring tide. It was as if the book spoke to him soul to soul, churning his heart and fevering his brow.

The package had been tightly wrapped in a gold silk cloth and tied with red cotton braid, a colour so bright and vivid that it shimmered and looked fluid. There was nothing to say who had sent such a fine gift and the coachman had, when questioned, been vague as to how it had come into his possession and who had told him to deliver it.

'A man just stopped me in the street,' he had said softly, avoiding contact with Blake's strong gaze and keeping the brim of his hat low over his eyes. 'He waved his arms about like a madman, nearly frightened the horses to death. Foreign man, could hardly speak a word of the King's tongue. French or Spanish. Could even have been from Persia. Never seen one that looked like him before.' The coachman sniffed and snorted a large dribble of mucus back up his nose. 'All he kept saying was Number 6, Bloomsbury Square. He gave me the package, Doctor Blake, pressed a guinea coin in my hand, and then turned and ran.'

Blake questioned him further. 'You know my name. Did the man tell you?'

'Everyone knows you, Doctor Blake. You are a man of letters,' the coachman smiled. 'In fact, I can now say that you are now a man of parcels!' At that he laughed, handed over the heavy gift, and walked promptly to the carriage. Blake watched as he picked his way through the filth and puddles, jumped on to the driving seat and slowly drove the horse and carriage up the muddy road of Bloomsbury Square.

Without hesitation, Blake tore at the parcel, unable to wait until he got inside. He sat on the white marble steps and quickly pulled open the silk wrapping. It was then that he first looked upon the Nemorensis: a book so splendid in appearance that it caused his heart to beat faster. The thick leather cover was encrusted in gold leaf; the tatty pages were etched in sharp black that had faded with the years, scratched in small letters. He had never thought he would ever hold the Nemorensis, he had even doubted if it really existed. Now he knew – now it was his!

Late one night, several weeks afterwards, Blake was leafing through the crusty old book with its thick parchment pages, trying to glean every piece of knowledge; and there in the sixth chapter of the sixth book, on the final page, written by an unknown hand in the margin, he read the words: *Wormwood . . . the bright star shall fall from the sky . . . and many will die from its bitterness.*

From that day he had searched every corner of the heavens looking for the new star, convinced that this would be the sign that a new age was about to begin, a golden dawn to enlighten small, feeble human minds. The illumination of the world was drawing near and he would be the first to see it, the first to tell the world.

Blake sipped a cup of hot tea and smiled to himself. He looked again through the lens of the telescope that rested on its fine oak tripod. The stars and planets remained the same, the universe was unaltered, in a few hours the night would be over and nothing would have changed. He stamped angrily on the wooden floorboards. 'Blast, bother and gibbor. Will it ever come?' he asked himself impatiently, his words echoing around the empty room. He began to doubt his calculations and wondered whether by some chance he had predicted the wrong day, week, or even year. He looked again and more anxiously into the night, hoping against hope that somewhere in a far-off galaxy a new light had appeared.

It was midnight; far in the distance he heard the sound of St George's church clock chiming out the hour. Suddenly the house began to vibrate and shudder. The whole world lurched forwards, then backwards, and then spun even faster. Blake heard a looking-glass drop from the wall of the downstairs room and smash to pieces. Tiles cascaded from the roof to drop the four storeys, smashing like leaves of baked clay in the road below. Plaster fell from the ceiling as the walls shook angrily, cracking the wooden doorframe and firing exploding shards of horsehair and limewash at him from all directions. At any moment he thought the house would fall to the ground.

In an instant the stars vanished. Without warning the sun rose, then set; night became morning, then night again, time and time again. Eleven suns came, followed by eleven moons, rising and setting from east to west. There was no chance to scream or cry out, no way to understand what was happening. Blake held fast to the telescope and tripod, hoping that each jolt would be the last, hoping that each dawn would not blast into daylight then into night – hoping that whatever was now striking the world would stop.

Then there was blackness – a still, sharp blackness surrounded by complete silence. There was no more day and no more night. There was utter emptiness, as if the world was over and the universe had imploded, sucked into some vast dark hole in space. Blake stared through the eyepiece but saw nothing. There was not even the smallest glimmer of light.

It was then that Blake became aware of the clamour and panic in the street. He could hear the screams from below as

5

men and women grappled in the darkness, hanging on to the iron railings of the newly-built gardens. Blake could not see the window. In the blackness he traced his hand along the metal of the telescope. Now there was nothing. He turned away from the telescope and edged the three feet across the room to where he knew the open window would be. The blackness was so deep, so intense, that it almost smothered and choked him. His feet tangled in the long belt cord of the thick, red dressing gown that he wore over his clothes to keep out the cold. It was cheaper than a fire or a warming pan, but now in the darkness he regretted his meanness and longed for even the faintest glimmer of firelight.

He fumbled his way to the window and looked to the other side of the square. His eyes were quickly drawn to the only source of light in the street, the soft candlelight from an upper-floor room in a house across the gardens. A solitary figure looked back into the darkness. This was the only light he could see, possibly the only light in the world.

In the street he could hear the cry of frightened horses stomping in the mud, their hooves nervously cracking against the stones. Far below him there was intense panic, as the inn on the corner spilled out terrified revellers into the night to grovel like so many blind mice squealing and screaming in the unending blackness.

In the darkness of his room Blake waited, but for what and for how long he didn't know. He listened to the noise from the street and wondered what to do next. Somewhere across the room was the door to the stair. Outside in the long hallway he knew a candle burnt. He stumbled across the room like a blind beggar. As he fell to the wooden floor, splinters from the newly sawn wood sliced into the palms of his hands. The only way he could know that the street was to his right was the sound of the chaos rising from there. He was a man of science, a seeker of the truth, but now even his immense knowledge failed him. For the first time in his life Blake realised that he was like the rest of the world . . . helpless.

From across the city he could hear the screaming growing louder and louder as the blind riot filled the streets. Pistol shots rang out as the militia fired recklessly into the darkness, aiming at the sound of people shouting. The whole world seemed to be on the verge of madness. He could hear people wailing, covered by the black hand of sightlessness.

Then, without any warning, a blinding flash filled the sky. Far to the east a shaft of pure white light penetrated the atmosphere. No one could escape its brightness as it cut across the heavens like a lightning bolt. London fell silent; the whole town waited. In his room, Blake managed to get to his feet and take hold of the telescope. Finding the eye-piece, he looked to the skies. The shaft of light came again, and again, flashing brighter and brighter, piercing the darkness.

Blake saw through the telescope what he had been waiting for. High in the northeast at the crown of heaven he could see a star, but this was no ordinary star – it was a sky dragon. A comet of such proportions the world had never seen before. Blake could clearly see a long white tail that streamed far behind the bright luminous head. He knew that it was far away, but something inside made him feel uneasy. Outlined against the deep black of silent space he could see that the horns of the dragon were pointed towards him. He stopped and looked away. He couldn't believe what he was seeing, couldn't believe what he was thinking.

'If it were true, if it could be believed . . .' he wondered aloud as he rubbed his face nervously with his hands. 'It can't be, I deceive myself,' he said in a strong voice, hoping to bolster himself against the rising panic that now gripped his feet and crawled up to his knees. 'The comet is coming towards the earth,' he muttered in disbelief. 'The dragon is coming home!'

In the east the sun began slowly to rise. It was a quarter past midnight but the dawn had come. Blake chuckled to himself and shook his head. Outside, the madness had ceased; the crowds that had gathered in the street looked to the sky. They ignored the injured and the dying, and the fires that burnt in tucked-away houses. Everyone looked up at the rising sun, which burnt bright against the fading black sky.

Blake could not contain himself and had the urge to shout the news of his discovery from the window to the gathering below. He danced around the room, banging and clattering on the bare wood floorboards and swirling his thick red dressing gown backwards and forwards like a pantomime dame. He danced and he laughed and he sang out loud: '*Wormwood! Wormwood! Wormwood!*' As he swirled he tripped and fell to the floor, wrapping himself tighter in his robe and laughing as he rolled around like some peculiar stuffed sausage. In the looking-glassed ceiling of the room he saw himself criss-crossed by shadows from the leaded pane of the window. He wanted to laugh until he was fit to burst – tears rolled down his face as his belly ripped and roared with laughter that echoed against each wall, then faded as it escaped the open window at the front of the house. Only he could see the comet; it was Blake's Comet, the bringer of his new age.

From the street below he could hear joyous shouting. People were spilling from their houses, and the stunned revellers from the tavern dragged their muddy forms from the ground where they had clung with fear and wrapped soiled arms around each other in relief that the earthquake and sky-storm were over. Blake got up and rushed to the window, where he joined in with the cheering, stripping off his dressing gown and waving it like the flag of some victorious state. 'Three cheers for the

King, may his madness bring joy to us all!' he screamed at the top of his voice.

Then Blake became aware that a sudden and deep silence had descended. The crowd had stopped looking at the sky, people were now staring to the open ground of Holborn and the fields that surrounded Lincoln's Inn. Far in the distance was the clatter of hooves banging against earth and stone; it was the growing fever of frightened horses. The beasts that had been left in the square quickly joined in, as if summoned by some unspoken call, kicking out at those who stood by, knocking one man from his feet with a blow to his spine that dropped him dead to the ground.

Echoing from Holborn came the sound of the horses approaching, neighing and snorting as they stampeded through the streets. Some still dragged the tattered and torn remains of the once fine carriages that they had pulled. Others ran free of rein or carriage rod as they kicked and bucked, as if to rid themselves of the unseen force that snapped and bit at their fetlocks. The stampede filled the street and moved through the gathered crowd on Holborn fields like a cavalry charge, cutting down all those that stood in its way, filling the roadway from railings to railings. They scattered into the narrow streets on the edge of Bloomsbury and ran at full speed through the narrow alleyways that cut through the neatly finished houses. Over a hundred horses turned into the square – grey, black and bay, once benign equines now transformed by fear, running for their lives.

Blake looked down from the window; he could offer no help. He shouted to the crowd but the noise of the horses drowned his words, and he banged his fists in despair against the window ledge. Below him people stood frozen, transfixed by the horses that bore down on them like a tidal wave. Within seconds the stampede engulfed all those who stood in its path.

Their victims made very little noise – no shouts of fear, no time to run. All that was left in the wake of the maelstrom was the broken flotsam of human bodies, a jetsam of cadavers washed up by a living tide. The only survivors were those who had clung to the railings, hidden in doorways or jumped into the basements of the tall row of newly built houses that overlooked the square. There they cowered in fear like so many rats packed into a barrel.

The reason for the horses' fear quickly became apparent. Chasing the horses into Bloomsbury Square came a surge of a thousand dogs that appeared to spill from the alleyways, runnels and every corner of London. The air was filled with barking and snarling as they bit and snapped at everything in their path, controlled by a power beyond reason.

The panic was intense, palpable and beyond imagination. Children who had come into the street to see the spectacular sky now screamed as the pack scented out their victims. Everyone ran, scrambled up trees, jumped over fences or climbed the stonework of houses to get out of the reach of the hounds. Street dogs, fine spaniels of rich men, deck hounds from river barges and preened lap dogs ran together, roused by some atavistic hunger.

Blake looked on as a young boy scampered the length of Bloomsbury Square. He was no more than twelve years old; his shoeless feet carried him quickly over the mud, chased by several dogs that snapped at his heels and coat tails. He screamed as he ran. To his right and lying helpless on the floor was an old woman. She was surrounded by a pack of dogs that grabbed at her arms and legs and pulled her across the ground like a rag doll. She made no sound, no resistance; the life had ebbed from her body moments before. The boy lunged for the low branch of a tree and, reaching out at full stretch, took hold and swung from the ground just as a large black mongrel jumped forward with bared teeth, trying to sink them into his flesh. Chaos covered the whole square as the dogs split into smaller packs to chase their victims into Gallon Place and Coptic Street. It seemed as if the whole of London was filled with the cries of people being savaged.

There was a sudden and loud banging on the door of Blake's house. The large brass tapping-handle was smashed repeatedly against the door plate, echoing through the hallway and up the circular staircase to the observation room. Blake looked out below. There in the street was Isaac Bonham, friend and Fellow of the Royal Society. He shouted loudly as he banged the door and tried to shake off a small brown deck hound that was gripping his leg.

'Blake, in the name of Hermes let me in!' he cried, the pain of the bite tinging his voice. 'Blake, shoot the thing! Let me in, do something!'

The dog let out a loud squeal as he kicked it against the iron railing of the house. But then three large mastiffs slowly walked into the square. They were wheezing and breathless, their mouths stained with fresh blood. They looked at Bonham, and even from such a distance they could smell his fear. Blake saw the creatures and realised that his friend was in great danger. He ran to the door, knowing he would have to move faster than the dogs if he were to save his friend. Down and down he ran, round and round, along each landing, his heart pounding in his chest.

Outside, the mastiffs stared at Bonham for several moments and then set off, covering the ground towards him a yard at a time. They slavered and growled as they ran, baring their large stained teeth, getting closer by the second.

Bonham screamed as he watched the dogs pounding down on him. He felt like a cornered fox about to be torn apart, ripped and eaten. 'Quickly man, let me in!'

Blake stumbled over his feet, fell one length of the stairs and crumpled on the landing of the first floor. He got up and ran again. 'Bonham, look out man, I'm here!' he shouted. He knew that he had one more flight and then the length of the hall before he got to the front door. And then panic hit him: *the key, where was the key?*

Outside, Bonham watched as the mastiffs pounded the mud with their paws, racing each other, their speed increasing with the prospect of a kill. He braced himself for what was to come. He squared his back against the door and drew a small flintlock pistol from his belt, knowing he would have only one shot, knowing he could not kill all three creatures. With both hands he aimed the gun at the hounds. Relentlessly they covered the ground before him. Bonham sighted the lead animal; it was larger than the others and led by a length. He aimed the gun a yard ahead and slowly squeezed the trigger. The hammer fell and powder exploded as the shot rang out, hitting the mastiff in the chest. The animal let out an ear-splitting howl but didn't even flinch. Bonham closed his eyes and waited. In thirty seconds he would be prey for the hounds.

Blake got to the door, which was made of thick oak, four times bolted and twice locked. He quickly began to slide away the bolts – one, two, three, four – counting as he went. '*The key, the key!*' he shouted, searching frantically for its hiding-place. Then, looking down, he spied the key on a small hook. He grabbed it tightly and pushed it into the top lock, turning as fast as he could, knowing he had only seconds before Bonham's demise. He fumbled in his haste and the key dropped to the floor. He grabbed it again and quickly turned the bottom lock. It was stiff and hard to turn, but opened with a reassuring clunk. He slapped the handle and the great door swung open.

Bonham fell backwards into the hall, and Blake was confronted with the sight of the three hounds bounding towards him.

The wounded mastiff summoned all of its strength as it leapt from the road up the marble steps towards him. Seeing his fate, Blake quickly slammed the door and slid the bolts. There was a loud thud as the door vibrated and shook with the impact of the hound, but it held fast. He heard the dog drop to the gound.

There was silence in the sanctuary. Isaac Bonham stared at Blake.

'Never be that late again,' Bonham panted. 'One more second and I would have said goodbye to this life.'

2 : Pulvis Humani Cranum

From the safety of the second-floor library with its polished floors and ochre walls, Blake and Bonham looked out on the devastation in the square. Pistol and musket shots rang out as the militia, dressed in their long red coats, white breeches and black boots, executed the last of the rampaging dogs and horses. They watched as the captain of the guard went from creature to creature. He drew his sabre over each one and with a swift blow made sure that they were dead.

The dead lay where they had fallen and the people who had sought safety in the trees were reluctant to come down for fear of yet another onslaught from some other beast. Those who had been attacked by the dogs sat in a huddled mass by the side of the road, waiting and wailing. A fine white mist blew in from the river, clinging to the house fronts and hovering like a funeral pall. It covered the ground at head height, hiding some of the people from view, covering their agony as a crisp fall of snow covers the dirt of the road.

Both men stared at the scene before them. It was now the third hour after midnight but the morning sun was in full blaze, casting thick black shadows on to the top of the mist. High above, a vivid blue sky obscured the sky dragon from view. Blake looked up, knowing that in a few days the secret would be out: others would be sure to see it and would claim it for their own unless he acted quickly. Blake could not allow that; it was *his* discovery, a lifetime's work.

It was Bonham who broke the silence. Trembling, still shocked from his nightmare with the dogs, he turned to Blake. 'They weren't as lucky as me,' he said as he pointed to the body of a young girl being dragged away by her mother into the ever-thickening mist. 'That could have been me, Sabian. By Hermes, I am so glad you were in.' Bonham patted Blake on the back. 'One more second and that thing would have had me.'

'You are blessed, brother, blessed. It was not your time,' Blake replied quietly.

Bonham sensed that Blake was distant, his mind far away, engrossed in some other world.

'But you – what of you, Sabian? Tell me, what do you think happened?' Bonham had a deep soft voice that was warm and friendly. It was rich, like chocolate and honey. He tried to smile at Blake. 'I could see its teeth as it ran towards me; I saw the look of hatred in its eyes. In those last few moments I thought I was staring into the depths of hell. What caused this? First the darkness and then the madness.'

'It was foretold,' Blake's reply came swiftly. 'As plain as the nose on your face, staring at us from the beginning of time and yet we couldn't see it.'

Blake knew that he had to share the finding of the comet with Bonham. They had known each other since Magdalene College; they had shared, and sometimes stolen, each other's secrets, but they were friends and brothers in the Cabala. He grew agitated. 'I have something to tell you, something that I have to tell the world. You must help me. My discovery will change everything.' He took hold of Bonham by the collar of his coat, gripping it in his fists and pulling his face close to his.

'Promise me, promise me one thing. You must –' He paused as he stared into his friend's eyes. 'I must know – will you believe what I tell you? Will you keep it a secret?'

'Sabian, you have known me since we were young men. Tell me, what troubles you so?'

Bonham pulled Blake's hands from his collar and walked him to the chair beside the fireplace. The fire had been covered with slack powder to keep it in for the night. It smouldered like a smoking volcano, drawn up and out into the London air by the strong updraft.

Blake sat down in the chair, his mood changing from excitement to trepidation. As Bonham prodded the fire with the brass poker, jets of coal gas leapt from the flames and burnt red and blue, hissing and spluttering.

'Now my friend, tell me what troubles you.' Isaac Bonham had never seen Blake like this before. He had always been a man who was in control. Blake led an ordered life, neat and precise.

'What happened tonight was no accident and certainly not an earthquake. The very foundations of the universe have been moved by some great power of which we know little.' Blake paused and looked at Bonham eye to eye. 'I saw something tonight that will change the way we look at the world. I found mention of it in the Nemorensis –'

'But the book doesn't exist,' Bonham butted in, his deep voice raised in excitement. 'It's a legend.'

'It exists and it is here, beneath this very roof. It came into my possession by chance, delivered by the gods, one could say.' Blake spoke quickly and in a hushed voice. 'I have read every word and finally I found it. The calculations said that last night something would happen. When the light vanished and just before the sun rose, I saw it: between Sirius and Aquila there is a comet, and it is coming towards us.' Blake waited for Bonham to reply but he looked into the burning coals, his mind unable to grasp what had been said. 'What you witnessed last night was not an earthquake or sky-storm,' Blake continued. 'It was time standing still . . . We were spectators to what it was like before creation, a black, dark, void, complete nothingness.' Bonham looked up from the fire, taking in his words for the first time. 'Today is the first day of a new age. Everything has begun again. As before, we have the coming of a star, a comet to light our way, and wise men always follow the star.'

'So the book is here and you really have it?' Bonham said, still not believing.

'It is, and I do! In fact, Isaac, you can see it for yourself.' Blake rose from the chair and stepped towards the fireplace. 'You too can look on the Book of Splendour. I will show you the secret.'

'And what of this comet? Why does it predict our fate?' asked Bonham.

'In four nights the whole world will be able to see it with the naked eye, in twenty-one days it will either pass the earth or strike a blow from which we may never recover. This sky dragon is Wormwood. The Nemorensis says it will poison the waters and many will die from its bitterness.'

'Can you stop it? The comet could destroy the earth and everything on it!' Bonham raised his voice as he stepped away from the fireside and walked to the large window draped in thick green curtains. 'If one sky-quake can bring all this destruction and madness, then what will the sight of a comet do to the people of London?' Bonham took the dandy gun from his pocket and with his powder flask filled the barrel with a charge. From his gold waistcoat he took a bright silver snuff box and then picked out a small pistol shot the size of a large pea. 'If the madness will come again then I will be prepared; I will go immediately and arm myself with weapons capable of killing any mad hound that ventures forth.' Bonham loaded the shot into the pistol and charged the hammer-plate. He aimed the pistol out of the window as if to shoot. 'The next time I face a dog from hell it won't be my leg it chews but this lead.'

'Your lead won't stop the panic and it won't stop the comet. If my calculations are correct then it will be a very close thing indeed. If they are wrong then we will be faced with the end of the world.' Blake walked to the window, and together they looked out over the square.

'I've never seen anything like this before, Sabian. Stampeding horses, mad dogs and now comets crashing to earth. And you believe you've the secret that will unravel all these things?'

'Not I, but the book. And this secret we must keep to ourselves. There are others who would find great power in knowing what is to be known. The Nemorensis has the potential to change us all. It is far more powerful than the alchemist's stone, and many will think it can turn their lead to gold. I know that somewhere in its pages is the secret of life itself.'

Suddenly they both heard a low growling coming from behind the cabinet door at the far side of the room. The door was made of book spines that looked like they were part of the library that covered the wall from floor to ceiling. Halfway down was a large green leather spine with the title etched in gold: *Opus Interacto*. When the spine was lifted the door would click open to reveal a large cabinet where Blake kept his supply of snuff, physick powders, gin and his most treasured possession of all, Artemisia absinthium.

Blake looked at Bonham and gestured him to be silent. The noise came again. It was the low guttural sound of a large dog with a grumbling growl that rattled through its teeth.

Bonham took the dandy gun and aimed it nervously at the

cabinet door. He looked at Blake, unsure of what to do next, then slowly pulled back the hammer of the gun, making it ready to fire.

The snarling came again, followed by frantic scratching that sounded like a large creature trying to dig its way from captivity. The growling was then muzzled, and the dog snorted through its nose.

Blake hesitated. He looked at Bonham, who now held the small pistol in two hands to steady his trembling. Then Blake slowly walked towards the door. On hearing the footsteps the hound growled even louder, pushing at the cabinet door in its attempt to escape. Blake reached out and took hold of the spine of the book and began to release the catch.

The door crashed open, and Blake was pushed from his feet. Bonham froze, unable to pull the trigger. In front of him was a large black dog with its right ear torn in half and its face scarred from years of bull-baiting. It snarled through broken and jagged teeth.

'Stop it, Brigand,' said a soft voice, and a girl stepped from the shadow of the deepest part of the cabinet. 'You're frightening the gentleman,' she said, holding tightly to the dog's thick black leather collar.

The girl stepped forward, her face etched in shadow and sunlight. She was tall and thin with long black hair that fell over her face. Over her shoulders was a black shawl; a white apron covered a thick green dress.

'Who in the name of Hermes are you?' Bonham asked in amazement, pointing the pistol towards the large mongrel dog that kept growling at him.

'That is Agetta Lamian!' Blake said, getting up from behind the heavy cabinet door. 'She is my housemaid.' He spoke angrily to the girl: 'I suppose you can give an account of why you were hiding in the cabinet?'

Agetta looked to the floor and held on even tighter to Brigand's collar. 'It was the earthquake, I was putting out the candles in the house, I knew you were upstairs and I always let Brigand in. He comes to meet me, protects me from the Mohocks as we walk home.' Agetta looked up at Bonham and tried to smile. 'I was frightened. The house started to shake, we hid in the cabinet and I held on to Brigand, he's all I've got . . .'

'Why then didn't you come out when I came into the room?' Blake asked icily.

'I thought you would have been angry. You never liked the dog, so I thought I would hide until you'd gone and then let myself out.' Agetta looked Blake in the eye and pushed her raven-black hair away from her face.

'Did you hear what we spoke about?' Blake asked.

'Some of it. Never made much sense, so I tried to keep Brigand from snarling,' she replied hoping the questions would stop.

'The some of it you understood you are to keep to yourself. Mention it to no one.' Blake looked at Bonham.

'Will sir put the gun down now? It's making Brigand nervous and I don't know how long I can hold him for.' Agetta struggled to keep hold of the collar as the dog pulled against her, hoping to grab Bonham with one bite and swing him like a captured rabbit around the room.

Bonham took one step back, clicked the hammer down and put the dandy gun into the pocket of his frock coat. An uncomfortable silence descended on the three. He looked to the dog and then to Agetta. 'Had it long?' he stuttered nervously. 'Had the dog for long? He's so . . . big. Does he bite?'

'Only Mohocks, and those who get too close to me. Just what I need when I leave here at midnight to walk back to Fleet Street.' Agetta stepped into the room, keeping the dog close to her side.

'And the Mohocks trouble you?' Bonham asked.

'Once they troubled me, now Brigand troubles them. They run a mile in their fancy suits. Dressed up and dangerous, that's what they think. Gang of idiots, I say, not a brain between them. Dress up and chase old men and harlots.' She began to fill the room with her presence. Agetta feared very little and there was something about Blake's friend that intrigued her.

'Then you'd better go forth into the day and trouble them some more.' Blake interrupted her gazing at Bonham. 'It's morning, you'll be able to see them clearly. Your hound can chase them to Hyde Park if he wants to,' he said curtly.

Agetta looked at the gold French clock on the mantelpiece. 'It's still night, sir, but the sun has risen.'

'My dear girl,' Blake said. 'You hid through an earthquake of such significance that it altered time. It is morning, the darkness has passed, it is a new day.' He looked at Bonham and then back to Agetta. 'Take the day off, come back tonight,' he said briskly. 'But tell no one of what you heard or you will need more than your dog to save you . . . I know you understand.' He looked to the room above, his voice obvious in its threat. Agetta bowed her head.

'I understand, sir,' Agetta said as she led Brigand from the room. She turned in the doorway. 'I know you think I'll talk about what I heard, but I won't. I may be many things, but I will keep my promise, Doctor Blake, I assure you of that.'

'I know you will, Agetta, I know you will.' Blake smiled, unknowingly charmed again. She had worked her magic once more and he hadn't even realised it.

Agetta left the library, carefully closing the door behind her. She let go of Brigand and ushered him down the stairs. She herself didn't move, but cupped her ear to the door and listened.

'That was quite a fright, Sabian,' Bonham said. 'Almost shot her and the dog. Do you think she'll speak of what she heard?'

'Not Agetta, she knows what would happen. We can be sure of that. She knows who the master is,' Blake replied.

'We could have kept her here until –'

'Her father would have been here as fast as that dog crossed the square,' Blake butted in. 'You would rather face the mastiff than Cadmus Lamian. If you think the Mohocks are the scourge of the city, then Cadmus Lamian would be your worst nightmare. He is a man you would never want to cross.'

Blake walked back to the window and looked out over the mist-covered square. 'It was old Cadmus who got me to take his daughter on. Twisted my arm and my purse strings. He said she would be useful but she costs me more than any servant I have ever had. There is something about the girl. When you look into her eyes it is as if you are staring at someone who has seen the world many times before, and knows more about life than you do. But she's good at her job and she knows when to keep her mouth shut.'

Outside the room Agetta raised one eyebrow and tightened her lips to a scowl. She had heard everything. The threats of the observation room held no fear for her. She had seen his companions parading through the house dressed in their fancy costumes and chanting like gypsies, and she had listened to their magical dances and acclamations. It was Agetta who cleared away the burnt-out candlesticks with their black wax and the incense bowls filled with bitter myrrh. While they danced, she lightened their purses a coin at a time, a sovereign from one and a guinea from another. All done with a smile on her face and a 'Thank you, sir' as they tipped her for holding their coats, dispersing at midnight into the gutters like the London rats they were.

Blake could believe of Agetta all that he wanted. He could fuddle her mind with stories of other worlds, mysterious charms and strange exhortations, but every day by midnight she had dripped one more piece of his wealth into her cup, and when it ran over she would be gone, for ever.

Agetta left the men talking in the room and stealthily made her way down the stairs to the back door where Brigand was waiting, his tail swishing backwards and forwards. The servants' entrance led into a narrow alley where even on the brightest day the sun never shone. It was damp and, in the chill of the morning, deathly cold. The mist from the river hung off the walls of the surrounding houses like giant cobwebs that clung to her face as she walked towards Holborn. The only other person in the alley was a derelict woman who was slumped against the gate of the house opposite. The bottle of gin in her hand was almost lost in the crumpled mass of ragged clothes, skin and bone which made up her human form. She was as ugly as the grave, with a lined face and blistered lips. She looked at Agetta through one open eye; the other was crusted shut with yellow flux.

'Give a penny to your old mother!' the woman cried out. 'Just a penny so I can buy a bottle of Geneva.'

Agetta ignored her and set off at a pace. Brigand ran over to the woman and sniffed at her face and then jumped back, unsure as to who or what she was.

'Brigg! Leave her!' Agetta shouted, her voice echoing along the dark alleyway.

The dog leapt away from the woman and shook itself and shivered, every hair on its back standing on end. The woman dropped the bottle from her numb fingers, and it clattered as it rolled over the cobbles. Brigand followed Agetta down the gentle slope of the passageway, stopping every now and then to turn and look at the old woman. It was as if he could see her in a different way, could look beneath the dirty, stained clothes and see the creature within. A creature that he did not trust.

The quiet of the alley quickly gave way to the bustle of Holborn. Wagons and carriages packed the street, heading for the safety of the Vauxhall countryside. Everywhere, throngs of people shocked from their beds by the quake were now mesmerised by the sun that was penetrating the layer of river mist. High above the dome of St Paul's the bright red globe burnt in a pale sky. A fresh breeze blew through the streets and brought with it the smell of the tide, like roasted nutmeg. Agetta stepped out along Holborn, picking her way through the noise and the hordes of people gathered outside the shops and taverns. She took the dark, narrow alley that cut through from Holborn to the Ship Tavern and the gambling houses of Whetstone Park.

Three nights before there had been a murder in Inigo Alley. Agetta could see the bloodstains on the wall from where the murdered man had tried to escape. His screams had been heard from the street, and even though people came quickly to his aid no one else was found. It was as if the murderer had simply vanished into thin air.

Cold shivers ran down her spine as Brigand pushed by her with a rumbling growl. Then he stopped in his tracks and started to bark. There was no one in the alley and yet he growled and snarled at something visible only to the eye of a dog, something that walked in another world.

Agetta knew they were not alone. 'Stop it, Brigg, you're frightening me!' she shouted. The dog was now jumping up and down and snarling louder and louder. 'Brigg, stop –'

Without any sound, Agetta was grabbed from behind, and a hand covered her mouth. She was pulled through a doorway that she hadn't even realised was there. The door slammed shut and she was trapped in complete darkness. Agetta could hear the heavy breathing of the person holding her. She could feel the dampness of the gloved hand that smothered her face.

'Don't scream, girlie, not if you want to see your dog or the light of day again.' It was the voice of the woman from the alleyway. 'I've been watching you, day and night. I know your coming in and going out.' The woman pressed closer to Agetta, who could feel the lice crawling from the hand and on to her face. 'I could have snatched you whenever I liked but it's not you I want. There's something I need you to do. When you leave Blake's house tomorrow night, come to Inigo Alley and you will find a message. It'll tell you what to do. If you don't, then I will get your precious dog and feed him to the rats . . . and then I'll get you.'

Agetta tried to speak but the strong hand kept her mouth firmly shut. She could see nothing, only smell the stench of gin, street dirt and rotten flesh. As the woman spoke her breath rattled through her body, sounding like she was on the verge of death.

'Not a word to Blake or your father. They can't help you, girlie. Tomorrow in the alley by the Ship Tavern, quarter past midnight. The clock of St George will tell you when. Don't be late.'

Before she could speak, Agetta was thrown into the alley and the door slammed shut. She landed face-down in the grime of emptied slop buckets. Brigg ran to her, barking. She turned. The doorway had vanished. All that was before her was the solid stone of the alley wall. Agetta gulped her breath as the mist was drawn around her and the light began to fade.

In front of her was a dark figure silhouetted by the light of the lamp from the Ship Tavern. Silently it came closer. It was a man wrapped in a deep purple cloak; his face was white and featureless. Agetta jumped to her feet and pulled a knife from her waist band to protect herself. Without sound or sensation the spectre rushed forward, passing straight through her and then fading away. Agetta could not speak. It was the first time she could remember being gripped with fear.

The noise of the street returned. Agetta looked around, dazed and unsure.

3 : The Apothecary

As she ran through the chaos of Fleet Street Agetta could feel her heart pounding. She brushed the lice from her face, looking ahead through tear-stained eyes. Brigand ran beside her, turning to look round every few paces to check that they weren't being followed, scenting the air for the damp, foul odour of the derelict woman.

In the distance Agetta could see the lodging house owned by her father on the corner of Ludgate Hill and Fleet Bridge. The thick smoke from its three chimneys mingled with the fading mist from the river. Its narrow bricks and beamed walls jutted out into the street and held up the thick tiled roof.

Agetta stopped to catch her breath, hoping that the fear would drain from her body. She didn't want her father to guess from her appearance that she had been frightened. This was a secret she could not share with her father.

Outside the lodging house three young boys wagered over two cockerels that fought in the dirt. Agetta watched as the birds danced backwards and forwards, throwing their spurs, trying to catch each other a fatal blow. They looked like two fat judges in powdered wigs.

The larger, fatter bird had a fine black comb on the top of its squat head. This fell from side to side like a black cap as the cockerel jumped and ducked, kicking out its claws against the smaller fowl that had fallen into the mud. The boys squealed with excitement as the black-capped cockerel leapt on its victim, slashing with its claws and tearing with its beak. There was hardly a movement from its prey. Death had come quickly. The eldest boy lifted up the winning bird by its bloodied legs and in triumph threw it in the air. The dead cockerel was carefully picked from the mud and examined by tiny fingers looking for its weakness. Then it was dropped back to the earth. Its wings fell open and its head crumpled to the side, a single drop of blood issuing from its beak.

All thought and fear of the sky-quake seemed to have vanished from the people of Fleet Street. It had been something beyond understanding, like a terrible nightmare, but now it was over. Life had returned to the commotion of before. The slop-covered road was swathed with discarded news-sheets; horse carts jammed the street as coachmen lashed out with knotted whips. In amongst the mud ran the sedan men, lifting a box-chair with its shuttered windows and secret passenger. They shouted 'By your leave' as they pushed through the crowds, running for the city. Agetta was surrounded by haste; the noise of the street burst her ears. Her heart churned, and the scent of the gloved hand still clung to her face. She kicked the dead cockerel aside and pushed the boys out of her way. As the boys lashed out in return Brigg snapped at them, snarling, and they stepped back, knowing that he would love to bite their flesh. In front of Agetta was the faded red door of her house. The sign above it read: *Lamian's Lodging House – clean guests welcome!*

Inside, the smell of roast lamb filled the air. From the kitchen the sound of chopping entered into the hall. Brigg found his place by the fire opposite the stairs, scratched and then settled down to stare at the flames.

Agetta dusted herself down, brushing the dirt from her clothes before she faced her father. Above the crunch of metal slicing through meat and dividing flesh from marrow his voice rang out: 'Agetta, is that you? Agetta! Come here, there's food to take to Newgate Gaol, half the town has gone mad and the other half is hungry, now get in here!'

Cadmus Lamian had a harsh, roaring voice. There was nothing gentle in his tone or appearance. He was a tall, brutish man with long, thin fingers a span in length. On the side of his temple was a large bulging growth that disfigured his brow and pulled the skin tight over his face.

Agetta went quickly into the kitchen. Cadmus stood by the long wooden table in the centre of the room, his apron smeared with blood and grease. The black oven bellowed out its smoke and heat. It softened the wax candles and scorched the eyes with the blistering fat that awaited the side of mutton he was now preparing. Next to the oven was the fireplace with its thick wooden mantel, a cauldron for boiling water and an iron log-rack. The fire burnt brightly, sending waves of hot amber light into the dark corners of the room.

Cadmus didn't look up as he chopped a stubborn leg bone that refused to be broken. 'What a night, hardly in bed before the madness struck. Rattled to the floor, shaken down the stairs and since then every man-jack has been to the door wanting to be fed.' He smashed at the bone even harder, spraying splinters across the room. 'Strange start to a day, lass. Don't like it, don't like it at all.' He stopped and wiped the sweat from his forehead with a bloodied hand. He saw the look in Agetta's face as a question about her mother appeared on her lips. 'She is in bed, says she has a fever – I say she drank too much gin.'

At that he raised the thick flat blade above his head and with all his force chopped through the remaining shard of bone, which snapped in two as the cleaver sliced into the table. Cadmus gave out a relieved grunt and laughed. 'All they want is meat wrapped in bread, and for the price of a penny that is what they will get.' He looked at Agetta. She was never this silent. 'Cat got your tongue?' he asked sharply.

'I need to sleep. It's been a long day and a short night. Blake will want me back by dusk, he hates doing candles.' Agetta couldn't tell her father what had happened. He would never believe her story. She thought he would laugh at her, he always laughed at her. She hoped her father would leave her be, leave her to sleep and face her future alone.

'There's plenty of time for sleep. Now there's work to be done and work means money.' Cadmus drooled over the words as he slipped the side of mutton into the hot fat of the long cooking pot. The flesh sizzled as the fat exploded the skin into crispy blisters. With one hand he opened the door of the black oven, from which bright red embers sent a surge of heat into the room. Cadmus slid the dish across the table, gliding it gently into the oven and slamming the door in a satisfied way. 'Done,' he said as he turned to Agetta. 'How is the old dog, Blake? Still got plenty of money?'

Agetta dropped her purse on to the table; it landed with a soft thud and a clatter of coins.

'Two shillings, that's all I dared take. He had no visitors today. I found one coin in his coat pocket, the other I took from his purse.' Agetta smiled, pleased with herself.

'And he pays you for doing it,' her father laughed. 'In the jar, with the rest. One day we will leave this fine London mansion and retire to the country.'

'He did have one visitor,' Agetta continued. 'Isaac Bonham. He was chased by some dogs when the earthquake happened. Just managed to escape. I heard them talking, said something about a star in the sky and a book. Stupid talk, that's all they ever do.' Agetta placed the two coins in the wooden box that they kept on the shelf over the fireplace. 'Said the book was full of secrets, would tell them if the star would crash to earth. I think they called it a comet.'

'Bonham, eh? Fellow of the Royal Society. A rich man, richer than Blake.' Cadmus mused over the thought of two wealthy men in one place. Agetta could see that his mind raced as he planned how to exploit this situation. 'That Blake is full of his own importance. He wants to discover the secrets of the universe,' Cadmus said as he pulled a tray of bread from the oven. 'Take care to remember everything he says; there'll be those who would give good money to know what goes on in that house.' He looked up from the table and smiled. 'Remember, Agetta, good things come to those who wait, and we have waited for long enough. Now come and help, we have guests waiting to be fed, and that quake might not have been the last.'

Agetta looked around the kitchen. She had known no other place. This room had been her world since she was born. Every smell, every mark on the stained walls, every cobweb that had hung off the ceiling for all her fourteen years were known to her.

She remembered the day when as a young child she had burnt her hand on the oven door. From then it had been the black monster that lurked menacingly in the corner of the room. She had stoked its fires with kindling and driftwood picked from the Thames at low tide when she mudlarked with her friends. As night came she would sit by the washtub that was always filled with pots and lard-crusted water. It reminded her of a ship she had seen sunk in the mud at Rotherhithe. The spines of the barrel stuck up like the planks of the vessel filling with the tide. In the corner of the room she would wait for the rats to scamper from their hole, searching for supper. With one crack of the fire poker she would smash at their heads as they peered from the darkness. Brigg would chase them across the dirty stone floor, catch them in his teeth and throw them against the wall like rag dolls. When they were dead he would prod them with his nose, hoping they would return to life to play a never-ending game of chase.

Her father's rough voice jolted her from her dream. 'Did you see the book that Blake spoke about? It could be valuable, and maybe we could relieve him of it . . .'

'He'd know it was me. Anyway, I don't know where he keeps it.' Agetta hesitated as she spoke.

'If we timed it right, when the chimney boy –' Cadmus was thinking aloud.

'We should just keep doing what we are doing and not bother,' Agetta snapped.

'Losing your nerve, are you, girl? Don't want to help your father any more, getting too fancy for thieving?' Cadmus stepped towards her, meat cleaver in hand.

There was a heavy knock on the kitchen door. Cadmus Lamian slammed the cleaver into the table. The door opened and a man stepped slowly and gently into the kitchen. Agetta noticed that his once fine clothes were now tattered and torn. His long frock coat bore the stains of the street, and its lining showed at the elbows and collar. On his feet she saw that the leather of his boots was gossamer thin, allowing the calluses of sixty years to push through. He was thinner and taller than her father; his worn, lined face was tanned and weathered by a foreign sun.

'Mister Lamian,' he said in a gentle voice, just louder than a whisper. 'If I might be so bold as to talk to you alone?'

Lamian gave Agetta a look that told her to leave quickly. She turned and walked to the door. 'I'll see to the other guests, father. They may need entertaining.'

The man made no effort to move from the entrance. Agetta squeezed uncomfortably past him as he grinned at her, obviously seeing her discomfort.

'A pretty girl, so young,' he said as she left, knowing that she would hear his words.

'What can I do for you, Mister Sarapuk?' Cadmus asked as he offered his friend a chair at the table. They sat together; Cadmus could see the whites of Sarapuk's eyes blazing red in the reflection from the fire. On his face wisps of fine white hair clung neatly to his chin, intertwined with crumbs of ship's biscuit.

'It's about my shop,' Sarapuk whispered. 'I have purchased a small property on Seething Lane, near to Hart Street. There are rooms above, so at the end of the week I will be moving in.' He paused. 'I will of course still require your fine food – say, every evening at seven?' He paused again and looked back to the door, listening intently. 'I wonder if it would be possible for Agetta to call on me? I seldom get to talk to anyone, she is such a charm and would bring a pleasant distraction to an old man's life.'

'Anything is possible . . . for the right price,' Cadmus replied with a smile that was filled with the prospect of money. 'This shop of yours, what will it sell?' he asked, eagerly searching for an opportunity to do business.

'I will not sell, Cadmus, I will cure. I am to be an apothecary and surgeon, so medicines, teeth and skull-tapping are my business. I have an interest in anatomy, but willing subjects are so hard to come by.'

'Must take a lot of learning to come to that, Mister Sarapuk. Those are higher things, higher than a man like me should think about.' Cadmus tried to look interested.

'Well, we all get sick, whether in body, mind or spirit. One day everyone will need a doctor and surgery is the art of the future. I intend, when the time is right, to open a small hospital – *if* I can find those sufficiently interested in making money.' As he spoke he looked Cadmus in the eyes. 'I have made so many mistakes in my life, been cheated out of so much, but this time things will be different. For a hundred pounds a man could make an investment that would be paid back many times over but, like corpses, men like that are hard to find.' Sarapuk slowly tapped a finger on the table as if beating out the rhythm of a secret concerto.

'I may know someone who could help you in both counts, Mister Sarapuk,' Cadmus replied, his interest awakened. 'The hundred pounds, what is the guarantee of its return?'

'All I can say is that for the right man there are always golden opportunities.' Sarapuk raised one eyebrow and smiled.

'There must be something driving you to do this, Mister Sarapuk. Caring for people, opening a hospital, these are high ideals.' Cadmus turned and leant towards him. 'For me, I strive to do the best for my wife and child. I know a good bargain when I see one and as long as the Lamian family are hearty and well fed then I am a happy man. But you, what spurs you on?'

Sarapuk looked around the room again. He checked the door and listened carefully. The room glowed red with the light from the fire, and candles burnt brightly around the walls. The tiny window at the rear of the kitchen struggled to suck in any light from the street. There was no night and no day visible. It was a timeless place with thick solid walls that had stood against rebellions, colliers' riots and the plague. Even the Great Fire had only charred its walls. Sarapuk thought carefully before he spoke, drawing in a long and measured breath.

'My dear friend, I have travelled the world in search of its secrets. From Egypt to Persia I have dug the ruins of many cities. My search has been relentless, but that for which I labour

34

is not to be found in the world, only in the deep recesses of the body. My search is for the place of the soul.' With a strong grip, Sarapuk clasped hold of Lamian's arm, pulling him towards him. 'I know that I will be the one who finds it, and when I do I will be able to capture a human spirit at the time of death and prove to the world that we are immortal. Think of it, Cadmus, think of it. What would people give to see a soul, the eternal essence captured in a glass jar and on view for two shillings? I would be a rich man. *We* could be rich men!' Sarapuk gave out a shrill, excited laugh.

'You think this is possible, that you could do it?' Cadmus asked, drawn into the excitement.

'It is like a jigsaw puzzle, for with every year I have found another piece. Now it is nearly complete.' Sarapuk stopped and looked nervously around the room. 'We can't tell anyone of this, it has to be kept secret. The authorities may frown on my research and I cannot be so choosy as to say where my *volunteers* come from.'

'These volunteers, are they . . . dead?' Cadmus asked hesitantly.

'So far, yes,' Sarapuk said quietly. 'There will come a time when I may need one or two who are, as you may say . . . leaving one world for the next.' He again drew in a long and loud breath. 'I would prefer them to be fresh. Some that I have bought have hung for too long and have been somewhat damaged.'

Cadmus mused. 'I may be able to help you. I have a friend, John Swift, who is the gaoler at Newgate. For a small fee he could be able to provide you with what you need. Have breakfast with the guests as my treat, and let me think this matter through. It is a most unusual business agreement and I would want our partnership to be kept a considerable secret. I wouldn't want people thinking that Lamian was having thoughts above his place in life.'

35

Sarapuk stood up, grabbing Cadmus by the hand and shaking it furiously. 'These are important times, the age of science and truth. We could bring a new way of looking at the world. In one year you could be the talk of London society, have your own supper box in Vauxhall Gardens, a carriage or river barge, and that daughter of yours would make someone a beautiful wife.'

The hallway had filled with the guests awaiting their food and jostling with Brigand for a place near to the fire. Agetta pushed through them and unlocked the door to the large dining room that formed almost the whole western end of the house. There was a cold chill in the room; a young fire struggled to blaze the damp coal into heat. It gave off a thick brown smoke that fought to climb the wide chimney and into the October sun.

A long table stretched the length of the room with wooden chairs clustered around it. Four large candlesticks lit the table; they had been burning for some time, the yellow tallow giving off the smell of pig fat. The candles provided a crescent of light over the top of the table, while underneath was the dark void and the stone floor. Agetta pushed open the heavy door as a scurry of long-tails fled to the far corner to escape through the crack under the floorboards.

She was pushed into the room by a tide of people. It was a gathering of the bedraggled, the lost, and those in descent from a higher rank to the gutter. Among them were street performers, ranters, and a man who claimed he carried the marks of the crucifixion and showed them to the public for sixpence a time. The lodging house was cheap. Shared beds, a slop bucket underneath and a farthing hang for those without the tuppence to lie down. The hangers would rest weary bones by kneeling against a long rope that stretched from wall to wall. They would suspend themselves against it, to be kept from the cold floor, and like so many hung birds would be gently rocked to an uncomfortable and broken sleep.

Breakfast was hurried. Slabs of hot meat, small round bread loaves and clay gin pots were carried from the kitchen. A clamour of eager hands snatched hungrily at the food, grabbing a penny-worth of hot meat wrapped in bread and washing it down with a mug of cheap gin.

Agetta waited at table, making sure that everyone was fed and that no one took more than their share. Mister Manpurdi wrapped his hands in two red cloths to cover the bright white bandages that concealed the bleeding marks of the stigmata. She looked at him closely. He would never allow anyone to see the marks without being paid. Watching him eat, she could see that he was in genuine pain: he held his hands in an uncomfortable pose as he tried to lift the piece of bread to his mouth. Agetta broke open a small, gritty bread loaf, snatched a piece of meat from the plate and placed it inside. She handed it to Manpurdi and smiled. He nodded, giving a small bow of appreciation.

Agetta had no need of religion. How could a loving God keep her in such poverty? She had no need or desire to see the marks on Manpurdi's hands. They meant nothing to her, they were not as interesting as the dromedary she had seen outside Gough's menagerie all the way from the deserts of Arabia, snatched from the ruins of Babylon. To her, Mister Manpurdi was like all the monster-mongers that stayed with them. There had been the boy with the skin of a beetle, a woman with three arms and a girl with ears so large that they called her the human elephant. She had seen them all. They had been bought and sold in that very room and then displayed in private collections and fairs and in Vauxhall Gardens.

Agetta knew that some of these strange creatures were of human creation. She had once watched a man insert duck quills into his face and claim he was half eagle. Another had filed his teeth to resemble the fangs of a wolf and dyed his skin with tea.

Mister Manpurdi was different; he was gentle and kind and made little of himself. All he had were the bleeding scars that would never heal – and the story of how they had come upon him one night in a vision that he had begged would go away.

Dagda Sarapuk walked slowly into the room and sat at the end of the table. He looked at Agetta and smiled as he helped himself to the breakfast. He leant towards Manpurdi and passed a comment that she couldn't hear.

Agetta noticed her father leave the kitchen and take a tray of food upstairs. He looked at her in a way that told her to get back to work. 'We have a guest, a special guest. A poet. He arrived last night. Doesn't want to be disturbed. He is staying in his room. Only I can take his food. Understand?'

With that Cadmus turned and trudged up the stairs to the top of the house. Agetta followed at a distance, intrigued by her father's actions, listening to his footsteps. When he got to the top flight he stopped and looked down the staircase, put the tray on a small table and then took out a key from his pocket. Agetta hid behind the wall at the turn of the stairs. She could hear the key being placed into the lock and quickly turned. The door creaked open. She held her breath so she could listen to everything.

'Do you eat food?' her father said clearly. 'It's bread and meat. I brought you water, somehow I didn't think the likes of you would drink gin.' There was no reply. Agetta began to breathe again as quietly as she could, listening out for any clue as to who was in the attic room. There then came the sound of chains being dragged across the wooden floor.

'Can you take these from me?' said a weak voice that she had never heard before. From her hiding-place she could not decide

38

if the voice was that of a man or woman. It was light, fragile and pure. 'I have neither the power nor the will to escape.'

There was a long silence before her father replied. 'I was told by Mister Gough that you would be gone before I knew it. *Never* take the chains off or he'll fly away.'

'Where shall I fly to? There are bars on the window and the door is locked. Am I to crawl under the door or sneak through a rat hole?' the voice replied.

'You are a strange creature and one who now belongs to me. I gave a good price for you and you may come in very useful. Only moments ago a scientist was saying that he could make good use of someone like you. But then, even he might be surprised as to what you are.'

Cadmus walked across the wooden floor. Agetta heard his every movement as he placed the tray on a table. 'I'll leave this here, take of it what you will. You could do to put on a few pounds. Scrawny chap, don't look too healthy. It was your teeth that sold you to me; they would look very fine transplanted in the mouth of a gentleman.' Cadmus laughed.

'So what is my fate? Will I be here for ever?' the voice asked.

'You will be here until I decide otherwise. You are a mighty fine creature and to reveal you to the world will be my making. What makes you special is that you really are an –'

The front door was flung open as a commotion filled the hallway. Brigand began to bark as the breakfasters spilled from the dining room and into the street. Cadmus Lamian rushed from the attic and Agetta slipped from the stairway to her room. In the street below, a condemned man sat silently in a rocking cart, dragged through the mire of Fleet Street to the gallows at Tyburn. The metal bracing of the large carriage wheels spat out the mud like a fop trap. The man's eyes were drawn to the top of the lodging house. There in the pinnacle of the eaves he glimpsed fleetingly a face pressed against the dirty glass of the attic window. In that small moment the heart of the condemned man was doubly broken. He saw a sadness on the face at the window that showed more grief than his own, and in some strange way he knew he had a gentler fate than the man into whose eyes he now stared.

4 : Inigo Alley

In Bloomsbury Square a dark, solitary figure leant against an old elm tree as its dry October leaves fell to the ground like a shower of golden coins. He coughed and spluttered as he pulled up the collar of his coat against the chill wind that blew the leaves across the grass. Grazing amongst the elms, several fat sheep kept a wary distance from the stranger, who drew on a long clay pipe, the burning embers lighting his face.

The clock of St George struck the quarter hour from its high marble tower that dominated the crowded streets. Rumour had convinced many that at midnight the sky-quake would come again. Boy vendors shouted the story as they charged through the streets with bundles of the *London Chronicle*, proclaiming the disaster and urging the world to stay calm. Outside the Bull and Mouth a crowd gathered to drink gin and wait for the earth to have yet another shivering fit, shaking the houses like the night before and turning the sky to complete blackness. Over the Thames a bright new moon hung against the rich purple sky, while the fire-ships of Holborn walked the streets, lifting their long hooped skirts and white shawls, stopping every gentleman in the hope of enticement.

Blake and Bonham had spent the evening in deep conversation by the open window of the fourth-floor observation room. They had dined on roast pigeons and mackerel, picking the meat from the bones and leaving the crusted skin on the side of their plates. Together they waited for the sky to clear. The strong breeze scattered the cloud, opening the heavens for all to see.

Blake fumbled with the long brass telescope, trying to set the lens so that they could view the comet. In Wormwood he placed his future and his reputation. For the first time he feared that he had deceived himself, that it had been a mistake, a smudge on the lens, a reflection from some distant light. As it drew closer to midnight, he searched the horizon more frantically for the rising of the comet.

Bonham waited patiently, wanting his friend to calm down. He watched Blake set the lens and the height of the telescope, and then moments later go through the whole procedure again.

'It'll be there, Sabian. Your eyes did not deceive you. Trust yourself, as soon as it is midnight the star will rise and you will see it again,' he said, trying to sound reassuring.

'We will wait,' Blake replied, walking away from the telescope and opening a large cupboard on the far side of the room. 'I have something to show you, and now is the time.'

Blake took out a large silk-covered package and walked back to the centre of the room, where he placed the object on the table lens of the camera obscura. As he slowly unwrapped the parcel Bonham grew more excited.

'This is the book, Isaac. Written so long ago that no one knows by what mind it was inspired,' Blake said. 'I never thought I would ever see the day when it would come to my house, but here it is and I must thank the stars for bringing it here.'

Bonham stared aghast at the book with its thick leather binding, its ancient gold writing and weathered paper. Blake turned the pages until he reached the sixth chapter of the sixth book and the final page. His finger darted to the writing emblazoned in the margin.

'There, look. It is true!' He read the words to Bonham. '"*Wormwood, the bright star shall fall from the sky, and many will die from its bitterness.*" It's coming to us, Isaac, we are the first ones to see it and there is nothing that we can do to stop it.' His eyes flamed with excitement verging on madness. 'We have to tell the world, but I fear that if we do then a terror will take hold and we will have unrest like we have never seen before. And if it is not true then I will be seen as the biggest fool that has ever lived.'

'Dammed if you do and dammed if you don't,' Bonham said urgently as he looked eagerly at the Nemorensis. 'You have to tell someone, and who better than the Society? Do you know where the comet will land if it strikes the earth?' Bonham leafed through the book trying to decode the strange letters and calculations embossed on every page.

'As it hits the atmosphere of the first heaven it will disintegrate into thousands of pieces,' Blake replied. 'The earth will be bombarded, and from my calculations everything from Paris to London will be destroyed, the seas will be poisoned and the earth covered in darkness for a generation!' He looked at Bonham, whose face was etched with shadow in the candle-light. 'How can I tell that to the Society? They're a bunch of over-fed intellectuals who like the sound of their own voices. To a man they'll think I'm stupid.' Blake paced the room nervously.

'Not if we show them. We can bring Lord Flamberg here, let him see for himself, and the others will take his word. I can arrange it for tomorrow night. If we wait any longer then someone else might claim the comet for themselves. It has your name on it, Sabian, all your work and calculations have gone into this moment, it cannot be wasted.' Bonham took hold of Blake's hand and shook it in a firm grip. 'I congratulate you tonight; tomorrow the Society and then the world will see your genius. Who knows, perhaps the Nemorensis will change the world, and you are the one entrusted with bringing its knowledge to us.'

In the square below the dark stranger kept watch over the house with eyes that stared up at the open window. Carriages passed him by and a watchman stabbed his staff to the ground with every step he took. No one saw the dark shadow beneath the elm tree, or the glow of the smouldering clay pipe.

Agetta could hear Blake's voice echoing down the spiral staircase. She opened the small back door that led into the alleyway at the rear of the square. To her left she could see the lights of Holborn casting eerie shapes on the walls of the houses. The old woman was nowhere to be seen. She looked for Brigand and called his name in the darkness. She was alone.

In an instant she decided to run to the street. Agetta picked up the front of her long skirt and gripped it against her apron, wrapping her shawl close to her. She dashed forwards, her feet clattering against the cobbles and slopping through the mud. Closer to the light she raced, knowing there would be safety among the mass of people who crowded the streets of Holborn.

Then, from the depths of her imagination came the hideous thought that she was being followed – that some dark creature was stalking not far behind, breathing down the back of her neck, whispering malice. A rising sense of panic made Agetta lose all strength; numbness gripped her face as imaginary hands took hold of her by the throat, squeezing out the breath. The hair stood on the back of her neck as she imagined icy fingers reaching out to her. She looked down to the ground to make sure she didn't fall as her feet sped faster and faster. A frightened scream erupted in her throat.

Suddenly Agetta was stopped dead in her tracks and knocked to the ground. All around her was the noise of Holborn. She looked up, dazed from the blow. There standing over her was a man dressed from head to foot in the deepest black. His frock coat was finished with a fine gold thread that matched the thick buckles on his boots. He stared down at her and held out his hand.

'Little people should look where they're going,' he said in a deep voice and an accent that Agetta had never heard before. 'It is very late, there are citizens whom you would not like to meet or run into.' The man gave a gentle smile as he pulled Agetta to her feet.

Agetta stared at him; he was over six feet tall with a thin face and large green eyes set beneath a black floppy hat. The collar of his coat was turned up against the chill of the night. Agetta tried to pull her hand from his, but he squeezed it tightly.

'So warm, so soft . . .' He paused and looked into her eyes. 'You are a girl who knows many things. For one so young that can be very dangerous.' The man let go of her hand. Agetta didn't move; she was rooted to the ground, unsure as to who he was or where he had come from. 'I see from your face you have a meeting that you must keep, someone who you mustn't keep waiting. Shall I walk you to your rendezvous?'

'Are you mad, or do you have maggots eating your brains?' Agetta replied fiercely.

It was then that St George's clock beat out the first stroke of midnight from the high tower. Agetta pushed the man aside and ran towards Inigo Alley. The whole of Holborn stopped and looked up to the sky, waiting for another quake. In the distance a ship's cannon fired and a low rumble of thunder rolled along the Thames. London fell silent and waited. Agetta pressed her way through the people on the street as she ran towards the alley. No one noticed her, no one cared – all eyes were fixed on the heavens. The new moon was high above the town, the sky had cleared and bright white spots of light decorated the universe like candles on a tree. There was newness to its beauty, as if the world had been born again and this was the first night of creation.

On the twelfth stroke of the clock Agetta turned into Inigo Alley. It seemed even narrower, darker and more sinister than before. The traces of blood still marked the wall. Every stone oozed a sensation of fear. Agetta hesitated in her step and looked behind her. She kept to the middle of the alley and looked about her, constantly ready for someone or something to leap from the shadows.

The noise from the Ship Tavern filled the alley. Agetta could hear the shouting of men as they gambled extravagantly on the turn of the cards. Their high-pitched laughter made the alleyway even more fearsome as it echoed from stone to stone.

The soot-blackened walls of the alley were sodden with thick green damp. From over the doorway of the Tavern a small lamp sent a thin beam of light that reflected from the low mist covering the ground at knee height. Agetta couldn't see where she placed her feet or if anything was hiding in the ground fog. The light danced around her as the swirls of vapour took on the appearance of faceless spectres. This was the deepest, darkest part of Inigo Alley and Agetta felt very alone as she searched for a message that the lice-ridden old hag might have left behind. She knew that it would be nearby, but didn't know what she was really looking for.

The door of the Tavern swung open as a fat old man fell into the cold night air. Agetta hid in the shadows and watched. The man picked himself from the floor and leant against the wall, giving out a satisfied groan as he stood in the ever-growing puddle of his own making. He didn't notice Agetta standing just a few feet away, and having again the taste for cheap gin, he crawled back along the wall until he found the Tavern door, pulled it open and clambered inside.

Agetta stayed in the shadows. She knew in her heart that she wasn't alone. To her right the low mist swirled as if an invisible force walked towards her. Above her on the roof of the Tavern she heard a scratching, like the sound of claws scraping on the old tiles. It was as if an advance guard was taking up positions around her. The cold damp climbed her legs like wet hands grasping at her flesh. All she wanted to do was run, to escape and turn back time. Midnight had passed and still there was no sign.

Then she heard the clatter of carriage horses pulling hard along the road from Lincoln's Inn. The sound grew louder as the metal-rimmed wheels ground against the cobbles. In the light from the Tavern Agetta watched as four silky black horses in funeral headdress came into view, striding through the ground mist as if they rode on the clouds.

Behind them they pulled a fine carriage. The driver sat in his high seat, the collar of his journey coat pulled up, and at the rear stood two footmen with deathly white faces and powdered wigs, their coats trimmed with gold cord and gilt shoulder knots. The carriage stopped outside the Tavern, blocking the exit from the alley. From her hiding-place in the darkness Agetta looked on as the coachman peered around him and then carefully got down from the high seat and opened the door to the carriage and leant inside. She could hear the faint whisper of a conversation. The man turned, dragging his long black coat across the floor as he walked to the door of the Tavern and looked down the alley. He was a small man with in-turned feet that caused him to waddle as he crossed the pavement. He reminded Agetta of a fat, flightless bird she had seen exhibited in the Piccadilly menagerie. His large pot belly pushed out the front of his coat and gave him an air of unsteadiness as he walked. At one point he stumbled and steadied himself against the slimy wall of the alley.

The man looked long and hard into the darkness. Agetta pressed herself fearfully against the wall, expecting to be consumed by it, taken into the grip of the old hag. The man was feet away and yet he didn't see her. He turned and shuffled back to the carriage door and again leant in before stepping back and holding out his hand to the single occupant.

Agetta looked on as a tall woman dressed in a long, black velvet hooded cloak stepped out of the carriage. The cloak glistened in the lamplight and swirled the mist with every movement. The woman wore a tiger mask with thick black whisker spines that jutted out from each cheek. Each stripe was crusted in gemstones, and around the eyes sparkled a rim of blue diamonds. Her long, sallow, powder-white neck shimmered in the half light.

She looked to the alley and called out: 'Agetta! Agetta Lamian . . . I have a message for you!'

Agetta tried to press herself closer into the wall as the woman signalled to her footmen to come down from the carriage.

'Come out, Agetta, or my men will have to come and find you. I mean you no harm, you can trust me.' The woman spoke with a fine accent. It was gentle and creamy soft and sounded as if it had never been raised in anger or spoken an unkind word.

Agetta didn't reply. Above her she heard the scratching on the tile roof, the sound of a large animal clinging to the tiles with sharp claws. She looked back along the dark alley to Holborn, wanting to run. The street seemed deathly quiet, the sound from the Tavern had hushed. It was as if there was only the woman and her left in the world.

'Agetta,' the woman said calmly, 'I will have to go soon and what I have to say is important. Your life and your father's may rest upon it. I know you are there so come out, girl!' The woman didn't wait for a reply; she turned and got back into the carriage. The driver climbed up the front steps and took his seat, picking up the reins in his gloved hands and steadying the horses before he drove off.

'Wait!' Agetta shouted as she jumped from her hiding-place and ran to the carriage door. 'I'm here, I'll speak with you.'

The door to the carriage opened. Agetta noticed a strange design that she had never seen before on the bright yellow-and-black door panel. It was not the crest of a nobleman that she would often see on the fine carriages that rattled through Fleet Street. The door of the carriage was covered with a large golden sun, inset with a bright red human eye that seemed to pursue Agetta with each step she took.

From the darkness of the coach the voice spoke quietly. 'Get in, Agetta. We have to go on a short journey, a journey that will change your life.'

The woman sounded reassuring. Agetta knew that to get into a coach of a stranger was complete madness. This had been the end for several girls she had known who had disappeared from the streets, never to be seen alive again. She looked back to the alley, and from the roof the cat-like scratching came again. Agetta put her fate aside and stepped quickly into the carriage as a cold shudder invaded her spine.

'Is it the cold or the fear of the night that causes you to shudder?' the woman said as she held out a gloved hand to Agetta. 'My friends have been watching you for some time . . . They think you can help us, in fact they believe you have what is needed to be one of us.' The door was suddenly slammed shut and the carriage jolted forwards through the cobbled streets of Lincoln's Inn.

A small lamp lit the carriage, its wick smouldering a dark amber glow that flashed off the leather canopy and gold-leaf door. The woman didn't speak for several minutes. She just stared through the diamond-encrusted slits of her mask, studying every feature of Agetta's face in detail.

'You have the lips of a liar,' the woman said above the noise of the carriage clattering through the streets. 'Do you tell lies, Agetta?'

Agetta hesitated. 'Sometimes,' she said warily. 'Doesn't everyone lie?'

The woman smiled as Agetta tried to stare back at her eye to eye. 'You have the eyes of a thief,' she said. 'Do you steal, Agetta?'

'Only if I want to,' Agetta snapped back as she looked to the carriage door, thinking that she could jump clear and escape. But the woman kicked out her foot, placing it between Agetta and the door.

'I wouldn't want you to fall from the carriage,' the woman said, her voice changed in tone and pace. 'Well, not yet, anyway. We haven't finished with you yet.'

'What do you want me for?' Agetta asked, trying to stay as calm and wishing Brigand was there to rip out the woman's throat.

'Sit back and listen and don't think about jumping out of the door and running away,' the woman said. 'If we'd wanted to kill you it could have been done by now, you could have been just another street urchin found in the Thames at low tide . . .'

Agetta didn't reply. She studied the woman intently as the carriage rocked backwards and forwards. There was a strong smell of expensive wine, and the fragrance of aniseed. Agetta had smelt this once before, when Blake had left out a bottle of his magical Absinthium. Agetta had looked at the dark green liquid, too afraid to touch it. She had sniffed at the cap and smelt the strong, sweet liqueur that had made her eyes water and stung her nose. Now the fragrance filled the carriage, hanging from the woman's clothes like a heavy perfume.

'Where are you taking me?' Agetta asked.

'Not far. You are safer in here than in the street. I want you to see the river. It'll help you to talk.' The woman rummaged in her cloak, bringing out a silver flask. 'Do you want some of this? It'll warm your heart and take away the mist from your feet.' She laughed as she offered Agetta the thick silver vessel.

Agetta looked away. She had no reason to trust the woman.

'It's not poison,' the woman said as she twisted off the silver cap and put the flask to her lips, taking a large gulp. 'See, do you think I would kill myself? Take it, we will be friends for a long time. You will have to learn to trust me and this is a good time to start.' The woman offered her the flask again.

'If we are to be friends then why can't I see your face?' Agetta asked as she cautiously took hold of the vessel.

'You might not like what you see. Anyway, it would be better if you only knew me by my *nom de guerre*, my name of war . . . You can call me – Yerzinia.' The woman smiled, Agetta saw her eyes light up behind the mask, as bright as the diamonds. 'Now, are you going to drink? It won't harm you; it'll do you the power of good. It frees the mind, releases the soul and warms the flesh.' Yerzinia gave a pleased shudder of her shoulders and giggled as she spoke.

Agetta knew what was about to come. The fragrance from the flask filled her nostrils with its vibrant odour. She hesitated before she put the silver vessel to her lips, knowing that once she tasted it she could never go back. With one drop she would be sealed in the friendship as if they had exchanged an oath of blood.

Yerzinia spoke as if she knew Agetta's mind. 'We will be sisters, I can look after you. You need never worry about anything again. I can set you free from the pots and pans, the scrubbing and serving. Soon you will never have to take a meal to a Newgate prisoner again.' She paused and smiled again. 'I know you don't like the way they stare at you. Take, drink to a new life.'

Agetta kissed the flask and drank the thick liquid. At first the fragrance danced across her tongue as she drank back the large mouthful. Then it began to warm her throat with its aromatic and mysterious taste that she had no words to describe. Agetta leant back for the first time and relaxed into the soft leather of the coach seat. The carriage rocked her like a ship at sea as the warming essence charged through her body, setting every nerve on fire and filling each muscle and sinew with new life.

Agetta felt more than alive as waves of pure joy washed over her. She had an overwhelming and tangible feeling of love for everything around her. Quickly she drank again, trying to swallow as much as she could in one mouthful, hoping that it would never end, that each drop would take her higher and higher.

Yerzinia slipped across the carriage and sat next to her, taking the flask from Agetta's hand and drinking some of the liquid herself. 'I remember it so well. You will never forget the first time you drink Absinthium. It has a magical power, it changes the soul and sets you free like a soaring eagle.' She took hold of Agetta's right hand and pressed her thumb into the palm. It began to burn as she pressed harder. Agetta, numbed to any pain, saw wisps of smoke leap from her skin and dance through the air like marsh imps. She cared not.

'Remember, Agetta, happiness and pleasure are more important than the will of any god. Tonight you come of age. Tonight you will live for yourself and not for your father or Sabian Blake.' Yerzinia lifted Agetta's hand to her mouth and blew on her palm. 'You have done enough in your short life to have your neck stretched by the Tyburn gallows more than once. I can save you from that. Stealing is for fools and you will soon find that another world will open to you, one that you once believed could never exist.'

'What do you want me to do?' Agetta asked as if she were talking to someone in a dream, unsure if she had said any words at all.

'You will know soon enough. It will come to you in a thought, an imagining that never leaves, a desire that has to be obtained, and a longing that can never be satisfied. Then you will know what to do, and we will meet again . . . soon.'

With that the carriage lurched to a halt, jolting Agetta from her seat. A footman jumped down from the carriage and opened the door. Agetta looked out to the dimly lit London street. She could smell the river and hear the cry of the boatmen shouting for their last trips. A street warden called out that it was one o'clock and that all was well as he tapped his staff along the wall.

'London Bridge,' Yerzinia said softly. 'There is a man here who you should meet. Come here on Sunday morning before you go to Blake's, and find the shop of the bookseller. He has something for you, something that you will need.'

The footman held out his hand and helped Agetta from the carriage, quickly shutting the door and jumping back on to the carriage. With the click of the lock the driver thrashed the reins and the coach rattled over the Bishopsgate cobbles, the four black horses in their funeral plumes beating out a trot with their metal-shod hooves, sparking against the stones.

Agetta was alone. The Absinthium waned like a setting moon, its power ebbing as Yerzinia's carriage faded in the distance. The night felt colder than before. Agetta huddled the shawl close to warm her chilled bones. She looked at her hand that now burnt like a hot scald. In the middle of the palm was a blackened thumb print that severed the life line. Agetta spat into her hand and rubbed the mark with her thumb. It burnt more intensely, growing in size before her, taking the shape of a large red eye etched in black. The pain pulsed with each heartbeat. Agetta quickly wrapped her hand in the apron, pressing the damp material into the wound as she set off unsteadily fom London Bridge to Bishopsgate.

5 : Burnt Wings and Periwigs

Cadmus Lamian sat at the long table and stared into the fading embers of the fire as it clung to its final moments of life. Dagda Sarapuk was slumped in a large wooden chair by the hearth. He dribbled frothy white bubbles down his long thin chin as he snored. A secret breeze scattered the dust across the stone floor of the refectory and wafted the candles that lit the room from their high place on the mantelpiece.

'You're not one for conversation, Sarapuk,' Lamian snarled as the gin rattled in his throat like some thin toad gulping for breath. 'Thought you'd at least stay awake until I had finished what I was going to tell you.' Sarapuk slept on, his head rolling from side to side as if troubled by the visions of his tormented dreaming. 'It's mighty stuff, not of this world. The sort of thing to lift you from the pit of this life with its leeches and lice, bloodletting and pox.' Lamian slapped the back of his arm, then picked the blood-fat lice from his skin with the precision of a man who had done this a thousand times before.

'I even brought you a feather, thought I would show it to you as proof.' He fumbled drunkenly as he brought out a long white feather from the inside pocket of his coat. Lamian held it up to the flickering candlelight and stared through the white beauty that in the darkness of the room glowed with a brilliance beyond this world. 'What's the good of having a secret and keeping it to yourself, I ask you? Here I am, a simple cook with an old lodging house, and yet upstairs, locked away from humanity, I am the keeper of such a beauty the world has never seen. But who can I show it to? Who can I boast with? That's the trouble with secrets – they're no good unless you can break them.'

Sarapuk grunted a reply, murmuring the words of a forgotten song in his half sleep. 'Purge me with hyssop . . . that I may be clean . . . Wash me and I shall be whiter than the snow . . .'

Lamian shuddered as if he had heard the words of a ghost. He grabbed the iron poker from the side of the fire and prodded Sarapuk in the chest three times. 'Stop your gibbering, man,' he exclaimed. 'You're giving me the shivers, that's church talk and there it should stay.'

Sarapuk slid from the chair, collapsing to the stone floor, grabbing hold of the wooden frame like a drowning man clutching for a line. 'Aaht! What!' he gargled as his knees smashed to the stone. 'Long way . . . forgotten so much . . . Comes back, comes back . . . Stalks me in the night, a hound, running after me, chasing me.' He woke quickly from his dreams, kneeling before Lamian as if he was about to pray to him. 'I saw it, Cadmus, and the words wouldn't save me. I could hear its feet pounding in the blackness, feel its breath chasing down my neck, there's a creature loose and it wants to consume me.' His eyes filled with tears as he sobbed the final words that choked in his throat. 'Say you'll protect me, Cadmus. Let us be more to each other than guzzlers of wine. You are my only friend and each night the hound gets closer to me!'

''Tis but a dream, a folly of darkness. There is nothing to fear.' Lamian clutched the bright white feather like an ancient wand. 'Look, this will protect you!' He thrust the feather towards Sarapuk urgently. 'Belongs to an angel. A finer creature you have never seen. Carried through the heavens on wings, and now it is mine.'

56

'Looks like a swan to me. I have had my fill of angel feathers, pieces of the rabbi's cross and dragon's teeth. The world is filled with such things, all to be bought for a guinea with a claim that they can cure all.' Sarapuk wrung his hands furiously, as if to rub off some hidden dirt that clung to him. 'You are a friend and now a partner in my business, but angel feathers are not what I expected. There are thousands of bald-arsed swans parading their pink rumps through royal gardens and not one of them has given forth an angel feather!'

'Ah!' Lamian exclaimed, furiously frustrated. 'This is not some trick from a menagerie, it is as real as you. I have seen the creature with my own eyes and plucked this feather from its wing with my own hands. It is not swan's wings pasted to the back of a man. It is an angel.'

Sarapuk jumped up from the chair and grabbed the feather, holding it to the candlelight. His eyes searched each thick strand of gold that pressed together to glow liquid white. It had the feel of rich, precious metal and for its size was incredibly heavy. Sarapuk wafted the feather in the candle flame, hoping to burn Lamian's fakery. The feather didn't even smoulder or char. In the centre of the flame it glowed more golden-white. He laid it in the palm of his hand to check the weight as his lined face revealed the workings of his mind. 'Who made this?' he asked, raising one eyebrow.

'I suppose it was he who made us all,' said Lamian.

'Rot! I believed that once but like so many things it was stolen away. Now I believe in what I can see and nothing else. When I find that which speaks of another world I will again believe.' Sarapuk tapped the feather against the side of the table, and with each strike it began to vibrate and resonate. At first the note was so high that it could not be heard, but then as the strikes increased so the sound pinched at the ears like the squeal of bats.

'It is a very strange thing,' Lamian said as he reached out for the feather. 'Do you believe me now?'

'If I could see the creature then I would believe. I have searched for years for the secret place of the soul. I have anatomised the dead of every race, looking for where the soul hides itself within us. Neither in the brain or the gut can it be found. The heart is not its resting place and it could be decided that the soul does not exist. Yet to find an angel, a real living angel, would change all that. Do you know of such a creature?' Sarapuk was impatient, his eyes hunting each movement that Lamian made for some hidden clue.

'I can show . . .' The front door slammed as a cold gust of wind rattled the windows of the room and blew bright against the embers of the fire. Lamian's eyes flashed at Sarapuk to be silent. 'Who is it?' he shouted into the hallway. 'Who is so late that they wake us at this time? We have no food till the morning.'

'I am late, father,' Agetta protested against his shouting. 'I was kept back by Blake and the walk from Bloomsbury was crammed with people watching for another quake. Have you seen the new moon?' Agetta spoke quickly, hoping to change the conversation as she hid her hand in her skirt. 'I'll be straight to bed,' she shouted from the hallway.

'Too big to say goodnight to your old man, eh, Agetta? Come in and bid us a good night,' Cadmus said.

Agetta half-entered the room. She smiled at her father and nodded to Sarapuk.

'You should be careful along the Strand, Agetta. It's a place of nighthawks and mollies and not for pretty young girls.' Sarapuk glared as he spoke.

'It would be a brave man who took on my Agetta,' her father replied. 'Either that or a fool. She packs a punch stronger than any bare-knuckle fighter.' Lamian raised his fists in mock battle.

58

'Come on, Agetta, show him your right hook. Knock this lump off the side of my face!' Lamian punched the air vigorously.

Agetta stayed on the other side of the doorway. She hid her right hand from view, not wanting her father to see the burn mark in her palm. 'I think I'll go to bed, I have done enough for one day,' she said curtly.

'Come on, girl,' Lamian said, his tone changing to the point of insistence. 'Come fight your old man!'

Knowing she could not refuse, Agetta stepped into the room, holding her right hand behind her back. She didn't want to explain how the mark had scarred her hand; its dull ache was a reminder of Yerzinia, the carriage and the Absinthium. Dutifully she took a long swing at her father with her left hand, aiming to miss and hoping to keep her other hand out of sight.

'With feeling, girl, hit as if you mean it,' Cadmus said as he clenched his fist. 'Come on, girl – you can do better than that.' He cracked the air with a punch that made Agetta leap backwards.

It was instinct and years of this fighting that made her lash out. Without thinking she quickly jabbed her right fist through the air, striking her father on the side of his face. He reeled back, laughing.

'Told you she could fight,' he said as he dropped his guard and drew his breath. 'She's a proper fighter is my Agetta. Taught her the hard way – spare the rod, spoil the child.'

Agetta winced in pain from his words and the wound to her hand.

'What's wrong with you, girl? Hit your old man too hard?' Cadmus looked at Sarapuk and laughed.

Agetta clutched her hand, holding back the tears. 'I burnt my hand. A candle,' she said. 'It caught me on the palm.'

'Let me see,' Sarapuk interrupted. 'I am a doctor, I can help.'

Before she could refuse, Sarapuk had taken two steps and grabbed hold of her hand and unfurled her fingers, exposing the palm to the candlelight. The eye-shaped sore stared back at him, the deep black line around the blood-red centre oozing thick green mucus.

Sarapuk quickly turned her hand away from her father. 'Keep this well wrapped, especially at night, and show no one,' he said as he put one arm around Agetta and pulled her closer to him. 'And stay away from the place where you got it from, they will want more from you than you could imagine,' he whispered.

'What is it, man? Let me see!' Lamian said sharply. 'She's my daughter, I should be knowing.'

'There is nothing to know, Cadmus. She must keep it covered and show no one, not even you. Agetta has a burnt hand; she must keep it wrapped and do nothing to make it worse.' Sarapuk looked at Agetta. 'As your doctor I tell you to wrap it in linen and go to your bed, you will feel better in the morning. I will bring something for you to ease the pain.'

Agetta looked to her father. She knew by his look that he felt cheated out of knowing the truth.

'You better do as *Doctor* Sarapuk says and get to bed. I will wake you in the morning. Be off with you now.'

Agetta left the room cradling her hand. Lamian slammed the door shut behind her, its thud echoing coldly through the house.

'Lot of fuss over a burn, Dagda. Sure it was just that?' he asked.

'I'm sure. I have seen many burns and that one is typical. Now tell me, what of this angel? For that I would certainly give a lot of fuss.'

'First we have a drink and let the lass settle. Then I will take you to a place that is the nearest to heaven *we* may ever get,' Lamian replied.

Agetta closed the door to the room she shared with her mother. It was small and cramped, containing two thin beds with shabby horsehair mattresses. A candle burned by the side of her mother's bed, giving off a dim light that made the room feel cold. She walked carefully across the cluttered floor, avoiding the slop bucket and the bag of flour that had been invaded by mites, then knelt on her bed and pushed against the stiff window frame. It gave way with a creak and the room was filled with fresh London air, bathing the walls in rich moonlight.

Her mother groaned in her sleep, and a hand reached out for the flagon of gin that rested on the table next to her. Mrs Lamian lay like a large whiskered seal stranded on a mound of shingle. Her head rolled from side to side, attached to her body by a long thin neck that disappeared into the ruffles of her sleeping coat. The sound of her rasping snores filled the room, broken occasionally by muffled groans as she waved her hands to brush away imaginary spiders.

Agetta looked out over the sparkling night. It was now bright and clear. Below, the fog clung to the pavement and weaved in and out of alley and street like a long white dragon, swirling its way to the river. She looked at her mother; the bed coat rose and fell with the timing of a clock. Jets of steaming breath blew from her nostrils into the cold air of the room, and the rattle of her lungs and her night tremors kept Agetta from sleep. She waited, watching each breath her mother took, even hoping it might be her last.

Rats scratched inside the wall, their gnawing adding to the cacophony of sleep as Agetta huddled herself in a thick blanket and closed her eyes, hoping the pain would go away and waiting for her mind to be invaded by the overwhelming desire that Yerzinia had said would come. She remembered the luxury of the coach with its soft leather seats, and the luscious fragrance of Yerzinia and her fine clothes. This was a world far away from the filth of her home. It was the world that she now wanted and would do anything to gain.

Her mother snored heavily, and each rasping of her nostrils stopped all possibility of sleep. Agetta watched the deep black shadows crossing the stained wall. She closed her eyes, waiting for the dawn, and the face of the stranger in Holborn filled her mind . . .

'*Little people should look where they're going,*' the man said in a deep voice, '*especially if they have already done this before.*'

Agetta looked up. Etched in dark shadow, the stranger looked even taller and more frightening as he towered above her, his black floppy hat wafting in the riverside breeze. The thought of fighting flashed into her mind but her arms and legs were dream-numb, she was unable to move.

'That is not a good thought,' said the stranger softly. 'Your face is connected to your heart and your eyes speak of what the soul can't hide.' He held out his hand. 'Why be frightened of me? You don't know who I am.'

Agetta couldn't speak, the words choked in her throat. She reached out her hand to take his. The pavement consumed her, she was falling. Faces flashed by, hands grabbed and tugged her long hair as tattered corpses fell towards her.

There was a sudden long, growling moan. Agetta clutched at the bedclothes as she hit the hard wooden floor with a thud. Her mother snorted loudly. Outside the room Agetta heard the sound of footsteps carefully treading on the wooden staircase. Quickly she leapt back into her bed and pulled the covers over her face.

The door to the room creaked open as long fingers held the wooden frame. Under the dank blankets that filled her senses with their musty smell, Agetta knew she was being stared at but didn't dare move.

'Sleeping like babies,' muttered her father as he turned to leave the room.

'It's good they don't know what you are up to, Cadmus. You can never have too many secrets,' Sarapuk whispered in his seething voice.

Agetta listened to the footsteps climbing the stairs to the locked attic room, her father talking to Sarapuk as they ascended the steep narrow staircase. She heard the key chain rattle against the door and the heavy lock clank open. He was too far away for her to hear what he said. Tiredness crept through her veins and soon the dark face of sleep overwhelmed her again.

'You can never be too careful, Dagda!' Lamian said as he shut the attic door and turned the key. 'I have to keep him chained to the floor with a set of irons. I was told he was faster than Jack the Lad and would escape twice as quick.' He showed Sarapuk through into an even smaller, darker room lit only by a faint light.

'So this is your menagerie?' Sarapuk asked as his eyes adjusted to the darkness.

'My prize specimen! For which I paid a king's ransom,' Lamian replied.

'So let us hope that he is real and not just a purveyor of swan feathers!'

Lamian pulled back a dirty curtain. 'My little angel,' he exclaimed proudly.

Sarapuk gasped with disbelief. There before him was a man dressed in a silver white coat without hem or seam, spun from a single thread and trimmed in shimmering braid. He had a thick-set jaw and dark skin with bright green eyes that sparkled like emeralds.

'He is a very fine specimen, but I see no wings,' Sarapuk said gesturing with his arms as if to fly.

'That is the beauty of a true angel. I saw one once at the Piccadilly menagerie. He had fine giant wings that stuck through his linen shirt. They could even flap, but what you didn't see was the leather straps that tied them to a human body. Six months later he was back again, this time as a centaur with the back legs of a dead horse strapped to him. Still people didn't realise . . . But my angel is real and his wings are as beautiful as he is.' Lamian gently stroked the creature's face.

The angel didn't acknowledge their presence. His gaze was firmly fixed to the floor, a look of deep sadness covered his face.

'Does he speak?' Sarapuk asked excitedly.

'He sometimes speaks, but neither sleeps nor eats. He just stares at the floor. When he first arrived he glowed, his skin almost shone like burnished copper, his wings were bright white, but now . . . Somehow he has lost his will, something has changed in him.'

'Something would change in me if I lived in such a place as this,' Sarapuk replied, his shoulders shivering. 'He looks like a man to me. I was expecting to see an angel at least.'

'An angel he truly is, he is no trick or jester. Underneath that linen shirt is a pair of the finest angel wings London will ever see.' Lamian spoke excitedly, his eye twitching as he rubbed the lump on the side of his head.

Sarapuk noticed that the creature was manacled to the floor with golden chains fixed to a metal band that clasped each thick bronzed wrist.

Lamian grabbed the back of the linen coat and lifted it high into the air. 'There you see – wings! Flying wings! Angel wings! Real wings!' Lamian laughed as he spoke, his eyes flashing over the creature's back, still disbelieving what he saw. 'What is amazing is that they can pass through the linen coat at will, and when he decides to do that they triple in size.'

The wings appeared to sit secretly in a recess in the creature's back shaped to the contours of his body. They were the size of an eagle's wings, with thick golden-white feathers that shimmered in the candlelight. Sarapuk's eyes searched for the straps that he thought tied them to its back. He reached out and slid his hand behind the wings, searching in the hidden part of the creature's back. Suddenly the wings of the angel flicked back and in a split second exploded in size, showering Lamian and Sarapuk in a wave of tiny silver sparks. Lamian dropped the back of the angel's coat, which fell through the wings as if they were not there. Both men jumped back, aghast at the sight.

The angel's wings filled the small room and towered over the creature like a shimmering peacock tail, each feather emblazoned with a bright blue eye. Sarapuk hid his face with his hands from the searing white light that now emanated from the wings, almost blinding him. He peered through the cracks in his fingers as the wings pulsated brighter and brighter. The whole room was bathed in a golden glow. Then, as suddenly as it had appeared, it was gone, and the room was plunged back into the light of just one candle. The creature sat, his face sullen, his eyes fixed on a cockroach that scurried across the dirty floor, as if more strength had drained from his impoverished and chained body.

Sarapuk tried to remain calm as his thoughts ran rampant through his mind. 'You can't show him to anyone,' he said quickly. 'The world would go *m-m-mad* at the *s-s-sight*,' he stuttered. Blood was pounding through the thin veins on the side of his face, throbbing with each beat of his fluttering heart. 'If I were you, Cadmus, I would sell him to someone who could use this to good effect. Someone who could get to the bottom of his power, someone –'

'Like you, Dagda? Someone like you?' Lamian interrupted him in full flow. 'He's not for sale, to you or nobody. He's going

on display for all the ladies and gents to see at a guinea a time
. . . and I'll be a rich man.'

'He's an angel, Cadmus, a real angel. He must be examined
properly. I have an electronic accumulator, we could see what
would happen if he were electrified. It is the best medicine about
and could cure his melancholy!' Sarapuk shouted excitedly.

'Quiet, man, there are lodgers here who would cut his throat
for a farthing, and are so stupid that they would chop off his
wings and sell them as swan feathers.' Lamian pushed Sarapuk
out of the room. 'He doesn't need any quack medicine, he is
my future – and yours if you want it, but on my terms.'

6 : Malus Maleficia

Mrs Malakin waddled along the long hallway of 6 Bloomsbury
Square. The clattering of the tapping-handle against the brass
plate echoed irritatingly through the house. She wheezed
angrily as she walked, gulping her breath and wiping the black
soot stains from her fat rosy cheeks with the hem of her apron.
The hallway was filled with a haze of smoke from a freshly-lit
fire in the drawing room, where the fumes struggled to escape
through the narrowed vein of the crow-blocked chimney.

'Yesterday! Everyone wants things to happen yesterday!' she
said as she struggled to the door.

'The door, Mrs Malakin! Can you get the door?' Blake's
voice tumbled down from the observation room. 'It's Bonham
and the others, ask them to wait in the drawing room.'

Mrs Malakin nodded to herself, muttering under what breath
she had left. She unbolted the door and let in the night. Before
she could give any greeting, Bonham pushed her out of the way
and stepped into the hall, followed by two men in fine wigs and
frock coats.

'Doctor Blake,' Mrs Malakin said as she gasped in the cold
night air, 'would like you in the drawing –'

Bonham didn't speak. He appeared to be deeply agitated as
he led the distinguished guests into the drawing room. He
sniffed the air, frowning at the small thin man who followed

closely behind. The ceiling of the room was obscured by a thick white cloud of smoke that hung in the air and stung the eyes.

'He wants you to wait here,' said Mrs Malakin as she slammed the door behind them and fought the urge to lock them in the room for ever. She tried to laugh, but lungs wracked by the fumes from years of bleaching cloth allowed her only a hollow cough.

Sabian Blake ran down the stairs clutching his small oriental cap, his blue silk house coat billowing out like a ship in full sail. Mrs Malakin lurched out of his way to avoid being cast down the stairs into the kitchen.

'Gentlemen!' Blake shouted loudly before he had opened the door. 'What a night awaits us all. Everything is set and –' He flung open the drawing-room door, and smoke wafted out into the hall. 'My friends,' he said, 'let us not wait here. The stars are rising and tonight I have something to show you that will astound even the hardest cynic.'

Bonham stepped out of the smoke into the soft milky candle-light of the hallway. The other guests appeared from the drawing room like ghosts from the grave.

Blake greeted each one by name. 'Mister Yeats . . . Lord Flamberg . . . Welcome!' He clapped his hands together and smiled. 'Let us wait no longer, what I would have you see is soon to rise from the depths of heaven.' He turned and gestured for them to follow up the stairs.

'I hope this won't take long, Blake,' said Yeats in a precise voice as he combed his long thick beard with his fingers. 'I have a table at cards waiting. I can't see what all the fuss is about. Bonham was most adamant it had to be tonight. Acting like a madman.'

'Let God preserve us from madness and Bedlam,' replied Blake quickly. 'If what I believe is true then what you see tonight may herald more insanity than anything you have seen in the King's madhouse.' Blake stooped on the stairway and turned to face the men. 'I must ask you before we go any further. What you see tonight is a secret to be kept until the proper time. You, Yeats, are here not for any grasp of science but for the fact of the scandal sheet you call a newspaper. In three days' time you can broadcast to the world what you see tonight. Is that agreed?'

Yeats looked to the floor and wiped his long thick fingers along the banister rail thoughtfully. He held out a dust-stained finger to Blake. 'Dirt! It's everywhere, and it's my job to tell the world about it. Kings and slaves, rich and poor. None of them can escape it. It fills our streets and it fills our minds and I am here to expose it to the world.'

'Yes, and to whoever wants to buy the *London Chronicle*,' Bonham butted in. 'Do you agree with him or not? If it is aye then we carry on, if not I will throw you down the stairs and you can go and play cards with your mollies.'

Yeats turned and towered over Bonham. He was a giant of a man with a thick, rugged brow, steel-blue eyes and the frame of a wrestler. Yeats feared no human adversary. 'You will *what*, Bonham? Throw me *where*, Bonham?' He seized Bonham by the collar of his coat and with one hand lifted Bonham from his feet and suspended him in the air. 'Would you like to fly? You could be the first scientist to experience the wonder of flight.' He lifted Bonham even higher, holding him towards the stairwell and the drop to the floor below. 'I am in this, Bonham, because I smell a good story and I'll keep your game as long as I have to.' Yeats laughed and dropped Bonham to the stairs.

'Gentlemen, let us continue. The stars will not wait, and we have so much to talk about and so much to see.' Blake quickly paced up the remaining flight of stairs to the observation room.

The large brass telescope pointed out to the night sky. It was set to the very crown of heaven where the sky was at its blackest and the dim light from the London streets could not penetrate. Far below, life went on as usual, unaware of the events taking place above.

'Come in, come in,' Blake said as he ushered them in excitedly. 'Gather round and I will explain what you are about to see.'

Blake spoke to Yeats as if he was the only one to be convinced. He knew that Lord Flamberg and Bonham would believe whatever he had to say. They were Royal Society men and knew Blake well. To convince Yeats was vital – he could tell the world of *Blake*'s Comet. For several minutes Blake spoke of what he had found, pacing the room vigorously, waving his hand and pointing to the sky. The gathering listened quietly. Even Yeats stood and watched his every move, intrigued as to what would come next.

'You see, gentlemen, this could mean the end . . . The end of life from here to Paris. Or the comet could miss the earth and shower us with rocks from space. How do you tell that to the world without them all going mad or hanging me as a liar if I'm wrong?' Blake stopped speaking and looked at the men.

'So how do you know it will strike here?' Yeats asked cautiously, pulling on his beard.

'From the height of the comet in the eastern sky and from the turn of the planet divided by the distance it has travelled so far it will either smash into the earth or pass five miles above our heads. Whatever happens there will be devastation never seen before.'

'The comet – if it is to strike the earth, when will it happen?' Lord Flamberg asked anxiously.

'I cannot be sure, but I know that in twenty days we will either still be here or the dust of Cheapside will be mingled with our bones.' Blake walked to the telescope. 'It is time for you to see for yourselves. There is some cloud, but the comet can be seen. It is getting closer with each day, much closer.'

Lord Flamberg stepped forwards and looked through the lens of the telescope at the monster that hurtled through deep space towards them. There was complete silence in the room. The candlelight flickered in the breeze from the open window, and the sound of clattering hooves in the street echoed coldly like the slow march of a funeral procession.

Yeats looked on impatiently, awaiting his turn. He rummaged in his coat pockets, turning out scraps of torn paper on to the floor and tapping the heel of his shoe against a loose floorboard. Finally Lord Flamberg stepped away from the telescope. Yeats saw a strange look sweep across his face. He stepped to the eyepiece and stooped down to look into space.

There before him was a ball of reddish-white light, a speeding mass the size of a fist, its long tail stretching off into the distance. To Yeats it looked like an exploding star, hanging against the black backcloth of space like the lights on London Bridge floating above the river in the October mist.

'Is that it? Is that what all the fuss is about? It's beyond the heavens, man! How can you worry about that?' Yeats asked in his deep northern voice.

'If you knew the first thing about science you would be greatly concerned,' Flamberg replied before anyone else could speak. 'From the shape of the comet's tail it is clear that it is coming towards us. Your job is to break the news to the world, but not the truth . . . That would be too much for people to understand – and we cannot have London alarmed, there could be a revolution.'

'So what do you want me to say? "Comet found, night spectacular to illuminate London"? I know, even better: "The hottest thing since the Great Fire and it's coming right to your doorstep!" Is that the headline you want me to write? Who's to say there isn't some other fool scientist watching the thing

71

right now and about to tell the world what you don't want them to know?' Yeats pulled angrily on his long beard.

'That's why on Monday next you must publish that Blake has found a comet,' Flamberg said as he closed the window to the room and pulled the curtains over the glass. 'Say that it will miss the earth, and that I have confirmed Blake's calculations. The Royal Society says –'

'The Royal Society, that wonderful collection of misfits and charlatans! Blind them with new science! Is that what you'd have me do?' Yeats asked. 'Look what happened the other night. One tremor and the whole city was in uproar, there were over a hundred people killed. Explain that to me. What caused that? Why did all the dogs in London go mad? None of you can give me an answer. Science, my dear friends, has been held in the balance and found wanting. You should all stick to trying to make gold from lead. Isn't that how it all started? Glorified sorcerers, the lot of you!'

Yeats walked to the door, pushing Bonham out of the way. 'You'll get your story, Flamberg, but I want to know what is happening, and if it is going to hit I want my carriage to be the first on the North Road out of this stinking city. Now if you'll excuse me, I have *pressing* business.'

Yeats slammed the door and stormed down the stairs. His heavy frame could be heard rattling each step and thudding towards the front door. There was a loud bang as he left the house.

The scientists stood in the dim candlelight and looked at each other. 'What will he do?' Bonham asked as he cautiously broke the strange silence that had fallen in the room.

'He is my man,' said Lord Flamberg, calmly. 'He will do what I say and he knows it. Without my money he would have no paper, but that is not common knowledge.'

'Why now, Blake? First the tremor and now the comet. Is

there more to this than we will ever know?' Bonham asked quietly, his eyes searching the room. 'If I were a religious man I would say this was the last judgement and this creature in space is the creator's way of bringing an end to us all. He promised never again to send a flood, but there was no mention of stars falling to the earth.'

'You are right,' Blake said. 'As you quite rightly say there is no mention of stars crashing from space, and what we observe is a scientific problem, not a spiritual one. As scientists it is our duty to our craft to give good, clear insight into what is happening and give a warning to the world in due season.'

'Or no warning at all,' Lord Flamberg said coldly. 'I don't think we should tell the people anything. The King as our patron must know so he can go to a place of safety, and our families, servants and fellow members of the Society. It should be done in a way as to not attract any panic, but I will tell Yeats that no mention shall be made of where the comet may strike. The *London Chronicle* will ridicule any scientist or quack doctor who dares to say the comet will strike the earth.' Flamberg paused, and a surge of dark inspiration rushed through him. 'We could invite all the people to a party to see the star pass the earth. Ours could be safely out of the way in the north, and theirs could be in Hyde Park by Triple Tree.'

'They would be condemned to death! It would be a disaster,' Bonham said in disbelief.

'Would that be such a bad thing?' asked Flamberg. 'It would only be finishing what we started with the Great Fire. There is a need for the world to be cleansed of ignorance, superstition and fear. This could be a way of achieving such an outcome. What you call a disaster I would call an *opportunity*.' Flamberg looked at the two men. There was a passion in his eyes that Blake had never seen before. 'Newgate can't hold any more prisoners and Bedlam is crammed with the mad. An apocalypse of this magnitude would clear London of every ounce of scum that litters its streets. Not a bad evening's entertainment.' Lord Flamberg smiled at Blake. 'Yeats and I will take chocolate with you at Nando's coffee house tonight at eleven. I bid you goodnight, and may we all keep this a secret.'

Flamberg walked to the door of the room and, pushing past Mrs Malakin, quickly left the house.

Bonham looked at Blake. 'You never told him what it said in the Nemorensis. You had an opportunity to tell him everything and you didn't,' he said angrily. 'What about the prophecy? Wouldn't Lord Flamberg think differently if he knew of the book?'

'Flamberg would think the same whether he knew of the Nemorensis or not. I cannot trust him enough to explain about what we know. He is a scientist, he knows little of faith. The Nemorensis is the truth of the universe, it is science, reason and all that is eternal mixed together in one perfect truth. Lord Flamberg has his feet stuck in the clay of human reason. The science of the Cabala is beyond him.' Blake looked to the cabinet where he had hidden the Nemorensis. 'It must be kept a secret.'

He looked anxiously at Bonham, his brow furrowed with worry. Blake drew in a long breath. 'I have something to tell you. You will think I am mad. Last night I read the Nemorensis from cover to cover, and as I turned the final page there before my eyes was another page with more inscriptions. They talk of a power coming into the world when Wormwood strikes, but that is not all.' Blake rubbed the sweat from his forehead. 'This morning I went back to check my work, I took the Nemorensis from the cabinet, unwrapped the book and then opened it at the last page. There were two new pages, new inscriptions with hand-etched words in the margins. Believe me, Isaac, I am not going mad.'

Blake rushed to the cupboard and, taking the long brass key from his pocket, opened the thick lock that kept the doors tightly shut. With much ceremony he took the Nemorensis from the shelf and carried it to the table.

'See for yourself.' Blake pointed to the new work.

Bonham stared in disbelief. 'Did you do this, Sabian?' he asked as he flicked the pages back and forth, his eyes searching for any clue as to how the pages had been inserted.

'You won't find a stitch or glue,' Blake replied. 'It is as if they grow from the spine like the leaves of a plant reaching for the sun. They are stuck fast. I tried to pull one from the book today, but with all my strength it would not move or tear.'

Bonham flicked to the final page. 'What does it say?'

'It speaks of torment and destruction, fire and brimstone. The earth will shudder and this will be the start of a time of great suffering. The Nemorensis speaks of a creature. A man who can fly and has escaped from the heavens. He has the answer to our questions.'

'Do you believe this, Sabian? Books that grow and comets that will destroy life?'

'I believe what I can see and experience. I search for truth.' Blake stopped speaking and walked across the room to the window. He pulled back the curtain, forming a small chink through which he stared out into the square. 'Come and see,' he called to Bonham. 'Every night, all night, under the trees stands a man. He is watching this house.'

Bonham peered through the gap in the curtain. There, far below in the shade of the elm trees, Bonham could see the dark figure of a man and the ember glow of a clay pipe.

'He's there all the time,' said Blake. 'Followed me to Piccadilly and back. He dresses like a Huguenot, black hat, long black coat and never a smile.'

'Perhaps he's just a refugee from the persecution. A refugee waiting to rob you for what money you have.' Bonham laughed.

'You may laugh, Isaac, but this whole situation grows stranger by the day. I believe there are powers at work that we know little about. If he is a Huguenot, then he will not be here on Sunday morning. The appeal of the church bells will be too much for him to resist.'

'So why don't you follow him? He will have to eat or sleep somewhere and even the French are not so blatant as to relieve themselves under an elm tree.'

'I have watched him, and he doesn't eat or sleep. He is there when I go to bed and again when I rise. He never moves unless I move. When the wind blows, he just turns up his collar and props himself against the side of that tree. If I hadn't seen him close to I would say the man was a ghost.'

'Even the living have a way of haunting us,' Bonham said as he stared down to the street. 'Shall I go and offer him supper? Perhaps he would be more comfortable if he came and rested with you, so you would both know where each other –'

'So he could slit my throat and have done with it?' Blake replied.

'Well, let us see the man's face,' Bonham said. He dragged the telescope towards the window and thrust the lens through the chink in the curtain.

'Look!' shouted Blake. 'What's happening to him?'

As the two men looked on, the stranger began to vanish before their eyes. First his legs turned to silver embers that danced like the sparks of the fire. Then his hands burnt white hot as the light engulfed his arms and torso. Then, suddenly, he was gone. The leaves of the elm tree blew across the grass. There was no sign of the man, he was no more.

Blake stared into the darkness. The light from the tavern cast eerie shadows through the trees. Dying leaves hung like dead men from the branches and rattled against each other. Through the square danced imps of river mist that swirled in the lamplight. He looked again and again, believing that his eyes had told untruths.

Neither Blake nor Bonham saw the small squat creature that hobbled through the dirt of the street below their window and scurried like a hungry rat down the cellar steps of the house and through the open scullery door.

7 : The Bibblewick of London Bridge

A tiny brass bell jangled above her head as Agetta tried to
sneak through the small opening and into the shop. The sign
above the door read in bold letters: '*Bibblewick Books –
Thaddeus Bracegirdle – Bookbinder & Seller.*' The words were
surrounded by the gold-painted pages of a large book. In the
swift river breeze it flapped backwards and forwards on its
hanging-post, welcoming all to a new world.

From the brightness of the crisp morning sun, Agetta was
plunged into the musty darkness of the shop with its smell
of damp paper. It reminded her of the beach at Rotherhithe
with its stink of rotting fish guts piled on the drying sand at
the end of the market. The large vaulted ceiling was like a
cathedral. Long strings of dusty cobwebs swayed back and
forth, shimmering in the light of the candles that lit each
aisle.

Agetta heard the words of Yerzinia echo in her mind: '*the
bookseller . . . London Bridge*'. Here she was in Bibblewick's
Bookshop. She had never been in such a place before. It was
a vast room of dark oak, made from the boards of ancient
shipwrecks. High on the wall was a ship's figurehead, a painted
lady dressed in fine purple and blue robes and staring down upon
rows of dust-laden shelves stuffed to bursting with volumes of
leather-bound books.

Gently closing the door behind her, Agetta shut out the tolling bells of the church on the corner of Grub Street. They beat and clanged the chorus that God wasn't dead, calling sleepers to wake up, rise from their beds and step into the light of the sun that would break the charm of darkness. Inside the bookshop the titled walls dulled the noise of the bells.

Agetta became increasingly aware that in this maze of tall shelves she was being watched. She looked up to the figure-head, whose dead eyes stared back at her. Mice scuttled across the floor around her feet and into the walls. She walked carefully and slowly between two long shelves of books that reached upwards from the floor to three times her height. She could feel a lump grow in her throat as she tried to breathe without making a sound, all the time feeling that someone was there, someone she could not see. There was no sign of the shopkeeper, just row upon row of book-cluttered shelves from which fell showers of fine white dust, blown by a draught through the cracked floorboards and clouding each aisle.

Agetta stopped, stood still and listened. From the corner of her eye she saw a small dark shape dart from shadow to shadow. The shop creaked and groaned. She could hear the faint sound of water far below. Then she felt warm breath on the back of her neck, blowing against the collar, and heard the sound of children whispering. She turned towards the noise; the shop was still empty.

Suddenly from the top shelf there was a slithering of damp leather against wood. A cloud of dust and mouse dirt welled up from the floor like a spiralling whirlwind. A large, leather-bound black book fell to the floor, its thick spine clattering against the dirty wooden floorboards and then falling open like a black swan shot from the sky.

The choking cloud engulfed Agetta as she pressed herself closer to the shelves. Again she heard the faint whispering of children's voices goading her in her fear. 'Who is it?' she shouted. 'Why are you doing this to me?'

A childish giggle sounded from behind the bookshelf. Agetta wanted to run, to escape from the shop and into the light. From above her head again came the slithering of another leather book being pushed from the shelf by unseen mischievous hands. The thick paper crunched against the hard wood, then the book crashed to the floor spine first, falling open. Again the sound of quiet laughter echoed in the aisles as if a hundred children surrounded her.

Agetta could feel a breeze blowing up and through each crack of the floorboards, bringing with it the smell of the river. The pages of the book began to blow like the October leaves, falling open at a page with thick, black writing.

Carefully, she edged her way along the side of the bookshelves, looking up to see if another book would fall upon her. Dust billowed around her feet like a thick cloud, then as soon as it had appeared it vanished again, leaving her staring at the book, its yellowed pages sprawled open. Her eyes were drawn to the bold black writing that appeared to have been scrawled by hand across the page:

> *Death be not proud, though some have called thee mighty*
> *and dreadful,*
> *Die not, poor death, nor yet canst thou kill me . . .*
> *Thou art slave to fate, chance, kings and desperate men!*

Agetta quickly read each line, her heart telling her that these were special, prophetic words, just for her. They were words spoken by creatures that had no human voice and chattered in children's laughter, playing games of chance with her imagination. She was a slave to fate, and trapped in a maze of secret knowledge. The sound of teasing laughter came again.

From far below her feet Agetta heard something or someone large being dragged across a stone floor. Candlelight jumped through the gaps between the large oak floorboards, and Agetta lay in the dust and peered down through a large crack into a cellar. Far below, a small chubby man with wispy hair and a balding head dragged a long fat sack across the cellar floor. The man dumped the sack in the corner of the cellar and turned to the door. Agetta saw him no more – but then she heard the muffled thud of heavy footsteps clodding on a wooden staircase, rising from the deep like the approach of some sea monster.

She ran into the next aisle. It was empty, there was not a sound. All around her were endless shelves and books, a myriad of confusion. She ran along the aisle, turned, and ran again, trying to find the door to the shop. With each turn she knew she was being taken further from freedom as the maze of books drew her closer to its centre.

The chatter of small feet began to chase her, and childish laughter filled the air. Agetta ran even faster as books tumbled from shelves to the floor behind her, clattering against the boards like heavy rain. She ran left, then right, and with each turn the footsteps got closer, the whispering of tiny voices growing louder and louder. And then, in an instant, Agetta was in the centre of the shop. A large three-legged desk overflowing with papers towered above her. At its side was a small set of steps set below a worn oak standing-plate. To the right was a large door, slightly ajar, through which the smell of the river spewed from the darkness beyond.

The laughter and the chase stopped, the small voices disappeared, and all was deathly quiet as an eerie stillness filled the room. The papers began to blow with the strong salty draught coming from the cellar. Heavy footsteps beat against each tread. Agetta knew she would not be alone for much longer, and panic flooded through her as she thought what to do. To run meant enduring the chase of ghostly children, to stay meant she would face her future alone. The eye-scar burnt brightly beneath a home-made bandage, its throbbing growing more intense as a rush of blood charged through her veins. The words of Yerzinia came again: '*the bookseller, London Bridge . . .*'

Suddenly the cellar door burst open, and before her stood the chubby man with wispy hair and balding head. He smiled at Agetta as if he had been expecting her. In his arms he carried a large bundle of books.

'Tides coming in, had to move these, they are precious, very precious. Didn't want to get them wet.' He looked at Agetta and smiled. 'Make yourself useful, come and give me a hand with these.'

The man struggled under the weight of the books. Agetta hesitated, then stepped over to help him, taking from him three large volumes of musty paper bound in linen. She read the gold letters on each spine: *Dialogues of the Dead, The Nature and Plan of Hell, The Art of Dying Well.*

The bookseller saw the look in her eyes. 'They're for a prisoner in Newgate,' he said. 'He's bound for the gallows. A proper gentleman who wants to prepare himself for what is to come.' He dropped the rest of the books on to the floor. 'You can put them on that chair. They are a special order to be collected.' Then he stopped and pulled out a large piece of white cloth from the pocket of his waistcoat and with it wiped his sweaty forehead. 'I'm Thaddeus Bracegirdle, but you can call me Mister Thaddeus. Now, what can I get for you?'

Agetta didn't know what to say. 'I'm . . . I'm . . . ,' she floundered like a dying fish gasping for air. 'I'm looking for something.'

'Aren't we all?' he said, as he looked her up and down. Thaddeus was a small man with a pot-belly. He had wiry grey hair that straggled to his shoulders and had been swept over his growing baldness. It was his sparkling eyes that intrigued Agetta. She knew she had looked into them before but knew not where. When he smiled she saw that he had false teeth that appeared too large for his mouth, though they were skilfully crafted from enamelled copper and fitted with strong springs that caused his mouth to jump open with every spoken word.

'Do you know what you are looking for? It always helps.' He tried to pile his hair on the top of his head. 'I'm an Oxford man myself, that's where I got my love of books. They can bring happiness to dull lives and be the transport to delight, taking us to places and giving us thoughts we could never achieve on our own.' He stopped and looked at her bandaged hand. 'What did you do?' he asked.

'It was burnt,' she replied quickly. 'A candle burn. Doctor Sarapuk said I have to keep it covered . . .'

Thaddeus looked at her as if the name of Sarapuk had registered within him. He grunted and stared at the books scattered around the shop. 'Been busy today, looks like *they* –' He stopped what he was saying as if he had realised he had given away too much already. 'Ah yes! Books! Did you know that they give you dreams?' He took Agetta by the hand and walked her to the low window at the back of the shop that over-looked the Thames. 'Read a book and dream for a week, that's what I say. Forget cheese or curdled milk, if you want to dream, read a book. Better still read one of mine!'

Thaddeus ran his finger along a shelf of books as if looking for a particular one. He grabbed a thin green volume and handed it to Agetta. 'This one's mine,' he said proudly. 'It started life as a dream, one of those dreams you have before you wake. I remember it well.'

'What's it about?' Agetta asked as she looked through the pages.

'It's about a man who spent years of his life looking for something and then he met someone and fell in love and he never had to search again.' Thaddeus looked at the river out of the window. A strange melancholy fell over them both, and for several minutes they stared in silence upon the changing scene. Far below, little red and green boats carried people back and forth across the Thames, and small waves lapped against the far shore. A pillar of cloud wafted up from a tall chimney by the leather-works in Southwark village, touching earth to sky and towering over the green fields that ran along the riverside.

It was as if they searched the horizon for something that they had lost, something precious that had escaped them. The tide changed; beneath them the old Thames sighed as deep swirls of white water broke against the thick columns of the bridge. Thaddeus looked down at a struggling boatman who frantically tried to escape the whirlpool.

'A wise man crosses the bridge whilst only the fool goes beneath it. They say that on the Feast of St Clement, just as the sun rises, a whirlpool appears under the bridge. As the sun strikes the water, if you dive from the bridge into the centre of the maelstrom you will be taken from this world and into another. A place of beauty and mystery where we are no longer slaves to fate, chance, kings and desperate men.'

The words sent a shudder through Agetta and broke her dreaming. Her whole body shook, as if gripped by a sudden force.

Thaddeus saw what had taken place. 'Happened to me once. Like someone had walked straight through you. You just have to hope they came out the other side and *don't start playing mischief with you*,' he said as he looked around. It was as if he wasn't speaking to her but to someone else, someone who was nearby and listening to their every word. He looked again at the book in her hand. 'Many a man's desire has come from the pages of a book. They are like fires to the imagination. A revolution can be started by one word, a single sentence can give man courage to fight any battle.' He stopped suddenly, as if he had forgotten something vitally important. 'In all this talking I forgot to ask your name. It's my fault, I always speak too much.'

'Agetta Lamian,' she replied dreamily. 'From the lodging house on Fleet Street.'

He looked again out of the window as if he hadn't heard her reply. 'There's only one book I need for my collection, and then I can die a happy man. It's a book so rare that if I were to have it then I could regain someone I lost so long ago.' He turned and stared at Agetta, his lips thinned and angry, and a tear rolled slowly across his cheek. 'I almost had the book once. Had a place set aside on my keep shelf, but before I could take it, it was snatched from me, never to be seen again. With it I lost the only person who I have ever cared for. She was a young girl just like you, a smile like yours and a heart of fire. She wanted more than a young scholar at Oxford. Her life was set for greatness, mine for obscurity. She left me something I could never forget and that I'll carry till the day I die.' Thaddeus rubbed the palm of his right hand.

'Does this book have a name?' Agetta asked, wanting to help him. 'I could search all the bookshops in London. I can read, you know. Then you could get the book and the girl you lost.'

'Why help me?' Thaddeus sat on a ledge and stared out of the window. 'You don't know me, never met me before.'

'But does it have a name?' she said insistently.

'The Nemorensis . . . It's called the Nemorensis,' he said thoughtfully. 'It's an old book written thousands of years ago. A beautiful creation.' He was suddenly animated again, his melancholy had vanished. 'Such a book would be worth all I had, such a book would be worth dying for . . .'

The name of the Nemorensis etched itself into Agetta's mind. It was like a key being fitted snugly into a lock and slowly turned. She repeated the word over and over again, and pictures of another world flashed across her memory. Her hand began to ache painfully as fresh blood seeped through the bandages. She held her hand close as the throbbing and the pain increased. Thaddeus grabbed hold of her to stop her from falling. Agetta sat on the window ledge, hoping the pain would go away. In her mind the thought of the Nemorensis churned and swirled over and over, welling up in her throat as if she was being forced to say the word.

'NEMORENSIS!' she shouted out like a woman strapped to a birthing chair. 'NEMORENSIS! NEMORENSIS!' Relief was etched in her face as the spell took hold and the pain ebbed away from her hand. She knew this was Blake's book, the one he had spoken of on the night of the sky-quake.

She looked down at the bloodstained bandages that Thaddeus began quickly to unwind. He lifted the linen swab from where the wound had been to reveal fresh new skin. Gone was the burn, there was no scar. Staring back at them was a bright red mark etched in black, in the shape of an eye. Agetta curled up her hand – there was no pain.

Thaddeus looked at her. 'I knew there was something strange about you,' he said as he folded away the bandages. 'I was meant to meet you today, you have been sent to me. I know that mark well. It burns into the hand like a seed and when the time is right it bursts forth to grow in the mind. These last days have been –'

'They have been dreadful,' Agetta interrupted. 'So incredibly strange, things that I have never experienced before have been around every corner. I have had no one to tell. My father would . . .' She stopped speaking and looked at Thaddeus.

'He would think you were fit for Bedlam and as far gone as a Vauxhall mollie. I know Cadmus Lamian. He's not a dreamer or a seer. Feet fixed to the soil and a belly washed with gin.'

Thaddeus and Agetta laughed. For the first time she felt a deep sense of relief, that in this man she had found someone who would understand her.

'I know what you have gone through, and in Mister Thaddeus you will always have a friend.'

There was a sudden and urgent jangling of the doorbell. Thaddeus looked at Agetta and gestured for her to be quiet. 'Go find a book. *They* will not bother you when we have a visitor in the shop. It takes special ears to hear where *they* are and not everyone has that.'

The sound of metal-tipped heels tap-tap-tapped across the shop floor, purposefullly heading through the aisles of books towards them. Agetta pretended to be busily looking at the bookshelf in front of her whilst Thaddeus returned to his desk, climbed the steps and stood on the waiting-plate, from where he could see every aisle of the shop. He took a pair of thick-wired spectacles from the pocket of his waistcoat, put them on the end of his nose and peered into the gloom.

Walking towards Thaddeus down the long aisle of history books was a tall man dressed from head to foot in black and wearing a floppy hat pulled down over his face. His tunic was etched in gold braid, his boots crisp and bible-black. The man turned the corner and stood before Thaddeus, who peered down at him over the top of his spectacles like some large ferocious

87

owl. The man stared at Thaddeus, raising one eyebrow and smiling through steely lips.

'I'm looking for a book,' he said loudly, his accent making Agetta turn suddenly to face him. The shock of seeing the man threw her back against the shelves, startled. It was the man from Holborn, the stranger from the dream. He looked at her and smiled.

'Three times in as many days,' he said in his soft voice. 'I would say that you are following me.'

Thaddeus interrupted quickly. 'Is it a special book you are looking for, sir? I see from your clothes you are not from these parts.'

'You are a very clever man and right on both counts. The book I am looking for is very special. It was once mine, but I somehow mislaid it many years ago.' He paused and stared at Agetta. 'Stupid of me, really. It is not the kind of book that should fall into the wrong hands, it contains too many family secrets.'

'You must come from a fine family to have books written about you!' Agetta said boldly. 'No one would ever want to write anything about me.'

'It is more important to be known well by one person than to have the favour of the whole world,' the stranger replied.

'So who wrote this book about you?' Thaddeus asked. 'Maybe I know it.'

'A sister . . . One who turned her back on the family. She was always too much of a coward to place her name on anything. Always hides behind someone else.' The stranger looked around the shop, as if listening. 'How many children do you have?' he asked, looking at Thaddeus. 'I can hear one of them calling you.'

'It's the waves crashing against the bridge, seahawks, something like that. I have no children,' Thaddeus said angrily. 'Is it

88

a book you want or something else?'

'A book, but I sense it is not here. My search will continue.' He stopped and looked at Agetta. 'Well, my girl, until I see you yet again. Our paths will surely cross – maybe, even in a dream.'

The stranger gave a genteel bow, turned and walked briskly out of the shop. The doorbell jangled as he slammed the door behind him.

Agetta looked at Thaddeus as she bit her lip nervously. 'He's following me,' she blurted out. 'I saw him once in Holborn and once in a dream. He wants something.'

'The man's a foreigner, they do strange things. Meeting him twice, well, London is a small place.' It seemed to Agetta he was not telling all he knew. 'The Huguenots are everywhere, and he is just another lost Frenchman, running from his king.' Thaddeus laughed and then rummaged in his pocket as if he wanted to take her mind off the situation. 'I have this, it is very special and very old, but it will help you read words you cannot see or understand. I knew you came for something, and *this* is it!'

Thaddeus reached into the depths of his pocket and produced a piece of polished crystal the size of half a goose egg. It was edged with silver holly leaves that held the glass in a garland. In the light of the window it cast a rainbow of coloured light across her face.

'I want you to have this. It's an Ormuz glass, a blessing to those who have aged. It was made by Al-Hazzan, and I want you to have it as a gift of our friendship, it will help you to understand that which you cannot read.' In three large steps he jumped from the high desk and stood in front of Agetta holding out the Ormuz glass. 'Take it, come back next week and I will tell you some more. Who knows, maybe you will stumble on the Nemorensis and make Thaddeus a happy man!'

Agetta had the urge to speak, to tell of her secret, that she already knew who had the book, but now was not the time. Thaddeus pressed the Ormuz glass into her right hand. It fitted the shape of the eye-burn perfectly. As she looked into the crystal Ormuz glass it magnified every line and mark on her palm. In amazement she saw every detail of the outline of the eye perfectly enlarged. It was as if each line was made up of tiny letters written so close that they looked like a solid line.

'It will show you many things. It has no magic or trickery, just the wonder of science.' Thaddeus took her by the arm and walked her to the door. 'I expect to see you again. I have but few friends and now I have one more.' He appeared sincere, his eyes glinted friendship. Agetta didn't reply and stepped into the street still clutching the crystal, wondering why Blake's book was so important.

London Bridge was crowded. The people pressed by each other, holding tight to their purses for fear of pickpockets. Agetta looked all around, checking each doorway for the stranger. She slipped the Ormuz glass into her pocket, still holding it tight with her right hand, and picked her way through the street dirt towards Bishopsgate. Consumed with her thoughts, she didn't notice the man staring at her through the thick dirty glass of the coffee shop. She was thinking of Thaddeus, his warm smile and startling eyes, and of the Ormuz glass. No one had ever given her such a gift as this before, and for no reason. She smiled, knowing life was changing and she was changing too. The distant memory of Absinthium danced across her tongue. She huddled tightly inside her coat and savoured the long-lost taste.

The sun was low in the southern sky and cast thick shadows across London Bridge. From his table in the coffee shop the stranger picked up his black French hat and quickly stepped into the light. From his pocket he took a pair of golden spectacles with deep blue lenses cut from the finest sapphire and polished to reflect the sun. He pulled down his hat and turned up the collar on his coat, sliding a thin black glove over his long white fingers.

8 : Liberato per Mortem

Blake staggered through a torrential downpour as hailstones like duck eggs plummeted from the thunder-black night sky and pounded into the mud around him. They splattered in the deep puddles and rattled on carriage roofs, beating the backs of the standing horses that jumped and twitched nervously with each blast of ice.

He held up his hands as he ran to protect his face. A sharp jag of silver-white lightning flashed from sky to earth, striking into the street and blasting the cobbles from the ground like smashed teeth. A roar of thunder rattled the windows and knocked the breath from Blake's body. A deep, thick, jet-black cloud rolled across the night sky, reaching down over Conduit Fields as if it were a giant fist about to smash into the earth; its edges were outlined in bright silver by the light of a struggling moon that momentarily broke through the clouds and then was engulfed again in blackness.

The last boulders of ice slapped furiously into the mud of the street. Picking his way from house to house, Blake could see in the distance the two bright lamps that protected the door of Flamberg's mansion in Queens Square. Guarding the door were two footmen dressed in gold braid and scarlet jackets, their white socks stained with the street mud, and holding large wooden torches wrapped in tallow rags that burnt bright yellow. He quickened his step, fearful that another bolt would crash from the sky as the storm fired its anger at the earth.

It came quickly. From all around came a rush of wind that lifted the water from the puddles and shot it like arrows through the air and up into the sky. A flash of electricity blanketed the street, sparking off the rooftops and turning the sky dazzling white. Blake pressed himself against the damp wall of a house as the lightning bolt fired past his face with brightness so intense it shone through his closed eyes. The heat steamed his wet coat, scorching the top of his hat and leaving his face with a red glow. As the lightning crashed to the ground it blistered the road outside Flamberg's mansion, sending the two footmen scurrying down the cellar steps, their burning torches cast aside and spitting in the mud as their light quickly faded.

Wet, bedraggled and intensely irate, Blake climbed the steep marble staircase that took him from the dirt of the street to the polished refinement of Lord Flamberg's mansion. Gargoyle lamps stood as sentinels beside the door. Each looked as if it had been cut from a solid piece of metal and was inlaid with fine white, red and blue glass. They were topped with the heads of helmeted snakes, and the light from thick beeswax candles shone an eerie glow through the red, cut-glass eyes. The spitting of the candles sounding like the hissing of snakes. In the centre of the oak door was a large gold tapping-handle forged from a single piece of iron in the shape of a dragon. Thick ribbed wings and green jewelled eyes shone in the lamplight.

To the north the sky rumbled with discontent as the storm swirled away into the night and the heavens began to clear. Blake looked up. There, for the first time, he could see his star with his naked eye. Its faint light and sparkling tail shone down from the depths of space. He smiled to himself as he took off his sodden hat and shook the rain from the brim. The two footmen clambered up the cellar steps and into the street, ignoring Blake as they ran to pick up their discarded torches, and then retreated again to the safety of the cellar.

Blake smashed the tapping-handle three times against the brass plate. The dragon felt unnaturally warm, the two eyes leaving a distinct impression in the palm of his hand. A tall, thin butler dressed in the finest blue silk coat opened the door. He had a pinched face and deep-set eyes encircled in dark, smudged skin that was crisscrossed with tiny wrinkles.

'Doctor Blake,' he said in a voice that matched the wrinkles. 'Lord Flamberg would like to see you in the dining room, they have been waiting for some time . . .' He looked down his nose at Blake as he gestured for him to come into the mansion.

Above Blake's head a large chandelier of candles lit the hallway, rocking slightly from side to side, slowly rotating and casting long moving shadows. In a large gilt looking-glass Blake somehow appeared much older than he had thought, his face lined and dishevelled.

Lord Flamberg stepped abruptly through the door of the dining room into the hallway. 'My dear Blake,' he said, wiping his long grey hair from his face. 'Thought you had been blown away in the storm. Quite spectacular. Come in, Lady Flamberg has been waiting.'

The room was brightly lit, with wooden shutters that blocked any chink of light from escaping. Lady Flamberg was sitting in a wing-chair at the head of a long polished oak table, two horse lengths from the door. She didn't move as Blake entered the room. Blake gasped at her incredible beauty – a black silk mantua gown was draped across her powder-white skin, and her fine, neat hands and long pure neck shone in the candlelight.

Lord Flamberg sat at the opposite end of the table and gestured for Blake to take the several steps towards the only other chair, next to his wife.

'She likes company, Blake. She'll want you *all* for herself,' Flamberg said. 'When you are finally comfortable we will eat.'

Blake held out his hand towards Lady Flamberg. 'I am Doctor Sabian Blake, it is nice to –'

'You may call me, Hezrin, Doctor Blake. I find Lady Flamberg so formal.' She smiled at him with her cold, steel-blue eyes and thin red lips.

Blake sat at the table and looked over the expanse of solid wood that stretched out like a polished fallen tree to where Lord Flamberg stared back at him.

'It is such a beautiful room, with so many pretty things.'

'And the prettiest of them all is my wife,' replied Lord Flamberg as he clicked his fingers. Two servants bustled into the room carrying large silver platters that gave off a thick steam from under their rims. They clumsily crashed the platters to the table and lifted the lids in a swell of fog. In the clearing mist, Blake could see the cooked head of a large animal, its butter-glazed eyes staring at him. On the other platter was a long black fish surrounded by a myriad of tiny writhing eels that wriggled and churned like a living sea. He gulped back his disgust and wondered how he could ever swallow such creatures and keep them from jumping from his stomach.

The smallest servant leant over the table and pointed to the dishes with the tip of a long, sharp stiletto.

'Which?' he said in a deep voice. 'I cut, you eat. Which one?' he asked again, impatiently.

Blake was holding his breath, not wishing to take in the fumes from the lightly cooked fish and the writhing fresh eels. He looked to the steaming animal head, unsure as to from what strange, tusked creature it had been severed. 'And this?' he asked expectantly.

'This is walrus – fresh, cooked walrus,' the man said in his broken English. 'I cut some for you. The best is the tongue or the eyes.'

'I will have some fish.' Blake said firmly. A look of disappointment crossed the servant's face.

'Fish?' he asked again.

'Fish!' Blake replied, pointing to the mass of eels that squirmed over the body of the long scaly creature.

'My husband tells me that you are a Cabalist. Does your magic help you?' Hezrin asked as the servant slit the knife into the fish and quickly sliced and slapped a long fillet of the squirming feast on to Blake's plate, accompanied by a large dollop of slithering eels.

'It is not magic but science,' Blake replied as the steaming plate of fish and eels was placed before him. 'The dark ages are long dead. This is the manipulation of forces that as yet we do not understand. I believe a day is coming when every mystery known to man will be explained away in science.'

'You leave no place for faith or mystery in your world. It is like art without the artist or music without an instrument. What can you do with your magic? Can you heal that fish?' Hezrin stabbed her table knife into the walrus's eye, gouging it from the socket.

'The universe is not without design, even that which you eat had a purpose and now that purpose has changed somewhat. Magic is about finding truths. The Cabala brings the infinite with the finite, the greatest to the least, everything is held together.' Blake looked up from the eels that now slithered from the plate and on to the fine white tablecloth, leaving behind a thick black slime.

'I believe in magic, Sabian. Not as you say, but as something wonderful that can transport us from the drudgery of this world.' Hezrin stabbed her fork again into the creature and tore off a strip of cooked skin, wrapping it around her fork. 'We live in a world where people believe in the strangest things, but you want to explain it all away and give a reason for every action.'

'He is a scientist, a discoverer,' her husband said from his faraway place at the end of the table. 'Blake has discovered something wonderful, and tomorrow it will be the talk of London. Yeats will see to that. The *London Chronicle* will tell every coffee lout in town what he has discovered.' Lord Flamberg saw Blake looking at the writhing plate. 'My wife has a peculiar taste in food. Sometimes I believe she would eat any creature that she turned her mind to. Why eat what beggar's eat? Who can say they have feasted on the finest walrus?' Flamberg said excitedly. 'Fine wine and the fruit of the ocean. I especially like the tongue.'

'Come now, Sabian. It's quite simple, stab them and eat them whole. They are wonderful for you and give a freshness to your complexion.' Hezrin laughed as she spoke, urging Blake to eat the eels. 'They are sea-fresh, caught on the mud-banks and kept alive for the table, they will do you no harm.'

Blake stabbed at the eels that writhed and squirmed and, spearing several, he quickly swallowed them whole, gulping the fish down as the taste of scales and salt gagged the back of his throat. Hezrin and her husband watched as he slowly chewed his way through half the plate before finally taking his napkin and folding it carefully over what remained.

'Delicious,' he said half-heartedly, swallowing mouthfuls of air as he tried to keep the contents of his stomach from churning. He was convinced that they were still moving, that they would never die and would be seen again. 'So what of the *Chronicle*? What news will it carry of my comet?'

'You are centre stage, the man of the moment. Yeats has billed you as a great scientist, the discoverer of the century,' Flamberg replied, chewing the fat from a long white tusk and wiping walrus grease from his face. 'They will be told that the comet will miss the earth, and that by your calculations we shall have the finest display of sky lights since the dawn of time.'

'Then they'll hang me when it crashes into London and kills half the population.' Blake's eyes flashed from Hezrin to Lord Flamberg, looking for some kind of reaction as they calmly continued to eat the rest of the walrus head.

'Then they'll never know!' replied Flamberg, coughing out pieces of chewed flesh on to the table. 'We'll invite the King and the Royal Court to our house in the northern counties and the rest can burn,' he said calmly. 'My friends and I believe that this would be a good thing for London. The city is far too crowded and some of the people are not worth the air they breathe.' Flamberg drew his hand across his throat as if to show the cutting of a knife. 'I think you know what I mean, Blake. London transformed into a new Rome or even a new Jerusalem, with the debris of life burnt up by your comet. Divine providence!' Flamberg laughed.

'That's not right!' Blake exclaimed. 'We have to tell them, we could save people.'

'There would be panic, Sabian,' Hezrin said. 'This way we can get all those that really matter away from London, and the rest will have to take their chance. To tell them now could spark a revolution.' She took hold of Blake's right hand and pulled it towards her. 'Let me see what the palm tells me of your life. I have the gift to see the future. Look at me and I will tell you what will happen.' Her hand was warm and soft. Blake could feel his face beginning to glow pink in the candlelight, and had no chance to refuse as she took his hand and turned the palm upwards.

Hezrin took her forefinger and traced the shape of a star into the palm of his hand. Taking her glass she dripped a large bead of red wine into his palm and then rubbed it into the skin. The candlelight flickered softly.

Flamberg folded his arms and slouched back into his chair, picking his teeth with the point of the table knife. He looked at Blake and smiled as he left him to the whims of his wife. 'She will lead you into something you may never understand,' he said as he chewed on half-eaten fat. Then he folded his arms and snuggled himself into the large wing-chair. He closed his eyes and rested his chin on his chest and fell fast asleep.

Blake looked at him in disbelief as Flamberg began to snore quietly with each pained breath. Hezrin tugged on his hand, pressing her nails painfully into his palm.

'I don't like to be ignored, Sabian,' she said angrily through her teeth. 'You and I have a future, don't you want to know what happens?'

'For my own future I have little concern. What I want is to tell the world what will happen,' Blake said as he attempted to take his gaze from her face.

'Those who matter know what to do. My husband has been very busy with his friends, leave it to them and all will be well.'

'For who? Your friends and the King? And the rest of London can burn?' he said loudly.

'What would you do? Have them all know now and thousands would die in the havoc that would follow. How would they cope? They would believe the last judgement was upon them. Would you see that happen? This way some have a chance to escape.' She paused and looked him in the eyes. 'Tell me, Sabian. How did you know the comet was coming? Was it by accident?'

Blake couldn't stop staring at her, such was the power of her fascination. She was dressed in rich purple and black, and had a deep dark beauty spot on her unlined face.

'I read . . .' The words froze in his mouth as if an icy hand had grabbed hold of his voice. He gasped the air as a burning pain raced through his hand, jolting pulses of torture along his arm, into his chest and up to his throat. Every nerve and muscle danced out of control. He tried to stand but the unseen force slapped him to the table and into the carcass of the half-eaten fish.

'Don't struggle, Sabian. I want to see the future, and for all knowledge there has to be a price.' Hezrin giggled as she held tightly to his hand, watching him writhe like the eels he had just eaten. 'Sit,' she commanded as she pressed harder into the palm of his hand. Blake had no control. He fell backwards to the seat, his eyes clouded with the dark vapour that now filled the whole room. 'Listen to me, Sabian. There is magic in your future and a power that will come to the world through you, it is clear to see. It is before you, and yet you cannot see it. Believe everything that comes before your eyes – but a foreigner will seek your life.'

The words thrashed in his head like a horsewhip, and his arm juddered and twitched several times more until she let go. He stared helplessly at Hezrin. 'What did you do?' he mumbled, his teeth chattering.

'A party trick, nothing more. Can your science not explain it away, Sabian? Or will you have to believe in magic as magic?'

Blake didn't reply. His arm burned like a tree struck by lightning. He tried to close his fingers but the pain was too intense, and the tiny blue sparks crackled across the surface of his hand.

'It will soon go away. Such is the power of knowing the future.' Hezrin paused and sighed. 'If only Flamberg had a mind like yours, things would have been so different. Look at him, snoring like a walrus full of fish on a sandy beach, happy in his ignorance. You, Sabian, have an enquiring mind, you will think for days about what has happened, you will torture yourself until you know the answer and work out by what power you were enthralled.' Hezrin laughed. 'Save yourself the time, it *was* magic.'

'Then, madam, I will depart. Your magic is far too bold for a man like me to understand and I fear that your husband's sleep may also be part of your spell.' Blake stepped unsteadily from the table, tripping and pressing his hand into the plate of dead eels.

'I have something I would like to show you, Dr Blake. Something that I have kept secret even from my *old walrus*. Oh for the day when someone will cut off his head and serve it on a plate!' Hezrin spoke quietly as she got up from the table and walked towards Blake. He felt the eels squirm in his stomach. He was sure they were still alive, and that before the night was over they would force their way out of his body by some circuitous route.

'I think I need to go to the –' Blake muttered, trying to speak without opening his mouth.

'Don't be so silly, not before I show you something that will excite your mind and stretch the imagination.' Hezrin took hold of his arm and dragged the unwilling Blake across the room. Flamberg didn't stir. He slouched in his chair, fatty dribble running down his chin and dripping on to his black coat. 'Sshh,' she said as she pushed Blake to the door. 'I don't want him to wake, this is our secret . . .'

Blake feared the secret, yet was overwhelmed by a desire and curiosity that burnt his heart. Hezrin overwhelmed him. She was powerful, intense, edged in darkness, and had a deep fascination from which he could not escape. They had just met, and yet she dominated Blake in every way. He felt like a blowfly about to be consumed by a giant black, silk spider, dragged to her lair, unwilling and yet unable to refuse.

'I have a surprise for you, Sabian. It is not only you that has a love for the sky and all that it will bring. I too have waited for this time, but for a different reason.' She gave his sore and burning hand a squeeze that made him wince.

'I don't think this is right,' Blake protested, trying to pull himself away from her. 'I would not be pleased if I were your husband –'

'Neither would I, but that is what makes it such fun. Who would want to be like him? Flamberg has always been so predictable, so boring. But you, Doctor Sabian Blake, Fellow of the Royal Society, Cabalist, and now discoverer of the planets – you make my mind tingle. Come and see what I have prepared for us.'

In the hallway of the mansion a large looking-glass filled the far wall from floor to ceiling. Its mercury was bright and crisp and reflected a sharp image in the candlelight. Blake stared at the reflection of Hezrin – she appeared ageless, without blemish or wrinkle.

'Behind the looking-glass is another world. Do you believe me, Sabian?' she asked.

'I would be a fool not to,' he said as he rubbed the growing red mark that burnt the palm of his hand. 'But I am a man of only one world and I would prefer to keep it that way.'

Hezrin laughed. 'Look into the depths and tell me what you see.'

Blake stared at the dim glass, across whose surface danced the candlelight from the large chandelier.

'So will you step inside this looking-glass with me, Doctor

Blake, and discover yet another world?' Hezrin asked as she gently pulled him closer to the glass. Blake did not speak, but nodded to Hezrin and stepped towards the glass, believing that in one step he would stand on the other side. 'No, Sabian! It is a real looking-glass,' she said as she lifted the catch on the side of the ornate gold frame that was decorated with monkey heads and the faces of frogs.

Blake noticed the gold ring on her finger, its comet tail wrapping her white skin with its golden band. 'Before we enter the chamber we must toast the future,' Hezrin said, taking two large blue glass vessels from the tall stand by the looking-glass. She handed one to Blake pushing it towards his mouth. 'In one gulp!' she said quietly, almost whispering. 'In one gulp and then together we can share what is to come.'

Hezrin put the vessel to her lips and tilted back her head. Blake watched as she drank the liquid and then crudely wiped her mouth with the back of her hand. 'Your turn, Sabian. Quickly.'

Blake drank from the cup. In two gulps he had drained the vessel. The thick green viscous liquid scalded his gullet, numbing his jaw, pushing his watery eyes from their sockets. and coated his voice, almost choking the breath from his lungs. Hezrin laughed to herself as she prised the looking-glass from the wall, slowly opening it like a gigantic door to some other world.

There was a sudden and cold blast of wind as the seal between wall and looking-glass was broken. Blake felt the coldness around him. High in the house a distant door slammed shut, and several footsteps tapped along the landing above their heads. Blake stared into the darkness of the room that lay beyond the mirror, searching the gloom with his eyes.

Hezrin gently prodded him to step into the blackness. It was then that Blake saw the tiny shape of shimmering blue essence that hovered in the centre of the darkness. It flashed and swirled like a thousand blue and white diamonds, spinning, making no sound as it floated three feet away from his face. Without thinking, Blake reached out to touch it, his hand helplessly moving towards the ball of sizzling electricity.

'Liberato per mortem,' Hezrin said, as she turned her face from the blinding light.

9 : Hebdomada Mortium

Agetta picked a large black bed-louse from the back of her hand, squeezing it till it splattered blood-red on her fingers. Beneath the scratchy blankets of her cold bed she had chased it through the night as it had scurried and bit.

To her left, her mother slept on, undisturbed by the constant gnawing of the rats in the wall as they chewed through daub-and-horsehair plaster. This was the full extent of life for Mrs Lamian – she never left the room she shared with her daughter. In between the long hours of sleep, she would eat the fickle food brought by her husband Cadmus and wash away her fear of the world with a quart of gin and small beer. The solid black door was the edge of her world, a line that could not be crossed. It was as impenetrable as any castle wall or high keep, with more power to stop her advance than the strongest lock forged in Spain.

In the darkness, Agetta brushed the crushed parasite from her hand and licked the small trace of blood from her fingers. It had a sweet taste like the memory of half-chewed honeycomb and bee spit. She tried to sleep, but the clamour of rats and the biting cold took from her mind any hope of rest. Brigand had vanished the night before. He wasn't there to protect her from the darkness with his rumbling growl, or curl up around her feet to keep her warm. She imagined him to be away over

Conduit Fields, heading out to the marshes chasing deer. His supper lay uneaten by the hall fire.

The lodging house moaned as floor joists pulled the boards and stretched and groaned. To Agetta it sounded as if the building was taking long, laboured breaths, stretching its ribs as it settled for the night. The candle on the gin table sent shadows scurrying across the room, tiny black shards of darkness that hid in corners and peeped from the side of the bed. She had always hated this room with its brown walls and dirty wooden floor; it gave no comfort, no happiness, it was only a place to rest after long weary days of cleaning and fetching and tramping through London's stink.

On the far side of the half-open black door she could hear the guests snoring and babbling in their sleep. The lodging house was full, even the hallway had been let off for sleeping. The only place of peace would be the kitchen and the large leather chair her father used as a bed, snug by the fire, clean and bright. She rubbed the damp from the window with her sleeve and looked into the night sky –and there in the height of heaven, surrounded by a million sparkling lights, was a star she had never seen before, its glinting blood-red tail stretching into space.

There was a sudden thud above her head. Dust from the attic room rained down upon her, filling the air with a sparkling white powder that reflected like falling snow in the candlelight. The thud came again, followed by the dragging of a metal chain across the wooden floor. A slate slipped from the roof and smashed into the street. Then again and again came the sound.

No one in the house stirred. Everyone slept on in deep oblivion. Through the floorboards above her head, Agetta heard the sound of weeping and the rattling of a metal chain. She slowly stepped from her bed and walked across the cold wooden floor. In the half-light she reached out to the door and listened to the crackling of the fire in the kitchen. Agetta knew her father would be asleep, feet warming by the fire and pee-pot squeezed under his chair.

She looked into the darkened hallway. A single candle burnt in its shelter on the wall, flickering with the breeze that constantly blew through the house. On the floor two crumpled piles of humanity groaned and gusted under thick, dirty blankets, scratching and picking at festering scabs in their sleep.

Agetta stared at the fat carcass of the derelict that now slept in her way. A short, rough, grey beard that twitched and rustled covered his pock-marked face. He lay on his back, half exposed by the blanket, his mouth wide open as he chomped at the air with loud snores. She fought the urge to take the candle and drip hot wax into his mouth to stop him from snoring and keep him quiet so she could get to the stairway at the other end of the dark hall.

The man muttered in his sleep, and she could smell his rancid breath. He moved suddenly and thrust out his arm, blocking her way along the hall. A large rat scurried from the depths of his coat and ran along the side of the wall and down the stairs to the kitchen. Agetta stepped over the sleeping fat body, trying not to touch him.

Her feet took her quickly along the hallway to the unlit staircase that led up two flights of narrowing steps. Agetta paused on each stair, a cold feeling of fear rising in her stomach like an ever-tightening knot. She could hear weeping from behind the attic door. It sounded far off, like the call of a lost seabird, and yet brought sadness to her heart as if she shared in the creature's grief.

Cobwebs hung thickly from the ceiling and grabbed at her face with strong gossamer threads. She brushed them away, untangling the fine grey strands from her hair. There was no light on the staircase, and she dare not take a candle for fear of being seen by her father. The blackness pressed in against her, whispering for her to stop, go no further, climb no more, turn back before it was too late.

It was on these stairs that she had seen Blueskin Danby on the night he had escaped from Newgate. In the half-light his face shone with the blue tattoo of a coiled snake that wrapped itself around each eye and slithered into his mouth. Danby had hidden in the attic, protected by her father. Two days later he was dead and stripped of his finery, a gawping corpse hung like a Christmas turkey.

The storm that followed his death raged fiercely for three days as his spirit clung to this world, refusing to be dragged to hell. In broad daylight tables had tipped over in the kitchen, coals were thrown from the open fire and plates were torn from the shelves and spun through the air by Blueskin's unseen hand. For three nights he had wailed on these very stairs, and from then on the attic had been a place of fear. Agetta had closed her eyes and crossed her fingers each time she had walked the landing, never daring to look up, never wanting to stare into the soulless eyes of Blueskin Danby. With each fearful step, she remembered more of that night. Her memory cursed her, speaking in whispers of all that she was afraid of.

At the top of the stairs the small door was chained and bolted from the outside. Agetta rummaged in her pocket and brought out a thin piece of bent metal. She slid it quickly into the lock and twisted the rod against the metal spring. She felt the lock twist and one by one she flipped the three metal snags that held the keeper tightly shut. The lock dropped open and Agetta quickly slid the two bolts back from the door.

Heavy footsteps thudded along the landing several feet below her. She pressed herself close to the wall, hiding in the darkness, fearful that Blueskin had returned. There was a long soft moan as the shadow of a tall figure ambled along the hallway, falling over its feet and mumbling to itself as it bounced from wall to wall towards the stairs.

She slowly crept down three steps and peered out from the darkness. Etched in the silver moonlight that shone in from the window, she saw the shadowy figure of a man. He was tall and wore a long tatty coat that trailed on the floor and a hat pulled down to his ears. As he staggered he lashed and kicked out at unseen creatures that infested his imagination and scurried around him. In one quick movement he fell backwards and slid down the plaster to sit on the wooden floor. He looked around in disbelief, thinking an invisible blow had knocked him from his feet. Closing his heavy eyes, he slumped down; then his legs crumpled beneath him and he curled up like a fat cat and shivered against the cold plaster wall, snoring loudly.

Agetta stealthily climbed the staircase back to the unlocked door. She listened for any sound, but heard only the beat of her own heart. She pressed against the door. It opened slowly and stiffly, scraping across the wooden floorboards. Quickly, she stepped into the attic.

Light from the city filled the room. In front of the high window, bathed in blue moonlight, she saw the silvered outline of a man sitting with his face in his hands, a glistening pool of tears around his feet.

Agetta gasped in surprise, the man looked up. He got to his feet, holding out his hands. From within him came a soft golden light that grew brighter as he stretched out his chained hands towards her. Suddenly the room was filled with blinding shafts of pure white light as two wings unfurled, filling the room, glowing and pulsating with every beat of the creature's heart.

Agetta peered through her fingers, shading her eyes from the intense, terrible brightness. It was as if all the light in the world was being sucked towards this figure, like time itself was being drawn deep within. Agetta could feel herself being gently lifted from the floor and pulled towards the creature. She held on to the doorframe, clinging tightly with her fingernails to the chipping paintwork, but with one, sudden, sharp jolt she was jerked from her anchor and she floated feet-first through the attic towards the creature's outstretched arms.

Frantically, Agetta waved her arms, trying to grab hold of everything that floated by her. Laughter filled the room, soft, cheerful laughter that glistened in the bright light. With a sudden and unexpected thump, she fell ungracefully to the hard wooden floor, and the room was plunged again into dim moonlight. Agetta looked up and stared first at the ceiling of the attic, where a hole had been smashed through to the tiles, and then at the tear-stained face of the man smiling down on her as she lay in the puddle of his lamentation.

'Don't say a word, Agetta,' the creature said, raising one eyebrow and the side of his mouth at the same time in a half-smile, and wiping the beads of salt tears from his face. 'Your father is still asleep in the kitchen, but his friend Sarapuk is on his way here . . .' The creature's soft, strong voice vibrated in her chest, penetrating her heart.

'How?' She looked at him, wondering what had just happened and searching every inch of his face for some hidden clue as to who or what he was.

'Fear not!' he said boldly, holding out his fine fingers to lift her from the floor. 'Your kind are either frightened or faint at the sight of me, but you seem to be different. There is something about you that –'

'Are you Blueskin Danby, come back to get my father?' She scrambled to her feet, trying to get away from him.

'Don't be afraid. I am Tegatus, a *guest* of your father, a victim of my own misadventure and a creature with a regretted past.'

He slumped back to the chair and held his head in his hands.

'Your wings, they've . . .' Agetta said as she brushed the floor dust from her coat, her eyes searching the darkness.

'They come and go. Alas, they are the cause of my downfall and the reason why I am here,' Tegatus muttered wearily.

'Was it a trick? Are they real? I've never known anyone with wings before.' Agetta attempted to peer over his shoulder, looking for the slightest sign of the large golden feathers that had filled the room with their bright glow.

'Real, unreal, what does it matter? They are a fascination to the world, and I am a freak to be sold and stared at, a powerless inhabitant of a menagerie from which I cannot escape.' Tegatus shuddered like a roosting bird with a pained expression on his face. 'I saw you climbing the stairs. I have tried to wake you so many times but you have always slept.'

Agetta looked at the hole in the attic roof. 'Did you do that?' she asked.

'I need to escape, but these chains keep me tied to this world.' Tegatus held out his hands towards her. His wrists were tightly banded in two gold manacles the size of shirt cuffs, each inscribed with small gold letters in a language that Agetta could not understand. 'They allow me to flex my wings,' he said angrily as he shook the manacles on his wrists, 'but whilst I wear these I am weak and helpless.'

'*Hebdomada Mortium*.' She whispered the words softly to herself. 'What does it mean?'

'It means I could be here for ever,' Tegatus said.

'I know a blacksmith who could smash them off and sell the gold,' Agetta said as she carefully examined each manacle from a safe distance.

He looked at her and smiled. 'It would take more than a blacksmith to take these from me. There is nothing forged that would have the strength to remove them. They are made of more than precious metal and are locked with pride and envy for something that would never be mine.'

She paused and took a step closer to him. Agetta was unsure as to what he was, but was afraid to ask the question that hovered precariously on her lips. 'Are you an –'

'I am whatever you want me to be,' he said, as if he knew the question before she asked. 'What I once was, is of no importance. My life has changed so much. I have been dragged through Europe and sold from one alchemist and thief to another. Now I am here, a *guest* of Cadmus Lamian.'

'What does my father want you for?' she asked, studying the labyrinth of silver wrinkles that covered his forehead.

'I am to be displayed on the Strand. A guinea a time and part of a menagerie of freaks. I heard him talking to Sarapuk. Together they have plans to collect the oddest and strangest creatures from the world. I suppose I will be the oddest of them all.' He saw the look of confusion on her face. 'Half of the guests in this house are destined for my fate, yet they do so with free will and the urge to make money. I . . .' He paused and looked to the floor, lowering his voice as he slowly spoke. 'I have no choice, I have to do what he says. He is the keeper of the key that binds me to him.'

Agetta fumbled in the pocket of her coat searching for the Ormuz glass. '*Hebdomada Mortium,*' she said to herself again as she looked at the golden shackles. 'I was given something to help me read that which I can't understand.' She pulled the Ormuz glass from her pocket and rubbed the clear crystal lens against her coat. 'See! This is what I was given, Thaddeus said that it would help and help it will.' She spoke quickly as she held the lens over the manacles and read the words that were embossed into the gold. '*Hebdomada Mortium!* It *hasn't* changed,' she said with frustration stinging her voice. She turned the Ormuz glass in her hand and stared as without warning each letter appeared to move in the crystal. There, captured by the glass, they changed shape and order, forming a long strand of words that whirled around before her eyes.

Seven ages we are born, captured for to live and die,
Seven ages I will stay, and watch the world through human eye.
Seven deaths I will endure, mortal and immortal behold,
Seven deaths of wasp and serpent; chance to decay and turn to
mould.'

Agetta spoke the words as they appeared in the Ormuz glass. 'What do they mean?' she asked as the writing danced around in the crystal. 'Who do they speak of?'

'It is my curse. Captured by my own heart, imprisoned by my own greed. I will wear these bands for the seven ages and then taste death.' Tegatus rattled the chains that were wrapped around the manacles. 'I just wanted to know what it would be like, one kiss from her, that was all. For one moment in eternity to know how it was to be –' The creature stopped and listened as if a silent voice spoke to him. 'We haven't long, Sarapuk is close by. You must return to your bed. Lock me in and say nothing of this.'

'I can't just leave you here, you're a prisoner.' Agetta stepped forward and with all of her strength pulled on his chains, trying to free him. 'What did you do to be put in this place?'

'I ask that every moment of every day and never get an answer. There is no one listening to me any more. I am abandoned.' The creature sighed, on the verge of tears. 'If only I had never been born, or could die now and no eye could see me. If I had never been I would be happier than I am now, trapped by my own deceit.' Tegatus turned his head as if he had heard some faraway sound. 'Your father is awake, he scrapes the fire and waits for his friend.'

'What about you? You can't stay here like this, you have to get away.' Again she pulled on the chains.

'When the time is right, then you can help me. Now go. If your father finds you here then I cannot answer for your fate.'

Agetta looked down on him as he sat with his face in his hands, staring at the floor. He looked small and frail, like an old man waiting for death by the roadside, a beggar with no one to feed him.

Tegatus looked up and motioned for her to go, waving her away with the back of his hand. The blue moonlight coloured his skin and cast a long dark shadow across the floor like a pathway from the room. Agetta didn't speak as she tiptoed gently across and out of the attic, locking the door behind her and standing on the top step in the darkness of the stairway. She had a sudden feeling that she was being watched, that somewhere in the dark night eyes stared at her.

A swift draught blew coldly around her feet, sending a sharp shiver up her spine, standing every hair on end and shuddering her whole body. In the darkness of the hallway Agetta could make out the tall shape of a man staring out of the gallery window. In the pale light of the moon she could see the etched and faded lines of his tattooed face.

Blueskin Danby. The thought flashed through her mind like a lightning bolt. The black shadow looked up, as if aware of his name being called by her spirit. His face was cold with deep, black, sunken eyes that stared like a mask of stretched parchment. A long black snake clutched to his face and slithered across the skin, through an empty eye socket and out through his mouth. 'I'm coming back for you Agetta,' he said, stepping towards her and holding out a thin white hand. 'Sometime soon in the dark of night when you least expect it. Nothing on earth will save you from me. I have your hound – he's payment for your father's treachery. Soon I will have you and my fate will be yours. A pretty neck will stretch and you will walk the night with demons as your companions.'

With that he smiled an empty smile, turned tail and disappeared.

10 : Handshake from a Golden Bough

The slicing of cold damp earth fired a dull echo through Blake's throbbing head. From where he lay in a freshly-dug shallow grave lined with straw he stared at the sky as the first shafts of October sun crept over the black horizon. A tall church spire reached into the clear sky, pointing its thin stone finger at his comet that hung in the peak of heaven.

Blake thought he was dead, and that he looked up from the pit with the eyes of a ghost. It was the skull-splitting pain and the thick rope-burns on his wrists that reminded him he was still alive. He tried to move but his legs felt heavy and numb. He lifted his foot – it dropped back to the ground, clattering against the lid of the coffin on which he was laid. He lifted his head and saw that he had been seasoned with a garnish of rose petals and holly leaves for the after-life. Pressing his body to the coffin was the carcass of a large dead dog with broken teeth, wild staring eyes and a long tongue that fell from its open mouth.

From the world above Blake could hear the distinct sound of a shovel that scraped the dirt, gouging chunks of fresh earth. Muddy clods shook the ground as they tumbled from a spade just feet away. He sat up, rolled the dog to the side of the grave, brushed the straw from his body and tried to understand how he had come to this place.

All he could remember of the night before was the ball of light that had exploded around him as Hezrin had closed the looking-glass door. In a split second it had engulfed him, growing so fast that he felt as if he would be thrust through the roof of the house and into the sky. He had been overwhelmed by its brightness as each molecule of the object beamed through his clothing illuminating his flesh in an iridescent glow. Then Blake had fallen into an inky black sleep.

He ran his cold fingers around the deep red burn marks on his wrists and felt the palm of his right hand that bleated with intense soreness. The fingernails on his right hand had been cut to the quick. A fleeting flash of the night before ran through his mind, a brief picture of Hezrin's steel-blue eyes and red lips as she laughed as he writhed in agony. Blake coughed and spat mud and straw, and the sound echoed through the grave and out, upwards into the world. The digging stopped.

'Was that you?'. A man's voice came from above him. It was rough and spoke of a life of street-corner fights.

'You're frit, man,' came the harsh but hushed reply. 'You'll be telling me you can see the devil next. Get digging, another foot and we'll have the body and the good doctor will have his plaything and we ten shillings.' The man gave a pig-like grunt as he spoke, urging his friend to continue.

Blake got to his knees to peer over the edge of the sepulchre. The body of the dead dog slipped further into the grave and slapped heavily on to the coffin with a loud thud.

The voice came again. 'I told you!' it said, shriller and more frantic than before. 'We shouldn't be doing this. They belong to the underworld and we've no right to take them back.' With that came a resolute scut as the shovel was buried defiantly in the earth. 'I isn't digging any more. The devil can keep his own 'cause I don't want him coming after me.'

'Dig, like I pay you to dig. It's just a noise of the night. There are no ghosts, no God and no devil. It would take a man to rise from the dead to convince me of any of them. Now dig!'

Blake heard the heavy slap of a hand across flesh. He slowly got to his feet and stood on the coffin lid, peering out into the churchyard with its broken gravestones and dirt paths. In the dim light of dawn Blake could see two men standing by a pile of freshly-dug soil and the discarded flower garlands of a fresh grave. Both men wore sea boots and frock coats. Their heads were freshly shaved and tinged with the blue of lice dip.

'I'll dig,' said the tall pot-bellied man who grasped the long shovel, 'but this is the last time. The devil's after me for stealing from his own, and you're not going to pay him off.' He grasped the shovel with his spindly hands tipped with dirty nails. His coat was a size too big, taken from the back of a stolen corpse before he had handed the newly dead gentleman over to the good doctor.

Blake looked around the churchyard. The stench of the grave filled him with despair and reminded him of his future. 'Good morning, gentlemen,' he said in a firm, loud voice, hoping to attract their attention. 'Could you help me from this grave?'

The pot-bellied man looked to the ground beneath him, believing the words had emanated from the wooden casket beneath his feet. The other leapt back, unsure if his ears had not deceived him.

'Help me from this pit and I will see you well paid and make sure the devil or the King won't catch you.' Blake shouted in deep frustration, scrambling with his feet against the side of the crumbling hole. The sound of earth clods drummed against the coffin lid with a thump, thump, thump as he tried in vain to gain a foothold.

'It's a devil!' cried pot-belly as he threw the shovel towards his companion and tried to run, slipping and falling. 'It wants your soul, and mine's not my own to give,' he screamed, as tears streamed down his face.

The thin man took hold of his friend by the sleeve and looked around the churchyard. He could see no one, only thick blue shadows cast by the half-light of dawn.

'Don't run, you fool!' Blake shouted. 'Help me from this grave. I'm alive, can't you see?'

Pot-belly could now see. He could see the blackened face of a dead man rising from the grave just a few feet away, shrouded in rose petals and holly leaves, and with straw billowing out from his coat neck. The hands of the corpse grasped strands of dock-leaf as if hopelessly trying to escape the bowels of hell. He felt an overpowering urgency to escape from the clutches of the emerging cadaver.

The thin man picked up the shovel and made ready to attack.

'I'll wrap that around your neck if you don't help me,' Blake shouted as he slipped back into the grave with a loud thump.

The threat from the now-vanishing carcass sent cold shivers through the man's body. The two grave robbers turned and raced to the churchyard gate, fearing Old Leather Wings himself was chasing them.

Blake slipped again and fell in a crumpled heap on the coffin. He stroked the fur of the somehow familiar dead dog. He knew he had seen the animal before, and there in the darkness of the pit it was his only companion. 'Oh dog,' he whined, 'as you are now, so soon I'll be. It is such a short time to live and full of misery, and to end it here talking to a dog . . .' Blake gave out a deep and forlorn sigh.

A voice rang out from high above him: 'Then talk to *me*.'

Blake, startled, pushed the dog away as if ashamed of his companion and looked up to where the voice had come from.

'Graves are not the best of places to spend the night. In the middle of life we are in death, and I now come to rescue you from the pit of torment.'

Standing above Blake, silhouetted by the dawn sky, was a tall stranger dressed in black and peering down through gold-rimmed, blue-glass spectacles.

'I heard you from the street and saw the two vagabonds running away and thought they had done you harm.' He gave a broad smile. 'And here I find you alive and . . .' The man paused and looked at the dog that lay crumpled against the side of the grave. 'You are in better condition than your friend.'

'I f-f-found him here,' Blake stuttered as he got to his feet. 'I woke up in the grave and he – er, it – was on top of me – dead. I fear it belongs to my servant girl.'

'So I have arrived in time, to save you from the same fate. We can't have two dogs sharing the same grave, can we?' The stranger reached down and clasped Blake's hand, and in one pull lifted him from the coffin lid and into the half-light of the shadowy morning. He kept hold of Blake's hand, opened his palm and stared at the red thumbprint.

'This is a very angry burn, one that will harm more than just the flesh. Where did you get it?' he asked as he looked at Blake.

'An experiment, I am a scientist, of sorts . . . Can we say that it was a misadventure that led me here and somewhere in the process I burnt my hand?' Blake wanted to end the conversation and get away from this man.

'You can say whatever takes your fancy, but would it be the truth?' The man continued to hold Blake's hand and lead him to the gate. 'It's best not to speak too much in places like this. I know that the dead listen more intently than the living.'

The stranger forcefully linked Blake's arm as he walked him through the streets of tightly packed houses with their overhanging galleries that surrounded St Bride's churchyard. Blake felt as if he was being led to a place he had been searching for, and that here in the crowded hovels of Blackfriars there would be an answer. They walked for several minutes through the grime, stepping over the drunken bulks of sleeping vagrants that littered the streets with their blistered bodies. Blake looked up to the sky – his comet was still there in the fading night.

The stranger tightened his grip on Blake's arm. 'It isn't far to where you live,' he said as they turned into Conduit Fields. 'I have seen you several times in Bloomsbury Square.'

'I have seen you also,' Blake replied, believing now was his chance to find out who the man really was. 'In fact,' he said, his confidence growing as they entered familiar territory, 'I have seen you come and go in the most unusual fashion. I have the impression that you have been watching me and that this meeting is not by chance.' He tried to pull his arm from the man but to no avail.

'I watch many people and my coming and going is a trick of the light. If I were you I would be more concerned as to what I had lurking in my house than to who watched over you.' He lowered his voice. Blake sensed the threat that filled each word.

'I keep nothing in my house that gives me concern. Only a thief would trouble me with such talk.' Blake again attempted to escape from the man, but they were locked together as if tied by invisible cords that couldn't be broken.

'When we have to go our separate ways then so be it,' said the stranger. 'But for the time being, Doctor Blake, you and I share the same journey, one predicted by that star that you have watched every night.'

'Star? I know of no star. I am an astronomer, a Cabalist. I search for truth.'

'You're a fool and a dabbler and it will be more than your hand that gets burnt if you continue with your magic. You have put your head in the dragon's mouth and it is about to snap shut.' The man took hold of Blake by the front of his coat and lifted him from the ground with one hand, so that he dangled by the neck as if in the hands of the hangman. 'I have looked over you for a long time, Sabian. Sometimes you have given me great joy, but now your stupidity fills me with despair. Yet your fate is in your own hands and the rope gathers around you and soon . . .' He paused and listened to something only he could hear. 'Soon, Sabian, the trap will fall and you will hang from a different tree.'

'How do you know me?' Blake asked, choking with the grip of the man's hand.

'I knew your father, and you could say I am the guardian of your family blood,' the stranger said quickly, lowering Blake to the ground.

'Does my guardian have a name?' Blake asked.

'You can call me Abram Rickards. It is a name that has served me well, and one which you will come to understand.' Abram tilted his dark spectacles and stared at Blake eye to eye. 'I don't waste my time on people, so don't disappoint me, Sabian. I am not someone who you should ever *think* of disappointing! I have my own way of dealing with people who dare to do that.'

Blake took a step back from his guardian and looked at the soft earth of Conduit Fields. He stood in his dirtied boots, his clothing covered in grave mud, the collar torn on his coat, and the pain of his wrists throbbing beneath his cuffs. Abram was tall, clean and neat. The gold trim of his black coat was fresh and vibrant in the first light of morning. From across the fields Blake heard the sound of loud conversation. Abram allowed him several more moments in which to think, to soak up the last embers of night before he had to face the light of the sun.

Abram turned and began to walk quickly towards the sound of raised voices breezing across from the far side of the sunlit fields. Blake followed, not knowing why or what lay ahead. In the distance he saw two small gatherings, their long shadows burnt into the baked clay and tufts of grass. He quickly realised that ahead of him was a duel, and he heard the seconds shouting the argument and demanding an apology.

The combatants stood grimly back-to-back, entrenched in their anger, unwilling to admit their guilt. Pistols were double-charged, cocked and raised to the heavens. Steps were about to be taken on a walk that for one would lead to death – either for the Squire with his long wiry hair and country coat, or for the Dandy with his powder wig and painted red lips. A drummer-boy began to beat out the slow drawl of the funeral beat. It came back as a whisper from the walls of the tall white houses that flanked the southern side of the fields.

The second in his white socks and long periwig shouted out the steps: 'One . . . two . . . three . . .'

Abram took long strides in time with each count, covering the ground at three yards to the beat. Blake feebly followed on behind, trying to catch up.

'Eight . . . nine . . . ten.' The second paused, covering his face with his hand, unwilling to see the outcome of his master's fate. Both men turned to face each other in the growing dawn. The wigged Dandy aimed feverishly, quivering, his hand shaking. He closed his eyes and fired. The hammer fell on dry powder that flashed in the chamber, igniting the charge and blasting the lead ball from the muzzle of the gun. The Squire stood his ground, feet firmly rooted in the dark earth as he waited, and the shot flashed by his head and whistled away behind him.

There was a long silence as the roar of the gunshot echoed and ebbed away. The Dandy opened his eyes and looked up. Before him the Squire raised his pistol and took a long, steady aim. No one moved as tears began to roll across the painted rouge cheeks of the young man in his French silk coat and fop-cuffed shirt.

'No!' shouted Abram. He strode towards the Squire, intent on stopping the gunshot.

With a flick of the finger the trigger was eased and the hammer fell. The Dandy clutched his chest. A wave of heat engulfed his body and the ruby grail splattered the green grass. The blast lifted him from his feet and cast him to the ground.

Abram ran to him and lifted his powdered face from the red earth. He stared into his dead, lifeless eyes lined in black kohl that matched the smudged beauty spot on his left cheek.

'He's dead, man. Leave him!' shouted the Squire, smoothing his thick country coat and wiping the embers of burning wadding from his chest. He held the smoking pistol in his other hand, tapping it against his breeches to remove the powder char from the barrel. 'He knew the price of an insult and he paid it with his life. From the north I may be, but I will never be wronged.'

'Was it worth a man's life, to satisfy such a trivial thing?' Abram asked as he knelt beside the corpse.

'This is our way. You foreigners will never understand. A man's honour is worth more than his life. I have my pride and for that I am willing to die. It was him or me, and my pistol prevailed.' The Squire handed the pistol to his second and turned away.

'So you walk away and leave him for rats and dogs to gnaw his bones?' Abram shouted at the man.

The Squire stopped and turned to Abram. 'Do you want some of what he got, Frenchman? My powder is dry and I'm sure he'd leave you his pistol as his will and testament. He was a mollie, a painted fop, a mad Macaroni who thought more of lip-paint than life. He was an insult to manhood.'

Blake looked on, transfixed. Here was his chance to escape his guardian, but all he could do was to stare at Abram as he knelt by the corpse.

'Lead may poison the soul, but he that gives life can assuage such passion,' Abram snapped at the Squire, who proudly gloated over the body. And then he ripped open the dead man's shirt and plunged his hand into his chest, forcing open the circular wound as he buried his hand deeper. Blake watched as Abram searched the innermost parts of the body with his fingers and then began to pull his hand from the bloodied cavity, lifting the dead fop from the ground. There was a loud squelch as the blood oozed and gurgled in the deep wound.

Suddenly, Abram's hand jumped from the wound. In his fingers he grasped the large, round lead ball that had smashed the Dandy's chest. He threw it at the Squire. 'Take your poison and turn it into gold. This will not end in death,' he said, wiping his hands on the man's fine white shirt. Then he paused and looked around him.

Blake stood frozen to the spot. Both seconds stared in disbelief as Abram formed a solid fist with his right hand and hit the Dandy in the chest with a heavy blow. '*Life!*' he shouted as loudly as he could, the sound shaking the ground on which they stood and reverberating through their bodies. 'Life for this man, not death!'

Abram grabbed the corpse and lifted him from the ground, standing him on his feet. The smell of burning flesh filled the air as the open chest wound began to billow sulphurous smoke into the fresh morning air.

The Squire grabbed a sword from his second. 'This is witchcraft and you both deserve to die.'

Abram held the corpse upright with one hand. 'Stand your ground, Squire, or you will stare in the face of my anger.'

The Squire didn't move. He pressed the tip of the sword into the ground and began to mutter under his breath, twisting the blade.

Abram looked into the eyes of the corpse. 'It is time to live,' he said quietly as he let go. Everyone stood still, no one dared move. The corpse teetered and rocked backward and forward. 'Don't listen to his moaning, you can have life and live to the full.'

Then the eyes of the corpse opened and stared at Abram. The man began to cough and choke, spitting blood towards his assassin. He coughed again, even louder, and babbled as he cleared his throat, trying to speak.

With one swift movement, the Squire lifted the sword from the ground and thrust it towards the body of the man. Abram snatched the blade in his hand, holding it firmly in his grip. 'He lives – and nothing you say or do will take his life again. Your honour has been satisfied and your pride still rules your heart.' He held tightly to the sword and twisted it from the Squire's grip. 'Now go. This is a place of life and your body sweats death. Go!'

Abram pulled the sword from the Squire's hand and threw it to the floor.

'I'll see you in hell for this,' the Squire shouted, stepping away and nodding for his second to follow. 'No man – do you hear? – no man has ever done that and lived. Who do you think you are?'

'I am who I am, that's all you need to know,' Abram replied, 'and hell is a familiar place to me.' He placed his hand on the Dandy's chest, pressing it to the wound. 'As for you, my painted friend, life will never be the same.'

Abram turned to Blake, who had stood speechless as he watched the morning unfold, then looked around Conduit Fields and saw that a crowd had gathered. 'There's nothing to see here,' he shouted. 'A near miss and a Dandy who can't shoot straight.'

The Dandy gripped Abram's shoulder and whispered to him as he wiped away the blood from his mouth. 'I know who you are, and I will never forget this.'

11 : The Kadesh of Blood

As Agetta woke from a fitful sleep the image of Blueskin Danby was still etched vividly in her mind. The morning sun burnt bleakly through the dirty glass of her bedroom window. Her mother was awake and taking breakfast. She was propped up against her pillow, a dirty white nightcap draped half across her face as she patted down the bedclothes and wiped the crumbs of bread from the bed.

'You're late up, Etta,' she said in the croaky voice of a woman twice her age. Mother Lamian had endured forty years and drunk her height in cheap gin several times over. 'Blake will be wanting you soon and so will your father,' she said as she slurped back the bottle that she cradled like a child, mumbling to it as she rocked it in her arms.

'They can wait,' Agetta replied as she brushed a long strand of hair away from her face. 'I have things to do for me and a call to make to a friend.' She jumped from her bed fully dressed, trying not to look at the furrowed heap that was her mother. 'You'll be here when I get back?' Agetta asked sarcastically as she stepped towards the door. 'Don't be doing anything that may tire you out. After all, father has plenty of time to look after you *and* run the house.'

'He knows I'm sick. Heart of gold, that's what he has. It's called love, maybe you should try it,' Mother Lamian shouted at her daughter.

Agetta felt her mind whirl as she was overcome with a coldness that clawed through her body. 'I know you are sick, but not in the way you think. As for love – this family has no knowledge.'

She slammed the bedroom door and jumped into the long hall, where she looked towards the dark stairway. There was no sign of Blueskin, just the lodger sleeping on the floor, gurgling and snoring beneath his frock coat, his muddy black boots twitching with each snort. As a cold shudder ran down her back and her mind took her back in time, she thought of Tegatus manacled and alone. She smiled, hoping that he could somehow see her, hoping that one day he could be free. Agetta shared his captor: pain upon pain and word upon word had forged chains from which she felt there would never be freedom.

A noise from the kitchen filled the hall and distracted her from her thoughts. She ran down the wooden stairs as loudly as she could, hoping that the sound would frighten away the ghosts of her mind. She charged into the kitchen, where Sarapuk sat like a large rook-faced bird at the end of the table. He gave a half-smile as she came into the room and shivered as if he rustled his unseen feathers.

'My pretty girl,' he said slyly. 'What a delight to see –'

'Don't even think it, Sarapuk!' Agetta said, unsure where the words had come from, as if they had been whispered to her by another voice. 'I've no time for you. Blake waits for me and at least he pays for my company.' She turned and grabbed a piece of bread from the table, deliberately brushing a large pile of crumbs and broken eggshells into Sarapuk's lap as she did so. 'Sorry, Mister Sarapuk, I am so molly-handed.'

Sarapuk grabbed her arm and gripped it tightly, pulling her close to him. She could smell the chicken breath that hung on each of his browned teeth. 'Careful, girl,' he said as he pulled her even closer. 'What the father doesn't see the heart doesn't grieve.'

Agetta quickly grabbed the large bread knife that lay next to the remnants of the morning loaf. In an instant, Sarapuk was staring down a long blade that hovered at the tip of his scaly nose.

'Another inch, Mister Sarapuk, and I will take this knife and carve the soul from your body. Doubtless I will be quicker at finding it than you will ever be.' Agetta spoke as if they were the words of Yerzinia speaking through her. She had no fear and the consequences didn't matter. 'You have two seconds to decide and then I will spill you across the floor and the rats can eat your entrails.' She stared Sarapuk in the face and smiled.

His hand let go of her arm and allowed her to step away. He looked surprised, as if he had heard the voice before. She noticed that his hand trembled by his side.

'I went too far. I . . . I am sorry, Agetta,' he muttered, looking to the floor.

Agetta walked to the kitchen door and turned, with the bread knife still clutched in her hand. Without thinking she reached back and threw the knife at Sarapuk with all her might. It twisted through the air, crossing the room in a second and cutting the shoulder of his black cassock coat as it spun by him and slapped into the soft plaster wall, embedding itself to the hilt.

'I need to try that again,' Agetta said as she stepped out of the room. 'It was aimed for your heart – if you have one.'

Fleet Street burned brightly; the sun warmed the stench of the gutter and steam rose from the tepid waters of the beck that fumbled its way to the Thames. It was high tide and the rubbish bobbed in the dirty water where two ragged children knelt in the mud playing with a broken pottery mug that sailed them into a new world.

Agetta walked briskly through the streets toward London Bridge. Blake would have to wait, Mrs Malakin could change the candles and scrub by herself. Agetta needed to see Thaddeus Bracegirdle and his ghostly children. Quickly she turned the corner and crossed the street and within minutes she stood at the entrance to Bridge Street. A large crowd filled the door of the coffee shop and spilled on to the cobbles, each man trying to hold on to a wide sheet of paper that was the *London Chronicle*. A newsboy shouted at the top of his voice as he held out copies of the *Chronicle*: 'Comet to pass the earth – King to announce a holy day!'

There was a burble of excited conversation as the people clustered together, arguing over the news. Agetta remembered what Blake had said on the night of the sky-quake, and suddenly it all began to make sense – the comet and the book were linked together. She quickened her step. She wanted to tell Thaddeus, but this betrayal battled against the promise she had made to Blake.

'Why me?' she shouted. 'Why do I have to carry this secret?'

A voice inside her head answered, a soft, gentle, warm voice that whispered against the wind like a far-off cry. Agetta stopped and listened, covering her ears with her hands to block out the noise of the street. The voice came again: *'Tell him . . .'*

The command made her shudder with delight and set her senses on fire. It was the right thing to do: promises were meant to be broken, secrets were to be whispered to friends and shared like the scraps from the table. Thaddeus could be trusted, she thought. He had kind eyes and a warm smile. To tell him would make his life complete, he could win back what he had lost and all would be well. Her heart leapt and her hands tingled, and she felt a rush of blood sweep across her face. She was in control of her future, and at last she could make someone happy.

The door to the bookshop was stiff, as if the wood had swollen and somehow knew of her desire to break her promise. She pushed and pushed until it gave way. Inside the shop there was complete silence. The smell of damp paper and the murky Thames tide filled her nostrils. The high vaulted ceiling echoed her footsteps on the wooden boards as she walked through the maze of shelves to the large wooden desk from where Thaddeus ruled the bookshop.

'Mister Thad!' she shouted. 'It's Agetta, I've come back to see you. I have some news of the book!'

There was a soft scuffle of tiny feet in the far corner by a narrow window. Agetta caught a glimpse, a slight shadow that darted from its hiding-place to behind the bookshelf. 'I can see you,' she said, stepping around the large desk to the mounting stool that led up to the waiting-plate from where Thaddeus could see down every aisle. 'Thaddeus told me about you, I know you are here. Show yourself!'

'They won't show themselves to you, Agetta!' a voice said, making Agetta jump and look anxiously around the shop.

The cellar door opened and Thaddeus walked in carrying a large pile of books. An elegant woman in a winter cloak made of thick, black wool followed him. She smiled at Agetta as she looked up to the desk. 'Be careful you don't fall, it's as high as the gallows,' the woman said, pulling up the hood of her cloak as she walked purposefully towards the door. 'Have them sent to Mister Hatchard in Piccadilly, he's the only bookseller I trust, apart from you, Thaddeus. He will send them to France to my cousin – she will be delighted with my latest find.'

There was something about the woman's voice that sent a wave of trepidation through Agetta. As the woman walked off, she felt her new-found confidence being sucked from her, as if a part of her soul was being torn out.

'It will be my pleasure, Lady Flamberg,' replied Thaddeus as he put the books down on the floor. He watched Lady Flamberg flow through the shop like poured wine, her black cloak billowing out behind her, before smiling and turning to Agetta. 'It's good to see you, Agetta.'

She interrupted him before he could say another word. 'I have some news – it comes by way of a broken secret. I promised not to tell but –' She paused and looked around the shop, hoping for some kind of sign that she could go on, listening for the voice that had told her to break the secret.

'If you promised not to tell then you should think carefully. Secrets are powerful things and words can have a life of their own, they are like arrows that fly off the tongue.'

'I want to tell and I want to tell *you*! It's about the book, the Nemorensis. I haven't stopped thinking about it. The word has been going through my head day and night and since I met you things have happened that I would never have dreamt of.'

'The book? You have heard of the book?' Thaddeus said impatiently. 'Don't break my heart, girl. I have had this conversation with many a man before and every time it has led to nothing.'

'I know where it is and who has it!' she blurted out, the words racing from her mouth quicker than her thoughts.

There was a long silence as Thaddeus paced the floor, rubbing his hands through the strands of his long thinning hair.

'I . . . I can get it for you,' she said quietly.

He looked up. 'For me? You could get the Nemorensis for

me? Bring it home to Thaddeus?' He smiled an excited, child-like smile. 'Who has the book?'

'It belongs to my master, Sabian Blake –'

'It belongs to me!' Thaddeus shouted back angrily. 'It's my book, always has been and always will be. Blake is a thief, he has no right.' He smashed his hand against the side of the bleached oak desk like a spoilt child quarrelling over a broken toy.

'I can get it back for you, and if it is yours by right then it wouldn't be stealing,' Agetta said as she stepped down to the floor. 'I could try to bring it tonight.' She had a sudden dark thought of Inigo Alley and the creature that had taken hold of her.

'Would you do that for me? For Thaddeus?' he said softly as he turned towards her.

'I had to tell you, Mister Thaddeus. It has been a secret that I couldn't contain any longer. So much has changed,' she said.

'A secret, and one that has brought such joy to your good friend. The Nemorensis is a special book and one too good for Doctor Sabian Blake. If you could get it back for me then you would be greatly rewarded.'

'I'll do it for our friendship and nothing else.' Agetta started to step backwards towards the door, constantly looking around, thinking she was being watched. 'If I can be back tonight I will. Leave the door unlocked and I will try to bring the book.'

'And I will prepare supper. A banquet that you have never seen before. We will celebrate a golden dawn,' Thaddeus said as he walked with her to the door. 'This is a special day and you have made Thaddeus a happy man.'

She stopped by the door and looked at him. 'Do you believe the dead can come back and get you?' she asked, her brow deeply furrowed.

'I only fear the living,' he replied. 'The dead are dead. I have nothing to do with them or they with me.'

'Have you ever seen a ghost?' she pressed him further.

'I have seen many things, some very strange, but ghosts are stories to frighten children. Remember this, the mind can play tricks and the eyes will often join in the foolery. It would take someone to come back from the dead to make me believe.'

Agetta turned and pulled on the door handle. The bell jangled and the morning air rushed in from London Bridge. She was confused, about to betray and break a promise, and yet it all felt so good.

Agetta checked the bridge, and the crowd that was still huddled at the door of the coffee shop. There was no sign of the stranger in black, only a large, dead dog-rat with broken teeth, lying on its back in the long gutter that ran the length of the bridge. She stepped outside and waved to Thaddeus as he closed the door.

He watched through the thick crinkled glass as she walked out of sight towards the city. A blind water-carrier with a small wooden barrel strapped to his back stumbled across the bridge behind her. A fat donkey that picked its way through the muck of the street led him on his way. Thaddeus checked he was alone and then turned the key in the shop door and pulled the shutter over the glass.

'I think that should do it,' he said proudly as he turned and walked to the cellar door. He descended the long flight of thick wooden stairs that creaked and moaned under his weight. The stairs took him deep into the bridge foot and further into the darkness. All around was the swirling sound of the tide as it beat against the thick stone pillars that held up the shops and houses clinging to the bridge high above the water.

Thaddeus took the lamp from its stand and held it above his head. The soft, warm glow was consumed by the deep black chasm that opened up before him, the steps descending deeper and deeper. Finally, he came to a large wooden door studded with the heads of a hundred nails. On the outside hung the skull of a cat, tied to the door with a pink ribbon stolen from a child's bonnet.

He pushed against the door and it slid open, disappearing into the wall. Beyond the darkness and the shadows was a large stone-clad room. Green algae spewed from each crack in the wall. The ceiling dripped with the brown water of the Thames that trickled in long stream fingers across the floor.

Thaddeus closed the door behind him and slid the three bolts into their keepers. All that was in the room was a large wooden chair, a tall brass candlestick and a thick iron ring pinned into the central stone and strong enough to hold a thousand horses. He slumped into the chair and looked around the room, smiling to himself. 'Show yourself!' he shouted as he brushed his hair with his fingers. 'I haven't got all day and we need to talk.' There was no reply, just the rushing of water high above his head. 'Do you always want to make me say those stupid words?' he said loudly as he stamped his feet against the cold stone. '*Hoc est corpus meum!*' he shouted, the words echoing from the damp walls. 'Isn't that enough to make you appear to me, you thane of wickedness?'

In the corner of the room a blister of blue mist appeared on the stone floor. Thaddeus could make out the shape of a long white shoulder blade and three bloodstained ribs that appeared to float in mid air. '*Hoc est corpus meum!*' he shouted again. 'Don't keep me waiting, I want to speak to you. Quickly!' He stamped his feet like a spoilt brat.

The spirit began to take form and substance as arms attached themselves to the trunk of a large muscular body covered in blue skin. The creature stooped as it was drawn together from the darkness and turned towards Thaddeus.

'At last,' he said, as the phantasm was complete. 'I have work for you. There is a young girl. She has the Ormuz glass in her pocket so she will be visible to you. Follow her and make mischief for anyone who tries to stop her from bringing the Nemorensis to me. I need her here tonight so be careful that she is not caught. Do you understand, Blueskin?'

Blueskin Danby looked back through his black, empty eye sockets. The snake swirled over his face and flicked through his mouth and out of his nostrils.

'It will be a pleasure, Mister Thaddeus. And then can I kill her?' he asked in his gruff, mournful voice.

'Not yet, she is still of great use to me.' He paused as he thought. 'I take it you are the ghost she was asking me about?'

'I had to see her, to be in that house again . . .' He gasped as the snake slithered in and out of his face. 'It was the last place I saw as a man, before . . .' He paused, his skin darkening in colour with his anger. 'Now I am cursed to walk this world as a spectre and Cadmus Lamian savours life to the full. One thing I know, she will never stare into the eyes of her hound again. It squealed like a puppy for its mother.'

'And you are tied to me for ever by three teeth and a piece of your severed finger,' Thaddeus replied. He took the velvet bag from his waistcoat pocket and jangled the bony contents before Danby's ghost.

'So when will you set me free?' Danby said. 'I have served you well for a year and a day and done your bidding in the afterlife.'

'Spells are not meant to be broken, Mister Danby, and I promised you a body so you could live out the life the hanging cut short.' Thaddeus folded the bone bag and put it neatly back into his pocket. 'Wouldn't it be droll to give you the body of Cadmus Lamian or Blake? You could choose what life you would want. The sweat of a London lodging house or the fine gentility of Bloomsbury Square. You could strut as a dandy with lip-paint and the taste of chocolate to coat your tongue. You could even keep the pet snake . . .'

12 : Widdershins

The large brass chandelier glistened with the light from seventy candles that warmed the hallway of 6 Bloomsbury Square. Mrs Malakin lit the final wick before slowly waddling down the ladder like an over-fed ape and dipping the flaming taper in the fire bucket. In the morning room Blake paced up and down, biting his nails, while Isaac Bonham sat in the large armchair with his face in his hands.

'It could be the end of me,' Blake said as he stopped momentarily to check the curtain and glare out of the window to see if he was being watched. 'I have no way of knowing what is the truth any more. As of last night my life is in the hands of someone who is quite mad, and if what I saw this morning is true then all my science is worth nothing, it does not answer the questions that I thought had already been answered.' He banged his fist on the wall as he strutted around the room. 'I am in a trap, Bonham. I am a fly caught in a web and the spider is about to suck my blood dry . . . And the trouble is Bonham, I don't mind. She is so dazzling that I don't care what happens to me. I could even agree with what they have planned, if only to sit at her feet and look into her eyes.'

'You're bewitched, man. Can't you see that she has you in some kind of spell?' Bonham asked.

'I don't care, Isaac. Whatever happened in that room has

changed the way I feel about life. I have cared for all the wrong things,' he said, looking at the eye-shaped wound in his hand. 'For years I searched the Cabala for the truth, an answer for the problems of the world, a chance to do some good. I neglected one thing – me! Now I want to live for myself.' Blake held out his hand for Bonham to see. 'Look, man. This is what Lady Flamberg left me with. Shot me through like fire racing through every muscle. I feel more alive than I have ever felt before and the memory of her face fills my mind.'

'A scald, a trick, a hidden electrometer to jolt some sense into you,' Bonham said, quickly slipping his own hand into his coat pocket. 'Hezrin Flamberg is a strange woman at the best of times, but a witch?' Bonham stopped and looked at the open door. 'This house has ears,' he said quietly, 'and Mrs Malakin is known for her slack jaw.' He rubbed the palm of his hand against the thick cotton sleeve of his jacket pocket as the seeds of jealousy began to grow.

'So what did happen last night that has changed your life?' Bonham asked, almost choking on the thought of Blake sharing a precious moment with Lady Flamberg.

'That's the point. I don't know.' Blake stopped pacing the room and stood by the fire. 'I can't remember a thing. All I know is that I was engulfed in a ball of pure white light that shone through me so I could see the bones in my hands, then all was complete blackness. I woke up in a grave with a dead dog and . . .' He stared at his palm. 'That man, the one who has been following me. *He* found me, lifted me from the grave, and that's not all,' Blake said excitedly. 'I saw him bring a man back to life, a dandy, shot dead in a duel by a vulgar fellow from the north. Back to life – blood, sweat and tears.'

'Are you sure he was dead?'

'As dead as the dog that I shared the grave with. And he was brought back to life, as alive as you are – a magic, the power of which I have never seen before. That's not all.' Blake gently closed the large oak door. 'The man who had been following me gave his name as Abram Rickards, and he implied there was something in this house that I should be afraid of.'

'You've lived here since it was built and know every stone, the man's a fool.'

'He may be many things but a fool is not one of them. I am beginning to think the man is right. He is coming back in the morning to talk again, he says he can answer a question that has been burning in my heart.'

'We all have questions. He is a jester who plays with your vivid imagination. He is coming tomorrow to steal all your silver and then vanish into the night. Such a man is not to be trusted.'

'I trusted Lord Flamberg, but he is hell-bent on creating a new Jerusalem, a London rid of every vagrant, buttock and poor man. From what he's said I am sure that his friends were the cause of the Great Fire.' He paused and looked at Bonham. 'I don't just think it was the rats they wanted to kill. The comet will do his work for him – he wants the people to die and for London to be destroyed. And then he and his friends can do what they like.'

'Surely you realised all that before,' Bonham said wearily. 'This city is controlled by Flamberg and his friends. You don't believe it's the King and Parliament who run our country? Our lives are in the hands of Flamberg, and the King dances to his tune, the madman isn't even invited to their gatherings.'

'I had heard such a rumour, but I thought it was the talk of the coffee shop,' Blake replied.

'Coffee shop it may be, but the truth is that they have our daily lives in their hands, from the price of corn to what we read in the *London Chronicle*. They have more power than all your magical science. Flamberg, that fat fiend, is the real king and Hezrin his queen.'

Bonham stood up from the chair and crossed the room and peered through the chink in the curtains. He looked around the square. 'Well, you are not being watched today,' he said, turning to Blake. 'Not yet.'

Five stone pillars marked the tip of each point of the star that had been carved out of the dry stone floor of the chamber. The vaulted roof was studded with tiny points of light, and at the highest point of the stone cavern a ball of oiled cloth burnt in a metal brazier suspended on a thick gold chain, sending flickering shadows across the high ceiling.

Far below, four masked figures, each with the face of a different creature, sat at the points of the star, with one empty chair at the southern point. Joining each point was a thick gold circle, at the centre of which was a tall clay figure of a creature with webbed hands that clutched its side and a face made of layered oak leaves.

'We cannot wait for him any longer,' the man in the fox mask said as he pulled the hood of his cloak from covering his head. 'The moon is rising and what we have to do shall be done tonight.'

'We are only four points of the star,' the soft voice of the tiger mask replied, shuffling uncomfortably in the chair. 'Do we have the power to work such magic tonight?'

'There is only one way to find out,' wheezed the old voice of the stoat's head. 'If we cast the charm and it works then we have bespelled the creature – we shall see it with our own eyes, here and now.'

'Then let us begin.' The owl head spoke in harsh tones.

Fox-mask slowly got up from his chair and walked to the

clay figure. In his hand he clutched a small silver tin with a pearl lid. As he walked he twisted the lid, swirled the cloak over his shoulder and put the lid in his coat pocket. He picked out several pieces of human fingernails and carefully embedded them into the fingers of the clay figure. 'With his bone he gives you life,' he said, stepping to the side of the creature and placing his hand on its cold, damp shoulder.

Stoat-mask got up from his seat and stepped towards the creature at the same time as the owl and the tiger. They encircled it, walking round and round against the direction of the sun, reaching out and touching its head and face with each passing.

The stoat reached into a small leather bag that he carried around his neck and brought out two gold coins. He stopped and faced the creature and placed one coin in each of its eye sockets. 'Guilt money, stolen from his pocket. Conjured by alchemists and now the element that will give you sight,' the stoat said, his hand trembling.

Now tiger-mask stopped in her turn. She took off her cloak and swung it around her head, covering herself and the creature in a thick shroud of velvet. It was as if she did not want to be seen by the others, that her gift to the creature had to be a secret even from them.

'I give you life, my breath shall be your breath, my blood shall be your blood. See for me, love me with all your heart, do always what I say . . .' She placed her mouth over the oak lips of the creature and gave a soft kiss as she breathed into it. 'Sekaris, creature of the earth, listen to me.' She slapped her hands against the side of its face. The cloak slipped quickly to the floor. Her mask was tainted in green mud, her lips smudged with paint. 'My blood shall be your blood!' With that she slipped a small silver knife from her pocket and cut the tip of her finger. Blood splattered the floor and spurted in pulses from the wound on to the creature. 'You shall have life,

Sekaris, and walk the dreams of humankind and inhabit the dark places of the mind.' And she chanted:

> '*Mud, blood and bone.*
> *Breath of the fallen one to bring life to stone,*
> *Chanting the name under a waxing moon,*
> *Sekaris, Sekaris, do what's to be done . . .'*

As one, they all stepped away from the creature and sat at the points of the star and waited. High above them the fireball spun on its golden chain, swirling the sooty light around the chamber. From all around came the call of jackdaws that pitched and fell through the air swirling and choking the light with their blackness. In the centre of the circle the Sekaris didn't move.

Fox-mask looked at the points to the star. 'The creature is dead, we need the serpent to be with us in this magic,' he said.

'Wait,' replied tiger-mask. 'Wait for him to breathe, listen to the blackbirds, hear them calling for his soul to come to him.' From high above them jackdaws swooped around the creature as if they brought with them a silver thread that would bring life to the statue of mud.

'Look!' cried owl-mask. 'It moves!'

In the faint light of the chamber the arm of the creature began slowly to move, each finger of its webbed hand taking on life with every passing second. A silver glow covered the creature like a thick sea mist growing from its feet and rising up over its body stiffening the mud skin and turning it to hard, green flesh. The chiselled oak leaves that covered its face changed from clay to a vibrant mask of living foliage with two golden eyes staring into the darkness that surrounded the circle. Ruby lips glistened with fresh dew as the Sekaris sniffed at the atmosphere and slowly opened its mouth to take in a long deep breath of the smoked-filled air.

'Sekaris,' said tiger-mask in her gentle voice, 'listen to me. I named you, brought you forth as my own child. It was my hands that formed your body, my breath that gave you life. Listen to my call. Go from this place and do my bidding, destroy the one whose nails you now carry. Let the night be your garment, go and find him and wait until the perfect time. Let no one stop you.'

The Sekaris shuddered with the new feelings of his living flesh. He twitched his shoulders and stretched his back as he bent forward and ran his rough hands over his body. He felt his face and rustled the leaves that covered his head with his thin fingers. A smile came to his dewy lips that glistened in the light of the fireball.

'I will, my mother,' said the faint voice that struggled gruffly to find tone. It whispered softly: 'Your desire . . . is my desire.'

Tiger-mask stood up and took a small dagger from her pocket and held it towards the creature in her bloodstained hand. 'Sekaris, go find the man! Destroy him, and bring the Nemorensis to me!'

A crack of blue fire shot from the creature and earthed along the blade of the dagger. The woman dropped the knife to the floor as the electricity quaked through her, making her legs tremble and feet shudder. The jackdaws flooded the air around her in a black mass, pecking at her hands and face as they swirled back and forth, lifting the Sekaris from the ground. The creature began to change, turning silver-blue in a vortex of bright coloured light. It screamed as if it were being dragged to another world, a cry so shrill that it pierced the hearing and scattered the birds in their flight.

The Sekaris hovered above the ground, and then without warning a deep black fissure appeared in the air above and fell like a black curtain, consuming the creature and all the birds.

The four sat motionless, looking to the place where the creature had departed the world. The floor of the chamber was thickly covered in black feathers and scattered with tiny black beaks and thin, spindly bird legs.

'It's dead,' said fox-mask, brushing himself clean of a thousand feathers. 'The magic was too much for it. We need serpent to be here, there was no balance in what we did.'

'It's alive,' said tiger-mask as she wiped the blood from her hand with her black cloak. 'I know it's alive, I can feel it.'

'We saw it destroyed with our own eyes – taken into some black hole like a fly into a web,' fox-mask replied.

'Does not a mother know when her child lives? The Sekaris is of my breath. I know it lives, I can hear him calling to me.'

Agetta Lamian snuffed out the light on the final wick of the seventy candles that had burnt for the last five hours. They had sooted the brass chandelier, coating it in a fine oil of dried tallow. She took the cloth from her apron and wiped every stem clean before pulling each of the hot stubs and dropping them into the candle bucket that she had carried from room to room. From the morning room the sound of Blake and Bonham crept through the thick oak door, their sharp tones hinting that they were locked in argument.

Mrs Malakin had told her they were not to be disturbed, and by that Agetta knew she would have plenty of time. Quickly, she ran down the ladder steps, propped it against the wall and picked up the candle bucket. She looked up the long staircase that led from the hallway to the observation room. She thought of her friend, Thaddeus, and knew she could fulfil his dream. If the Nemorensis were in the house then it would have to be there. She had seen Blake dressed in his scarlet cuffs and strange silk cap, one foot slipshod and the other bare as he chanted incantations and mixed the elements in clay jars and silver goblets that spewed dark flames. Somewhere in the attic of the house the Nemorensis was hidden, and Agetta knew she had to find it.

Taking two steps at a time, she ran up the stairs to the landing at the top of the house. She constantly looked over her shoulder, but there was no one following. Stepping into the top corridor with its delicate white plaster cornices and hand-etched walls, she stopped yet again. This time she waited as she tried to regain her breath. She listened to the sounds of the house.

From far below, Agetta could hear the muffled sound of shouting. Carefully she stepped along the soundless, finely woven carpet that ran like a deep blue pathway to the observation room. In the distance she could see the candle that lit the doorway to the room. It was a daunting, gloomy, narrow corridor, the width of a man's shoulders. It led into thick blackness like a tunnel taking her to hell. She knew that if caught there would be no escape, there was only one way out. Her imagination mixed the shadows to conjure creatures that did not exist yet were so real they tore at her soul, and her daylight reasoning battled with the ogres that invaded her every thought.

Turning quickly, she looked behind her, convinced she was being watched. She again heard the voice of Blueskin Danby rattle through her head. In her mind's eye she saw the figure of the ghost with the black serpent weaving through his rancid flesh.

Beads of sweat trickled down her spine like a procession of long white slugs. Brushing her hands against the sides of the corridor to steady herself as she walked, she tried to banish all fear from her mind, to think only of Thaddeus and what she could do for him. She was determined to succeed; she would never let him down.

147

Agetta edged her way towards the door. The candle stub flickered on the small table. With each step, the lump grew in her throat. Her hands began to tremble as the darkness of the house began to creep around her.

13 : Sui Sudarium

The door to the observation room had a large, round brass handle with a polished brass fingerplate that shone like gold in the candlelight. Fresh, deep scratches had been cut into the surface, and flakes of metal littered the floor. Agetta pressed against the door, which quickly sprung open. Inside she could see the large telescope pointing through the open window to the sky.

At the far side of the room she saw that the large cupboard door had been left slightly open, as if by someone who had been disturbed. It rocked slightly back and forth. She had never seen inside before – Blake had been secretive as to its contents, this was his magical room and not for those whose minds were earth-bound. Thinking only of the Nemorensis and how Thaddeus would be so pleased to get it back, Agetta opened the door further and looked inside. There on the only shelf was the book. She rubbed her hand over its old skin and traced her fingers around the strange shapes etched into the cover. Slowly, she slid the book from the shelf and lifted it to her chest, squeezing it as tight as she could, wanting to absorb the book deep within her. Dust fell from the pages as if a bright white cloud were billowing forth from each chapter. It fell around her like a growing fog as she retraced her steps to the door.

It was then that she heard the muffled sound of breathing coming from behind the curtains. Agetta paused, unsure of what she heard. The sound came again as the curtains rustled, and the solitary candle cast long shadows across the wooden floor. She clutched the Nemorensis, completely transfixed. From where the sound of breathing had come there appeared a long, thin, webbed hand that slowly began to pull the curtain away from the window.

Moonlight flooded the room, and Agetta dared not move as she stared into the face of the Sekaris. The creature's golden eyes glared at her like two glistening lanterns.

'My book . . .' it said softly, holding out its long webbed hand towards her.

Agetta's mind raced. She knew she could not fail Thaddeus. 'Nemorensis,' she replied defiantly. 'It's the Nemorensis and it belongs to Thaddeus Bracegirdle.' She took short, precise steps backwards towards the door, drawing on every ounce of strength to defeat her fear.

The Sekaris walked awkwardly towards her, dragging its heavy feet across the wooden floor, its eyes flashing. Agetta clutched the Nemorensis tightly with one hand, turned and ran as fast as she could, slamming the door to the observation room behind her. She stopped outside the door, her eyes searching for some way to block the creature from following her. Seeing the key in the lock, she quickly turned it, securing the door. Then she leant against the wall of the long corridor and took a deep breath as panic rushed through her body, setting every nerve and sinew on fire.

'Agetta,' shouted a voice from the hallway far below. 'Is that you?' It was Blake. 'What's going on, girl? It's nearly midnight!'

'I'm fine, Doctor Blake, it was a breeze that slammed the door,' Agetta called down, knowing that this was her only chance to escape the house with the book. These were just words, and deception came so easily that they fell from her lips like honey. She stood in the darkness and listened – there was no reply, no sound of footsteps from the hallway. She looked back at the lock, which began to move slowly as the creature attempted to pull the door open with its clumsy hands. She began to edge away from the doorway.

It was as she turned that there came an ear-splitting sound of rupturing wood and, faster than a shot from a gun, the long, strong arm of the Sekaris blasted through the broken door and grasped her by the throat, pulling her to the splintered hole. The creature tried to pull her through the fist-shaped opening before it thrust her away and then pulled her back again, slamming her against the door again and again like a rag doll.

Thick, sharp splinters stuck into her face as the Sekaris smashed her back and forth. Agetta gripped the Nemorensis even tighter, knowing in her heart that she would never let go. She kicked against the door and with all her strength she smashed the book against the creature's hand, hoping against hope that its ever-tightening grip would be broken.

'In the name of heaven, what's going on, girl?' shouted Blake from far below as he and Bonham began to climb the stairs.

Agetta could feel her legs growing weaker and her eyes bulging from their sockets. The creature's arm was squeezing the last remaining breath from her. A thin red mist began to numb her mind and she slipped down the door, but with one last effort she lashed out with the Nemorensis, thrusting the book as hard as she could against the hand that gripped her so tightly.

For one moment she felt the creature loosen its grip. Agetta twisted away and fell to her knees. The Sekaris lashed out with its arm, trying frantically to get hold of her. She crawled along the carpet, clutching the book with one hand, as the beast tried to smash the door from its hinges.

'What are you doing, girl?' Blake shouted, his voice getting closer.

Agetta got to her feet as the Sekaris destroyed the wooden panels, showering the corridor in fine oak splinters. She ran, panting, towards the light and Blake's harsh shouting. Two paces in front of her was the door to the scullery stairs that spiralled down three floors to the kitchen and the servants' entrance. She could hear Blake and Bonham pounding across the landing below her, their heavy feet clattering across wood and carpet. She looked behind her – the Sekaris was about to shatter the last panel from the door, which shuddered in its frame. Agetta jumped the last step and grabbed the handle of the door to the stairway. It opened easily, and the smell of boiled cabbage billowed upwards. She stood on the narrow step at the top of the stone staircase and hurriedly closed the door, leaving a narrow opening through which she could see the corridor.

She had a view of the stairs and the doorway. She could see the Sekaris beating out the panels and trying to drag itself through the hole. It fell clumsily on to the carpet and rolled into the table, knocking the candle to the floor.

Blake raced ahead of Bonham and was the first to see the creature. 'Isaac!' he screamed, as Bonham struggled to run up the last few steps as he gasped for breath. 'Get your pistol, man!'

Bonham fumbled awkwardly in his pocket for the small dandy gun. The Sekaris got to its feet and looked at the two men. It stared at Blake and shuddered, then looked at the fingers of its hand. It held them to its thin mouth, which was almost hidden in the vibrant foliage that covered its face, and slowly tasted each one.

'It *is* you . . .' the beast said as it stepped towards the men. 'You can make this easy for yourself and I promise I will kill you quickly, or struggle and it will take a little longer.'

Bonham took the gun from his pocket and aimed it at the creature as Blake stepped back. 'One more step, demon, and I'll shoot!' Bonham shouted, holding out the small pistol in front of him.

'Don't talk to it!' Blake shouted in despair. 'Shoot it!'

'It's not you I want,' replied the creature as it took slow steps towards them. 'It is *him*.' The Sekaris pointed to Blake.

Bonham hesitated and looked at Blake. 'Shoot the thing!' Blake shouted again, backing away. 'It wants to kill me.'

Bonham cocked the pistol, raised his arm and fired. The narrow corridor echoed with the blast as the dandy gun spewed forth shot and red, burning wadding that together hit the beast, knocking it backwards to the floor. The Sekaris lay motionless, a growing patch of skin turning back to white baked clay.

'Is it dead?' Bonham asked, reloading the pistol from the dandy bag he carried at his waist.

Blake leant out from where he had cowered behind him. 'It doesn't move and makes no sound. Wait here and I'll get my sword,' he said, and he ran down the stairs to the room below.

Agetta slipped quietly down the spiral staircase walking in complete blackness, knowing each step from the thousand times she had walked them before.

Bonham kept guard, keeping his pistol pointed at the prostrate beast that filled the floor of the narrow passageway. Blake quickly returned, clasping a sea cutlass given to him by his father. 'I never thought I would see the day when I would want to use this,' he said eagerly as he approached the beast. 'This creature is surely stranger than anything we have ever seen, and not the product of a menagerie.'

Bonham stood at the end of the passageway as Blake edged closer to the creature holding the sword out before him. He prodded the body of the Sekaris with the sharp tip. It didn't move. Taking strength from the brightly polished blade, he stabbed the beast firmly in the leg. The razor-sharp tip cut deep into the mud-like flesh. Blake watched as the wound began to dry like baked clay.

'You killed it, Bonham, come and see.' He looked at the leaf-covered face and cold, gold eyes. 'This is a creature from hell if ever I saw one. Now do you believe we are more than just flesh and blood? My science will prove it, now that I have a creature to show to the society.' He looked at Bonham. 'I'm convinced all this has something to do with the comet. It is as if the whole of the underworld is being stirred up by its presence. We will have to be careful, Bonham. The closer the sky dragon gets to the world, the more strange things will assault the senses.'

'Do you think it has eaten your servant girl?' Bonham asked as he looked around for Agetta.

'Whatever has happened we shall soon find out. I care not for her welfare – servants can be replaced and we can explain to her father that she lies in the belly of an angel from hell. Oh, to see the look on his face when he hears that!' Blake laughed. 'Knowing her, I'm surprised the beast was still alive for you to shoot it. We will soon find out her fate, for I intend to cut the creature in two and anatomise every piece. A chance like this may never happen again.'

Blake knew that something had brought the Sekaris to him. He quickly scanned its flesh, looking for any sign or talisman that would speak of its origin. His mind raced with avarice for understanding. This was a gift from heaven, a child of another world sent by the comet to broaden the mind of man.

'Help me carry it to the table and then we'll cut it to pieces and dine on the knowledge.' Blake was overcome with desire. He visibly glowed as he took hold of the feet of the Sekaris and began to drag the creature into the observation room. Its body felt cold and clammy, like damp earth covered in morning dew, and its silky fluid covered his hand in a bright emerald green like thin paint. 'Come on Isaac, the thing is heavy.'

Bonham stood rock-still, holding the dandy gun and pointing it, finger ready, at the Sekaris. He had an air of melancholy about him, and appeared to ignore what Blake had said. He looked at the phantasm before him and eyed each feature as if it reminded him of someone he knew well.

'Isaac, it *is* dead,' Blake snapped. 'You don't need to shoot it again.' His voice was edged with anger. 'I don't want to wait all night, Isaac.'

Bonham snapped out of his dream. He looked at Blake and he put the gun back into his pocket. 'What kind of creature is it?' he asked, as he took hold of its heavy arms as together they dragged it into the observation room. He studied the creature's face. 'It looks like it has been hand-made, like a statue come to life.'

Blake was speedy in his reply. 'If I am right then the creature is something that I have longed to see. I heard of one created in Prague, but rumours of its birth were quashed in the pogrom. They destroyed half the city trying to find it and killed anyone they felt had been involved in its creation. Some say it is still alive, locked in the high vault of a hidden temple, away from prying eyes.' Blake laughed to himself as they dragged the creature to the middle of the room. 'I never thought I would see the day when a Sekaris would call upon me for supper.'

'It said it was going to kill you,' Bonham said.

'It would, if you hadn't been such a good shot. This creature was sent to kill me by someone who wants me dead or wants what I have.' Blake looked at his hand, examining his fingernails. 'Last night I lost my fingernails, cut to the quick while I lay unconscious in the grave.' He looked to the hand of the beast. 'If I am not mistaken and remember the formula correctly, I should find them imbedded in this creature's hand.'

Blake examined the hand of the Sekaris, and from the tip of each finger he picked out a single piece of human nail. 'I told you, Bonham. There is my evidence, I rest my case.' He nodded smugly in self-approval.

'Who would want to do that to you? You're a man of science,' Bonham asked.

'I have my suspicion, Isaac, and one thought especially that I do not wish to believe. It is best for your sake that I keep it to myself. You are my only friend and companion, but I would not want to share something with you that could result in your death.' Blake smiled at Bonham. Here was a man for whom he had deep affection, a friend loyal to the last, and even in anger and difference they shared a bond that nothing could break.

As they lifted the corpse of the Sekaris on to the table, Blake looked towards the cupboard where he kept the Nemorensis. The door swung fractionally open. Blake dropped the corpse on to the table with a loud thud and looked disbelievingly at the open door. 'It's gone,' he said in a murmur. 'The Nemorensis has been stolen from me.'

He opened the cupboard door fully. There was nothing to be found. The book had vanished. 'Someone has stolen the Nemorensis!' he shouted, and he ran to the passageway.

Bonham grabbed him by the shoulders, pulling him back into the room. 'In the name of Hermes, calm down, Sabian.'

'She stole it, I know she did!' Blake shouted. 'That thing found her when it came looking for me. It hasn't eaten her – she ran off with my book. Knowing Lamian and his hell-child, they'll cut it up and sell it as privy paper.' Blake steamed in his anger, his face burning red with rage. 'Give me your gun, Isaac, and I'll save the hangman a job. She may be a child but for this she will die by the lead or the rope, it'll be her choice.'

'Agetta Lamian is a child, she knows no better.'

'She is old enough to know that if you steal from your master then it is a capital offence. She has had enough from me over the years and I have turned a blind eye to her hand in my pocket and fleecing my guests, but for the Nemorensis she will pay with her life or be transported to the colonies.' Blake spat his reply. In the Nemorensis, Bake believed he had found the answer to every question he could think of. It had predicted the comet and grown before his eyes. It was precious, magnificent and powerful. It had snared his imagination and taken hold of his soul.

'Then we must find her and get back the book before the inmates of Newgate sample the softness of its pages,' Bonham replied as he let go of Blake. 'If we go now, we can be at the lodging house before she has time to destroy the book. Your creature will have to wait for its anatomisation.' He took out a large red handkerchief from his pocket and covered the creature's face. 'I hate to see the eyes of the dead, they have a habit of staring at you . . .'

Blake and Bonham stepped into the hallway. Bonham turned and looked momentarily at the Sekaris, and for a split second he was sure he saw the beast move. He looked again, convinced he had made a mistake, and after closing the door they walked to the scullery staircase.

14 : The Chimera

The fog that filled Fleet Street was so impenetrable that the link-torches lighting the shops and houses failed to brighten the gloom. Agetta ran quickly through the mist, jumping over the rotting carcass of a slaughtered goat that had been thrown into the gutter outside the butcher's shop on the corner of Chancery Lane. Its bones had been picked clean by dogs and men who had sucked and gnawed raw flesh in their hunger. The skinned head flopped to one side as if to bite at her heels as she speeded by. She looked down at the creature, expecting it to spring to life and give chase like some night dragon.

As she kept a tight grip on the Nemorensis, she could feel the book becoming hotter. She stopped and wrapped the cover in her coat, to keep the heat from burning her hand. Then she noticed that the Nemorensis was getting heavier, pulling at her arms to let it go. Agetta sensed the book had the power of another world. Sudden, deep dread sent soul-blistering thoughts flashing through her mind: it was as if the book wanted her to stop running, and to fill each approaching face, shadow and alleyway with such terror as to frighten her to give it up to the gutter.

The vision of the goat haunted her as she dashed across the cobbles towards the lodging house. It flashed through her mind's eye time and time again, changing from goat to lion to dragon. 'Stop it, stop it!' she shouted as she ran by a crowd of old men gathered on the corner to drink gin. They laughed as she passed by, one man lunging at her dark flowing hair with his flaking hand. Agetta was sure the book was calling to everyone she saw to thwart her escape. The weight of the book grew with each pace and the heat scalded her flesh. One more step! One more step, she thought to herself, as she ran towards the door.

Agetta jumped from the mud of the street to the freshly scrubbed steps of the lodging house. Suddenly the Nemorensis tripled in weight and pulled her to the floor. She crashed on to the step and crumpled against the wooden door as she spilled into the hallway. 'Brigand!' she shouted as she tried to get to her feet and lift the book again. No one came. 'Father, help me!' There was no reply. The house made no sound.

Leaving the book by the fireplace, she ran into the kitchen. Cadmus Lamian was slumped in his chair by the remnants of the fire. The smell of roasting beef filled the room. Agetta ran to him, grabbing his shoulders to shake from him every ounce of sleep.

'Wake up, father. I have something to show you,' she said urgently.

Cadmus snorted, grunting a low reply and brushing her hand from his face like a summer fly. Agetta saw the keys to the attic on his belt. She thought for a moment and then bent over and unhooked them, sliding them quickly into her pocket. 'Will somebody please help me?' she cried out.

The door to the kitchen slammed shut. Agetta realised she was not alone. She turned around and there, sitting in the darkness in a rocking chair, was Dagda Sarapuk.

'No one will help you, because no one *can* help you. They are all charmed. The whole house sleeps through my spell, and the Hand of Glory.' Sarapuk pointed to a severed wax–covered hand that stood on the mantel over the fire. Each tallowed finger burnt with a faint blue flame. 'This one is very old, cut from the body of a hanged man. Once I had the pair, both right and left, but I left the right with a dear friend. I am always surprised by its power; it has never let me down. Everyone will sleep until I blow out the light and then they will awake as if nothing has happened.' Sarapuk rocked back and forth, quietly sniggering to himself.

'So why don't I fall for your charms?' Agetta asked as she looked around the room for a way of escape.

'You were not here when the spell was cast. I couldn't check your room, and your father and I were busy upstairs with his guest.'

'Tegatus! What have you done to him?' Agetta shouted.

'So you know of the angel? Don't worry, for the moment he is still alive, but that may not be for long.' Sarapuk kicked a large black sack by his feet, which appeared soft and light. 'Feathers. He has been stripped, plucked, trussed like a Christmas turkey, and I shall sell each one, every strand of his golden hair, every lock and quill. They will make potions, mulls and quibdykes. Poultices for the young, sops for the blind, a cure-all that I shall have pleasure in selling.' Sarapuk smiled at her. 'Then I will grind his bones for angel dust and search his entrails for the origin of the soul, and if I can't find it in an angel then what hope for us mortals?'

'You'd kill him for that?' Agetta asked as she looked for a weapon.

'I would kill him for less. In all my years of robbing graves and dissecting the dead whilst I look for the human soul I have yearned – no, cried out – for such a creature.' Sarapuk paused, his teeth chattering, and looked at her with a small smile that cracked his long, thin, white face. 'Perhaps you would consider joining me in my quest? I have always needed an assistant and you are so pleasing to the eye.'

'What would I gain from such a union?' Agetta asked cautiously.

'I would keep you as a lady and you would never need to work. You could have a servant of your own to order around the house. Doctor and Mrs Sarapuk could be at home to entertain . . .' Sarapuk glowed with the idea that ached in his mind. 'We could live in a new London. I have friends in high places who may soon be even higher.'

'Strung from Tyburn gallows with a rope around their necks, that's as high as your friends will get. You have mighty ideas for a tuppenny quack.'

'Things will not always remain the same. A star is coming that will give us all a new future. London will be destroyed, my friends told me just last night. They are to build a new golden city, great, powerful and free from rats and ignorant people.' Sarapuk rubbed his hands together. 'I am part of their plans. Imagine that, old Doctor Sarapuk sharing a table with the likes of them!'

'Your friends have bad taste. I wouldn't let you eat from the same bowl as my dog,' Agetta replied bitterly.

Sarapuk rubbed his chin. 'As for that creature, where is it?'

Agetta thought before she spoke. 'He's away. He goes away from time to time but always comes back,' she replied anxiously, her face giving away her true feelings.

'Well, if that is the case then I have nothing to fear. Your father is charmed, the dog has gone and I have you all to myself . . . without interruptions.' Sarapuk got up from the chair and walked towards her.

With all her strength Agetta suddenly lifted the table and tipped it towards Sarapuk, sending huge billows of white everywhere as the flour sack spilled on to the floor. Sarapuk dived for her across the upturned table, but Agetta hid behind her father and then pushed his chair on to Sarapuk as he tried to chase her across the kitchen. The unconscious body of Cadmus Lamian fell on to Sarapuk as he grovelled on the floor, pinning him with its dead weight to the cold stone. But as Agetta ran for the door, Sarapuk lashed out and grabbed her ankle. He held her with a sturdy grip, so powerfully that she could feel his icy fingers digging deep into the flesh.

With one hand she managed to grab the bone door-handle and tried with all her strength to pull herself free from his grasp. Sarapuk held firm, gritting his teeth as he tried to free his other arm that was trapped beneath the gasping body of her father. 'I won't let you go,' he panted, tightening his grip. 'Give up now, girl. Give in to me now!' Sarapuk pulled himself and her father closer to Agetta across the stone floor.

As Sarapuk freed his other hand and clamped it around her leg, Agetta was forced to let go of the door handle. The double grip dug into her flesh. She grabbed a small brown bottle from the fire mantel and threw the liquid into his face. Sarapuk screamed as the strong vinegar burnt his eyes. He released Agetta and tried to wipe the liquid from his face as she ran to the door.

'May you burn, Sarapuk, may you burn in hell for this!' she shouted as she slammed the door shut and stood panting in the hallway. She reached to the top of the door and pulled the thick iron key from the wooden lintel. She locked the door and threw the key across the hall. It jangled as it slid and bounced across the stone floor, landing by a rat hole in the corner by the fire.

The Nemorensis was in the hallway, sucking the last embers of heat from the fire. In two paces, Agetta crossed the hall and tried to prise the book from the floor. But the heat from the Nemorensis scalded her skin, it was too much to resist. From the other side of the kitchen door she could hear Sarapuk fighting with the sleeping body of her father. She looked into the refectory. Every chair was filled with a sleeping guest, some slumped in their food as if they had fallen into a deep sleep as they chewed on their supper, others curled up on the floor like fireside cats full of mice. Mister Manpurdi sat at the long table – the bandages that covered his stigmata were unravelled and had dropped to the floor in a heap of matted cloth. Agetta watched as a thick red drop of blood spilled from the hole on the back of his hand, dribbled across the skin and ran down his finger.

In her anger she kicked the Nemorensis and then ran up the stairs. As she opened the bedroom door she could hear her mother snoring loudly – she too was fast asleep, either drunken or charmed. As Agetta turned and faced the stairs that led up to the attic, she was aware of a sudden, sharp drop in temperature that chilled her spine. She looked around for Blueskin Danby. Lying against the wall was a lodger wrapped in his coat, his dirty boots sticking out from underneath. She took the several paces to the stairs and slowly climbed until she stood by the door. She took the key and quickly turned the lock and stepped into the room.

Tegatus sat in chains, his head shaved, his tunic covered in blood. His hands were held locked together, the blood dripping into his lap. Agetta could see what her father and Sarapuk had done.

The angel looked up and tried to smile at her. 'I heard you call for help, but somehow I couldn't rouse myself to come. I didn't think you would want to see me like this.'

'I have seen Sarapuk, he told me what he will do with your hair and the feathers from your wings,' Agetta said quietly.

'He cut off my fingernails, so deep that they bleed. They laughed as they did this to me.' He paused and looked at Agetta forlornly. 'I fell from grace, a fallen angel. I am here because I wanted to be. I fell in love with the woman whose life I had been sent to save. I lost myself in her eyes and forgot who I was. What I didn't realise was that she was lost for ever to a creature that seeks to destroy us all.' Tegatus rattled the length of chain against the wooden floor. 'I thought that angels were beyond his power, but even we can be caught in his snare.'

Agetta spoke quickly. 'I need you to be strong, Tegatus. I have found a book. I am taking it to my friend at London Bridge. I need you to help me.'

'I can't even help myself,' the angel replied. He stopped and listened. 'Mister Sarapuk is trying to get out of the kitchen, I can hear him smashing against the door.'

Agetta ignored his reply. 'I want you to come with me, to my friend Thaddeus, he is a man who will help us both.' She took the keys from her pocket and offered them to Tegatus. 'There must be one here that can undo those chains.' She found a small bronze key covered in tiny chiselled letters in a language she couldn't understand. Finding the Ormuz glass in her pocket, she looked at the lettering and read the words aloud: '*The Angels who surrender their glory will be kept in darkness, bound with everlasting chains for the Day of Judgement.*' She looked at Tegatus. 'What does it mean?'

'It is a warning to me – that even if you release me from these mortal chains I will never escape. I will be bonded for ever until the Day of Judgement. I gave up everything and this is my reward.'

'Is there no way out of this for you?' she asked.

'Only to go back and seek the blessing of exculpation, and I have gone too far for that.' Tegatus stopped and looked at Agetta. He saw the crystal sparkle in her hand. 'Where did you get the Ormuz glass? I have only ever seen one before.'

'From Thaddeus,' she said proudly. 'He said it was a special gift just for me.'

'Thaddeus is a clever man and someone I would love to meet.'

'He asked me to get the book, and I found it,' Agetta said. '"Bring me the Nemorensis and you will make Thaddeus a happy man." That's what he said and that's what I want to do, make him happy.'

'You like Thaddeus because he's kind to you?'

'He's kind, quiet and thoughtful. He said he would make supper, a banquet he called it, and we'd watch the dawn together.'

Agetta put the key in the lock and turned the hammers, which fell one by one. The manacles dropped away from his wrists – Tegatus was free.

The angel got to his feet and stretched out his arms. 'Sarapuk is breaking down the door,' he said, as if he knew what was happening in the kitchen. 'If you want to escape from here we had better leave now.'

'Quickly,' replied Agetta, grabbing him by the hand. 'You'll have to borrow my father's clothes from his room, if you go into the street like that they'll think you're from Bedlam and have you back in the madhouse before we get down the street.'

She had no fear of Blueskin Danby as she ran down the stairs, clutching Tegatus by the hand. It felt as if he was weightless, that the pull of the world had no hold on him.

They got to her father's room and Agetta bundled him through the door and waited outside. She had told him to take the best boots he could find, a frock coat and thick winter shirt. Cadmus kept these for special days, for the finer times when he would follow a coffin and celebrate the death of a friend. He loved a funeral with its fine horses and the long carriage with the weeping widow and a grieving hound to lead the way. Funerals were worth getting dressed up for.

Tegatus changed quickly and came through the door looking every inch an English gentleman in his fine frock coat and ruffle shirt, French boots and wool breeches. Agetta smiled.

165

As they entered the hall, Tegatus saw the Nemorensis on the floor by the fire, its pages steaming with the heat. Without hesitation he picked up the book with ease and held it firmly under his arm. 'It needs to be controlled,' he said. 'The Nemorensis can sense your mind and play on your fears. If you let it, the book will take control of you and play tricks with the imagination.'

'It's just pages in a book, isn't it?'

'The Nemorensis is the heart of magic, stolen from heaven, and to heaven it must be returned.' Tegatus looked as if he had been strangely transformed. His emerald eyes shone with a passion that Agetta had not seen before, his steps had a purpose and his voice a new-found strength. 'I want you to take me to see your friend,' he said as he walked to the kitchen door. 'Peace, be still, Mister Sarapuk. If you do not cease banging on the door I will come in there and rip your ears from your head and your tongue from its mouth. I suggest you sit and wait till the house is free from whatever charm you placed it under. Do you understand?'

Sarapuk stopped banging against the door.

'It's done,' Tegatus said, turning to Agetta. 'To the street, and may the stars shine a blessing on us!'

Together they left the house and turned towards the Fleet River. The fog was still thick and clung to the houses, blotting out the night sky. Behind them a carriage rattled to a halt outside the lodging house. Agetta and the angel hid in the doorway of a draper's shop and watched as Blake and Bonham leapt from the carriage and ran through the swirling mist into the house.

Tegatus looked at Agetta in the half-light. 'I fear they are looking for you and this book. Did you steal it?'

Agetta looked away in her guilt. For the first time in her life she felt ashamed. It was as if her lies were written across her face and nothing could be hidden. All that she had kept in darkness was now exposed to the light that shone from the angel's life.

'Who are they?' Tegatus asked, sheltering her in his frock coat as they walked quickly towards London Bridge.

'There was a creature tonight at my master's house in Bloomsbury. It was like a man with a face of oak leaves and a skin like wet earth. It smelt of the forest and its eyes shone like fire. It tried to stop me taking the Nemorensis. They shot it and I ran away and I took the book, I had to.'

'It was not yours to take, and neither was it his to keep. The Nemorensis is a book of prophecy; it is not for the eyes of mankind, the secrets that it holds are beyond their imaginings.'

'I know it speaks of a comet coming to the earth. I heard Blake talking of it after the sky-quake. It's here, high above us.' Agetta pointed up through the fog.

'Did he give the comet a name?' Tegatus asked anxiously.

'Wormwood . . . He said it was called Wormwood.' As she spoke her lips faltered.

'Then we have very little time. Each hour seals our fate. As the sky dragon draws near so we will see a madness taking over the earth and air, and forces will be released that the world has not seen since the beginning of time. I pray that your friend Thaddeus will be a man who can help us.'

15 : Timeo Daemones et Donna Ferentes

Sarapuk stuffed the Hand of Glory into his coat pocket and then thrust himself on to the floor of the kitchen as Cadmus woke fitfully from his charmed sleep. A loud crashing in the hallway brought him quickly to his senses as doors slammed and lodgers were roused from their reverie. Mister Manpurdi awoke in a pool of blood. Throughout the house the spell was broken.

Blake smashed his gloved fist against the kitchen door and, seeing it was locked, kicked at the wood. He was watched by a small crowd of tired and bedraggled spectators who had spilled out of the refectory.

'Hold them back, Isaac!' Blake shouted as he kicked, trying to batter down the door. 'If any of that menagerie even move, shoot them like the dogs they are.'

'Help us,' cried Sarapuk in the feeblest voice he could find. 'She's gone mad, attacked her own father in his sleep and made off into the night!' Sarapuk then swooned and moaned, hoping that his performance would not go unnoticed and that the door would be broken down before he had to repeat his act.

A tall, fat, wallowing man covered in a thick mat of black hair with gigantic hands and long dirty fingernails pushed his way from the refectory into the hall. He quickly eyed the scene, and upon hearing Sarapuk's dying eulogy ran the three paces across the stone floor, pushing Bonham and Blake out of the way and smashing into the door like a huge ox.

The door bent in the frame, then sprang back into shape. The man stared at the door, screwing up his eyes and furrowing his brow. He towered over the gathering that waited expectantly for him to strike the door again. He was a giant, orphaned at birth, who now entertained the gentry in Vauxhall Gardens. In his first week of life he was named after the flowers that filled the wicker basket in which he was found and now Campion, the Human Bear, was known for his large size, profuse hair and teeth that he had filed into a row of sharp brown fangs.

'Do it again!' shouted Blake to Campion.

'I have the . . .' whined Manpurdi quietly, fumbling with his bandages.

'By Hermes,' interrupted Bonham, 'knock the thing down, man.'

' . . . key,' said Manpurdi, in a way that he knew no one was listening.

Campion growled from the depths of his enormous stomach. His whole frame vibrated as the long moan echoed off the plaster walls. He rushed at the door, jumping the last pace and landing against the wood with a heavy crash. The door shot from its hinges, falling back into the kitchen and crashing against the wooden table.

Sarapuk lay on the floor, entwined around Cadmus like some large snake about to engulf its prey. He moaned and squawked, writhing in false agony. 'Look what she has done,' he cried. 'She's gone mad, attacked her father and tried to kill me. She's eloped, run off with the stranger from the attic.'

'What?' Cadmus mumbled half to himself. 'She's what?'

'Run off! Attacked you and locked us in and run off with the brute from the attic.' Sarapuk nodded to the gathered crowd.

Manpurdi stood in the corner of the room, listening intently and holding the key in his hand.

'Who did she run off with?' Blake asked as he pressed his way through the crowd and lifted Sarapuk from the floor by the front of his coat. 'Tell me, man, before I throttle you.'

'Agetta has run off with the man from the attic, Tegatus, a lodger from . . .' He paused and looked at Cadmus, hoping that he would help with the word he struggled for.

'The man was from . . . Italy!' Cadmus said. 'Tegatus – pretended to have wings, part of my menagerie. A new acquisition.'

'So, Sarapuk, are you telling me that this Tegatus has run off with Agetta into the night?' Blake demanded, holding fast to his collar.

'I am, Mister Blake. He's a thief, completely no good.'

'Did she have a book with her when you saw her?'

'Book?'

'Yes, man, a book. Large, with thick pages, engraved cover.' Blake let go as Sarapuk slumped to the floor.

'Ah, that book. Yes, she did. She said it was hers to sell,' Sarapuk lied, hoping to bring felony to Agetta's door.

'Cadmus Lamian, your daughter is a thief,' Blake protested over the mutters of the crowd that now filled the kitchen. 'She has stolen something precious from me and I want it back. It was entrusted to me and has a value beyond what the world could give. I will see you and your daughter hanged if it's not returned.'

'She has stolen from me!' Cadmus replied. 'She tried to murder me and Sarapuk as we slept.'

'I am disappointed that she failed in her task,' Blake said bluntly. 'I'll search London for her and if I find her I have a mind to save her from the gallows and drown her in the Thames.' Blake's feelings flashed with anger. The loss of the Nemorensis burnt in his heart, and a boiling desire for vengeance crept through his soul.

'I can't control her, Mister Blake. She is a woman now, takes after her mother. You can't hold me responsible for what she has done. Look at me – I am a victim of a ruthless child, an innocent party in the bitter twist of life.' Cadmus scrunched up his shoulders and held out the empty palms of his hands.

'You can't even stand by your own child. You're a feckless halfwit who only thinks of himself,' Blake snapped in reply.

'Feckless and half-witted I may be, Mister Blake, but she has stolen from me again and again, and others too.' Cadmus scrabbled in the deep pockets of his frock coat, bringing out a handful of silver coins. 'Look at this! I found these in her room. Sadly I think they are stolen from you. See, Mister Blake, she even steals your bread.' Cadmus tipped the coins into Blake's hand.

'Paying me off, Lamian? Hoping I save you from the gallows with thirty pieces of silver?'

'Just giving you what is yours, Mister Blake. I am an honest man and have been hard done to by my own child.' Cadmus lowered his head and stared at the floor. 'If you catch her I will happily testify for you at the Bailey.'

'Then you can take her bread as she rots in Newgate Gaol before the hangman ties her thumbs together and watch as the trap drops.' Blake turned to walk out of the door.

'What must be, Mister Blake, what must be . . .' Cadmus replied slowly. The picture of Agetta hanging limply from Triple Tree haunted his mind.

Blake and Bonham pushed through the crowd and into the fog-filled street. The lodgers stood in silence, looking at Cadmus. The Great Bear furrowed his brow even deeper as he took the door key from Manpurdi. Sarapuk smiled to himself, his face reflecting the glimmering red embers of the fire.

'Get out, get out!' shouted Cadmus as he ushered all but Sarapuk from the room. Campion hauled his huge frame through the door, stooping under the lintel and into the hall, and Mister Manpurdi bled his way out of the kitchen. Sarapuk picked up the broken door and propped it across the doorway to shield them from inquisitive ears.

'What have you done, Sarapuk?' asked Cadmus, his face filled with anger. 'If Blake catches Agetta she'll hang, and if the truth is out then you and I will swing with her. I have committed too many wrongs that could surely bring me ruin. I like my neck the length it is, and the thought of Erasmus Duvall getting to strip me of my clothes and sell them for gin leaves me cold.' Cadmus coughed nervously, his face twitching. He could see the grubby fingers of Duvall, the Newgate hangman, picking off the buttons of his shirt and clipping a lock of his hair to sell to the charm widows who made talismans to ward off the pox. 'Once you're dead he nails you through the heart with a bolt of holly to make sure you don't rise again.'

'You should have done that to Blueskin Danby, then you wouldn't fear him troubling you again,' Sarapuk muttered.

'I had nothing to do with his death. He hung himself.'

'Strange how you can hang yourself with a bludgeon wound on the back of your head and your hands tied together,' Sarapuk replied slowly.

'Rumours, all rumours,' Cadmus protested.

'Just look upon it as doing society an act of kindness, ridding the world of a nuisance, cutting a carbuncle from the big toe of life.' Sarapuk dribbled with excitement. 'He was a soulless man, a thief and a rascal. Who would miss such a creature as that? Sired by the devil and born of a donkey.'

'I won't have you speak ill of Blueskin. He was a good friend, even though we had our differences.'

172

'Differences that meant he met with an unfortunate . . . accident,' Sarapuk said, smoothing the palms of his hands. He leant closer to Cadmus and spoke to him in a hushed voice. 'I've been thinking, Cadmus. We have been friends for a long time, but our business has now faltered. The angel has flown away and will be hard to find. I have been privy to some information that lathers my thoughts on life and London. I will be leaving soon and moving to the north. The air is better for the spirit.' He looked around the room as if listening to another voice. 'It is time for us each to go our own way, my dear friend, but I will always think of you.'

'We had plans,' Cadmus replied angrily. 'We had such great plans to build a hospital, to make wealth out of sickness. Can it all change because of what your friends have told you?'

Sarapuk thought, his face racked with indecision. He held a secret that broke his heart and scarred his mind, which he had sworn he would share with no one. 'Oh, if only the stones would speak,' he cried out. 'If only I could tell you what the future held for you and everyone else who inhabits this dung heap then my heart would be lighter.' He looked solemnly at Cadmus. 'London has done you no good, you need a change of air. Leave as soon as you can, I tell you this as a friend. A time is coming when these very stones will speak out agony and death.'

'The laudanum speaks through your veins, Sarapuk. Have you gone mad?'

'If only I had,' he said, holding his face in his hands. 'If it were someone else I wouldn't care, but for you and your daughter, my little Pisces . . .'

Then a sudden swirling of dust blew around the kitchen like a windstorm, spiralling and twisting, knocking the furniture out of place and sending the rocking chair spinning across the room. Pewter plates crashed from the side table and half-burnt candles and vinegar pots crashed to the stone slabs.

Cadmus jumped back in fright as the table shuddered and shook its way towards the door, pushed by unseen hands. Sarapuk leapt out of the way as it shot past him and wedged itself against the door, blocking their escape. Pans torn from hooks on the ceiling rained down upon them and the slop bucket was thrown across the room, blasted like shot from a French cannon.

'What is it, man?' Sarapuk asked feverishly.

'It's another sky-quake, the whole world is groaning like it's strapped in the birthing chair,' Cadmus replied as a soup ladle flew across the room and hit him in the chest. To his side the knife drawer began to rattle, and then the front of the drawer was violently ripped apart and thrown into the fire, sending bright, exploding red embers scattering across the floor. Sharp, flat blades flew from the felt-lined case, just missing Cadmus and sticking in the wall above his head as he ducked to the floor and cowered behind the washtub.

'It wants to kill me, Sarapuk,' Cadmus shouted. 'This is no sky-quake, it's a creature from hell.'

Sarapuk hid by the table as Cadmus leapt upon it and tried to pull it away from the door to make his escape. He prised his fingers between the door and the frame and pulled as hard as he could. Slowly the wooden door began to give way and he could see a chink of light streaming into the darkened room from the hall.

'Campion, we're trapped!' Cadmus shouted for help as he squeezed his hand into the widening crack. There was a sudden loud snap as the table jumped back, then sped forwards at an unthinkable speed. Cadmus screamed from the depths of his soul. His legs gave way and he hung by one hand, pinned to the wall by the door and frame.

There was an eerie silence. A cold breeze swirled under the kitchen door and picked up the dust from the stone floor. It moulded particle upon particle, slowly taking the shape of a man. First the outline of his coat, then his feet and finally the blurred face and head. Sarapuk saw the phantasm and pressed himself against the wall. He pulled a small stiletto knife from his pocket and clutched a dried henbane sprig with his other hand. He muttered the oath to the dead over and over again, calling upon the saints to protect him.

The table juddered away from the door and Cadmus dropped to the floor in a crumpled heap. He lifted his head and stared disbelievingly at the vision before him.

Sarapuk held out his knife to the ghost and swished the henbane sprig back and forth. 'Go, creature, back to the world of darkness, leave this place,' he shouted, hopping nervously from one foot to the other. 'I command you in the name of Saint Venerious to go!'

The phantasm sucked all the particles of light from the room as it took form and substance. The spirit stood before them, its face veiled by a dark mist that hung in the air. It shuddered and twitched as it gained form. Finally, the features of its face became clear.

Cadmus recognised the spectre by the taint of its blue skin and the living tattoo that crept over its flesh. His heart pounded as he waited for the ghost to speak. Cadmus knew that the apparition was Blueskin Danby, and the mere thought of his resurrection chilled him to the bone. He could feel the strength bleeding from each sinew of his body as the creature stared at him through lifeless eyes. It was as if Danby could not yet see him, as if he searched the room but saw it in another time.

Sarapuk, cowering by the table, broke the silence. 'It's not me you want but him,' he shouted to the phantasm, which now looked eagerly around the room. The serpent swirled over his flesh, parting his dead hair and sliding between his thin lavender lips as it slithered back and forth over his head.

'I can hear you, foul fiend, but see you not,' Danby said as he peered into the darkness. 'Your voice is known to me, but from what time I am unsure, and from what place I cannot recall.'

'It's Sarapuk, Doctor Sarapuk. I was your doctor.'

'Sarapuk . . . Yes, I remember Sarapuk. Always drunk, never a penny of your own and killed more people than you cured. Arsenic and laudanum with a cabbage cake, a pound of quicksilver to a pint of ale shall take away a winter chill. That was Sarapuk.'

'Yes, and it did take away the chill,' Sarapuk interrupted.

'And killed the poor woman that drank it. I remember her well, Helen Fury, the Black Lion, Drury Lane, Michaelmas Eve. Watched her choke to death the next day and you were too drunk to help her.'

'It's not me that you visit, Blueskin, I never meant you any harm,' Sarapuk whined.

'I watched you anatomise me. I gripped the old life and refused to let go. I had been spelled, caught by a magician in the Stygian world. As in life, so in death I hung between health and damnation.'

'It's me you want, Blueskin.' Cadmus got to his feet as he confronted the ghost. 'I'll play no games with you. I never hid from you in life so why should I fear you in death?'

'How sweet the sound of your voice. You have been blinded from me by death and now I hear you again.'

'What do you want of me Blueskin? Let us not jest.'

'I bring you a gift. Though my hands are too feeble to carry it, I can tell you where it lies. You killed me for it but never found it. You see, Cadmus, I suspected what you were doing was a trap so I dug up the gold and hid it in a bookshop. Trapped under the bottom shelf and entombed by a volume of *Micrographia*, there you'll find it. I have no use for the gold, there are no pockets in this shroud.' Blueskin let out a deep mournful sigh.

'You bring gifts and not vengeance . . . why?' Cadmus asked.

'Death treats you to many virtues, I cannot hold on to bitterness. There is no place in my heart for human schemes. I would give everything for a year and a day in human form, to have the sun touch my skin and the taste of gin on my lips. That would be paradise regained. The pleasure of the flesh is all I know and it was stolen from me.' He looked to where Cadmus stood. 'The years have been good to you, Cadmus. Take my gift and use it, for as I am now so soon you'll be.'

From all around came the faint sound of children screaming in the distance, as if tormented in play. Their voices grew nearer. 'My guardians come for me,' Blueskin said as he began to turn to dust. 'See that you heed my words, Cadmus. You wanted the money in life, now have it in my death.'

Three small dark figures walked through the wooden door as if it did not exist and encircled Danby, joining hands and dancing around him. They had no features, just the small shape of young children lost to death like running shadows. The grey, lithe spirits danced faster and faster, round and round to the beat of a silent drum. Danby began to fade, and the spiral of wind came again to shatter its way through the dark kitchen and rattle the pans across the floor, scraping the table to the centre of the room.

Sarapuk shook with fear as the creatures joined as one, growing into a ball of pure white light that sparkled and fizzed in the centre of the kitchen. The blinding light etched his face in long, dark shadows and he covered his head with his hands. Cadmus endured the light as long as he could before shielding his eyes from its glare. In an instant it was gone, and the room wallowed in thick blackness, lit only by the fire and a soft chink of candlelight that crept into the room through the door crack.

'Are you there, Sarapuk?' Cadmus asked feebly, stumbling

like a blind man trying to find a chair. 'I can't see you, my eyes are burnt by the ghosts.'

Dagda Sarapuk crept stealthily across the kitchen to the door and quietly slid the wood from the doorway before slipping into the hall and then out to the street.

'Dagda, I can't see, where are you?' asked Cadmus as he floundered around the kitchen, lurching into the table and crashing to the floor. 'Help me, man. Help me!'

In the darkest corner of the room, pressed against the wall, a shadow waited for Cadmus to stagger closer.

16 : Herba Sacra

On the corner of Bishopsgate a tattered woman clutched a bundle of herbs as Agetta and Tegatus walked quickly along the street towards London Bridge. A fat candle in an open-topped bell jar lit her midnight stall. The night-light flickered and spat, casting an orange glow into the fog like the eye of a fox as her shrill voice called out into the night. 'Vervain! Rue! Herba Sacra! Herb of Grace, keep away the scourge of death, taste the bread of repentance . . . All a penny,' the woman shouted as she held out a long vervain wand with its tall, woody stalk tipped with slender, tiny blue flowers. 'Dip the flowers in November frost, chase away the midnight ghost.'

Tegatus looked to the ground, trying not to catch the woman's eye. He was weary and his feet dragged in Cadmus's boots as if he were not used to walking such a distance.

'For the young lady, sir? It will protect her from many things,' the woman said as she waved the wand feverishly at him. 'I have a sprig she could wear as a garland, keep her safe, no charm can hurt her, nor mad dog or snake, even takes away the plague.'

Agetta pulled on his arm and looked at him. 'Please, Tegatus, I have always wanted to wear a garland of vervain,' she said, rooting in her pockets for a penny.

Tegatus clutched the book tightly and looked away, fearful that something in his expression would give him away.

'Just one sprig,' Agetta said to the woman, handing her the money.

'Not much of a gentleman, making you pay,' the woman said as she gave Agetta the garland of dried blue flowers. 'Can't even look me in the eye,' she whispered. 'Not the kind of a man to be out walking with.'

'So what herb would you give for that?' Tegatus snapped. 'Sage, to colour my bile? Or marigolds to get rid of warts? I don't look at you because I care what I cast my eye on.'

The woman didn't reply. She shrugged her shoulders at Agetta and slid the penny into her pocket. Agetta smiled and took the arm of Tegatus to lead him down the street. 'He's not from these parts, he's a stranger to London.'

'He's no stranger to hell, mark my words, girl. That man has the hand of death firmly grasping his shoulder and he'll take you with him given half the chance.'

A large black carriage clattered through the street towards them as the coachman lashed out at the four horses with his long whip. It rattled furiously over the cobbles as Tegatus pulled Agetta out of its way.

'He drives with a purpose!' Tegatus said, stepping out with expanding pace. Agetta ran to keep up with him.

'I told you the madness was coming closer,' Tegatus said as they finally went through the great arch on to London Bridge. 'Superstition and magic fills the heart and no one can be bothered to search for truth.' Tegatus stopped and turned around, and for several moments he waited in the doorway of the coffee shop to see if they had been followed. 'I sense we are being watched,' he said. 'It doesn't seem to be human, somewhere in the fog by the arch, I feel it's there . . . waiting.'

'No one knows we are here, so how can they follow us?' Agetta asked as she pressed herself against the door.

'This book speaks darkness, it cries out to the night and

your human ears cannot hear it. Every spirit in London will be drawn to it like a flea to a candle. They'll come to gloat at your fate to steal your energy.' Agetta clutched the vervain tightly in her hand. 'That won't protect you, it's just a dried flower,' Tegatus said as if he could read the very thoughts of her heart. 'The leaves will take away the melancholy and ease the pain, but it won't stop the devil chasing your soul.'

'What did the woman mean when she said death had a hold of you? Do you think she could see anything?' Agetta asked quietly.

'It was the book speaking through her, telling her what to say. It's mischievous and was written in wickedness. The Nemorensis has the power to change the way we think, to take control of our minds and seduce our understanding. It lies with its own ink,' he whispered. 'Many people have fallen for its beauty and have believed everything it has said, but with every prophecy there comes a lie. It twists the truth, adds a jot here, an iota there. It tells a man to watch for trouble by night and then surprises him by coming like a thief at dawn. I think you will hear more before this night is out . . .'

'It told Blake it would be twenty-one days from the sky-quake to the comet's coming to the earth,' Agetta said as she peered out across the bridge towards Bibblewick Bookshop. 'I heard him tell Bonham before they found me hiding in the cupboard.'

'Wormwood is closer than that, I fear. It would seem that Doctor Blake doesn't realise what powers he is playing with.' Tegatus looked back and forth up and down the bridge. 'I know it's here, I can feel it, but it cannot be seen,' he said as he looked towards the candlelit bookshop. 'Tell me, Agetta, when was your friend expecting you?'

'I said I'd be back tonight.'

'Alone?'

'Yes. I didn't think you would ever come with me.' She paused. 'You and Thaddeus have been the first people that I would call friends. You've both been so kind. In a way I have found you both by fate. I found you in the attic, and if it wasn't for Yerzinia telling me to go to the shop I would never have met Thaddeus.' She wrapped herself tightly in her shawl.

'So Yerzinia is a friend?' Tegatus appeared shocked by the mention of her name.

'The best friend you could ever have, so fine and dandy, with her own carriage,' Agetta said, smiling. 'You know what, *she* found me. It was fate, she said I would become like her.'

'She said you would be sisters and that you would never want for anything again?'

Agetta didn't reply but looked to the ground. She had the intense feeling that her mind was an open book, that everyone who just looked at her could read her thoughts and know her deepest secrets.

'What sealed your friendship with her? A drinking-cup of fervent liquid or was it the moon mark that burns blood red on your palm?'

'Both,' she replied.

'Then you are twice cursed. This Yerzinia of yours wants more than your friendship.'

'I know,' Agetta interrupted. 'She told me, that I could leave my life behind and –'

'Be sucked dry of every ounce of your life and then discarded in this open sewer you call the Thames, to be washed up on a distant strand with no one the wiser or ever caring.' Tegatus gave a sudden deep breath as if a sharp blow had struck him. 'I need to rest. I will see this friend of yours now.'

He was sharp in his demands and Agetta felt uncomfortable in his presence. She even began to regret helping him escape and sharing with him the secrets of her newfound friendships.

Tegatus had taken them and cast his light upon them, he had corrupted that which to her was beautiful, good and true and tainted it with deception and intrigue. She could feel a bitter resentment growing against the angel. She wished she had left him to rot in the attic, she thought to herself, trying to cover the resentment with a myriad of other thoughts to disguise her feelings so he couldn't read her mind. She thought of her mother, of washing plates and swimming in the Thames. She allowed her mind to dance from one dream to another so that he would not be able to see the growing dislike she had for him.

Tegatus appeared distracted, distant. His mind was far away as he stumbled across the cobbles to the Bibblewick Bookshop. He held his chest as he walked as if a dark, painful memory had stabbed him in the ribs. Agetta followed at a distance.

The shop door was slightly open, wedged with a piece of folded paper. Agetta bent down and pulled it from the door and instinctively put the torn parchment into her pocket. Again Tegatus stopped and peered through the mist back towards Bishopsgate. The fog swirled as two jackdaws chaffed in the darkness above their heads. The bridge was empty. In the distance they could hear the mournful, weary voice of the herb seller calling the faithful to buy Herba Sacra.

The angel reached up and took hold of the bell and pulled it from its metal spring.

Agetta allowed her face to speak the anger that brewed in her heart. 'Why did –' she whispered.

Tegatus put his hand roughly over her mouth to stop her speaking as he slowly slid the door open and dragged her into the shop. Once inside, he held Agetta against the wall as he looked down the long dark aisle of books. She saw his eyes searching every inch of the shop, flashing from the rough wooden floor to the ornate plaster ceiling. Very slowly he let his hand slip from her mouth, gesturing with his long white finger for her to be completely silent.

At the end of each tall aisle of books a bright candle lit the way through the maze of crammed shelves. There was a constant swirling of dust, blown through the floorboards by the breeze of the Thames that gushed up from the river below. The sound of the ebbing tide filled the shop, echoing from each wall as it flooded each narrow passageway of books with its groaning.

It was a sound that Agetta didn't care for, reminding her of a time past, one Christmas Eve, when she had watched as the Thames watermen had struggled to drag out a boy who had fallen through the ice and into the fierce current that rushed underneath the snow-white crust that shut in the river. They finally heaved him from the water and rested his bitter-blue body on the ice. A thickset boatman had then lain on the boy, trying to warm him through, as the child coughed and choked up the icy sludge that filled his lungs. Yet what disturbed Agetta most was the absence of kindness from the crowd that huddled around the nearby fire of the Frost Fair, where they watched a bear being baited to death by two large mastiffs. She had stared tight-lipped as the crowd laughed at the dying bear whilst behind them the child gripped on to life, cared for only by the fat boatman who gave up his coat.

The river sounded as if it were all around them, louder than she had heard it before. Tegatus crept along the side of the bookshelves and Agetta followed close behind. She felt that something had changed. The bookshop had lost its charm. The atmosphere now shouted a stark warning.

'I hear children,' Tegatus said in a whisper, as he peered around the end of the aisle. Agetta could hear nothing but the roaring of the water as it flooded through the narrow arch beneath the bookshop. 'They are speaking of Thaddeus . . . he is not here!'

Agetta panicked – he had promised to be there. She thought that her only escape would be through him, that Thaddeus would be to her a new life. Without thinking, she ran ahead of the angel towards the tall desk in the centre of the bookshop. She had memorised each aisle, first left then right through the labyrinth of wood and paper. She ran until she reached the desk and jumped upon the waiting-plate and looked out over the shop. For the first time she became aware of how vast the bookshop was. With its vaulted ceiling and walls with thick columns growing out of the oak shelves and topped with ram's horns and garlands of oak fruit, it was like a church.

The angel appeared quite small as she looked down on him from the desk. She thought how he had changed since Sarapuk had stripped him of his feathers and shorn his hair. She wanted to goad him into showing her the angel-wings, to mock the featherless bones and joke that he was a Gravesend goose, plucked whilst still walking. Bitterness surged from her like a spring tide, and the closer he came to her the more she despised him.

'We'll have to hide the book,' he said as he looked round, 'and what better place than in a bookshop?' He laughed. 'Can you see the children? Perhaps they are playing games with us. They will come out when they are not frightened.'

'They were here before, when the stranger came. He could hear them like you, even when I couldn't,' she said indifferently, wanting him to go and leave her to find Thaddeus on her own.

'This man, what did he look like?'

'Like you . . . but older. Same kind of eyes. Looked like a hawk and wanted to know my business.' She looked around the bookshop. 'Thaddeus didn't like him, and I don't think he'll like you either.'

'Did the man say what he wanted?'

'He wanted a book, written by a sister or someone who'd turned their back on his family.'

'Did he say his name?' Tegatus asked as he put the Nemorensis on the bottom shelf of a long bookcase next to a dusty old volume with a crusted cover etched in green mould. He looked at the faded name printed in gold: *Micrographica*.

'No, he never mentioned his name. Should he?' Agetta asked.

There was a sudden crash as a pile of books tumbled from the top of one of the shelves in the distant corner of the shop. Agetta leapt from the waiting-plate and ran down the aisle, quickly followed by Tegatus. By the front window of the shop, lit by a tall green candle and bathed in its gentle light, was a crumpled pile of books.

Tegatus grabbed Agetta by the back of her coat and pulled her towards him. 'Listen,' he said sharply. 'They are near to us.'

They stood in silence. From behind the shelves could clearly be heard the sound of a child weeping. The angel carefully edged his way to the end of the aisle and around the corner. Agetta followed, not wanting to be left behind – the thought of being alone chilled her soul. Somehow she now felt she had been wrong about Tegatus, and she could feel her anger ebbing as she reached out and touched the hem of his garment.

Standing before Tegatus, barefoot and ragged, was a young boy. His face was pale and drawn, with deep black bruises under each eye. Tegatus stared at the child, who could only have reached his eleventh year. The boy held his long grey fingers against his face as he tried to wipe away the salt dew from his eyes. He stared at a pool of thick red blood on the wooden floor and slowly shook his head from side to side, unaware of their presence.

'Mister Thaddeus,' Tegatus heard him whisper, as a long rumble of thunder filled the night air.

'Has Thaddeus left you alone?' the angel said, as softly as he could yet wanting to be heard.

The boy turned and looked in his direction and peered through his deep blue eyes, unsure if he could see the creature that spoke to him.

'Who's there?' he asked. 'What do you want? I can hardly see you.' The boy looked on the shimmering outline of the angel and reached out as if to wipe away a mirage.

'I can see you child, and hear you,' Tegatus said as he stepped towards him. 'What has happened to Thaddeus?'

'Who are you talking to?' Agetta asked, unable to see the boy.

The child hesitated and stepped further away. 'It wasn't me,' he said as Tegatus looked at the blood that was splattered over the floor. 'They came for him, a creature from my side, looked like the gargoyles from the Tower, and a man who could speak the rhymes.' The child stopped and stared at Agetta, who was looking out from behind Tegatus, still clutching the hem of his coat. 'I saw her before when she came to the bookshop. Can she see me?'

'No, not yet. She stands too much in her own world,' Tegatus said as he stared at the apparition. 'What happened to Thaddeus?'

'They took him away, dragged him from the shop and into a carriage.' He looked at the blood again. 'I followed them to the arch, but I can't go any further, that is the end of my world. This is where I left the earth life . . . Beneath this shop I drank from the water as it sucked me further and further down. I live on the Gemara, it is a place of near-completion, there are lots of us.'

'Why didn't you go on to the next life?' Tegatus asked.

The boy hesitated. Tegatus saw his image tremble as if about to disappear. 'Mister Thaddeus gave me a home. He's a kind man. He is my family now.' The boy looked at Tegatus even more intensely. 'I can see you so well . . . You're not from her side, are you?'

'I am not from any side, I am from another place.'

'You're not human, and you're not a Diakka creature what took Mister Thaddeus,' the boy replied.

'I heard the voice, Tegatus,' Agetta said. 'What's his name?'

'Do you have a name?' Tegatus asked. 'She wants to know.'

'I had a name,' the boy said, 'but so soon on crossing to the Gemara it slipped from my mind and has not returned. It was stolen from me. If only I knew my name, then maybe . . .'

There was a crashing of wheels on the cobbles outside the shop. Through the misted window and the tiny beads of rain that sparkled on the glass, Agetta could see the large black carriage. From the open window of the coach, in the cover of darkness, two small red eyes stared into the bookshop.

'They've come back,' said the boy, and a look of fear flashed across his face. 'It's the Diakka that took Thaddeus. You must hide.'

He waved for Tegatus to follow. The angel grabbed Agetta by the hand and they both chased the spirit-boy through the shop. They weaved in and out of the aisles and between the cavernous cases of books that nearly touched the ceiling until they reached the large fireplace by the window over the river. 'There's a hiding-place,' the spirit-boy said. 'I heard Thaddeus call it a priest-hole. The girl can hide in there and we can pass to the Gemara, they won't see us there. Press the stone at the base of the pillar and she will be safe in the wall.'

'I cannot pass to your world. I too am bound to a place I don't want to be.'

The shop door slid open and the sound of heavy breathing filled the bookshop as a large creature scraped at the floor with long, sharp claws. Mist from the street flooded into the

188

bookshop and began to blot out the light from the candles. In the doorway stood a tall man with long wiry hair and a thick country coat. In one hand he clutched the reins of a squat black creature, half-dog, half-monkey, that sniffed the air as it panted in its harness and stared into the shop through blood-red eyes.

'If they are here then the Diakka will find them,' the man said as he looked back into the carriage.

Tegatus pressed the long flat stone at the base of the fire-place and pushed Agetta through the gap between the stone pillar and the brazier that sizzled as it consumed a fresh holly log. The back of the fire tilted and they both stepped through the opening into a small room filled with wood smoke. In the corner, a narrow set of steps led up into the wall and the darkness. The boy stepped through the wall and stood between them, his outline etched in smoke for Agetta to see for the first time.

From outside they could hear the Diakka dragging itself across the wooden floor, getting closer and closer.

17 : Aurora Sanguinea

The thick black mud of the Holborn streets stuck to Bonham's boots as he scraped them against the iron scouring plate outside 6 Bloomsbury Square. Blake scurried by and into the house, clasping the golden hilt of his sword and cursing the night under his breath. He didn't wait for Bonham to follow him, but stamped up the stairs leaving a trail of black footprints across the fine weave of the Turkish carpet that covered the wooden boards of the long hallway. He fumed with anger at not finding Agetta and the book. He could feel himself being drawn deeper and deeper into black bitterness and resentment. The world is full of fools who delude themselves and critics who cannot see the poisonous warts that sprout from their own faces like rat droppings, he thought to himself, his hatred growing towards everyone who had ever condemned his new science as magic.

He turned and looked at Bonham, who prodded precisely at the dirty soles of his riding boot. Blake had known him for many years, but their friendship had been tormented with misunderstandings to which he had turned a blind eye. Like a saint he had carried Bonham through deep water, allowing Bonham to steal his own ideas. Now as he stared at him he saw someone who could never have an original thought of his own, a man for whom he had nothing but contempt.

Blake took the sword from his belt and stabbed it into each stair as he climbed towards the observation room. The long passageway was littered with the debris of violence from the night before. Wood chunks stuck out from the plaster walls like hedge-pig spines, and a harvest of green, leafy fungus grew from the place where the feet of the Sekaris had trod. In the observation room, Blake looked at the empty shelf where he had so preciously hoarded the Nemorensis. All his hope had gone, he thought, and his quest for understanding now rested within his imagination. No longer could he rely on the Nemorensis to guide and direct him.

The Sekaris lay on the table, the fine red handkerchief still covering its leafy green face. Blake crossed the room and prodded the creature with the tip of his sword. Its skin was hard and firm against the blade. They would have to believe him, all those preened poodles that masqueraded as scientists. The Royal Society could not laugh at him now, Blake thought as he contemplated slicing the creature like a cured ham and serving it to them with cold cabbage. He bent over and examined the hide of the creature, looking at the glistening drops of dew that slowly seeped from its skin. He picked at the thick leaf that formed its ear, pulling it from the head with a sharp tug. He held it to the light of the candle as he rubbed the waxy covering between his fingers. It had the touch of chocolate and the smell of rough tobacco. The skin-leaf reminded him of Oldenberg's Coffee House on the night they had taken a goat and transfused its blood into Joshua Oldenberg. The man had become a marvel of London society, bleating and butting from that day on, transformed by the sanguine elixir from server of dark rich coffee to a chewer of lane grass and parsley.

'My sole is rotten,' Bonham said as he walked unannounced into the room. 'I gave a fortune for these boots and one hour in the mud has eaten its way through them like paper.'

'It is a sign of the times,' Blake replied.

Bonham stood uncomfortably close to him and looked over his shoulder as Blake examined the creature further. 'Where did it come from?' he asked casually, prodding it with his finger.

Blake didn't answer, trying to bury the conversation in silence.

'It must be some new creature from Africa,' Bonham said. 'I once saw an animal with a neck so long that it could eat from the top of a tree. It had horns on its head like a devil and a tongue that could lick its own eyebrows.'

'Interesting,' Blake replied in a whisper.

Bonham wandered across the room to the telescope and peered into space through the brass eyepiece.

'How many days until mayhem comes to London?' he asked.

'Fifteen, sixteen. There is plenty of time to get out and leave for safety.'

'Your comet looks closer than I would expect,' Bonham said as he turned from the telescope.

'So you're an astronomer now, Isaac?' Blake replied, irritated at Bonham's concern for *his* comet. 'Let me see.' He stomped across the room and pushed Bonham out of the way.

He stared through the eyepiece at the comet. It was now the size of a fist in the centre of the lens and bright enough to be seen clearly with the eye. The dragon tail had vanished, and Blake saw for the first time that the comet had changed course and was several days closer to the earth than the book had told him.

'Isaac, we have a problem,' he said as he stared into space. 'The sky dragon comes at us from a different part of the heavens, and by dawn it will be visible in the morning light. The Nemorensis was wrong . . . or *I* was wrong.' A look of panic flared across his face. 'We have two days at the most before our judgement is upon us.'

Blake stepped back from the telescope and rubbed his eyes as if to rid them from the sight of the dragon. He trembled as he walked to the window and looked down on the square.

Outside, London woke from its slumber. In the growing light people began to fill the streets with their daily clamour. Already at this dark hour coachmen clattered across the cobbles in their carriages. Children gathered barefoot on the corner to beg from passers-by, and milkmaids waddled under the weight of the large churns they carried on ox-yokes that dug sharply into their shoulders. All were oblivious to the impending fate that hung in the sky above their heads.

'They have no idea,' Blake said remorsefully as he watched the people pass by beneath him. 'There is nothing we can do. If we tell them it'll cause even more death.' He paused and looked at Bonham. 'Flamberg *is* right, better for them to die suddenly in ignorance than slowly, knowing that the heavens are going to fall upon them.'

Bonham didn't reply. He looked into the mirror above the fire as he warmed his feet.

'I have this overwhelming desire to tell them all what is going to happen,' Blake said as he opened the metal clasp and flung open the sash to lean out in the street. 'There's a comet coming and you're all going to die!' he shouted as loud as he could above the cacophony. There was no response, not even a turning of one single head. Blake shouted even louder to the groundlings. 'In two nights your lives will be blasted from the planet and all you care about is food in your belly and gin on your tongue!'

'Leave it, Blake,' Bonham said, pulling him away from the window. 'It's of no use, man. How can you be so certain it will strike sooner? The book said –'

'The book was wrong, I was wrong. I don't know how it happened. It was very clear. When I read the Nemorensis it told me that from seeing the comet to it striking the earth would be twenty-one days. Now when I look through the telescope it is clear that we have very little time. The beast has turned and I think it comes to devour the earth.'

Blake stopped speaking and closed his eyes. He felt as if his mind had been torn in two and strange hands had pulled his brain apart. He gripped his head with both hands. 'I feel there is a battle taking place for my mind, Isaac. In one breath I have to help them, in the other I care not if the whole world is destroyed. I am going to tell Yeats what has happened – he will tell the world through the *Chronicle,* and then I can leave this life with a clear conscience.'

'That's a rash thing to do. The man can't be trusted, he's not one of us. Surely you should tell Flamberg and allow him to spread the news.' Bonham spoke quickly, his eyes flashing from Blake to the open window. Suddenly he rushed towards Blake, his arms outstretched as if he were about to push him from the window to the street below.

'I brought you gentlemen some breakfast,' Mrs Malakin commanded as she burst into the room with a tray of hot meat and coffee. She saw Bonham lurching forward to push Blake. 'No!' she shouted, and Bonham grabbed Blake and pulled him back from the window.

'By Hermes, Blake, I thought you were going to fall,' Bonham said as he looked sharply at Mrs Malakin. 'You were swaying with the madness that has taken your mind, all that you have endured has been too much for you.' Bonham looked again at Mrs Malakin. 'Make ready his bed chamber, he needs to rest,' he said, guiding her from the room. 'Come, Sabian, you need sleep. There's plenty of time for you to meet with Yeats if you must. Come to your room and rest a while. I will take care of you.'

Bonham led him quickly from the observation room and along the passageway to where Mrs Malakin busied herself making ready his chamber. Blake sat on the bed as Bonham

194

pulled the doctor's muddy boots from his feet and covered him in his night coat, then fed the fire with several small logs.

'Sleep, my dear Sabian, and soon the light of day will ease the troubles of your mind.'

'What of the comet?' Blake asked wearily, his mind overcome by waves of anxiety that he had never known before.

'The comet will still be there and together we can devise a plan for the city.'

'Dear Isaac, I even began to mistrust you. Now I know true friendship,' Blake said as he tried to make sense of the confusion in his mind. 'I feel as if I am fit for Bedlam.'

'This madness can even creep into that which we hold most precious,' Bonham replied as he ushered Mrs Malakin from the room and led her along the landing to the servants' stairs. 'He is not to be disturbed, do you understand, Malakin? No nursemaid for him. The doctor needs his sleep.'

Mrs Malakin was pushed into the dark, twisting stairwell and the door was slammed and locked behind her. Bonham hurried back to the observation room and pulled the window shut, firmly securing the black metal catch. He turned to the mirror and preened himself in the reflection of the mercury lens, wiping away the dark stains of mud from under his eyes. In the looking-glass he saw the Sekaris on the table behind him, a lifeless hand dangling towards the floor. Bonham smiled to himself in the mirror.

With his left hand, Bonham checked his pocket, feeling for a small glass bottle with a wooden stopper. He reached further and, clasping the rim carefully, lifted it from his pocket. The thick, deep blue glass shone with the light from the fire. Bonham gently pulled on the wooden stopper and stared at the opaque liquid that filled the bottle. Still holding the top in one hand, he dipped his little finger into the fluid and touched his tongue, tasting the salty solution.

Bonham crossed the room and pulled the handkerchief from the creature's face. He looked down at the Sekaris and saw the wound from the pistol shot. It had grown crisp and hard, its outer edges flaked with green mud. With his little finger he dripped several drops of the liquid from the bottle into the wound.

> *'Angel tears shall bite your wound, like the teeth of the hound.*
> *Salted water, tears of Grace, holpen spring of new life,*
> *Fire for spirit, earth for shelter, bring this temple down with*
>   *strife.'*

Bonham repeated the spell several times as he washed the wound with the angel tears. He dipped the tip of the handkerchief into the bottle and wiped the eyes of the creature as he spoke aloud long incantations. Then he poured the remaining liquid over the lips of the beast and put the bottle back into his pocket.

The angel tears glistened on the green skin of the Sekaris. Bonham examined the creature for any signs of life and listened for the sound of a beating heart. It was cold, damp and very dead. Bonham knew that this was not a worldly beast; its hardened flesh and golden eyes spoke of a dimension beyond his understanding. Foolish meddler, he thought to himself, as the lifeless creature stared back at him.

Bonham searched the room with his eyes, believing that somewhere in amongst the cupboards and papers would be something he could use to complete his task. He had once seen Blake use an electrometer on a dead frog and had watched in awe as every muscle in the tiny creature juddered and jerked as Blake churned the handle of the osolator, sending sharp sparks of internal lightning through the electrometer and along thin strands of copper wire into the frog. There had also been the time when Blake and he had summoned the spirit of a long-dead soldier as they recited rhymes from the Book of Nebukathosiz. It had appeared like a shadow and had spoken to them for several minutes, telling of how the soldier had been murdered in the Two Brydges Inn and no one had yet found his body, entombed by a layer of bricks in an upper room. Together, he and Blake had journeyed to the boundaries of science, magic and understanding. They had shared more secrets than brothers.

A sudden thought now gripped Bonham, filling him with the great desire to see the creature alive and to release it. He frantically searched every cupboard until he found the electrometer. Bonham unwound the reel of copper wire and led it across the room to the table. He entwined the strands around each wrist of the Sekaris, then crossed the room and quickly whirled the handle of the machine. The smell of smouldering mud filled the room like sulphurous spewings from hell. Bonham looked up and saw the charred wrists of the beast burnt like tinder-dry flax. The electrocution had failed; it brought only the stink of a Spitalfields butcher.

He cleared away the experiment, making sure the wire was wound precisely around the coil and the instrument placed carefully back as if it had never been disturbed. And then an idea came to him, to breathe his own life into the beast. It was a thought conjured from the depths of his soul, placed in his mind by a silent hand.

He looked at the Sekaris with its leaf-mould face, sunken eyes and crispy red lips that allowed marsh gas to rise through its blackened teeth like a will-o'-the-wisp. He knew what he had to do, and it was a feeling that left him in no doubt. Bonham kissed the creature and breathed into its mouth as deeply as he could, nearly choking with the stench that blew back into his face. It clung to his skin and hung from his mouth like a gossamer beard of swill. He ran to the window and fought with the catch to gasp the fresh morning air and clear his lungs.

Nothing happened. There was no life in the creature. It stared at the coved ceiling with its white moulded plaster and embedded pictures of Greek gods. Bonham spluttered in his failure and held his face in disbelief. He picked the sword from the fireplace with a mind to cut the head from the Sekaris and lay it at the feet of Lady Flamberg.

In the room below, Mrs Malakin rattled the furniture as she set the fire and polished the grate. Bonham placed the sword in the stand by the fireplace and walked from the room, pulling the broken door behind him. He looked back through the smashed panel, but the creature didn't move, death gripped it in its velvet glove. Bonham ran quickly down each flight of stairs and on towards the front door, slamming it behind him, shuddering the whole house. He looked left and right through the morning mist that draped itself over the trees in Bloomsbury Square. Without warning a jet-black carriage stopped before him, its windows black-boarded and locked. The driver was wrapped in a thick oilskin coat with a collar that hid his face.

Bonham reached into his pocket and took from it a bright white pipe. 'Is your lamp well lit?' he asked the driver, who nodded back without speaking a word. 'Then we shall drive together. They say that London Bridge is a fine place to find your future.'

High above, Blake still lay in his four-poster bed with its dark green curtains, red canopy and thick horsehair mattress. He slept fitfully, his mind tormented by monsters.

In his nightmare he was trapped in a long cold cellar, and he knew that somewhere in the surrounding dark a stranger lay in wait. He could hear his breathing but couldn't see his face. He was a child again, lonely and afraid, with no one to help him or take away the dread. Then came the tap-tap-tapping of the blind man's stick against the cold wet stone. Blake could feel his presence filling the cellar and oppressing him.

In a sudden sweat-filled panic he decided to run. But he was rooted to the spot, his feet clasped to the earth with oak roots that burst from his boots and into the brick-tiled chamber. He tried and tried to lift his feet from the surface but they were drawn deeper into the ground.

As the tapping of the stick got closer and closer, Blake knew he would be discovered and that his shame would be known. But there was one word that, if proclaimed, would take away the stranger that searched for him. Frantically he tried to remember what he had to say, and as he reasoned with himself he felt the thick bark spreading from his feet and climbing his legs, encasing him in a coffin of oak as his legs turned to wood.

Then he realised he was on a driftwood raft, being rolled though a chamber on a strong current as rats dropped from the roof to escape the flood. They jumped over him and clung to his back. In the distance a bright light burnt in the tunnel, sending its rays through the blackness and blazing into the water.

Blake tried to drag his soul from sleep and shook himself to rid his mind of the terrors that beset him. Finally he awoke and looked around the darkened room. He couldn't be sure if he was still dreaming or transported to another world that in some strange way looked like his own. By the curtains at the far side of the room, he could see the outline of a man.

'Bonham, is that you?'

'No,' replied a dark voice. 'It is the guardian of your blood.'

18 : Rumskin Ashmodai

In the deep darkness where nothing could be seen, Tegatus shook himself like a large broody bird. There was no sound to be heard but the low rumble of the Thames as it roared through the narrowing of the stone arches.

Agetta shuffled on the low stone seat that ran the length of the wall in the priest-hole as she listened for any sound from the bookshop. Strange thoughts invaded her senses, and a deep regret for allowing the angel to escape and sharing her journey with him. She felt as if she had been charmed, that some magic had taken control of her mind and made her help him. It was as if beneath the angelic smiles was the working of some hideous demon.

In the blackness she thought of killing him, of finding some weapon with which to strike him dead. But even that brought a quandary of new visions: was it possible to kill an angel, and if so, by what means? Was there a special way? Did she have to use a silver knife or stitch his eyelids shut with golden thread? She edged further away from him. Did she have to know some magic word that would aid his death? Were angels just humans with wings?

Agetta tried to picture his face. In the short time she had huddled in the priest-hole the darkness had robbed her memory. She tried to think of the first time she saw him. There had been something so powerful in his face, a hidden light that shone from his eyes, something so attractive that it had taken her breath. Now her mind had been changed, and she hated the day she first saw him.

'How does the book speak to people?' she whispered into the darkness, not sure if Tegatus was still there to hear her.

'It allows you the freedom to think what you really want. It can take a harmless thought and magnify it so that it becomes the shout of a dying man. A word of hatred is transformed into a litany of spite and malice. It allows you to be fully human.'

'So why do they all want it so badly?' she asked as quietly as she could. The darkness made her feel she was speaking to herself, or to some god who could actually reply in a way she could understand.

'They want the Nemorensis because it tells them secrets. That is the greatest human failing: wanting to always know that which is hidden. It was written by someone who has more power than she should.'

'What of the boy, will he always be a ghost?'

'Questions, you ask many questions of someone you harbour so much hatred for.' There was a long silence as Tegatus allowed the words to permeate the barren soil of her mind. 'I can feel what is going through your mind. Angels are like fish, we can sense the vibrations that come through the air. You speak far louder with your soul than you do with your mouth. Your seething will tell every spirit in the city that you are here.'

'You changed my life,' she snapped in reply. 'If you had never been here then I would still be with my father and wouldn't have stolen the book.'

'You forget Yerzinia, Blake and everyone else who has influenced your actions. You are not so innocent, you knew what you were doing.'

'So how come an angel can end up with his wings clipped and caught in a human menagerie?'

'Because I fell from grace. That I cannot deny. I was a fool who allowed the way I felt to take over my mind and drag me away from that which was perfection. Love is a powerful thing and to be in love with the unlovable is the worst thing of all.'

'Could we ask the book what will happen to us?'

'It would lie to you, because it was written by the greatest liar of them all. The father of all lies scrawled on every page and has led the world a dance ever since.' Tegatus pressed his hands against the stone wall. 'You see, child, your kind is obsessed by secret knowledge because they think it brings the power to influence their lives. Give a man a secret, write it in some ancient language and bind it in an old book. Then tell him that it is from another world and if used in the right way will bring him wealth and power, and you have the Nemorensis. It is a book that loves to be loved, a book that thinks it's a god. That's why so many have died to find and keep it. With every turn of the page it demands a sacrifice, for every word read it demands payment and its wages are paid in death. Touch it and it will burn your hand, read it and it will burn your mind, and once read it will have you in its grip.'

'Then what of Blake?' Agetta asked, concerned for her old master.

'Done for. Poisoned through the eyes and a man with a burning soul.'

'Thaddeus said it was once his,' she replied.

'It is all he can think of. It has become his passion, with every waking moment it will cry out to him like the voice of a lost child. He would give everything he had and everyone he knew to have that one book.' Tegatus stopped speaking and listened. 'He would even sacrifice you.'

Before she could speak he quickly put his hand over her mouth. From the bookshop came the clear, crisp sound of the Diakka scratching at the floor by the fireplace.

'Dead rat,' said a loud voice. 'Come on, my beauty, there is no breakfast here.' The words filled the priest-hole and echoed up the chimney. 'No one here for you,' the man said loudly as he pulled the beast away from the fireplace.

The sound of the slamming door echoed through the shop, then all was quiet. Tegatus pulled at the back of the fireplace. It opened in once piece, flooding the room in the warm light of the holly fire.

The spirit boy suddenly appeared by his side and smiled at him. 'They have gone,' he said. 'We are alone.'

Agetta heard the faint trembling of his voice and in the swirling smoke had a momentary glimpse of his face before he faded away. 'Is it safe to leave?' she asked, her face bathed in the orange glow of the fire. Tegatus listened intently to the sounds outside.

'I'm not sure, there is something not quite right . . . but I know not what it is.'

'They've gone, all gone, not here,' the boy said, as if demanding Tegatus to follow him.

Agetta heard him clearly and with each word he grew brighter, as if the passion of his anger made him visible. 'We have to go with him,' she said, pulling on the angel's sleeve. 'I want to get out of here to find Thaddeus, we have to find him.'

Agetta pushed by Tegatus and squeezed herself through the narrow gap and into the large fireplace. The stones burnt red-hot against her back and the heat of the fire quickly dried her face to parchment. She stumbled into the room, followed by the boy, who walked through the flames as if they were not there.

'I don't want to come out,' Tegatus said from inside the priest-hole. 'You go if you want to but I will stay here.'

'You have to come now,' the boy said eagerly.

'Let him stay if he wants to,' said the man as the cellar door was pushed open by the Diakka. 'I can always get my little friend to go in and get him. Angel meat is far more succulent than gnawing on the bones of young children.'

'Tegatus!' Agetta screamed as the Diakka crawled towards her, rasping its long claws into the floor. The man let go of the creature and it scurried to Agetta and with its monkey hands took hold of her by the collar, pulling her towards its face. The Diakka breathed on her with its warm stench-breath as it examined her through one of its murky green eyes. It sniffed at her skin through its fat squat nose, then slowly and carefully licked the beads of sweat from her face with its long blue tongue. Its face crinkled in a crooked smile as it turned its head to look at the master who held tightly to its long leather lead.

'Not yet,' he said in a tired voice as he brushed the dust from his frock coat and with one hand straightened the mask that covered his face. The creature sighed as it sniffed Agetta again, burying its face in her hair. The man pulled on the lead. 'Enough, Rumskin. She is not for you, I have instructions to take her to see the Temple Master, maybe then you can take her bones.' He looked at the fireplace. 'The boy tells me there is someone else in the priest-hole, an angel if I remember rightly.'

'The spirit told you?' Agetta asked.

'He had to, couldn't resist the temptation of knowing his name. As soon as we came into the bookshop he was waiting to tell us. We have Thaddeus and we also have his gathering of ghosts. My little bloodhound is good at catching ghosts.' He laughed.

'So why should he give us away to you so quickly? His name can't be that important.'

'My dear child, it is the only thing of value he has. With his name are all his memories of his true life. Now he stands twixt life and death with nowhere to go. His name was stripped from him when he was first enticed. With his name he can be released from this half-life and find whatever awaits him in the next.'

'You hold him in death without a name?' she asked.

'Not I, but he who caught him at the point of death. All that is necessary is to charm him as the soul leaves the body or have some piece of bone or hair, and with the right words he can be kept for ever.'

Agetta looked away from the Diakka as it continued to press its cold, clammy face against hers. She searched the room for any sign of the poltergeist that had betrayed them.

'Rumskin likes you,' the man said as he pulled back on the lead. 'All we need is a priest and we could marry the pair of you.'

'My father said that anyone who married me would have to be paid well,' Agetta said as she tried to pull away from the beast.

'Oh, he is paid well, he eats all he can and who he can. He is a creature of great appetites, some of which food will never fulfil.' The man looked again at the fireplace. 'Angel!' he shouted. 'Come from your tomb or you will rest there for eternity.'

'Can you kill angels?' Agetta asked.

'They can be *transformed*, turned from glory into . . .' He paused and looked at the Diakka. 'Well, just look at Rumskin. He wasn't always this beautiful.' Rumskin shuddered and shook his wet fur. The creature held Agetta firmly in its grip. 'The trouble with angels is that they soon begin to love themselves.

Take them from heaven and the prying eyes of their master and like the rest of us they discover they too are not immune from desire.' The man paused and looked at the Diakka. 'Rumskin was once such a creature, as fine as any, but he was overtaken by his passions and transformed into my beautiful Diakka.'

Rumskin jumped on to his hind legs and let out a ferocious scream that shook the building. He threw Agetta to the floor and twisted and pulled at the leash as he bared his white fangs, spitting drops of deep red blood across the room. The man pulled a wand of yew wood from the top of his boot and hit the beast across its back. Each beat sparked blue lightning across the room, making the Diakka twitch and writhe in pain. Then it settled to the floor, growling deeply like the rumbling purr of a large cat.

'Enough!' shouted the man. 'We have work to do and a winkle to pick from its shell.' He looked towards the fireplace. 'Come out, little cherub,' he mocked.

Tegatus stepped from the priest-hole and into the bookshop. His face was sullen and drawn, his eyes filled with sadness. Agetta noticed how uncomfortable he looked in her father's clothes. The funeral coat clung to him like a sod of wet earth.

'An angel – how beautiful!' the man said as the Diakka nervously jumped up and down like an anxious dog. 'Will you do one thing for me?' he asked. 'Show me your wings.'

Tegatus looked at Agetta. She could see the grief in his face as he screwed up his eyes and looked to the ceiling: 'He has no wings,' she said. 'They were clipped so he couldn't fly. My father wanted him for his menagerie so he took every feather from him.'

'Your father will be a rich man. Angel feathers are nearly as rare as angel teeth, and how I would love to see Rumskin with a necklace of freshly pulled angel teeth.' The Diakka growled at Tegatus, pulling on the leash. 'I think he wants you to come with us. We have a carriage outside and there are people waiting to meet you.'

Suddenly the boy stepped from out of the oak panel of a bookshelf, and for the first time his form was clearly visible in the light of the fire and the growing dawn that crept in through the thick glass of the window.

'What of me?' the child asked. 'You promised me my name.'

'I lied,' the man replied coldly as he smirked at the boy. 'You'll be here for several more centuries and can haunt all those who are still to come. Play your games, child, but don't get in our way.'

The Diakka swiped at the boy with its arm, hitting his ghostly body as if it were completely solid and filled with substance. The boy spun across the floor, sliding through several bookshelves and vanishing from view. Rumskin looked gleefully at his master and grunted.

'Now we leave,' the man said. 'I don't think you will give me any trouble, but if you do I will allow Rumskin to chew on your bones and spit out the fat, understand?'

He nodded, as if to tell them to walk to the door. Tegatus held out his hand towards Agetta. She looked at him and then to the floor as she turned and followed the man. The Diakka snapped at the angel as he walked by, then scurried behind him as they walked through the aisles to the front of the shop.

Through the half-open shop door, Agetta could see the black carriage that waited for them, and could hear the stamping of the horses' hooves as they scratched on the cobbles of the bridge. The thought of escape invaded her mind as Rumskin pulled at her coat and sniffed the air. Tegatus walked slowly behind her like a solitary mourner at a funeral, crestfallen and fatigued. In the front of the procession the man walked boldly on, the long leash draped casually over his shoulder.

'Will my captor tell me what he is called, or is ignorance one of his virtues?' Tegatus asked.

The man stopped and turned and pulled the yew wand from his boot and gently tapped the side of the angel's face. 'My name should be of no consequence to you, but you may call me . . . Komos. Not my birth name, but good enough for an angel.'

'A man with such a festive name and a raven-mask to cover his lies. Strange business, catching children and mastering a Diakka. You are obviously a man of other worlds.' Tegatus looked up at a stack of books that teetered high above his head.

'Taming creatures such as this comes as second nature to us. London is a place of many such beasts, and when you two have been disposed of and business here is done then Rumskin and I shall go to the country to catch sheep. And eat them.'

As he spoke the final word the front door slammed shut. Above the man's head the pile of thick volumes fell to the floor, knocking the leash from his hand and cascading over his back. He held his arms above his head to protect himself as books flew at him from every direction. Rumskin leapt angrily against the shelves, as if trying to catch some invisible mischief. Komos was beaten away from the door as every shelf emptied itself upon him.

Agetta and Tegatus cowered by the door. They watched a thick hail of bound paper soar through the air. Flying from the vaulted ceiling a large, black book hit Komos in the chest, knocking him from his feet. There was a giggle of childish laughter. Komos looked around, his humourless face steely beneath the mask.

'Rumskin!' he shouted loudly. 'Bring him to me!'

For the first time he slipped Rumskin from his tether. The creature looked about the high shelves, searching the ceiling for a sign of the boy. His ears twitched to unheard sounds as his eyes followed something that appeared to walk unseen across the top shelf at the far side of the shop, just beneath the vaulted roof. The Diakka fixed its gaze and licked its lips as every muscle in its body twitched. Suddenly it leapt from its stillness and scrambled up the bookshelves.

In several strides and leaps it crossed the room, then perched on the top of a bookshelf high above them. It looked around, stalking its unseen victim. Then it leapt to the floor, crashing into a shelf and sending all the books falling to the floor. It began to chase the ghost-boy as he ran in and out of the corridors of books, trying to escape. Komos jumped about and shouted to the beast to run faster, and from each aisle they could hear the sound of the Diakka as it panted and growled in excitement.

The ghost-boy ran through a shelf of books, appearing in front of Agetta and then disappearing into the wall. To her horror the Diakka did the same, keeping pace with the child as it too vanished through the shelves and into the stone wall.

From the cellar came the noise of a struggle, and childish screams burst from beneath the floor. The boy exploded through the floorboards and into the shop as if blasted from the barrel of a cannon. He hung momentarily in the air, then fell to the floor as the Diakka burst through the door and into the shop, its white fangs bared for the kill. It leapt towards the ghost-boy, but the boy rolled and melted into a wooden shelf, vanishing completely and then appearing on the other side.

Komos lashed out at the boy with the yew wand, striking him across the face. A blinding crack of thunder filled the room. The boy was frozen in time.

'Leave him!' shouted Agetta. 'Hasn't he suffered enough, what more can you do to him?'

'He'll be absorbed like his friends,' Komos replied as he put Rumskin back on his leash. 'That is all they are good for.' He looked at her. 'You may never understand, but he will not fulfil his life. There will be no paradise for this pest, no heaven, no hereafter. For him his time is done, annihilation is all his soul deserves.' Komos turned to Tegatus. 'Take the girl into the coach. I will be with you presently. Rumskin will see that you do not run away. After all, we don't want to frighten the people of London Bridge. Who would believe the sight of an angel being chased by a demon?'

19 : Carriages and Comets

'How do you walk into a house without a key?' Blake demanded as he chewed on a crust of yellow cheese that crawled with mites. 'I was alone, and Mrs Malakin didn't let you in. You saw the look she gave you when she brought my breakfast.'

Abram Rickards had woken Blake from a dark sleep filled with blackness and death and with one sweep of his arm had banished the nightmare from his mind as he pulled open the thick curtains to let in the light. He had refused the several cups of thick black chocolate offered to him by Blake as the doctor had sat quietly and listened to him.

'Keys mean very little,' Abram said. 'A lock is meant to be overcome, and I am entrusted with your welfare. I am your guardian.'

'From what do I need protection? I can look after myself and I have a sword to rid me of quarrelsome fools.'

'I protect you from yourself and some of your friends,' Abram replied as he looked out across the square.

'So what gives you this right to protect me?' As Blake bit hard on the cheese, the scurrying mites covered his lips.

'Remember as a boy when you fell into the river? You couldn't scream as the water sucked you under. Then as the sun broke through you saw yourself floating down and down. Did you realise you were dead, that you were passing from one world to the other?'

Blake spat the cheese on to the bed. 'How did you know? I was alone and told no one. I waited until I was dry before I went home. You meddle with my mind.'

'I meddle with nothing,' Abram shouted as he hit the wall with his fist and plaster dust fell from the ceiling. 'It was I who pulled you from the depths. What man can save himself from the power of the grave?' Abram held out his hands towards him. 'Seé these? They saved you from the watery tomb and pulled you from the murky depths. It was these hands that brought life back to your dead, breathless corpse, my breath that filled your lifeless lungs. I have watched you grow. Wept for you, spoken for you in high places and pleaded your case in time of trouble. What of the time when you tried to turn lead to gold and blew the roof from your house? Who protected you from the fire? What spirit banished the creatures you conjured and could not get rid of with your failed magic as you danced in your silk cuffs?'

'You meddle with everything,' Blake shouted back. 'What you know of me has been tricked from my mind, robbed whilst I slept.' He threw the plate on the floor and jumped from the bed. 'Now you come to me and torment me like some Shibbetta that throttles the life from my bones. You're a warlock, a demon –'

'I am an angel. I am *your* angel,' Abram said quietly.

Blake stared at his reflection in the gold-framed looking-glass that hung over the fireplace. His face began to change as if another merged with his. It slowly cracked with a smile that grew broader as a laugh bellowed from the pit of his stomach. 'An . . . An . . .' He tried to speak the unspeakable, his laughter breaking forth from his mouth and filling the room. 'You are a liar and should leave now,' he said, bent double with the fever of mirth that weakened every muscle. His body shook and quivered as he fell backwards laughing and giggling. 'An angel! The man says he's an angel! A charlatan, a vagabond, a Huguenot rogue come to steal my money. These things yes, but an angel? *No*.'

'Then how do I know that you still weep and mourn your mother's death? That you poisoned your cat with mercury to cure it of fleas, then stuffed the corpse under the floor of your bedchamber to stink for weeks? I know these things because I was charged with watching you, and at every turn you have done your very best to go your own selfish way.' Abram grabbed Blake by the throat and lifted him from the floor, holding him with one hand above his head. 'What did you think when I healed the dandy after the duel, that it was a trick?'

'Yes,' whispered Blake meekly as his feet kicked the air like a lifeless puppet.

'I knew it,' exclaimed Abram, throwing Blake to the floor. 'Not even if someone was brought back from the dead would you believe. Don't you trust your own eyes? Can you not see the truth or has the god of this age blinded you with unbelief?' Abram turned and walked to the window. The atmosphere of the room suddenly changed, and Blake felt a desire within his heart to listen to Abram. 'There is a plan for your life, a plan to prosper you and not to harm you, to give you hope and a future. These are not my words but from the one who sent me, but you have to obey. Gone are the days of rebellion, of going your own way. Listen to me.'

'You're a master of words and a craftsman of cunning, but you don't fool me. Look at you. You are barely my age and yet you say you have known me since I was a boy. Do you take me for a fool? You're not an angel, you're a frog-eyed Frenchman on the run from your king. I don't want or need an angel.'

'So shall I leave you to your fate? To a comet that will bring poison to your sea and destruction to the city?'

'You know of the comet?' Blake asked as he walked towards the window. 'How do you know?'

'I *know*, because the time was set long ago, as was the purpose. I *know* that you have read the Book of Nemorensis and have been taken in by its lies, and I know that even you don't want to see the destruction that is set to come.' Abram faced Blake eye to eye as they spoke. 'So can I still be of no help to you?'

Blake stared at him, searching the lines on his face. If this is an angel, he thought, then why does he look so like a man? 'I don't know what to think,' he replied, walking back to the bed. 'There is so much at stake, so much to lose.'

Abram ignored him. He walked to the door of the chamber, opened it and looked into the long passageway. He closed the door and turned the key in the lock. 'We can't be too careful. You are being watched by a creature sent to find the Nemorensis.'

'I have met the beast when it tried to kill me last night.'

'The Dunamez tried to kill you?' Abram asked.

'Where were you then, O guardian of my blood? Thankfully Bonham shot the thing and it now lies dead in the observation room.'

'Dunamez can't be shot, they are spirit and have no substance.'

'This had substance, lots of it. Green mud-like substance that stank like a full privy. It knew who I was and was intent on killing me. It is a Sekaris.'

'Let me see your hands,' the angel asked as he took hold of Blake and inspected his fingernails. 'Did you clip these?' he asked.

Blake didn't reply. It felt like the start of a nightmare. He knew what would come next and in his mind pictured the scene that would spill out before him. He shook his head and looked at the floor, feeling like a scolded child in front of his father.

'When did this happen?' The angel asked, letting go of the hands and searching through Blake's hair. 'Do you have a mark? It is the shape of a moon. A burn on the skin?'

Blake held out his hand. 'Is this what you search for?'

Abram looked at the wound and smiled to himself. 'Did it hurt?' he asked. Blake nodded in agreement. 'Good! Next time you will think twice about offering your hand to a woman.'

'I had no choice, Lady Hezrin Flamberg is quite persuasive.'

'So *that* is what she is calling herself, I know her by another name, though she has many. Igrat . . . Kettevmiria . . . Lillith . . . Yerzinia . . . Like a dog she answers to any of them.'

'You speak as if you know her well,' Blake answered.

'She is a collector of angels and any other trinket that takes her fancy. I have known her for an eternity, century to century, Paris and Rome, Constantinople and Babylon. The thing with Igrat is that she never changes, always those same deep, beautiful eyes that capture the soul – and hands that will tear out your heart.' There was a long silence as Abram looked about the room. He sniffed the air and looked closely at the skirting board. 'She isn't human, far from it,' he said, as Blake was about to ask that question. 'Lady Flamberg, as you know her, has gorged on the blood of noblemen since the beginning of time and you are entranced by her.'

'How do I know what you say is the truth?' Blake asked, following Abram as he paced about the room.

'Just look at your hand. That burn is a beacon to her treachery. It is a mark to tell the whole of hell that you belong to her. Look at it, man, closer.'

Blake stared at the fine black line that surrounded the deep red burn in his palm. He could see that in amongst the deep

215

black were flakes of white and red that formed linear squiggles and appeared as words on a page.

'You are right in what you are thinking. It is text. A language seldom spoken by men or angels.' Abram answered Blake's next question before it was asked. 'You will find that these are the words of the Nemorensis. They bind you to her, she has access to your heart.'

Blake stared at the wound, trying to read the miniature inscription that encircled the red moon on his palm. 'You are a liar, she would never do that to me.'

'She would have you dead. The creature with the stink of mud *is* a Sekaris. It was sent to kill you. Your bones brought the Sekaris to you.

Mud, blood and bone.
Breath of the fallen one to bring life to stone,
Chanting the name of a waxing moon.
Sekaris, Sekaris, do what's to be done . . .'

'Rhymes and magic is all I hear,' Blake replied. 'The Sekaris was sent to kill me, but I don't want to believe it was Lady Flamberg. You may be my guardian, you may know all about the future and the comet, but knowing you have been my nursemaid makes me feel cheated in life. I feel that you have lifted me up in your hand so that I would never strike so much as my toe against a rock. When I fell in the Fleet I thought I rescued myself, and now I know it was an angel. You are as good for my pride as a rusty mirror glass.'

'So you would have me leave you to whatever peril is to come?' the angel enquired.

'Yes,' Blake replied firmly.

'Very well, until you ask again I will leave you be.'

'I will never ask again, my blood shall be my concern.'

The angel turned the key in the chamber lock and opened

the door, stepping into the hallway. 'I would like to see the Sekaris. It has been a long time since I last saw one . . . Prague, I think, 1662. That too was Lady Flamberg, or did she call herself Baroness Manrique de Moya?'

Blake walked with Abram to the observation room. His eyes quickly explored the room. The table was empty; there was no sign of the creature.

'It was here!' Blake said as he wiped his finger across the top of the muddied table. There was a thin layer of green algae and spawns of minute fungus that clung to the damp wood. 'It was dead, truly dead,' he said unable to believe his own eyes. He looked for some excuse, some reason why the creature was not there. 'I saw Bonham shoot it. The Sekaris dropped to the floor and its skin grew like baked clay. I know it was dead.'

'Now it is alive, or Bonham has taken it for himself,' Abram said. He walked to the large window and looked out over the city. 'The Sekaris has gone, but the comet has come . . .'

High in the dawn sky, the comet was visible to the naked eye. It hung like a small moon, a diamond set in a clasp and surrounded by seven smaller lights that flickered against the rays of the sun. Blake hurried to the window.

'It will drive them all to madness. They will fear for their lives and think the appearance is a sign from the heavens. I must tell the truth to the *Chronicle*,' Blake said as he rubbed his face feverishly. 'Yeats will tell the world and they can escape.'

'The comet is only two days away. It will strike on the night of the full moon. Fear not, Blake. Fear not.'

'Isn't that what you always say, "Fear not"? It may be good enough for shepherds and young girls, but I am a man of science. My fear is proven by fact, calculated by reason and with very little place for faith in angels.' Blake looked out over the city.

'I will see Yeats today and in the morning he can warn the people.'

'There is more at stake than the comet. Yerzinia has a plan, and you are a key to that plan. She has friends who plot and scheme and –' Abram paused and looked at Blake. 'Find the Book of Nemorensis and bring it to me, it is something that you can do alone. I give you one warning: do it alone, trust no one.'

'Where do I find you? On a pinhead? Hiding in my pantry?'

'Speak my true name.'

There was a sudden and loud rush of air as the door to the observation room slammed shut. The fragments of the battered door fell to the floor, leaving the frame empty of everything but the brass hinges. Abram scanned the room as if he searched for a rat in a grain store.

'You have a guest, Doctor Blake, and finally it shows itself.' Abram ran to the far corner of the room and pressed himself against the wall. Blake stood silhouetted by the shaft of sunlight that burst through the window. He was wrapped in a blanket of swirling dust that hung in the sunlight like a swarm of bees.

'I see nothing, what's there?' he asked as he looked about the room.

The scurrying came again, louder and to his right, as if a creature ran against the side of the wall and dragged itself across the floorboards. Abram gave chase, knocking everything out of his way as he swiped his hands at the floor as if to grab some small but invisible beast. In the swirling dust Blake caught a glimpse of a small beast that scrambled along the floor like a small dog.

Abram grabbed at the creature, laughing as he ran after it. 'They are such good sport,' he cried as he chased round and round the room, caring not for what he smashed. Blake hung on to the brass telescope for fear of it falling over. 'Join me, Blake, this is fun . . .' Abram jumped on to the chair near to the window and swung from the curtain before crashing to the floor, struggling with something invisible in his hands. 'Never in the whole of eternity was there anything better than chasing a Dunamez,' he cried out gleefully, holding on to a writhing mass that slowly began to materialise before Blake.

'What is it?' Blake asked.

'This is proof. Proof that I do not lie. It's a Dunamez, sent to invade your brain, inhabit your body and steal the book. It would have waited until the right time and then jumped your bones and pushed your soul into a corner of your mind. Then it would have walked you down the stairs into your carriage and away to its mistress. And, knowing the Dunamez, it would have drunk all of your best wine before it went.'

The creature began to grow in size as it took form. It grunted and pulled against Abram as he tightened his grip. It growled and snorted through its thin nose and small mouth filled with long sharp teeth.

'What can I give you to let me go?' it said, trying to turn its head to look at Abram.

'There is nothing that I want from you,' he replied sharply, twisting his grip on its neck. 'I am going to send you away to a place where you will do no more harm.'

'No – not for me. I mean no mischief, I was charmed and told to come here for this creature, promised his warmth and his body as a sepulchre,' the creature wheezed.

'Who commands you?' Abram asked as he twisted the neck even tighter.

'I cannot say the name, she could reach me in hell and do to me more hurt than anything your hands can do.' The Dunamez winced as the angel held it in his strong grip.

Blake weakened at the sight of the beast. He realised he had seen it before, carved in stone. There before him was the face of the gargoyles that lined the roofs of Newman's Row. They had stared blindly down upon him every day with their long noses and thick squashed eyes and he had given them no thought. Now one was before him – living, breathing. His heart raced with several beats at once as the panic of blood rushed through the veins in his neck.

'What else is there for a man to see? Does heaven hold more surprises for my eyes?' Blake asked as the Dunamez struggled to be free. 'What of the Sekaris? Where will it be?'

'Your friend took it, I saw him.' The creature gloated as it spoke in its raucous voice, slobbering over each word. 'Whilst you slept he picked it up and carried it from this place. Talked to himself as he went down the stairs . . . I followed and listened. He took the creature to a Society, said it would make him famous, said that the *Chronicle* would make him rich . . .'

'They lie, Blake. I wouldn't believe a word,' Abram said, picking up the Dunamez from the floor with one hand.

'It's the truth,' the creature cried as it became even more visible and solid. 'The other man even searched the room before he went, took out some kind of instrument and tried to pass lightning through the beast.'

Blake looked at Abram, his eyes confirming the existence of such a machine.

'Your friend isn't as trustworthy as you have always believed,' Abram said. 'I will return, there is much to tell you and so little time. First I have to take this creature to its appointed place, from where it will never return.' He gripped the beast even tighter, almost choking what life it had left from its body.

'No, no, no!' the Dunamez screamed as Abram began to disintegrate in front of Blake. He watched as the angel appeared to grow opaque and beams of sunlight absorbed his flesh. He faded and faded, carrying the creature with him, until he finally disappeared.

Blake looked around the room. It felt cold and foreboding, the morning sun casting stark shadows over the wooden floor. It was then that he saw the flake of mud wedged in the doorway. He noticed for the first time a trail of living fungus footprints that led from the room towards the dark spiral staircase.

20 : Morbus Gallicus

The wooden windows of the carriage shut out all but one small chink of light as its metal-bound wheels rattled over the cobbles and through the muddy ruts of the London streets. Agetta sat crunched against the carriage frame, pressed in by Rumskin, his cold fur itching against her skin. The smell of the Diakka filled the dark coach and hung in the air like the taint of some dying animal. Komos puffed on his long white pipe, the bright amber glow of hemp tobacco lighting his eyes and forehead.

'Where do you take us?' Tegatus asked as he was squeezed against the door.

'To a palace . . . of joy and pleasure . . . beyond your imagination,' Komos replied between each draw on his pipe. 'It's not far and the view is quite amazing. But where you are to be lodged will be somewhat mean and lowly and not what you are used to.' He laughed, coughing on the smoke. The Diakka made a noise like the giggle of a small child gurgling on warm milk.

The oppressive darkness jolted Agetta back to a time when she had once found a large black beetle scurrying across her face. In the darkness she had picked it from her skin as it held on tightly with barbed claws, leaving one of its legs stuck into her nose like a black fish-hook. She had kept the creature locked away, imprisoned in a small black box, and had sometimes watched it scuttle and hobble along the floor of her bedchamber.

Now, locked in the rumbling carriage, she feverishly idled away the time by twisting curls in her hair and staring through the darkness at the embers of her captor's hemp pipe. With each breath his mask would be lit by the deep red glow. Agetta knew she had heard his voice before, and although some dark force blocked her mind from knowing who he was, yet deep within her she understood that he was a part of her past and a key to her future.

The carriage came to a sudden halt. Agetta could hear shouts from the street, and the Diakka gripped her arm to stop her trying to escape. Tegatus fell forwards into the lap of the creature, burying his head in its fat stomach as the Diakka kicked him back to his seat.

Komos laughed, not caring what was happening. He stoked the pipe with more strands of the thick green tobacco and feverishly sucked on the stem for fear of it losing its light. 'Morbus Gallicus!' he shouted. 'Get this carriage going and to Fish Street Hill, quickly.' He banged on the roof with his fist.

There was a muttered reply from the street and the carriage jolted forwards and continued to rattle along the broken road. 'The man is half blind, half deaf and completely mad,' Komos said, continuing to giggle to himself as if he was the keeper of some incredible humour that only he should know. 'He also has only half . . . a . . . nose!' He spluttered out the words in between shrieks of laughter.

The others sat in the darkness, not knowing why he laughed so. The Diakka grunted to himself as he rubbed his face against Agetta, trumping out loud flatulence accompanied by belches of fish-scented breath.

'How long to this place?' she asked, trying to hold her breath so as not to take in the creature's stench and the hemp fumes.

'Not long,' Komos replied. 'Don't wish away what life you have left. Savour each moment, breathe each breath as if it were your last . . .' The carriage rocked and twisted over the rotten roads and carcasses of fallen stock left where they died.

'For what purpose are you taking us?' Tegatus asked.

'That would be telling.' Komos laughed as he spoke. 'This is the divine experiment, the *gamma draconis*, the meeting of time, the coming of the dragon. Call it what you will, but soon your eyes shall see it. In fact, you will be a part of it.'

Several minutes later and after many churning turns, the carriage stopped and Komos pushed a small spy-hole in the wall of the carriage and pressed his eye against it. 'Here,' he said with a relieved expression in his voice. 'Now to get them inside . . .'

Agetta could hear someone scramble from the top of the carriage and drop with a splash into a large puddle by her side. The man let out a long, low moan as he gathered himself from the mud, complaining bitterly.

'Blast, bother,' the man screamed. There was a crack of a whip. 'Don't look at me that way, you broody mare. I'll get the twitch to your lip and you won't be so cheery then, will you?' he said as the whip cracked again.

'Morbus Gallicus,' Komos shouted above the sound of the fish-market and the shout of traders outside the coach. 'Get the trap and let us out of here.'

The man outside ducked under the coach and could be heard scrabbling about, tugging on a large flat stone and pulling it across the cobbles. Again he bobbed under the carriage and with two clicks undid a panel in the floor and slid back the wood.

Agetta stared down into a deep black hole. At the very bottom she could make out the flickering of a small lamp. Strapped to the side of the hole was a wooden ladder that appeared to grow narrower as it plummeted into the dark depths.

'Who's first?' Komos asked, tapping the pipe against his foot and watching the red embers fall away into the chasm like a spray of vanishing stars. 'It is a dark fall but great beauty awaits us all in the depths of the p–p–pit.' He giggled and stuttered.

Rumskin jumped wildly on to the seat next to Agetta and without warning fell into the gaping hole and grabbed the ladder. He vanished into the murk, blocking out the light from the lamp in the narrowing tunnel.

'I th–th–think it should be you two next.' Komos faltered as he spoke, trying not to laugh. 'Morbus is waiting with his hood and whip, *if* you're thinking of escape. He is not a man to be seen in daylight for he has a face made for darkness.'

Komos nodded for Agetta to go next, and held out his hand as her feet slipped from the carriage and fell to the top of the ladder.

'You're next,' he said to Tegatus, 'and no trying to fly. Morbus will pick you from the sky like a flea from your face!'

Tegatus dropped to the floor, using the seat of the carriage to lower himself into the top of the hole. Before he took hold of the ladder and descended further into the deep shaft, he peered into the street. He appeared to be at the base of some large monument surrounded by wooden stalls and set on a small hill. In the distance he could see the river and the bright shafts of light that sparkled on its surface. At the side of the carriage he could see the long leather boots of Morbus. They were black and stained with mud. The hem of his long wax coat brushed the muck, and trailed around his feet was the double tail of his long horsewhip.

Tegatus blinked in the light and then stepped down the ladder descending into the dark pit. Komos followed, nearly standing on the angel's hands to make him climb down faster. High above them the light began to fade as the scraping stone was pushed back in place with a solemn thud.

The sound of running water came from below. Tegatus shuddered as with each step he thought of what might be in his future. He was angry that he had allowed himself to be taken, that he had given in so easily. As he descended deeper and deeper he became urgently aware of how far his life had changed. Once he had carried the standard of the Most High in the Battle of Heaven, when the dragon had been defeated and cast down to earth; now he skulked in an old sewer like some flea-chewed rat. The shame covered his face, and he was glad it was veiled by the darkness of the pit.

From far below he could hear the grunts of the Diakka as it splashed merrily in the shallow water. Soon he was standing next to Agetta in a few inches of clear spring water in the light from a tallow lamp burning on a small shelf. A tunnel dropped steeply to his left in the direction of the river, and a set of stone steps led up to a wooden door with a large brass lock.

Komos took a key from his pocket, turned it in the lock and slowly opened the door. 'You may enter your chamber,' he said as he filled his pipe yet again, his eyes bulging like two red sores. 'There is already a guest, one whom I think you know well, my dear girl.' Komos laughed as he pushed them both towards the door, and Rumskin splashed in the water.

Agetta lifted her soaked feet from the cool stream. The fast-flowing water had washed away the mud from the street and its coldness had soothed her senses. She stepped into the room, looking at the white marbled walls and large grey stone flags that fitted together like some strange jigsaw. There was no furniture apart from a thick marble shelf that formed a long seat in the far wall, and a large seven-crowned chandelier that dripped hot wax on to the stone floor. At the end of the shelf sat a man, his unconscious body slumped to one side, his head covered in a hemp sack, his hands tied with thick bindings.

Komos sucked on his clay pipe. 'You can make yourself comfortable. Morbus will bring you some food and then later the fun will begin.' He nodded to Rumskin, who slid the two brass bolts into their keepers, then melted through the wooden door and into the tunnel. Agetta gasped as the Diakka vanished. 'He is not bound by philosophy or physics and can come and go at will. My little pet is an entity not controlled by the rules of this world, only by the voice of his true master.'

'So what does your lap dog do now?' she asked as she sat on the long marble shelf.

'He waits and guards the tunnel for intruders and those foolish enough to think they can escape.'

'Where are we?' she asked urgently.

'Not that it matters to you in your shortened life. You are fifty feet below Fish Street, at the base of the Pillar. We built it to commemorate the Great Fire, the fire *we* started. The fire that meddlers stopped from completing its purpose. Now we are at the time when the fulfilment of the law will be complete, and you two will help us in that task. Girl unblemished . . . angel's wing . . . eye of toad . . . and all the usual things that the blind blentish think we put in our rhymes . . .' Komos chuckled to himself as he walked from the room. 'I will let you get acquainted with your old friend. Don't think of escaping, Rumskin hasn't been fed.' He slammed the door behind him, and they were left alone.

There was a long, loud growl from the tunnel that echoed and faded into the distance. Rumskin pushed his head through the middle of the door as if it wasn't there; it hovered like some disembodied skull floating in the dark shadows, then vanished before their eyes.

'The creature plays tricks with you,' Tegatus said, pacing the room in his wet boots.

'Agetta, is that you?' said the groggy voice of the hooded man.

It was Thaddeus – he was alive. Agetta rushed across the room and pulled the hood from him. The crown of his head was smeared in blood, he had a short silk noose around his neck, and his feet were wrapped in blue canvas parlour shoes tied with yellow threads.

'What did they do to you?' she asked as she propped him up against the wall and tried to untie the bindings around his wrist.

'They came for the Nemorensis. They thought I had it. Do you know where it is?' Thaddeus asked anxiously. 'It's all I seem to think about.' He stopped and looked at Tegatus. 'Who's that?' he asked suspiciously.

'It's Tegatus. I found him in the attic of my father's house.' Agetta smiled at Thaddeus. 'He's an angel.'

'So why is he here? Can't he escape and fly away?'

'Sarapuk saw to that,' she replied. 'He stripped him of every feather and it took away his power. He's done something wrong, something that makes him nearly one of us.' She spoke as if he wasn't in the room. 'I got the book for you, but it is best that we don't tell you here. Rumskin may be listening.'

'Never has the darkness given us anything so foul. That was the beast that dragged me here, taken like a kitten from its nest and spat down those stairs. It came again this morning to torment me, brought by its malodorous master, Morbus.'

'What will they do to us?' Agetta asked.

'They will not say, but you must tell me all that you now know.'

There was a banging on the door to the stairs and heavy footsteps thudded on the landing outside. A shadowy hooded creature peered through the iron-barred casement in the top of the door.

'Morbus,' exclaimed Thaddeus as he tried to get to his feet. 'Stay back, he has a temper that flows from him like a torrent. Stand close behind me, Agetta, he hates children.' Thaddeus spoke as if he knew the creature well.

The door was kicked open and in stepped a man dressed in a thick floor-length carriage coat. 'Food,' he croaked, his deep hoarse voice rasping like crunching flint. 'I don't know why they feed you, waste of good food, 'tis as bad as giving breakfast to a condemned man before the gallows.' He stepped into the light of the chandelier, carrying a dirty linen sack bulging with bread and cheese.

Agetta peered from behind Thaddeus and gasped as she saw his face. His lips were blistered and swollen, his eye drooped with large black ulcers, and in the centre of his pock-marked face was a small black fissure partially covered by a flap of skin that blew in and out as he breathed. Never had she seen anyone so grotesque. Morbus looked like a living corpse, a man being eaten slowly by the stink of death. He saw the look on her face and knew her thoughts.

'Never seen the likes of Morbus before, girl? Do I smell as bad as I look?' He lunged towards her, spitting his words. 'Bracegirdle won't always be here to look after you . . . I may come at night and steal a kiss from your pretty lips and then you can share in my discomfort and carry my christening sickness.' Morbus stepped back and looked at Tegatus. 'Well, well, well,' he said as he walked slowly towards him. 'If I am right then you must be an angel, marked with lamb's blood on your right ear. 'Tis a long time since I have seen that mark – a long time, and in a different place to this stink-hole. You must be the one for tonight's party, the pretty chicken to be dressed and trussed, stuffed and plucked, then fed to Rumskin. This will be a night to remember,' he croaked.

Morbus took his cloth cap from his head. A long, thick lock of hair fell to the floor, as if plucked from the root. About his skull were large festering sores that broke through the skin like a field of volcanoes oozing yellow puss. Agetta tried to bury herself in Thaddeus, turning her head from the sight of the pestilence.

'You can't hide from the likes of me, not when you're here. This is a place where you are not even safe when you sleep. Even when you dream they can look inside your head. I warn you, Lamian's child – don't share your imaginings with anyone.'

'You know who I am?' Agetta said nervously.

Morbus looked at Thaddeus and gave him a thin smile as a tear of thick mucus dribbled across his cheek.

'You don't have an inkling, do you, girl? All that has happened and you still don't know what is going on.' Morbus grunted, trying to clear his swollen throat. 'We've been waiting for *you* for many years, watched you as a child and kept your guardian as far off as we could. All for this time. You forget, girl, 'tis your birthing-day tomorrow, you'll be the age, the time when belief leaves you and the doubts of adulthood start to cloud the mind. So the rite will take place and you will be transformed before our eyes . . . with a little help from an angel.' Morbus laughed, threw the bread sack on to the floor and turned to walk out of the cold marble chamber. He stopped at the wooden door. 'You have twelve hours of childhood. Use them well, child.' He looked at the angel. 'As for you – think of a name for yourself as tonight you become the brother of Rumskin.'

Morbus slammed the door and double-bolted the thick oak beams. Agetta looked at Thaddeus. His eyes seemed to know more than his mouth would ever speak of.

'What are they going to do to me?' she asked as she looked for the knot in the bindings that were holding his hands tightly clasped.

'I wouldn't worry, I don't think they will harm you. As for the angel, well, for some reason his end has come. He will be transformed into a Diakka – that is the only fate for a creature who would leave the abundance of grace for earthly greed.'

Tegatus slowly slid down the white marble wall and squatted on the cold stone slabs. It was as if all the life had suddenly drained from his bones. A look of despair was etched across his face.

'I knew that one day it could come to this, but not so soon,' he said, holding his face in his hands. 'I found heaven so dreary . . . I looked at the world and all of its glory and wanted to be a part of it. Then I found *her* – she was looking in the great river, on the banks of the Euphrates, staring at her own reflection. From that moment I was prepared to leave everything behind.' Tegatus looked up at them both. 'What startled me more than anything was that she could see me. I remember her first words – "*Staring at your own reflection will never equal looking into the eyes of a Seruvim.*"'

A sudden long, low snarl broke into his story. The door to the chamber began to rattle and judder with each breath of the creature that tried to force its way through the tiny crack between the stone floor and the thick oak beams. The beast jumped and kicked at the wood. Tegatus leapt to his feet and ran to the door to look through the iron-barred casement.

There was no warning – the beast attacked like a cobra, impaling its victim with two long, fang-like claws that pierced the angel's cheek to the bone. Tegatus was gripped like a toy puppet, then thrown to the floor. He scrambled backwards as the creature pressed its snout through the iron bars. Licking angel blood from its long bone fingers, Rumskin stared into the chamber and sniffed the air, growling and snarling.

21 : Salve, Regina, Mater Misericordiae

Grub Street smelt of rotten seaweed, a bitter smell borne on the breeze from the drying mud-banks of the Thames. With every step that Blake had taken from Bloomsbury Square, he had passed clusters of people staring to the sky and looking at the fist-shaped comet high above them. In a strange way he felt proud that he had seen it coming, yet he knew that no one would see it his way – the blentish would look upon it with fear and the rich would care only for themselves and their bellies. In his loneliness he pulled up the collar of his coat against the wind and the words of his fellow man and banged his swordstick into the ground, sparking the metal tip against the cobbles.

In three quick steps he left the street piled high with bundles of news-sheets and entered the office of the *Chronicle*. The door was open and the front shop unusually empty. Gone was the old woman who sat at the desk with her one front tooth like a pinnacle of yellow rock jutting from her wizened bloodless lips. No newsboys scampered barefoot in the room, uttering Newgate curses to the passing gents. The house was completely empty and silent.

Blake picked up a copy of that morning's *Chronicle*. There on the front page, under the long reports of yesterday's hangings and ships lost at sea, was the news of his comet. In a paragraph of nearly impenetrable words the whole of his life's work was summed up in one line: *'Scientist discovers new star visible from earth, no danger to city . . .'*

Blake scanned further. In his reading he could hear the voice of Lord Flamberg reducing his discovery to nothing more than another quack remedy or exhibit at the menagerie. What the readers looked at in the sky would be of no consequence to them, just another star passing a lonely planet, a wonder of the same magnitude as a hanged man.

'Do not fear. Enjoy the spectacle as it passes.' Blake looked at the last line as if it fell from Flamberg's own lips.

He angrily crushed the paper in his hands and threw it into the street as he looked around for Yeats to explain himself. From the floor above, Blake heard the sound of footsteps scraping over the rough wooden floor. Then a door slammed shut and all was silent. Blake gripped the silver handle of his sword-stick. The lion's head fitted neatly into the palm of his hand and soothed the burning from his palm, and the knowledge that inside the case of the stick was a sharp blade reassured him. Blake didn't want to be taken by surprise as he carefully climbed the narrow staircase to the upstairs room.

He crossed the landing that led into the small writing room at the back of the house. The walls were dark and grimy, stained with the dull yellow of tobacco smoke. The strong smell of Virginia leaf hung in the air, mixed with the fragrance of stale wine. There was complete silence. Blake called out, 'Yeats where are you, man?' His voice echoed around the lifeless room.

He stepped further into the room and to his left saw the large oak desk with its high-backed leather chair. Slumped on to the desk like a sleeping bear was Yeats, his head resting on a pile of papers that littered the top.

'Yeats, man – wake up!' Blake prodded him with his sword-stick.

There was no reply. Yeats slept on, his head falling limply to one side, a long dribble of blood-tinged saliva coming from his mouth.

'Wake up!' Blake prodded him even harder. 'Now is not the time to sleep.' In his frustration he pushed him hard in the back to wake him from his dreaming.

Yeats slipped slowly to the floor and sprawled spreadeagled across the rough boards. He was dead – his blue-tinged lips showed as much. His face was contorted with a shocked stare that gawked at Blake through lifeless eyes. In the centre of his chest was a neat fist-shaped hole, as if someone had used a searing ladle to precisely scoop out his beating heart. The wound had been burnt through his thick waistcoat and double vest, through the skin and deep into his chest, cauterising the flesh.

Blake coughed, choking at the sight of the corpse that he knew so well in life and now terrified him in death. From the next room he heard the shuffling of heavy feet on wooden boards, then the quick slamming of a door. He turned and drew his sword from its case, holding out the glinting blade before him. He thought of Abram – he wished for the angel to be with him in what he could see was to come. In his mind he saw the other room. He knew that there would be a small cupboard set with a thick panelled door, and that there he would find his fate.

Walking swiftly and quietly, he made his way from the room and turned through the narrow doorway. This was Yeats's study; the room was littered with paper and opened books thrown across the floor. A large sofa was placed under the tall window that looked out over the dark alleyway, and in the corner a table was set with one place, a half-eaten meal still waiting on the Dutch plate, a small candle lighting the victuals.

Blake's vision became clouded, misted by strange thoughts

of the Nemorensis and by a strong desire to see it again, to search it out from its hiding-place. It was as if the book called out to him in a song outside of time. Blake thought of Agetta and in great anger lashed out at the sofa with his sword-stick, cutting through the thick fabric and bursting it like cooked pig flesh, spewing white feathers across the study. They billowed through the air like spring snow, deep and white, covering the floor with a coating of down. He kicked the seat again and again, laughing as he did so and watching the pulsing waves of feathers rise higher and higher into the air, covering him in a dusting of plucked goose.

Blake fell to the sofa laughing, but in an instant his reverie vanished as he heard the sound of gentle tapping coming from the dark oak panel in the wall just a few feet away. The patter got faster as fingers beat in rhythm. The whole room began to vibrate with the beat, every panel juddered and shook, and the noise now sounded as if it was coming from every corner of the study.

Blake jumped to his feet, holding out his sword before him, flicking it back and forth as if to cut down some unseen enemy. 'You can come out, creature. I have no fear of you,' he said, his voice cracking with the final words, spoken through parched lips. 'Let's finish it here and now,' he shouted, hoping Abram would hear his words and forget his sullen pleading to finish one task in life without his guardian.

The tap-tap-tapping continued, growing louder with each beat, banging from panel to panel around the room like a regiment of ghostly drummers. 'Leave me be,' Blake shouted as the noise grew louder and louder. 'Come out and fight face to face . . .'

The drumming suddenly stopped, leaving an eerie silence and the swirling of goose down in whirlpools of air. Blake knew that his adversary was nearby, and his emotions swirled from the passion of courage to the despair of panic as he tried to imagine what was to come. He wanted to run, but something held him to the undertaking – he sensed that what he was about to endure was not of human origin, that some phantasm and creation of darkness was at work and was about to make itself known to him.

Blake didn't see the long thin panel that guarded the passage-way to the river slowly open behind him. It was the low screech of the tight hinges that alerted him to the presence that now stood behind him. Turning, Blake saw the Sekaris leaning against the wall and gnawing on the blood-red heart that it held like a fresh apple.

'Blake,' said the Sekaris in a soft voice like the sound of a purring cat. 'Finally we meet when we are alone.' The Sekaris smiled at him as it chewed on tiny mouthfuls of Mr Yeats's heart.

'Why did you kill him?' Blake asked, stepping back from the creature that blocked his escape through the door.

'I was told to . . . And the idea became appealing to me.' The Sekaris stepped towards him.

Blake could see the pistol wound had healed in its chest and a patch of darker skin covered the lesion. 'You heal well for a monster made of dirt,' he said as his eyes flashed around the room, looking for a way of escape.

'I had a good healer, one who came to me by night and blessed my wounds with angel tears and the longings of his heart.'

'Angel tears?' Blake asked. 'The medicine of some quack magician, a charlatan and a liar.'

'Strange way to talk of your friend,' the Sekaris said as its eyes burned like the sun. 'You could make this easy for yourself and just give yourself to me without a fight. I could make it as quick as I did for the other man. He died so readily, with such grace, he almost choked on his own tongue when he saw me. Lost for words and now so . . . heartless.' It took another small bite from the heart. 'It would be over very quickly, I promise.' The creature gave a sharp giggle, and the leaves on its face rustled as if moved by a swift breeze.

'I am a man – it is forged within me not to give up without a struggle. So come and take what you want from me, but you will fight for my flesh and my soul knows no price.'

'So you think you have a soul? That you will live on beyond death? Don't flatter yourself. Your kind is skin and bone with a mind that deludes them. All you are good for is eating and then only good in parts.' The Sekaris laughed as he threw the last of the heart at Blake.

'Then my steel against yours,' Blake said as he swung his sword back and forth, halting the Sekaris.

Several black feathers fluttered to the ground in amongst the white down that continued to spew from the slashed sofa. More and more they came, floating down like a dark fog that filled the room, and from every part of the house came the squawking of jackdaws that flocked and swirled all around him.

Blake lashed out at the birds as they swooped and dived, lunging at his eyes. He struck one, then another and another as they exploded into black dust with every blow of the blade. With each stroke the Sekaris bided its time, waiting for Blake to tire as the birds pecked at his flesh and grasped at his hair with their razor claws. More and more birds filled the air as Blake staggered backwards to the far corner of the room, the Sekaris watching his every move.

Blake turned, jumped on to the sofa and smashed the window with the hilt of his sword. The noise from the street flooded in and the squall of jackdaws billowed from the room and out into the bright London morning.

Blake jumped to the floor. 'You and me, Sekaris – face to face with none of your hawks to help you now.'

The Sekaris stood and laughed. 'Your bravery comes a little too late, Blake. Dust to dust, ashes to ashes.'

It leapt towards him, snarling. In one step it had him by the throat, digging its long thin fingers into his neck and biting at his face. Blake stumbled backwards, falling across the couch and on to the floor. The Sekaris followed and gripped its prey, forcing its hands deep into his chest. Blake screamed as the pain burnt through the skin, his waistcoat and jacket charring and bursting into flame.

'Give in, Blake, let me take your heart and I will tell you the truth about your soul!'

Blake smashed the hilt of his sword into the face of the beast, scattering dry leaves across the floor. He saw fresh green buds quickly blossom in their place. The Sekaris twisted him against the wall, dragging Blake to his feet with incredible strength and holding him upright with one hand. It drew back its hand and made ready to kill Blake with one final plunge to grasp the heart and rip it from his flesh.

A final, furious swipe of Blake's sword smashed through the clay and yew wood, severing the arm of the Sekaris above the wrist. The green-encrusted hand dropped to the floor and its writhing fingers slowly dragged it across the boards like a dying spider. The Sekaris dropped Blake, who lashed out again with his sword, striking a glancing blow to the side of its head and scattering leaves like an autumn gale. It fell back on to the couch, reeling from the blow. Blake jumped towards the beast, stepping on the creature and leaping from it across the room towards the door to the secret passageway. He dived into the darkness, slamming the door behind him and fumbling for the bolt. His nostrils were filled with the stink of the river as he ran down the crumbling steps and the sound of the Thames got closer. High above he heard the crash of splintering oak as the Sekaris smashed its way through the door to give chase.

Running in complete darkness, Blake barged from wall to wall through thick cobwebs that smeared his face. In the distance was the faint light of the tunnel entrance. He ran even faster, trying to escape before the creature's echoing footsteps caught him. The light grew brighter and Blake could see the outline of a narrow door etched with sunlight, growing nearer was the sound of the Sekaris, squealing excitedly like a stuck pig as it chased him.

Slamming into the door, he grappled for the key to turn the lock. It was stuck fast, corroded with rust, and snapped off in his hand. The shrieking got closer, like the sound of an eager child, as the Sekaris ran through darkness. Blake struggled with the door, unable to open it to gain his freedom, then turned to see the creature getting closer by the second, splashing through the dew puddles that littered the floor of the tunnel.

Blake couldn't escape. He saw the eyes of the creature glowing in the darkness as its teeth flashed white. In ten paces it would be upon him. He braced himself, and in one final effort lashed out with his sword-stick. He struck the beast across the chest as its momentum propelled it towards him. It smashed into him, crashing him against the thick wooden door, and with the force of the impact the door suddenly gave way, its rusty hinges breaking under the strain, and Blake and the creature spilled from darkness to daylight.

For a moment they both lay stunned on the sodden steps matted in kelp that led to the river. Then the Sekaris sprang to its feet, and Blake looked up at the beast as it stared at him through day-blinded eyes. It lurched back and forth, the wound to its chest pulsing green blood that flowed down its stomach like a mossy veil. He lashed out again at the creature, striking a blow to its legs and cutting through to the yew bone. The Sekaris staggered and slipped backwards, falling several feet into the deep water of the old river. Blake spun around and looked over the edge and saw the beast bob in the water face-down, then swirl and twist as it slowly sunk beneath the thick brown stew.

'Interesting,' said a voice in the shadows. 'I wondered how you would conquer the Sekaris.' Abram Rickards stepped into the sunlight, perching the blue glass spectacles on the end of his nose and flicking the wire straps behind his ears. 'A creature like that can survive many things and I have never known one to have ever drowned. To kill a Sekaris it is often best to strip out its chest and find the oyster shell placed as its heart. Tear it out and smash it, then the creature will truly be dead.'

'So you were there all of the time, like some wet nurse waiting in the darkness for her child to cry out,' Blake said as he got to his feet and stepped back into the entrance of the tunnel.

'I would prefer to say I was intrigued.' Abram smiled. 'I promised you that I would not interfere and I kept my word. When I knew you had won, then I made myself known to you.'

'So what would you have done if it had got the upper hand?' Blake asked.

'You would be dead. I promised not to intervene and I would have walked your soul into its future and listened to you complaining that I allowed you to die.' The angel looked up to the sky. 'But you have a greater problem than the Sekaris,' he said, pointing to the comet that could clearly be seen high above them. 'The advance of the star is upon us and nothing can now stop it.'

Blake looked up and to his horror he saw white steam trails blasting across the morning sky as hundreds of pieces of celestial ice began to rain down upon the city. From every corner of the heavens came the deep groaning wail of mini-meteorites that vaporised and exploded high above them, and within seconds London was being blasted with a myriad of hailstones that had broken from the comet and sped as harbingers of what was to come. They shot through the atmosphere, hissing and bubbling as the heat burnt off the many tons of frozen mud and chalcedony that had travelled through time and space to bombard the planet. The sky burst open in a spectrum of colour as the crystals fell to the earth.

Blake ran to the top of the steps. From the quayside he could see the great dome of St Paul's, its vast roof like an upturned plum dish, glistening with the colours of the exploding sky.

There was a long thunderous roar as a sphere of sizzling ice and rock spluttered through the atmosphere like a huge ball of fat thrown through the flames. It crashed into the church, and shrieks echoed through the stunned city streets. The shockwave surged through the lanes and alleyways, pushing aside all that stood in its path and devouring the feeble who were too old to run. It seemed as if the whole city was now fleeing towards the river, and as the final sky-stones plummeted earthwards the panic and roar of the crowd came closer.

Blake looked at the angel, his eyes filled with hopelessness.

'Into the tunnel,' Abram said calmly. 'The madness is about to strike.'

22 : Gemara Ge-Hinnom

Far below the Great Pillar the clamour of the falling sky-stones rattled through the underground chamber and its walls shook with the final impact on St Paul's dome. The chandelier trembled and the floor of the chamber moved back and forth, throwing the captives to the ground and lifting the door from its hinges. Rumskin blasted into the room and spun around, grunting like a caged monkey and lashing out at Tegatus, then vanished through the doorway to the stairs, screeching into the distance.

'Another calamity has struck the city,' Thaddeus said as he got to his feet. 'Perhaps this will change their plans for you.'

'What plans, Thaddeus? Who are they and why have they chosen me?' Agetta asked.

'They are builders of a new future, a new society. From what Morbus Gallicus said to me there is something happening of which you and I are a vital part. Something that my feeble mind cannot understand, but I know that they will do us no hurt.'

'I don't want to stay here, Thaddeus. You'll have to help us escape. We can give them the book, it's of no use to us.' Agetta grabbed him by the arm.

'We should stay, child, and see what they will want from us. I don't think they mean us harm, just the angel,' Thaddeus replied.

'It isn't you who will be transformed into a friend for Rumskin, is it?' Tegatus said, taunting Thaddeus. 'I will take my chances out there rather than wait for them to come and make chicken-meat of my flesh.'

'I'm with Tegatus,' Agetta said, letting go of Thaddeus. 'You saw what that creature did to him. He doesn't deserve to die, we have to get out of here.'

'I say we wait. We could talk to them, tell them where the Nemorensis is hidden and bargain for our freedom. We would be fine, it would only be the angel that suffered.'

Tegatus stepped towards the door and pulled on the hinges, prising them away from the wall. The lock snapped open and the door fell backwards as a rush of cold air blew in from the tunnel.

'I'm going. I have suffered enough. Come if you will, but being here has made me realise where I belong and what I have left behind, and there may be a way of making right with my master.'

'Where's the book, Agetta? Tell me where it is!' Thaddeus said. His voice was transformed and filled with anger. Gone was any hint of tenderness as he glared at her. 'I want to know before you leave here. Rumskin could always be called on to come and find you.'

Agetta realised that something was not right. Thaddeus spoke loudly, as if he hoped to be overheard. In one sentence he had changed, sounding more like a father than a friend, and she just a girl to be used for what she knew and what she could do. She stepped backwards, trying to get closer to Tegatus, and all her thoughts of hatred towards him quickly evaporated.

'If I told you where to find the book, would you let me go?' she asked as she held out her hand to the angel.

'It would be considered,' said Thaddeus. 'I could convince them to save your life.'

'Are you truly captive?' she asked as she got closer to the doorway.

'A captive guest, bound by a party trick, but still a friend and one who knows your future,' Thaddeus said gently, tilting his head to one side and smiling, knowing that his harsh words had wounded her heart. 'It would be safer for you to stay here. Let the angel go and we can have that meal I promised you. In fact I was going to ask if you would consider coming to work for me and becoming a bibblewick, London's greatest purveyor of fine books.' Thaddeus spoke proudly, raising his eyebrows and beaming a smile as he twitched his thin nose like a large rabbit.

Agetta let go of the angel's hand and smiled back at him. Her eyes searched his face for the slightest trace of a lie. Thaddeus held the smile long after its worth had gone as he waited for her to reply.

'I'll go with the angel,' Agetta said, and she walked backwards to the doorway. 'I want nothing to do with these people. Life is more than what I shall eat and the fine clothes of the ladies in Fleet Street.' She stopped and thought for a second. 'I think your shop is beyond me, I would never make a bookseller.'

Agetta turned and looked at Tegatus. He plucked two of the largest candles from the chandelier and gestured towards the open door, and silently they left the chamber and stepped into the darkness of the tunnel.

'Wait, I will come with you,' Thaddeus shouted as he slipped the bindings from his hands and ran after them. 'I can't stay here. I am a prisoner to more than Morbus Gallicus.'

Agetta and the angel ran through the tunnel, the sound of the Thames getting closer with each footstep. Thaddeus fumbled on in the darkness, trying to maintain pace with their flickering shadows, keeping close to the echoing footsteps and sound of splashing feet. Tegatus held tightly to Agetta's hand as he pulled her along. They whispered to each other, hoping Thaddeus would not overhear their words.

'If we escape the tunnel we can return to the bookshop and take the Nemorensis,' Tegatus said as he pushed through the deepening water. 'It has to be returned to heaven or destroyed. I cannot leave it in his hands, there is something I cannot trust in your friend.'

Agetta didn't reply, but she found herself agreeing with the angel. She had thought so much of the friendship, dreamt of what it could be, but now she realised that there was more to Thaddeus than he would have her know.

'Wait for me,' he said faintly in the distance. 'You have the light and I walk in darkness.'

They ignored his words and strode through the flow. Agetta looked up and in the light from the candle she saw a large white rat perched on a flat stone that stuck out from the wall. It looked at her through its one black eye, twitching its whiskers, shaking water from its fur. From high above them in the streets they could hear the ever-growing panic as people abandoned their lives and fled the capital. Cartwheels rumbled over cobbles and the shouts of the poor dug beneath the clay and echoed through the labyrinth of tunnels linking every part of the city.

'How much further?' Agetta asked as she waded through the knee-high water.

'Until we find the way out,' the angel replied, losing his patience. 'Soon we will reach the river and from there we can find the bridge.'

'I know the way,' Thaddeus shouted from far behind. 'Wait and I will take you there.'

They pressed on. Tegatus stopped and listened to the distant rumbling, not sure if he could hear the sound of footsteps far behind Thaddeus.

'He'd better come with us,' he said to Agetta. 'At least then we will know if he plans any mischief.'

Thaddeus walked as quickly as he could to catch up with them. 'We could always go back, Agetta, I could talk to them . . .' His deeply furrowed face was outlined in the candlelight as they stood at the crossroads of two tunnels.

'We go on,' said the angel, pointing ahead to where the tunnel dropped sharply towards the river. 'You can stay here if you want but the girl doesn't want any part of your scheming.'

The dull shouts of the rampage above them echoed harshly along the tunnel, the sound coming at them from all directions. Agetta felt a long cold shiver shoot up her spine, making every hair on the back of her head jump like a jackrabbit. 'What's happening?' she asked as they walked on in the waning light.

'Another sky-quake or something even more terrible,' said Thaddeus miserably, taking her by the arm. 'We should turn back, it will be safer for us.'

'For you but not for me,' said Tegatus, and he pulled Agetta away from him. 'We go on, but you can stay. I sense that you don't really want to come with us. So why don't you stay? Why don't you stay and play with that fat dog you seem to be so friendly with – Rumskin, wasn't it?' He rubbed the claw marks on his face, then pushed Thaddeus in the chest. 'He's not here to look after you, is he?' the angel asked. 'Nice to have a friend to look after you, a demonic lap dog to pant over you, Mister Thaddeus.'

'What do you mean, Tegatus?' Agetta asked.

'Ask him – ask him what is really going on. If he can tell the truth you may get a surprise.'

'Don't listen to him, Agetta, he just wants to set you and me apart. Angels don't know the ways of men. They are born to interfere, born to fall from grace at the slightest sniff of the barmaid's apron . . . What got you, then? Was it the Absinthium or the Geneva or was it something more subtle than that?' Thaddeus asked as he stroked the side of the angel's face.

'This is where we part company,' the angel said, and he grabbed Thaddeus by the throat and lifted him out of the water, kicking and scrabbling to be set free.

'Are you going to use magic?' Agetta asked as the angel sat Thaddeus on the rat-infested shelf that ran the length of the tunnel.

'No, something far more powerful than that,' he exclaimed. He punched Thaddeus twice in the face with his fist and dropped him to the cold wet stone. Rats crawled all over the unconscious Thaddeus, and Tegatus saw the look of surprise on Agetta's face. 'He is one of them, it was all a trick. Thaddeus was the bait in the trap and you are the one they are really after.'

'They said they were going to transform you.'

'And they would – it is part of my future. When an angel falls, when it takes on the things of the world and desires to be human, that is what happens. We delude ourselves that it is so far in the future that it is of no consequence, we try with all our heart to taste human life, but once we take that step, like every addiction the pit becomes our home and the body we then inhabit is an expression of our vice.'

'So will you change anyway?' Agetta asked as they quickly walked on, leaving Thaddeus to sleep with the rats.

'In the chamber, when the creature took hold of me, I saw what I would become. In an instant I could see how I had given my life over to the desires of my heart and forgotten my purpose. I was trapped by the Queen of Darkness, not because of her power, but because I wanted to be. I had tasted the fruit and saw it was good.'

247

'In the shop, I hated you, wanted you to die or to go away . . .'

'That wasn't you but the book – it has power to alter your mind and from that you have no protection.' Tegatus stopped and looked at her face, holding the candle above their heads and letting the light flicker on the low roof of the tunnel. 'I'm going back to the shop. I will take the Nemorensis and destroy it. I would take it to heaven, but I have no idea how to get back. My mind has been so long on earthly things that I have even forgotten how to fly.' The angel laughed. 'But then I have no feathers so even in that –' He stopped. Far behind came a cry that he knew well. The wail of a beast ricocheted through the tunnel as Rumskin called out to them in long, loud howls.

Tegatus gave a look to Agetta that shouted for her to run. Together they sped through the tunnel, splashing through the water and almost snuffing out their candles. The angel protected the light with his hand as he ran, and the flame cast shadows in the shape of long black claws that seemed to crawl over the roof. Far in the distance was the small light of the entrance. With each step it got closer, and with each step so did the sound of Rumskin.

Agetta reached the door first. It was smaller than her, the height of an infant. She managed to squeeze through into the bright morning light. Tegatus pushed himself into the opening, the frantic splashing getting closer by the second. 'Quickly, pull me through,' he shouted to Agetta as she threw the candle into the river below them. Agetta pulled and pulled on his coat, trying to prise him from the tunnel entrance. But Tegatus was stuck, trapped by his size, wedged in the doorframe. 'You'll have to go on alone,' he shouted. 'At least they won't get by me, unless they eat their way through.'

Agetta grabbed him by the head and put her foot against the wall and pulled as hard as she could. 'Now push,' she shouted, and suddenly he popped like a cork and fell on to the towpath. Agetta quickly pulled the door behind him.

All around people were running, and on the quayside came the sound of shouting and crying as the blentish filled their barrows and carts, piling them high with chattels. The chaos could be felt like a cold wind that blew through the streets. Everywhere was shouting and screaming as the panic inflamed people's minds and the desire to survive stripped each of their dignity. For what seemed like an eternity, Agetta stared at the scene. In the distance the dome of St Paul's looked like a giant fractured egg, its roof smashed through and wisps of thick smoke billowing from the wound. On the river the boatmen rowed furiously for the south bank, dragging the flotsam that hung to their vessels to escape the fury that had fallen from the sky.

'We have to get to the bookshop, quickly,' Tegatus said, pulling Agetta back from her dreaming.

At that moment Rumskin hit the door to the tunnel. His grotesque head burst through the wood and stared at Agetta, snarling and spitting blood. Tegatus grabbed a small barrel and threw it at the creature, which recoiled back into the darkness.

'It won't follow,' Tegatus said as he began to run. 'It's daylight, and he won't risk the sun. Once taken by darkness the radiance becomes a place of pain. It will be tonight when he will try to track us down.'

Agetta didn't feel reassured. An overwhelming sensation of dread filled her body, making her feet turn to lead and her stomach twist and turn with every fearful thought. As she ran behind the angel, trying to keep pace amongst the madness, all she could think of was the destruction that had come to the city and the terrifying change to her life. There came a painful feeling of guilt and despair. It sharply reminded her of the dissatisfaction she had with her life. It poked fun at her thoughts for a better way, a higher ideal. This was the result, it whispered. Agetta had desired something more – the riches of Yerzinia, the life of a lady. Now her wishes to be lifted from her mundane life were being answered. Now this terror was the payment for her dreaming, a reminder that everything she touched would wither and die.

As they ran, her thoughts blocked out the sights of the dead, crushed in the human stampede. They reminded her of what Yerzinia had said, and she knew that she had to find her, to tell her of all that had happened and accept all that she offered. The vision of the alley came to her mind: Yerzinia dressed in her long black coat, the fine carriage with its silky black horses. She would find her again, and tonight she would take the Nemorensis as a gift, a token of service and friendship.

Along the road towards London Bridge there was no space to run as the mass of people moved like a slow, dirty river, funnelled and crushed together through the pillars of the gate and on to the stones of the bridge. Agetta held tightly to the back of the angel's coat as they struggled to move through the seething bodies that carried them along like a summer flood against their will. At the far side of the bridge she could see the entrance to the bookshop, where the sign squeaked and called as it swung in the fresh breeze.

Tegatus pushed his way closer to the door of the shop as unseen hands dipped into and out of his every pocket, dismayed by their emptiness. Agetta held tightly to him, staring at the sea of faces, the feeling of floating became overwhelming as she was pulled like a bobbing cork closer and closer to the bookshop. She looked up. For the first time she realised that the roof of the building was like a peculiar castle with high ramparts and tiny arrow-slits for the upstairs windows. Set high on the battlements were the familiar faces of the Diakka cast in stone, gargoyles protecting from an unseen enemy. High above was the comet, shimmering in the bright morning sun, the upper heavens glowing silver with the fragments of the exploded sky-stones.

Her hand was torn from the angel as she moved further away from him in the surge. 'Tegatus!' she shouted, and she began to drown in the crush, slowly sinking down, to be trodden underfoot by the frantic throng. Tegatus turned and saw her hand reaching up as gradually she became submerged beneath the crowd. Quickly he reached out and grabbed her wrist, pulling her towards him against the human flow. She screamed in pain as her arm stretched with the weight of the people. An old man with a long stick and grey beard lifted her from the ground and pushed her higher as the angel tugged her towards him. Agetta saw the man stumble, and their eyes met as he was sucked into the seething mass, the crowd slowly engulfing him inch by inch beneath them, unaware of who or what he was. His screams went unnoticed in the cries of the throng.

Tegatus held on to the shop door, using it as a safe anchor, and with his other hand he dragged Agetta towards him. She fell into his arms, safe in the solitude of the doorway, an island set against the tide.

They stepped inside the bookshop and bolted the door against the tide of people, locking out the noise and chaos. Row upon row of dark volumes breathed complete silence and the knowledge of ages.

There was a scurrying of tiny feet against the wall, and in the corner of the shop by the old fireplace a darkening of light began to shade against the stones. A small creature began to form, slowly taking shape, drawn together bit by bit as dust fell on dust. First two bright eyes, then the shape of an ear, a mouth and a small button nose – all were wrapped in a sheath of matted blonde hair as an urchin materialised before them.

'You must go,' said the child in a whining voice. 'It is not safe for you here.'

23 : Le Grand Dénouement

'I met a man the other day who would not believe in angels,' Blake said, staring out over the Thames as it pushed relentlessly to the sea. 'He said there was no such thing. It was the day before the sky-quake, and the comet.' He paused and looked ruefully at Abram. 'If only he could be here now and see what I see.' Blake replied as he looked at an upturned boat that swirled and turned, sucked towards London Bridge, its passengers floating like basking otters face-down in the water. 'My imagination has been stretched to breaking, and now I will never be surprised by anything. My eyes cannot deceive me for my mind is shattered and I feel my life will never be the same again. Tell me one thing – why all this?'

'You have read the Nemorensis, you are the master of the Cabala – tell *me*, O wise one.'

'I thought I knew, thought I could predict what was to come, but since I had the book I was a changed man, obsessed with my calculations, distracted to know the truth.'

'Scientist, Cabalist, always looking for the answer and never just accepting,' the angel replied. 'I am always amazed, every time you reach out for illumination you fervently grasp some old belief. Look at you – you're a scientist, a man who has lived his life in fact, and you search for truth in some whimsy. The more you discover, the more you bury your head in the ways of the past.'

'The more I discovered, the more I concealed myself in magic,' Blake replied. 'It was as if I was running away from the modern world to some better place in the past. I have always been afraid to live in the here and now. I have found myself either looking to the future or living in a world of what could have been. There is too much to face in the present moment, it's demands are greater than I could ever bear.'

'It is a calumny on life to live like that,' Abram said almost whispering. 'Each breath is a sacrement of the present moment, it is precious and unique and has to be savoured. Living in the past has to be savoured. Living in the past leads to bitterness, wanting to be in the future is a waste of life. You cannot afford to squander one second, it may be your last . . . And all you could think of was the pages of the book and what you would discover?'

'It began to be everything,' Blake replied, as if at last he was being understood.

'That is the Nemorensis. It finds your weakness and makes it grow. Those who desire knowledge will be led astray with its power. Those who seek power will be made drunk with its influence, and those who are bitter will be shrivelled like the praecoquum. It will call out to you from its hiding-place, it will want you to discover it again. The Nemorensis needs the adoration of its slaves, for that is what you are. It will shout its presence and drag you from the ends of the world and all I have to do is follow you and then it will be mine again.'

'Again?' Blake asked, surprised by what he heard.

'I was its keeper. I stole it from the one who wrote it. The book started life as the history of our family, then its creator began to fill it with desires that leapt from her heart. Filled the book with talk of our master lying to us, cheating us out of our inheritance. She said we were equal to him, that we were not his creation but just the same. Dust from dust, ash from ash.'

He stopped speaking, hoping that Blake would grasp the consequences of his words.

'Hezrin was such a fine angel, so beautiful, and in that came her deceit.' The angel looked up to the sky and the comet that hovered high above them. 'She has called this comet from space. As her power has grown, so has her greed. She wants to be the queen of two kingdoms – earth, then heaven – and she will rule them with her brother Pyratheon. The one good thing about the book is that it will predict what she will do next. With it we will know how to defeat her. And there is something that she needs to do. Every thousand years she has to be transformed. Once we come to live on earth and the pull of the world controls our spirit, an angel will soon be changed into a snarling demon. She is near her time again; she will have to take on another identity. The only way of doing this is by stealing the body of the person she is to become. It has to be their birthing-day and it has to fall on the full moon. Tomorrow is such a moon and somewhere very near is the one who is to have their very life stolen from them.'

'How do you know who it will be?' Blake asked, as the screams from Cheapside flitted like leaves across the city spires and wind-blown bells chimed without help of hands.

'It has to be a girl, in her prime, pure and faultless. Hezrin has always taken those who have a streak of violence. They are chosen at birth and watched through their lives. Her advocates will observe the child for years and then at the right time will snatch the child from life and Hezrin will be transformed.'

'Tomorrow is All Souls' Day, it's the birthing-day of my servant girl Agetta Lamian. I always give her the day off. She stole the Nemorensis and took it away.'

'Then she could be the one, and the real reason why you were given the book. Did you never doubt as to why such a gift should come to you?' the angel asked, keeping his meeting with Agetta a secret.

'I thought it was a gift from the gods, handed to me for safe keeping.'

'It was given to you so the child would fall under its influence, that she would have her mind opened to the things of the spirit and her youth stolen from her. You are a pawn in her game, a passing folly for Lady Flamberg.'

'She wants to see the city destroyed and all the people with it,' Blake said as the madness of howling dogs grew louder.

'They fear the sky, they sense what is to come and in their anger do what any creature does in fear . . .' the angel said as he pulled the collar of his coat. 'It attacks – it scents down its victim and then attacks.'

Blake replied quickly as the howling echoed around the streets. 'Her father said she had run away with a man from his menagerie. They said he was a foreigner, from Italy, a man with wings.' Blake laughed. 'They would have me believe that she eloped with a man with wings.'

'Did this foreigner have a name, by chance?' Abram asked.

Blake tried to remember. 'He did. He was called . . . *Tegatus*. That's it – the man was from Italy and was called Tegatus.'

'Then all is not lost, for this man is not an Italian or even human – he is an angel, a heavenly emissary sent to search out Yerzinia and bring back word of her life. Like a moth to the flame she enticed him and scorched his wings. I pray he has not fallen too far and that blackness hasn't covered his feet. What good is it for him to gain the world yet lose his eternal life?' He looked at Blake. 'Tegatus is like a sheep that has gone astray and has turned to his own way. There may still be a chance for the girl and for us all.' Abram walked several paces to the quayside and looked down the swollen river to the houses on London Bridge. 'Do you know a book-seller called Thaddeus Bracegirdle?' he said as he edged closer to Blake.

'I know the name well, a strange man with beady eyes and the nose of a pig.'

'Is his shop a place that the girl, Agetta, should frequent?' he asked slowly.

'She is a bright girl, self-taught, but not one for bookshops,' Blake said, firm in his reply.

'I was in that shop and met your servant. She acted if she knew Bracegirdle, as if he were a friend. There were other creatures in the shop – children.' He waited and looked around, not wanting to be overheard. 'Dead children, their spirits trapped and sealed in the building. It was like walking over the chasm of Hades, never have I felt such a powerful presence of malevolence. Do you know a reason for this?'

Blake seemed surprised and faltered in his answer. 'It was a church once, a small chapel for travellers coming into the city. There is a legend that at a certain time of the year as the rays of the sun touched the water, a whirlpool would appear under the bridge. To jump into the maelstrom would take you through a gateway to the next world. When the plague came to the city many people, fearing death, would jump from the church into the water, never to be seen again. It became a place of death and not life. The last one to jump into the water was the priest – he rang the bell for matins, locked the door and threw himself into the water. They say the river never freezes at that part of the bridge, the boiling fires of the underworld heat the current and the steaming breath of a dragon rises from the depths.' Blake tried to see the connection. 'It became a bookshop after that, and Thaddeus Bracegirdle is a friend to many a strange character.'

'Lady Flamberg?' the angel asked.

'Everyone in the city knows Lady Flamberg,' Blake replied with a smile. 'She has always been around.'

'And she has never changed, never grown old. Whilst her husband has become fat and wizened she looks like the girl he first met fifty years ago.' Abram looked towards the bridge. 'She fears this transformation will be her last, so in this she must not fail. The comet is all part of her plan, a new life and a new city.'

'They said they would go to the north, to a house in the country, and watch from there,' Blake said, recalling what Lord Flamberg had said.

'Yerzinia will not go far from this place. She has surrounded herself with loyal followers and tomorrow, as the full moon rises from the sea, the comet shall strike and the transformation will be complete.'

'And London?' Blake asked quietly.

'Will be destroyed, and the bowels of the underworld will spew forth their spectres to torment the living – well, those that are left.'

'What of the girl?'

'She will be stripped of her body and cast out to wander the wilderness for ever. Hezrin will use her like a carriage and the wasted body of Lady Flamberg will become a rotting corpse. Lord Flamberg will wake to find his wife a putrid mass of skin and bone.' The angel laughed. 'But there is more than the transformation. You were right – the comet *is* a sign of a new world, one poisoned and darkened, ruled by a foreign power that will enslave you all. She will build a new city of corruption and fear, a dragon shall be its herald and will sit at its gate.'

'What will you do?' Blake asked the angel.

'What will *I* do?' The angel seemed amused. 'Am I expected to do anything? I was just going to sit back and enjoy the spectacle, see the human race disintegrate before my eyes. What do you

258

expect me to do? You are a man of magic and science, surely *you* have some power to stop all that is about to happen.'

Blake was silent, staring across the city. Black crows swirled above the streets that were littered with corpses and the remains of broken carriages.

The angel looked at him closely. 'What do you see, Blake?'

'I . . . I see that we are lost. All it has taken to bring this city to an end was the coming of the comet. Scattered like the cut grass, thrown to the wind, as if we were the husk from the threshing floor.' He looked around at the devastation. 'This place is all I have ever known, and it has been stolen from me. What can I do?'

'Children of dust, blown by the slightest breeze, feeble and frail like an old dog ready for destruction. Is that what you believe?'

'I believe that we have been discarded by whatever force sent you. The decrepit Immortal has given us over to the power of a fallen angel,' Blake shouted at Abram.

'Can't you see that this has come about because you rejected the one that could redeem you?' the angel shouted back at Blake, and he kicked over a barrel of salt fish that was stacked on the quayside. 'Blentish have always relied on their own instincts to do right. You have searched for power and wealth for yourselves, you have starved your soul with your fancy philosophies and none of you have noticed. It would be better that you believed in nothing than everything served to you as belief.'

'But what –' Blake tried to interrupt.

'You make me sick. As soon as calamity strikes you raise your hands to the air and cry out to the sky for help. You hope that all will be forgiven and goodness will come running like a frail servant bound in chains of your making, bowing and begging and tugging at his old grey beard, thankful that he's been remembered. *Well, it's not like that!*'

Abram's words, screamed at the top of his voice, echoed around the empty streets, rattling the panes of glass in the shattered windows and booming like the first coming of the sky-quake. Blake felt the angel's hot breath blast his skin, pushing him backwards, as tongues of fire shot from the angel's mouth and engulfed him in bright orange smoke. 'The best that you can aspire to in your own strength is like dirty rags to us. Humanity has no goodness within itself – that is a delusion of the faithless, the blind that lead the blind. Your noses are so far into the dirt that this world is all you see and you tremble with fear when it is being taken from you. Open your eyes, you ape of Eden, and see what is really happening.' The angel suddenly lashed out at Blake with his boot and kicked him with a shattering blow to the backside. Blake was lifted from the floor and thrown through the air as the angel panted gusts of smoke from its nostrils.

Blake sat on the floor, dazed by the burning images that filled his eyes. He felt as if he had stared at the sun, blinded by its glare. 'We do only that which we know,' he said sorrowfully, like a scolded child.

'You do what your greed dictates and expect the Immortal to pick up the pieces of your detritus,' Abram said as he picked Blake from the floor. 'Changed your mind, have you? Want me to leave you to this fight by yourself? Go on, Blake. You could find her and stop her if you wanted. Your friend Bonham would help you, if he wasn't so busy snuggling in her bosom with the rest of them.'

The sound of howling dogs got closer, and the screams of those too fearful to leave the city could be heard in Grub Street.

'It is time for us to leave,' the angel said as he looked to the sky. 'Or you will be meat for the dogs.'

As they turned to go, several men ran along the quayside. Far behind, a large pack of dogs gave chase, spurred on by their shouting. The men's screams for help became drowned in the howls of the creatures that ran faster and faster. A large fat man in a white nightcoat stained in blood, unable to run any further, threw himself from the river bank and into the brown water, only to be sucked beneath the bubbling stew, his bald head bobbing amongst the broken boats before finally disappearing into the deep.

Blake raised his sword-stick and braced himself. He was too confused to run, and the hope of ending his nightmare here, by the side of the river in the city he loved, grew more alluring with each second.

'So we fight dogs?' the angel asked, rummaging in his coat pocket.

'In this country we help our fellow man, regardless of what it costs us,' Blake replied defiantly. He waved his sword and growled, grunting like an old bear about to be baited.

'This I shall enjoy. But forgive me if I have to disappear before its conclusion, I have never enjoyed the pleasure of canine company.'

'If I die here, I die for something worthwhile,' Blake shouted, lashing out with his sword.

'Then perhaps I should wait and escort your soul to wherever you are going,' the angel said, smiling.

The mob ran faster as the hounds gained ground. A judge still decked out in his wig and red coat lagged far behind. Blake watched as his little legs ran nervously in boots too big for him, his feet slopping about in an expanse of old leather, as if in the panic he had seized another's boots from the hangman.

It was a deerhound that caught him first, pushing him to the ground with a sharp prod in the back, tearing the long wig from his head and shaking it like a captured rabbit. As the hound chewed on the hair, holding it with one paw to the ground and ripping it with its teeth, the judge got to his feet, kicked the oversized boots from his feet, and ran bare-foot towards Blake and the angel. The men ahead of him scattered and ran into the buildings that backed on to Grub Street, disappearing like frightened rats, slamming the doors and bolting out the animals that chased them. From there they looked down, unwilling to help the man who had once stood in counsel for them.

'Run, man!' Blake shouted as he set off towards the judge, brandishing his sword. Abram walked behind at a leisurely pace, admiring the architecture of the fine houses that fronted the river.

The judge ran slowly and painfully towards Blake, gingerly lifting his feet as broken glass pierced his skin. Following the scent of blood another, larger hound quickly took up the chase and pounced through the air. With one swipe of its paw the hound knocked the judge to the ground, grasping his head firmly in its teeth and tearing at the flesh.

Blake caught the beast a blow to the head, dropping it to the ground, dead. Again the judge got to his feet, panting and breathless, his face steaming with tears and his words choking like hot stones in his throat. Sword in hand, Blake waited for the approaching hounds that bounded towards him. In a final act of defiance he let out a scream that shook his whole body. Abram quickly reached into the deep pocket of his black frock-coat and grasped a small, round object. With great speed he aimed the crystal and with a sudden flick of his arm he threw the pulsating ball towards the stampeding animals.

There was a blinding flash of light as Blake was blown from his legs and somersaulted several paces towards the river, landing against a stack of barrels. A thunderous roar sucked the air from his body and dragged him helpless across the ground, pulled in by the force of the blast.

All was silent. Stunned, he lifted himself from the earth, but could hear nothing but the loud ringing in his ears. He looked around. The pack of dogs lay dead, scattered by the blast and torn limb from limb. Abram Rickards sat on a low wall, smiling and wiping white dust from the shoulder of his long black coat. Slowly, the sounds of the world returned to Blake, the echo of the blast jumping from building to building and rolling across the Southwark fields and around the tannery tower far over the water.

'I had to join in, I just couldn't resist. I find that Abaris crystals are such fun. They come in so useful and *nothing* can resist their power . . .' Abram laughed. 'Tell me, was it science or magic or something more powerful than either of them?' The angel got to his feet. 'Now, can we go in search of the Nemorensis?'

24 : Optime Disputasti

It was the fourth hour of the afternoon and the dark embers of night were already stealing the sun and casting long shadows across the city. Agetta huddled by the fire in the corner of the bookshop and watched as Tegatus paced the floor, holding the Nemorensis in his hands and slowly turning the thick parchment pages. Since the time of their arrival she had felt its power growing within her. Every ounce of bitterness bubbled to the surface of her mind and twisted her heart – she sweated and cursed her mother for every false word and deed she had done to her, and the anguish of jealousy stung her lips with words that brought pain to her tongue. Dark words, words that could only be spoken under her breath for fear of being heard by the angel or by the child spirits that ran through the shop in their chasing games.

The urchin had sat by the fire and stared at Agetta through the long afternoon. They were waiting for nightfall, and for the streets to clear of the refugees who now trickled across the bridge and out to the fields of the south. The spirit had at times faded, almost to the point of invisibility, and then as if lit like a new candle had burst into light, becoming as solid as Agetta. She was now opaque, and the fire glow beamed through her face.

'Why won't you go?' she said angrily. She had said little else throughout the day. 'It isn't safe for you here, they will be back, and there are others who will do you harm.'

Tegatus sharply interrupted. 'We will stay till dark, and then you can haunt this place to yourself and perhaps you will be happy.'

Agetta had never spoken to a ghost before. She had heard tales of their existence and had laughed and scorned the stories as fancy. Now before her sat a ghoul, its sallow face and deep black eyes looking out mournfully, its lips curled at the edges in despair at its condition.

'You must go, or you will end up as one of us,' the urchin said again, its cold shrill voice filling the room.

'What is it like to be dead?' Agetta asked, pulling her chair closer to the fire.

'I'm not dead, I'm alive as you,' the creature said.

'But you were once alive and now you run about as a spirit, so you must be dead. What was it like?'

'The changing was easy – I jumped out of my skin and left it behind. Found myself here and things were different.'

'What's your name?' Agetta asked.

'*He* has it,' she said, scrunching up her shoulders and shivering. 'Got it locked away somewhere, I saw it once but I can't read. If I had my name then I would be out of here and going on. Don't want to be here for ever.' She gave a little laugh that sounded like the chattering of teeth.

'You are not meant to talk with spirits,' Tegatus said as he closed the book and put it back on the shelf. 'Once they have left the world they are not your concern. Even angels try to keep them at arm's length, and those who conjure them.'

'Did Thaddeus steal your name?' Agetta asked quietly.

'The book-keeper enjoys our company, it's like we are his family.'

'Then why doesn't he let you go?' the angel asked quickly. 'Surely that would be the kindest thing to do?'

'Maybe we're all he's got, he ain't got a family of his –' The spirit suddenly went rigid, her eyes bulging from her head. 'Someone's coming,' she said, and she quickly vanished.

Tegatus pushed the Nemorensis back on to the shelf, grabbed Agetta and pulled her quickly behind the fireplace into the priest-hole. He snatched a candle from the table and they climbed into the chamber. High in the wall was a small hole cut between the stones with a clear view of the shop. Drawn by the chink of light, Agetta pressed her eye to the spy-hole and saw, amongst the yards of shelves and piles of books, Dagda Sarapuk. Walking through the aisles like a tall thin beetle, Sarapuk made his way to the back of the shop, getting closer to their hiding-place.

Tegatus said nothing; it was if he didn't need to see what was going on, as if he had some deep insight into these hidden things. 'My feather trimmer,' he whispered to Agetta. 'Come to steal the book.'

Suddenly Sarapuk stopped and raised his head, looking around the large vaulted room to see what had made the noise. Agetta saw the urchin appear high above his head, edging towards a pile of books that perched on the very top shelf. Agetta wanted to shout out, to tell her to stop, knowing that the ghoul would make the books fall. There was a sudden tremor of the shelf above his head and Sarapuk looked up as three thick, black Bibles fell one by one like a shower of truth. They clattered against his skin and fell to the floor. Sarapuk dropped to his knees with the final blow, and a shrill echo of glee danced high above his head as the urchin danced across the rows of books.

Sarapuk screwed up his eyes and looked around the room before putting his hand in his coat pocket and pulling out a pair of gold spectacles with deep blue lenses. Agetta gasped – they were the same as the man wore who had been following her. Sensing her unease, Tegatus pushed her roughly to one side and peered through the tiny slit.

266

'My Chezzed eyeglass,' he said in a whisper, stepping back from the spy-hole. 'Your father took them from me when he bought me as a trinket in his menagerie.'

'The man who was here the other day, the one who was following me, he had some just the same,' Agetta said.

'He had eyeglasses just like those?'

'Exactly the same – thick blue glass that masked his eyes and hung from his nose.'

'Then I am not the only angel abroad in London, and I fear even more the reason why one should be stalking you,' Tegatus whispered. 'Through them he will see things that human vision was not meant to behold.'

Tegatus watched as Sarapuk ran his hand along the spines of the books on the shelf where the angel had hidden the Nemorensis. He stopped, his finger poised on the cover of the book. His body shuddered and twitched as if he had been suddenly charged with electricity. The eyeglasses dropped from his nose, landing on the floor, and he shivered with shock and backed away from the tome. His hand darted out again to grab the spine; again it was jolted back by a blue arc that flashed in the darkness. Sarapuk giggled like a small child with a new toy as he plunged his hand back and forth and blue sparks shimmered.

'The Nemorensis has found him,' the angel said as he peered down.

Sarapuk played on, his hand jumping as each spark stung his fingers. But suddenly his eyes fell upon the gold leaf that encrusted the next book on the packed shelf. '*Micrographica!*' he shouted, springing to his feet and realising that he had found what he was looking for. 'Blueskin Danby didn't lie, his truth is here for me to behold.'

As Sarapuk grabbed the small panel of wood beneath it, the book slid from the shelf, revealing a void that vanished into blackness. Sarapuk tried to peer into the depths, but could see nothing. In his frustration he thrust one arm deep into the hole, squashing his head against the bookcase and pressing his long thin nose against the wood. With the tips of his fingers he could feel the soft touch of a velvet bag. He strained to get his fingers deeper into the void, and the cord of the bag tantalisingly slipped across his hand several times. Sarapuk kicked against the far wall and pushed himself deeper, the urge for gold driving him on.

'At last,' he said as he finally took hold of the bag and pulled as hard as he could. The bag moved three inches and then stopped, as if caught by some hidden obstruction or ghostly hand not wishing to let it go. 'What stops me?' Sarapuk shouted angrily. 'Don't play games with me now, Danby.' His words echoed around the darkening room as he let go of the heavy bag and tried to squeeze his hand another inch deeper.

Blindly, his fingers fumbled across the smooth, cold marble that lined the hole. He thought of the gold and imagined counting the thick yellow coins and dropping them one by one into his pocket. He gave a quiet chuckle to himself as he recalled Cadmus looking like a frightened pig at the sight of Blueskin Danby. What was a friend, he thought, but someone to be cheated when the opportunity came to pass?

With this fleeting thought he ran his fingers over a small, sharp catch that held the bag to the bottom of the hole. With a flick of his little finger he freed the bag, and in that instant Sarapuk felt one side of the chamber spring open, as if he had flicked the switch to the entrance of some hidden compartment. His eyes widened with anticipation, and a rush of lust choked his throat. 'What joy!' he murmured, sliding his hand into the long narrow hole that opened to one side. 'The bag of gold, and now erstwhile treasures to behold! Soon, soon, soon,' he sang to himself.

As Tegatus spied on him, suddenly Sarapuk went rigid. He jumped from the floor, pulling his hand from the hole and looking down at his clenched fist.

In between his fingers a scorpion twisted and turned, pushing its way between his finger and thumb. Sarapuk turned his hand to look closely, and the creature's long spiked tail twitched and arched around his fingers. Then it flexed back and struck several sharp blows to the back of his hand.

Sarapuk's hand flashed open like a sprung trap and the scorpion was thrown into the air, landing at his feet unharmed and snapping its pincers as it scurried towards him. Sarapuk began to hop from foot to foot as he tried to crush the creature. He grasped his right hand at the wrist as the venom inched its way through his veins, and his brow gushed with droplets of thick white sweat. The scorpion danced around his feet as he attempted to squash its thick brown shell, screaming as he jumped about. And then the poison pulsed into his heart and he stood bolt upright and clutched his chest. In two seconds his face drained of its colour as the skin tightened and stretched across his sallow cheeks. Sarapuk struggled to speak, opening his mouth and gawping like a fish as he sucked the air into his frothing lungs.

There was a swirling of the dust on the floor. Slowly the phantasm of Blueskin Danby began to appear, sucking all the particles of light from the room as it took form and substance. The snake slithered through Danby's empty eye socket and darted at Sarapuk, wrapping itself around his long, thin, white neck. With a flick of its tail it anchored itself around his shoulder and began slowly to squeeze the breath from his body.

'Wonderful thing, this snake,' Danby said, half-laughing. 'Given to me at my demise as a token for the afterlife, a skin-picture come to life, and now it will herald your death.'

All Sarapuk could see through his venom haze was the

bleary outline of Blueskin Danby. The rushing of blood filled his ears and made Danby's words but a faint murmur in a faraway world.

'What's the matter? Snake got your tongue?' Danby joshed the man as he choked and spluttered. 'I thought it would be Lamian who came for the money, but greed got the better of you. I see you found the surprise. It was my last action in life, setting that trap.' He looked around the room. 'Strange, really. I never thought I would see it work, but death has been kind to me. I bought the scorpion from the docks; it had been kept in a silver cage. Would have pawned the silver, given half a chance, but the rope got in the way with my sudden misfortune.'

Sarapuk struggled to free himself of the living noose around his neck that coiled itself tighter and tighter. Death was inching its way through every fibre of his body as Danby walked slowly around his victim, taunting him as he savoured his downfall. 'Tell me, Sarapuk. What do you expect will happen?' He stroked the long black snake that hissed loudly. 'Come on, man, you hang on to life like a frightened child. Give in and join me, then we can embrace as damned brothers.'

Holding out his hand like a blind man, Sarapuk grabbed the bookshelf by his side. His hand had swollen sevenfold and throbbed with the final pulsing of his weakening heart. With one last, final effort he dug his nails into the soft wood, hoping against hope that he could hang on to life. Like a drowning man he gasped his frantic breaths, snorting against the rising waters of death.

'Come on, man,' shouted Danby as his snake slithered and coiled itself over Sarapuk's face. 'Come to me and we can take our revenge together . . .'

In one last effort of life, Sarapuk grasped the snake and pulled it from his face, his eyes searching the high wall as if he knew where Tegatus was hiding. With his final breath he shouted out his last words: 'You never helped me . . . never . . . Hell.' The words stuck in his throat as he dropped to his knees and then on to his face with a hollow thud.

Danby stared down at the corpse, then picked up the adder by its tail, stretching its body until it became completely rigid like a long thick staff. With the head of the creature he tapped Sarapuk on the back three times. 'Wake up, sleeper, and rise from the dead,' he said softly, waving the snake-rod over the body and snatching a clump of hair from the back of Sarapuk's head. 'Mine be the spirit, mine be the death.'

Sarapuk's ghost slowly got up from his body and looked around the room. High above him, on every bookcase stood the child spectres. Turning slowly he came face to face with Blueskin Danby, who smiled softly.

'I have waited a time and half a time for this and your death does not seem as sweet as I once thought it would,' he said. He twisted the head of the snake to break its trance and return its litheness. Then he held out the tattered lock of Sarapuk's hair. 'You join me in Styx, and with this mark of your flesh I take your name . . .'

With deep desperation, the ghost of Sarapuk tried to form the familiar word that he had carried since childhood, but it was as if it had been stolen from his thoughts and hidden from memory. He was nameless.

The ghost of Sarapuk looked around him. The grey drabbery of death veiled all he saw. He could no longer feel the heat of the fire that embered brightly with its spitting logs. Everything was drained of colour, tainted with half-light. The scorpion scuttled across the wooden floor, snapping its claws as it scurried along the side of the bookcase, and disappeared into the mouse-hole in the corner.

Danby chuckled to himself. 'People will call your name and you will not know that they speak to you. I am your father in hell and I give you the name Kashal.' He touched him on the shoulder. 'We have work to do and *my* soul to regain.'

Danby began to disappear, melting into the spirit of Kashal, who suddenly looked up to the spy-hole as fragments of his flesh fell away and turned into particles of light before vanishing completely.

Tegatus didn't speak. He had seen this fate before, far away on the banks of the Great River. The body of Dagda Sarapuk lay face-down on the wooden floor, its spirit gone. The angel turned and sat in the darkness of the chamber and now knew what he had to do. He yearned to stretch his shaven wings and fly home. But these hope-filled thoughts blistered with despair as he realised how far he had fallen from grace. He had left all charm behind, squandered in the pursuit of one he could never embrace.

In the cold, silent blackness of the place where no mortal eye could behold or ear understand he spoke the words of his birth. Penitent tears gouged acid sores across his cheeks.

'*Ga-al et ha-shamayim*,' he said, again and again, each word growing on his tongue. His voice faltered but then grew stronger with each utterance, resonating around the dark chamber.

'It is time,' he said to Agetta. But there was no reply, just the hushed sound of the girl sleeping.

25 : Seidkona

Agetta stood in her dream outside a large mansion house at the top of a long flight of marbled steps, unsure of how she had arrived at such a place. Her last memory was looking up at the dark shadow of Tegatus as he stared down through the spy-hole and into the shop. She had felt the power of the Nemorensis once more as it twisted her mind, stirring resentment and anger for everything and everyone. Then voices called her to sleep and the vision appeared, stealing upon her like a thief in the night.

There, surrounded by a blinding light, was the figure of a girl not much older than herself and dressed in fine purple. She had held out her thin white hands to Agetta, who felt she was being dragged from her body, and that with the coming of her birthing-day she now had the right to wander and leave behind the frailty and decay of flesh and explore other lands of perception. With trepidation she had reached out to the girl and stared into her deep green eyes. Then there was a sudden crack of thunder, the girl had gone and Agetta was outside a mansion house, staring at the chipped wood of the door.

The sky was darkening and two bright gargoyle lamps, topped with the heads of helmeted snakes, guarded the door of the house. A footman dressed in gold braid and scarlet jacket stood to one side, looking across the square. Agetta smiled at the man, wondering if he might know why she was here and what had called her to this place. She looked around. The familiar sight of Conduit Fields stretched out to the north, and across the newly-laid gardens were the tall houses of Queens Square with their neat iron railings and polished steps. She waited to be challenged by the footman, to be tossed down the stairs and into the mud like some guttersnipe. The footman turned suddenly and Agetta tried to step out of his way – but then, to her amazement, he stepped straight through her. She convulsed as the man strode boldly into her chest and then out of her back, as if she did not exist or was now some ghost. She screamed, but the footman didn't turn or even notice as he scurried down a flight of steps that led to the basement. Across the square an old man turned and stared at the house, unsure if he had heard a shout, but could see nothing.

In the half-light of the torches, Agetta noticed that the mark on her hand burnt blood-red and that the small letters that surrounded the scar had now been turned to a deep gold. They appeared to rotate against the direction of the sun. She watched, entranced, as the words spun and danced on her palm, then stopped. Before her eyes the words *Ga-al et ha-shamayim* hovered around the edge of the burning skin.

Agetta felt as if she was being dragged backwards, as if she were hooked like a flounder pulled from the sea. In the centre of the large oak door was a gold tapping-handle in the form of a dragon, forged from a single piece of iron. Its thick ribbed wings and green jewelled eyes shone in the lamplight. Agetta grabbed for the handle, but her hand slipped through as if it didn't exist. Turning her head, she saw her reflection in the glass of a side window. Stretching from her back and away into the blackness was a thin silver cord embossed with glinting diamonds. With every second the cord grew tighter, pulling her from her feet as she slid across the marble step.

Just as she was about to be dragged back into the darkness a white hand pierced the door and grabbed her firmly by the wrist. Another broke effortlessly through the wood to take hold of her arm. Then she saw the girl, her piercing green eyes shining as bright as the lamplight, snake-like and charming. The girl pulled Agetta towards her as she stepped backwards through the closed door and into the hallway of the house, dragging Agetta with her. She shuddered as she passed through the wood, and tiny blue sparks flashed from her skin. She gasped with an overwhelming delight that surpassed any sensation she had ever felt before.

'I enjoy it too,' the girl said, her eyes glinting in the light of the hallway. 'You can never get over the first feeling of utter joy that shudders your body.' She spoke in a low voice and smiled as she led Agetta onwards.

Agetta noticed the long silver thread trailing behind the girl that snaked up the long stairway until it vanished through a door encrusted in gold leaf.

'You don't know where you are, do you?' the girl said as she led Agetta through the hallway of the house and into a large room. Agetta was speechless as she tried to comprehend all that was happening to her. This was more than a dream – there was a tangible, lucid presence that made her feel as if it were all real, as if she were some ghostly spectator looking in on reality from another aspect. Agetta passed a large mirror and was startled that she had no reflection.

The girl laughed. 'You will never see yourself in the glass, but you are not dreaming. Come and see.'

In the dining room a finely dressed man chomped like a starving pig on the thin tendons of a monkey bone. Thick grease smothered his face as he sucked every drop of marrow from the thin femur. He never looked up, staring contentedly into the long thin bone shaft.

'We are bound only by time. We cannot see the future, nor can we go to the past, but here we can do what we wish and when we are finished we can return to our bodies and take these memories with us.' The girl pointed to the man with her long white fingers. 'He can't see us or hear us. But sometimes it is as if we are seen as phantasms caught in the corner of the eye as we pass by.'

'Am I a ghost?' Agetta asked as she tried to touch the winged chair on which the man was sitting.

'It's your spirit that walks whilst you sleep. You are joined to your body by the life cord. This is only broken at death. But beware, if it is severed at the spine then you will never return to your body.'

'How should that happen?' she asked nervously.

'This is not a place where we humans should tread. You are here through desire. When we sleep we stay with our bodies, but tonight you were liberated from mortal reverie and brought here.'

'Is this your home?' Agetta asked. 'Why didn't you leave London when everyone fled?'

'I am a servant to Lord and Lady Flamberg. She taught me this secret, she would visit me by night and play tricks upon me. I am sleeping in the room upstairs and walk the corridors at night and listen to their conversations . . . When the stones fell from the sky we hid in the cellar. We will be safe from whatever devastation it brings.' There was a glint of excitement in her eyes as she spoke. 'There are others here who can do this, they knew you were coming and wait upstairs.'

She took Agetta up the long flight of stairs to the upstairs landing, where a small barge dog trundled along the corridor to meet them, its tail wagging with delight and anticipation.

'It can see us,' Agetta said as the dog began to bark and leap along the landing.

'Not only that,' the girl replied. 'It is with us in this world.'

Agetta felt the life cord pull her back with a sudden jolt.

'You are being woken from sleep, there is nothing that can be done to keep you here,' the girl said anxiously.

Agetta reached out to the girl as she tried to hold on to this spectral sphere. 'Don't let me go back, I don't know your name.'

'You are being woken from your dream. You will have to go. Tell me where you sleep and I will come to you.'

'I am in the priest-hole, behind the fireplace at Bibblewick's Bookshop on London Bridge, that is where you will find me,' Agetta said quickly as the cord was pulled tighter, as if wound by some unseen hand that stirred her from sleep. 'Come and find me. Bring me back to this place. I need to know more,' she said as she was pulled from her feet and dragged backwards down the stairs.

The dog gave chase, barking cheerfully as if this were some spirit game. Agetta soared effortlessly through the air, then slipped through the door and into the street as the life cord sped her faster to her waking body. She flew through streets and alleyways, slipping in and out of the narrow streets and getting ever closer to London Bridge. The life cord began to slacken as she drew near the bridge and calmly floated along a narrow ginnel.

Then, with a suddenness faster than the eye, the alley was lit with a bright silver light. The sky exploded as a ball of fire hurtled from heaven, falling from the northern heights. An ear-splitting roar filled the air and the buildings around her shook with the explosion as the fireball crashed into the river, evaporating its dirty waters to a bright steam that hung in the air like a funeral shroud.

Helplessly Agetta drifted along the banks of the Thames, looking at the silhouettes of the fine houses that lined its banks, their deep blackness edged by the glow from a fire that overwhelmed the village of Hampstead to the north. In this half-dream, half-reality, she had no care for the chaos that engulfed the city. She stared at a church spire that broke from the horizon like a defiant finger pointing in rage at heaven. It was as if the buildings had been designed for darkness, that their creator had known that this hour was to come and that only at this time and in this place would their true beauty be perceived. She stared to the pinnacle of the stars and watched the quick flash of fragments of rock and ice as they broke free from their source and were sucked to earth. The broken dome of St Paul's lay as a testament to its failure of salvation. The place that once echoed to the sound of traditions made by man now resonated to the low hum of the ice boulders as they stormed through the outer layers of the high heaven towards the earth. The comet was being drawn closer, the world was luring its slayer nearer with each turn.

In the distance, etched by the moon, Agetta saw the girl running along the banks of the river and the small dog jumping by her side. The girl waved and shouted out in words that were stolen away as Agetta was pulled silently through the air. Her heart raced, knowing that her friend had sought her out and that she would see her again in her sleep. In her floating slumber Agetta tried to move her arms in a gesture of reply.

Then there was a sudden tug on the cord and Agetta crashed quietly and painlessly through the thick stone walls of the bookshop and sunk back into her cold body with a long shudder.

Tegatus shook her to bring her back to wakefulness. She held her head and rubbed her face groggily.

'*Ga-al et ha-shamayim*,' Tegatus repeated again and again, as if reciting a charm. 'You have been talking in your sleep. What place were you in?'

'I don't know,' Agetta said quietly as she tried to gather her thoughts. 'I saw another sky-stone strike the earth and the northern sky lit by a fire. I was at a house near Conduit Fields, a large house with marble steps. I met a girl, a servant just like me, she said she could walk in her sleep as if she was a ghost and I did too. It wasn't a dream, was it? And the words you spoke were written on my hand.'

'You have a seeing-stone. Maybe this would be a time to discover for yourself,' Tegatus said as he slumped down next to her.

Agetta took the crystal from her pocket and placed it carefully over the scar with its black-etched letters. She looked on as the small black shapes changed before her eyes. '*The heavens he has redeemed*,' she said quietly, staring at the words. 'So that is what you were saying when I woke up. What does it mean?'

'It means you are safe and away from danger. You are the centre of something even beyond my understanding. It is as if all this is for you. While you slept Sarapuk was killed and his spirit taken captive by a demon with a blue face. They have now left this place.'

'*Danby!*' Agetta gasped, realising the ghost of the highwayman had found their hiding-place. 'He was a friend of my father, a cheat and a murderer, and now in death he stalks me.'

'Fear not, child. There is a chasm fixed between heaven and hell that no spectre can cross and I know the name of one who can cast this creature to the pit for ever.'

'He said he would kill me to punish my father, and he will,' she said desperately. She got to her feet to run from the hiding-place.

'No. There is something I must do before you go outside.' Tegatus grabbed her by the arm, pulling her back into the room. 'I will go first and do what is right for Sarapuk. Even though he is a dog he cannot be left to rot in this place.'

Tegatus left her in the chamber and went into the shop, where the urchin was stretched out on the back of the body as if reclining on a fashionable French sofa. 'He won't be needing this any more,' she said as she saw the angel. 'I wanted to get inside and see what it would be like to live in a body again but all the life had gone. It's what my master has done to us all, he captures our spirit then tips our bodies through the trap door and into the Thames.'

'The book-keeper knows more than books,' he replied.

'He is a master of many things and has many friends. He knew the girl was coming here. I listened to him talking to the woman with the carriage. They wanted the book you carried and the girl together and they want them here tonight. You thought you were helping her escape and you have brought her to the place and to the time. Perhaps you are not such a clever creature after all.' As she spoke the spirit faded to almost nothing but a thin outline.

'They will be searching the whole of London. This is the best place to be, somewhere they don't expect us.'

'She has been dream-soaring. I was on the roof, I saw her. Tell me this, angel – she didn't teach herself to fly, so they must have charmed her out of her body. If they did that they will know where she is . . .'

'Then we will leave and you can tell your master that we have gone,' Tegatus said, stepping towards the urchin and pushing her from Sarapuk's stiffening body. 'Now tell me where the entrance to the river is hidden.'

The urchin pointed to a thick brass hoop that was fitted neatly into the wooden floor by the fireplace. Tegatus lifted the ring and pulled the three boards that formed the trap door. Beneath, the thick brown waters of the river bubbled between the narrow arch of the bridge.

'Brings back memories, that does,' the urchin said as she looked on. 'I remember the night it happened to me, I watched as my body went into there. Best thing that ever happened. Miserable life, miserable death, what's the difference?'

Tegatus picked Sarapuk from the floor with one hand and dragged him across the room. Without ceremony or comfortable words he tipped the body through the trap door, listening for it to splash into the surge. There was nothing, no sound but the bubbling water and the clattering breeze that whistled above the river.

The urchin vanished through the floor, then materialized moments later next to Tegatus as he peered through the trap door.

'He's not gone,' she said in her shrill voice. 'He's stuck, hanging from an old beam. He'll be there till Christmas, or till he rots and the seahawks pick him clean,' the girl said cheerfully.

'Then hang he will until Christmas and let the dead take care of the dead,' the angel replied sternly. He lifted the trap door and slammed it shut in a smoulder of thick dust. Far below, the body of Sarapuk dangled like a forgotten puppet as the quick breeze blew it back and forth.

Tegatus turned and called out to Agetta. 'It's done,' he shouted. 'Come, we have to go before we are found. The urchin saw your flight and fears you were followed by those who seek you.'

Agetta appeared from behind the fireplace. Her face had changed, and the angel thought how much older she looked, aged by the tribulation and now a woman.

'I was followed . . . by the girl in the dream . . . and her dog.

281

I want them to find me, they will do me no harm. I want to know more of her magic.'

'Where are they now?' asked the urchin.

'I saw them by the church with the spire towards Blackfriars.'

Tegatus ran to the window and looked out. To the north the glow of the fire filled the sky, etching the houses in deep black. He could see no one.

By the gate to the bridge a small barge dog snuggled into a discarded coat and, turning several times, made its bed. With one eye closed it peered sleepily across the cobbles to the entrance of the shop it guarded.

In the house by Conduit Fields, Hezrin Flamberg discarded the shadow of the girl as she woke from her sleep. She clicked her fingers, and Morbus Gallicus crawled like a dog before her.

'I will leave Rumskin where he is. I am sure he will tell us if they try to leave. Go to Thaddeus Bracegirdle and take him to London Bridge and make sure they never escape.'

26 : Hamartia

'Think, man, think,' Abram said as he pushed Blake through a narrow alley that had been wrecked by an exploding fragment of celestial ice. 'Do you not having any feeling in your bones as to where the book is?'

'I can't think, there is too much to think about,' Blake replied. A cascade of slates fell from the roof of a nearby house, crashing into the narrow alley and splattering in the dung that littered the ground. He looked around in the half-light. Every weakness was here to see. 'Just look at us. What do you think, you're an angel from another world, what do you think of this wonderful creation?' Blake shouted, his harsh words echoing through the darkness.

'You wouldn't want to know what I think,' Abram said as he pushed Blake further on. 'I have tramped the sewers of this world too often, lifting the drunken carcasses from the morass and putting them back on their feet. And what thanks do they give you? None. Maybe you yourselves are to blame for all of this. You were given free will to do what your hearts desired, and you desired to care only for yourselves. If only he had broken your selfishness then Yerzinia and her dogs would have had no one to feed on. Your kind are easy meat. From generation to generation I have seen you grow in knowledge – I was there when the first wheel was made from twisted wood, I have seen your kind create new inventions and wonderful machines. Yet you have spread your diseases of murder and greed wherever you go. Perhaps there is more hell in you than heaven.' He stepped over the corpse of an ass that lay across the way. 'I often wonder if you would all be happier if we left you to the devices and desires of your own hearts and didn't strive to bring you that which you call goodness. I once said this to the creator – but then he had seen my thoughts before I spoke them, he never replied he didn't have to. It was all in his eyes, those all-seeing, all-knowing eyes that strip you bare – they said it all, spoke of some deep, strong bond that only he knew.'

The angel slipped into melancholy as he took hold of Blake's arm and they turned into a deserted street that ran along the back of Fleet Street. 'We're jealous of your kind,' he said. 'We can't understand why he feels for your world so much, but then we soon realise that we are messengers, his messengers, and unlike you we can stare into his face and live.'

'Then why all this?' Blake said urgently as the thought of the book began to burn in his mind. 'The city is torn by madness, struck from the sky by a comet predicted in an old book, and the world is to be the conquest of a harlot. Doesn't the all-seeing, all-loving care about that? Is he so impotent that he's unable to help us?'

Then his feet suddenly stuck to the cobbles as if they had been charged with a shot of lead, and his body convulsed and writhed in pain. Blake fell to his knees as icy fingers pulled at his face and a harvest of dead hands groped up through the stones and mud, clawing their way to the surface from the pit that had been their tomb since the first plague.

Kicking at the hands that grasped his feet, Abram strode towards Blake, who was being dragged closer to the sodden earth. 'It's a plague pit come to life!' he shouted, taking hold of

Blake by the shoulders and lifting him from the bony fingers that tore at his flesh. '*She* has done this. Graves will give up the lost and the streets will be filled with the souls of the dead. It will soon be time, Blake, and she knows you will try to stop her. We must leave this place.'

Abram pulled Blake from the ground and carried him along the alley, blood streaming from his face, a broken finger embedded by a long brown nail hung limply from his skin.

'Where are they from?' Blake asked as Abram propped him against the broken door of the shoemaker's shop and pulled the corpse nail out of his face.

'She has called the dead. They will rise from the grave from now until the time of her transformation. Lady Flamberg will try to stop us from finding the girl, she knows there is a force against her. We have to discover where your servant is being kept and then I will find Tegatus and we can put an end to this whole event.'

'And you have the power to do this?' Blake asked as he drew his breath and looked back on the writhing mass of tormented hands that swayed back and forth like a silent crop of corn. 'Look, they reach out like blind men and still the grave holds them to its breast.'

'Given time they will break free and pull themselves from the pit, trapped in a half-life of rekindled madness. Evil is not limited to people, there are wicked strongholds that occupy the land itself. Every act of violence or tragedy charges the very particles of the earth with its presence. There are powers that feed on this and pitch their tent, making their dwelling place amongst men. Then you wonder why the trials of the ages repeat themselves time and time again in the same place, every generation cursed like the one that went before. Whatever people do makes an impression in the land. Wherever you tread you leave behind the scent of your sweating feet. So too with the spirit, its groanings are absorbed by the stones, to be played again and again.'

Abram set off to walk, casting a look back to the swaying mass of hands that reached out towards the dark sky. 'Come, my dear scientist, we have the city to search, and the Nemorensis will call out to you as the moon begins to rise. On a night like this it will want the adoration of its followers.'

Blake turned his gaze to the alleyway. Long shadows cast by the northern lights danced across the rooftops as the swathe of dead hands struggled to be rid of the earth that entombed them. They made no sound; all that could be heard was the grinding of the stones as the loathsome bones rubbed one against the other. Blake was transfixed. Never had he ever thought he would see such a spectacle.

'Does this not frighten you?' the angel asked Blake as they watched the plague pit slowly give up its dead.

'I wish I had seen this long ago. My quest would have altered and I would not have wasted so many years searching for that which would never be attained. To me this is the proof that I have longed for, proof that my scientific magic never gave to me.' Blake laughed. 'Who would believe that I would stand in the presence of an angel and the clambering hands of the dead in a Fleet Street alleyway?' He touched his face and wiped away the smear of blood that trickled across his skin. 'I am even marked by their presence.'

'There is more than this,' Abram said as he took hold of Blake by the arm and turned him away from the alley. 'Some days ago an attempt was made to destroy the world. The first sky-quake and the madness of the animals was a sign of what happened. Far to the north I fought with Yerzinia's brother. He desired a golden statue, a Keruvim, with which he would have overturned the throne of heaven. He failed in his undertaking and cannot trouble us here. But Yerzinia is far more wicked than he will ever be. She is a plague on the human soul, and will not rest until she has conquered heaven and the heart of every man she desires. She wants the world to bow at her name.'

'Then tell me this,' Blake asked, striding alongside the angel as they picked their way through the tormented street littered with the bodies of those who could not keep up with the human tide that had fled the city. 'Why does this evil seem so powerful and good so weak? If you are all-powerful then why can't she be destroyed in the twinkling of an eye? I have seen the power of the sea. I have watched as lightning crashes to the earth with such force that even buildings crumble with its power. So why not her?'

'It is not for power that the universe was created, but for love. Each abides by its own rules. Power seeks itself, and those too weak to follow the way of truth it corrupts, eats away like a vicious cancer of the mind. Choose power over love and soon you will believe phantasms as truth and delude yourself for ever. The ways of the creator cannot be understood, and I sometimes wonder myself the reason for this madness, but I know that what we now see is the last fight of wickedness as it clings to this world.' Abram stopped and looked around the street. It was as if he could hear a sound pitched beyond human ears. 'There are others . . . they are hiding from the comet.'

Blake strained to hear what Abram had discovered. All he could hear was the distant echo of the crackling blaze far to the north and the faraway rumble of houses crashing to the ground. Abram walked on, led closer to the sound. A thin silhouette crossed the street and clung to the shadows of the houses and shops that ran in broken file towards the river. Abram pointed to Blake and bade him be silent. Together they hid in a doorway.

Footstep followed footstep as whoever approached them crept closer, stumbling in the black shadows and muttering in a low, deep voice. Blake held his breath, he could hear the being close by, only feet away, skulking towards them. Abram waited, holding Blake against the door with one hand to stop him bolting. The buildings opposite were silhouetted and tinged in the red of the fire that raged in Hampstead. They reminded Blake of the Chinese theatre he had seen in Vauxhall Gardens and the mystical creatures cast in shadow by silk-clad puppeteers.

Suddenly a black figure crossed the doorway. Abram leapt from their hiding-place and like a spider quickly lashed out and pulled the figure back down. He held him like he had held the Dunamez, his hand firmly over the mouth, smothering the breath from its lungs.

Blake saw in the half-light the frightened eyes of a young man whose hands grasped at Abram, trying to loosen his suffocating grip.

'Quiet, man, or you will breathe your last in this place,' Abram said softly in his ear.

'You're going to kill him,' Blake said, and he made futile attempts to pull Abram's hand from the man's face.

'It wouldn't be the first time and perhaps would not be the last,' Abram replied menacingly as he slowly released his hold on the man. 'For someone who has so cleverly researched the supernatural, you have a very strange view of angels. The little cherubs you paint are far from what we really are.'

The man sucked in the cold night air as he coughed the fear from his lungs and squatted on the ground. 'I mean no harm to you g-g-good gentlemen,' he stuttered.

'Then tell us why you never fled this place,' Blake asked.

'I am from Newgate Gaol, a prisoner freed from his chains by the blasts from the sky. The gaoler thought it was the end of time, that the last judgement had come upon the earth, and he let us all go free. There has never been a finer time to be a thief in London as this night. Fortunes are to be made, riches found on every corner.'

'And the rest of you?' Blake asked.

'We hide in the old church at Blackfriars. You can join us, there are plenty of takings for us all to share. Eat, drink and be merry, for tomorrow –'

'In the morrow you could be dead and where would your thieving have got you?' Abram asked as he squeezed the man tighter.

'Are you a magistrate?' the man asked angrily.

'Some would say I am a judge, jury and executioner, but that is a matter of opinion. For you I am a gateway to freedom, so who do you say I am?'

'You play games with him, Abram,' Blake said. 'Let him go. He will do us no harm.'

'But *I* will,' came a voice, followed by the quick click of a hammer-lock being pulled on a pistol. 'Bad things always come in threes,' the man said as he pressed the muzzle of the gun into Blake's temple and turned to Abram. 'Give him his freedom or whatever brains your friend has will dangle from your coat like a Spanish medallion.'

From the corner of his eye Blake could make out the shape of two men. One held the gun to his skull whilst another skulked behind, darting his head from side to side.

'Freedom?' asked Abram calmly as he lifted the man to his feet. 'You can be a slave and yet free, poor and have the world as your home, but are *you* free? What wrongdoing binds you in perpetual night and eats away in the dark hours when you entertain yourself in self-pleasure and loneliness?'

'He speaks like a Garrick bard whilst I hold the gun to his friend's head,' the thief said, and his companions laughed, the former captive taking Abram by his collar and pushing him back against the door.

'I wouldn't do that,' Blake said, attempting to step away from the pistol. 'He is not one to be pushed around. My friend is an angel, and they don't appreciate that sort of thing.'

'Did you hear that? He's an angel and won't appreciate it,' the man with the pistol said mockingly as the others laughed. 'What a fine voice you have, just like the Vauxhall dandies we had so much pleasure in robbing. Now gentlemen, as you can see we left Newgate in rather a hurry and we would like your coats and your boots and of course your purses. So, my dear angels, take off your clothes.'

'If we give you these things then you will not have a world in which to spend your gains. Your fat will boil and bones turn to dust, so put the pistol down and go on your way.' Abram straightened himself and pushed the thief away with an out-stretched finger.

'And where are your weapons to make us do these things? Isn't it I who has the gun and you nothing?' The man spoke firmly, looking Abram eye to eye. 'Give us your clothes and I will consider your life, argue with me and I will gladly take both your life and your coat.'

'You don't understand,' Blake said feverishly. 'He *is* an angel and he can stop the madness.'

'This madness is not such a bad thing, it brought us our freedom and will give us all we need for a new life. We will take our chances with whatever is to come, and as you will not give us what we desire alive then you will both be dead.' The man took the pistol from Blake's temple and placed it to Abram's forehead. 'Alive or dead, what is it to be?'

'In your heart you have already chosen my fate and I yours.' Abram took hold of the pistol in his right hand and slowly squeezed the metal, which began to glow white-hot in the man's hand. 'Pull the trigger and see what will happen. *Do it!*' Abram shouted.

The man released his grip and stepped back under the cover of a long arcade that stretched along the row of shops.

There was a sudden crack like the snap of a horsewhip. Abram hardly moved, yet the thief crumpled before him, bent double and with a look of disbelief etched over his wrinkled brow.

The angel looked down at his clenched fist and then at the other two thieves. 'Would you like to share his experience?' he asked, raising one eyebrow.

'You've killed him!' one exclaimed.

'Not yet, but I could do if you so required me. I suggest you take him and go. Tell no one of what has taken place and I will not come looking for you.' Abram stepped out of the doorway and into the street.

'You ain't no angel,' one said as he drew a long cooking knife from his belt and stepped towards him.

Abram turned and without speaking held out his out-stretched hand. The man lashed out, cutting the tip of Abram's forefinger.

'See, you bleed like any mortal,' he said as he pulled back his arm to strike again.

'And you combust like a dry mattress,' Abram replied as he flicked his bloodied hand at the thief.

Two drops, thick as claret, landed on the man's dirty white shirt and began to smoulder in plumes of dense blue smoke. The man dropped the knife as he vainly tried to quell the flames that sprang from beneath his skin. His screams echoed from building to building as he was engulfed in a fire that fed from his bones and welled up out of his mouth like the billowing of a baker's chimney.

Abram looked on as the man slowly crisped into an unrecognisable mass of bubbling flesh. 'I give you my peace, now go,' he said to the spirit that hovered over the flames.

As Blake stared at the fire, he could in his mind see the Nemorensis, its golden letters glinting in the soft embers of another hearth. He had the overwhelming sensation that he had seen that place before. Abram had been right – the book was drawing him closer.

'We must leave this place,' Abram said as he turned away from the flames. Blake was silent and walked head-down towards the river. 'They had set their hearts on killing us. But tonight was not the time for you to die.'

'You see our thoughts?' Blake asked.

'Sometimes before they come to your lips.'

'And you know what I think of now?'

'That I am a murderer and a demon not to be trusted,' Abram said as he put his arm around him. 'I know that you are taking me to the river, and I can see that our journey together is nearly complete. From what I know of your world, what we seek is at Bibblewick's Bookshop. The hearth you see in your mind is in that place, and where else but in a bookshop would such a possession be hidden?'

'You guard my blood and yet yours explodes like gunpowder.'

'You forget, I am an angel – a warrior.'

27 : Summis Desiderantes

An eerie stillness consumed London as if the whole of the city was being dragged into a large bell jar. The stiff breeze that had blown feverishly was suddenly calmed as the fire in the north began to die away, seemingly starved of the very air it needed to burn.

Blake rubbed the stiff sweat from the palm of his hand and saw that it had dried as bright white salt crystals. His eyebrows were etched in ageing salt that cut lines in his face like deep furrows and crusted his cracked lips.

Abram looked at his companion, then wiped the salt from Blake's face with the soft palm of his hand. The angel's own skin glowed in the ebbing light of the northern fire.

'I'm as dry as a salted herring,' Blake said, licking his lips. 'Must be something from the ice crystals changing the atmosphere.' He hunched himself forwards as he walked in the shadow of a row of empty buildings. Ahead, the arch to the bridge was outlined in crisp white dust that shone in the clear night sky. He felt the book calling to him, whispering his name. A sense of deep excitement welled up in his stomach, twisting his gut to the point of nauseous expectation. He swallowed, gulping down the burning gore that was a manifestation of his growing fear.

'It will soon pass,' the angel said. 'You have coped with

much and soon it will all be over. You will either be dead or free to lead your life again.'

'And what of you?' Blake asked the angel. 'Will you die also?'

'And you a Cabalist! Angels do not die – well, not in the way you think of death.'

'And what of tonight?'

'Its secrets have not been revealed, nor shall they be. But I do know we shall recover the book, an angel and the life of a young lamb waiting for slaughter. That is work enough for you and I. Then I shall leave you to your world, your failed magic and desperate science, and return home.'

'And leave me a man of constant sorrow?' Blake replied earnestly, as the power of the book covered him in doubt and darkness. 'It all seemed so simple, pursuing magic and science, wanting to be the one who would discover all that humanity needed. Now I ask myself, was it for them that I searched for these things or for my own glory?'

'You have been held in the balance and found wanting. The proverbs you learnt in the Nemorensis will do you no good now. What you thought was a book of light is a book of darkness sent to mislead you.'

The angel stopped and pressed himself against the side of a drinking house. The front door swung back and forth on a broken hinge. He edged himself along the painted wooden wall clinging to the black shadow, Blake following his every footstep. 'There is a creature ahead by the gate, a sentinel the like of which I have not seen for sometime.'

Blake peered into the darkness but could see nothing. The fine rain of salt powder had stopped. It had covered the streets in a tissue of white dust that shimmered on every surface like cold white frost cast on a winter night.

'I see the salt mist but not the creature,' Blake whispered, looking over the angel's shoulder.

'It is a Diakka, a fallen angel,' Abram replied. 'Its presence here means that they too search for the Nemorensis and the girl and know where it is.' Abram edged his way closer. 'I need you to walk to the gate. If you walk quickly and ignore the creature it may let you pass. I don't think you have much to fear.'

Something in his words did not ring true. Fear rooted Blake to the spot and his knees began to quake. 'Walk by a creature that I cannot see? What if it should attack? I have been bait for too many night beasts. Is there no other way?' he whispered.

'It may let you pass,' Abram said quietly as he pressed Blake forwards. 'If it should attack I will be there for you. When have I ever let you down? I am the guardian of your blood, I do not want to see it spilled.'

Blake stepped from the shadows and kept his gaze fixed on the centre of the gate. High above, the grey stone gargoyles stared down, fixed in their stone skin as they guarded the bridge. He saw the dust swirl and twist in a myriad of tiny tornados. As he approached the bridge gate he could make out the shape of the creature on the stone mounting block where it sat waiting, black and squat, with a powdering of crystals covering its long black spines.

With every step his gut twisted. Blake kept his attention on the gate and what lay beyond whilst keeping the creature in sight from the corner of his eye. The dust wafted around his feet, covering his boots in snow–white crystals. He heard the low, guttural moan of the beast as he walked by. It licked its thick lips with a long blue tongue that swept across its face and over its pug nose, as if tasting the air for the scent of its victim.

A shiver juddered down Blake's spine as he crossed its path. He knew that the creature could leap from its hiding-place and swoop without warning upon him from behind. Fighting the urge to run to the bookshop, he checked his gait and counted the paces to himself as he calmly strode on.

In one second his legs were swept from under him and he was spun through the air like some discarded rag doll. He crashed to the ground, his fall broken by the arm of the creature as it plucked him from the air and grabbed him by the back of his frock coat. The Diakka, fully visible now, stared bleakly at Blake with its bulging eyes and bared its long white teeth, holding him now by the scruff of the neck and facing him eye to eye.

It purred like a giant cat filled with cream as with one hand it stroked the salt powder from Blake's face and then, with its tongue, licked his eyes and nose. The creature appeared to grow larger with each breath that Blake panted. He waited for his guardian to strike as the Diakka breathed its foul stench breath into his face, beads of moisture dribbling across its thick black chin. The creature opened its mouth and gave a loud gasp that rattled its tongue in its throat. Fit for a menagerie, Blake thought, as he sought to control his racing mind and fight the growing panic that welled up inside him.

In the darkness Blake heard a sullen thud like a distant cannon. The Diakka suddenly gave an ear-splitting scream and thrust its head awkwardly towards him, its mouth opening wider than before as it spat out its tongue like a fat snake. It groaned and closed its eyes, rolling its head backwards and twisting Blake in its grip as its fingers unfurled. Dropping to its knees, it let slip its hold of Blake as it slumped to one side clutching its stomach and rolling back and forth.

The angel stood behind the creature, a radiant smile fixed across his face. 'What joy!' he said as he fumbled in his pocket. 'It never expected that when it took hold of you. I thought it would have bitten off your head straightaway, but thankfully you intrigued the beast and it gave me time.' Abram took out a bobbin of red cord with which he began to tie the creature's hands and feet.

'Is it dead?' Blake asked, stepping away from the trussed creature. 'What did you do?'

'It is not dead as you would know, but will be of no trouble to us for some time. As for what I did, all I can say is that I am thankful to an Abaris crystal and a stink hole in the back end of the Diakka. I don't think it would ever have thought that something like that would happen. It brings a tear to my eye just thinking about it.'

'You shoved an exploding crystal up the creature's –'

'Yes,' Abram interrupted. 'It was such an obvious place. There was no time for second thoughts – it was the creature or you.'

'Then I am thankful for your absence of morals and your physiological understanding of demonic powers,' Blake replied as he looked at the writhing creature rolling in the dust. 'Do you leave the beast here?'

'Wait in the shop doorway whilst I see to the creature. Its future should not be your worry.'

A strange look crossed the angel's face. Blake turned, fearing something terrible was about to be done of which he wanted no part. He strode to the doorway of the bookshop and peered in through the frosted windows. A light glowed behind the shelves and a tall shadow moved across the far wall.

From the bridge gate, Blake could clearly hear a loud gurgling and a sound akin to the grinding of teeth. It came at him sharp and cold through the night air and carried a short, final cry at the height of hearing. He had heard this sound before many times as bleating lambs had cried out before the butcher's knife. Though he shuddered, not wanting to know what the angel had done to the creature, its cry pierced his heart.

Abram appeared through the dust, wiping his hands on a piece of torn coat picked from the back of an old man who lay crushed in the street. He looked at Blake and read the concerns of his heart with one glance. 'The ways of man are not the ways of angels. I am nothing but an assassin for righteousness, never forget that. There is war in heaven, and for us to lose would mean the diabolical would have power over the world and we would all be destroyed.'

The angel barged past Blake and pushed against the barricaded door of the bookshop. His feet gripped the stones as he forced the wood to bend, snapping the door in two and pushing the timber to one side. '*Tegatus!*' he shouted as he stepped into the shop. 'It's Raphael, come to take you home and deliver the girl from her oppressor.'

Blake and the angel made their way through the narrow bookcases as they followed the light of the glowing fire towards the back of the shop. At each careful step Abram looked around the high vaulted room, as if searching for something that could not be seen.

'*Tegatus!*' he shouted again, and this time the whole room vibrated with his voice.

'We're by the fire,' Agetta replied faintly.

Blake and Abram turned the corner of the final set of high shelves, then walked by Thaddeus's high desk and into the open space by the fire. Tegatus stood with his back to them, looking into the night through the tall leaded window. Agetta sat hunched on the stone hearth, warming herself on the fire.

'Tegatus, my friend,' Abram said softly. 'Turn and come back to me.'

'I have fallen too far, Raphael. The wholeness you bring cannot save me from that which I have come to know.'

'It is the evil of your heart that ensnares you. The cords of hamartia hold you fast, you will be waged as dead and soon transformed into a Diakka. That is no fate for one such as you. You have not fallen so far that you cannot put to death the rebellion of your heart and turn once more.'

'Turn to what – to the life I had before?' Tegatus said, still with his back to Abram. 'I have come too far. A vast chasm separates you from me that neither of us can cross. I have chosen my fate, of my own free will. It was a decision of my heart, to wander from the path and follow the ways of another.'

'Then it would be better for you to be dead than fall into the hands of the harlot.'

'If only that were possible, to fall into her arms, then life would be complete.' Tegatus turned to face Abram. 'I am not so stupid that I don't know I have been a fool. It is my pride that keeps me in this place. If only it could be different, if I could change time . . . Take the Nemorensis, Raphael. You are its keeper and can control its ranting. I will make my own way back.'

'Don't listen to him,' Agetta shouted at Abram. 'Take him from this place, he wants to go back, he told me. Can't you see he is too proud to ask that from you? If he stays they are going to kill him and turn him into a monster. You can't let them do that, I won't let you.' She turned to Blake, looking him sternly in the eye. 'You do it, Blake, you're a magician. I've seen your conjuring. Tell him to take Tegatus away before Morbus Gallicus gets him.'

'Gallicus? Morbus Gallicus?' Blake asked as he brushed the white dust from his coat. 'When did you meet this man?'

'At the Great Pillar, we were taken there by a man in a mask and a creature called Rumskin. They kept us there and when the stars fell we escaped. Thaddeus tricked us, he said he was with us – but he was with *them*.' Then she giggled. 'Tegatus used his magic and we left him in the tunnel with the rats. He saved me from them, that's why he has to go back. They're going to kill him and make him like Rumskin –'

'*Magic*, Tegatus?' Abram asked. 'An angel using *magic*?'

'It is not what you think. She jokes with you.'

'He hit him, right in the face, knocked him from his feet and into the water, then he picked him up and left him to the rats,' Agetta said excitedly.

'I am concerned about the place of your captivity. Did you see anyone else?' Blake asked.

'Why your concern, Blake?' asked Abram.

'The Great Pillar is a secret experiment known only to the members of the Royal Society, and in particular to Isaac Bonham. It is a vast sunglass used to capture the power of the sun and then funnel it to a marble room in its depths. Bonham believed that he would find a force so powerful that he could end all war. He would have known of your captivity, for he is there every day.'

'Then he is a conspirator and a traitor to your friendship,' Tegatus replied.

Blake looked ruefully at Abram. 'I was wrong. The deception goes deeper than I first thought. I have been manipulated at every turn and now even those who are close to me surprise me with treachery. I was used to find the comet and to trap you, Agetta. This is *my* fault. My greed for knowledge has enslaved us all.'

'How could you enslave me?' Agetta said. 'I stole from your pocket every day. I pitied you for taking me on.'

'Agetta,' Abram said, stepping towards her. 'You are the reason for all of these happenings. The woman you know as Yerzinia is a fallen angel. She has come to a time in her life when she needs to be transformed or end up like Rumskin. She needs *your* body. She will become you and cast out your soul to live in darkness. Remember, Tegatus, the command of our master at the Battle of the Skull. Tonight we fight again an evil stronger than before. Will you join me in this?'

'For what else was I created?' Tegatus smiled as his spirit leapt within him.

In the darkness of the street a long black carriage drawn by black horses creaked to a stop outside the shop. Morbus Gallicus jumped from the coach, whip in hand and his long wax cloak flowing out behind.

'They have come for you, Agetta. We must leave this place,' Abram said as he took off his frock coat and threw it into the fire. 'Quickly – to the roof. We should not be here when the Abaris crystals explode.'

'The book!' Tegatus shouted as he grabbed the Nemorensis and followed Blake, who was already running after Abram and Agetta to the stairs.

Bonham, wearing his raven mask, rushed into the bookshop and ran towards the fireplace. 'They'll be in the priest-hole,' he said hurriedly to Morbus Gallicus. 'Spare the girl and kill the angel,' he shouted as he chased through the shelves, pistol in hand.

In the hearth, Abram's coat burst into deep blue flames that grew brighter and brighter. An Abaris crystal fell from the burning coat and rolled across the floor towards Bonham, who dived headlong through the cellar door, rolled down the steps and emerged in the dank room at the foot of the bridge.

The growing blaze of the comet lit the cellar through a small window, on which Bonham heard a steady tapping. He looked up and saw the silhouetted body of Sarapuk hanging in the moonlight, his black-shod feet knocking against the glass.

28 : Lunar Lustrum

The narrow stone staircase twisted higher and higher. Agetta fumbled her way, holding tightly to the rope that led her upwards. Taking three steps at a time, Abram pushed by her in the darkness. She could hear Blake and Tegatus bolting the door to the stairs and then making their way quickly towards her. The blackness thickened and pressed against her, squeezing the breath from her, choking and fearful. As she tried to make her feet gather haste, they caught the lip of each stone step, causing her to jar against them in her panic.

'Help me!' she shouted, the words echoing upwards.

Tegatus took her by the arm and led her on. 'Walk slowly, take one step at a time. The darkness will not hold you for long.'

'They will catch us and Gallicus will kill you –'

'I don't fear what is to come. They can kill my body but I will be free.'

'Quickly!' Blake shouted as he stumbled up the stone steps. 'The Abaris will soon explode and I don't want to be anywhere near –'

There was a sudden loud explosion as, in the room below, Abram's coat burnt through and the Abaris crystals fell into the fire. It was as if every stone shuddered, leaping from the wall and then dropping back to its place. The door to the stairway was sucked from its hinges with the blast as a ball of white fire burst into the darkness and billowed upwards towards them.

'*Get down!*' Blake shouted as he leapt on to Agetta, pressing her to the cold steps as the fireball roared across his back, singeing the fabric of his coat and burning the hair from the back of his neck. Tegatus was consumed by the blast and fell backwards, his face blistered and charred.

'Leave me . . .' he muttered as Blake lifted Agetta to her feet. 'You must take her from this place, I will stop anyone who follows.'

'No!' Agetta cried as Blake dragged her higher. 'We can't leave him!'

'Do as he says, we cannot help him. You have to escape.'

'Quickly,' shouted Abram above them, fumbling with the lock to the roof door.

'Tegatus is wounded,' Agetta panted as she finally stepped on to the landing where Abram was pushing against the door.

'Nothing can withstand the Abaris, not even an angel. Tegatus will know what to do.' Abram took two steps back and leapt at the door, smashing it from the hinges and sending a shower of splintering wood across the flat roof. 'Follow me and whatever happens, do not give into fear.'

The Archangel – for such was his position among the angels – stepped from the darkness of the stairway into the glow of the full moon that outlined the rooftop castellation in deep silver. The fire to the north had dulled to an amber glow that lit the sky, and as he looked upwards he could see the comet drawing closer with each second. The roof was like a battlement of a castle, its stone walls towering high above the river. At each corner sat a large stone gargoyle perched on a high pinnacle, guarding the place at every compass point, and below them smaller gargoyles peered down to the city and the river, their bulbous eyes gawking blindly.

The surface of the roof had been etched with the points of a large five-pointed star, the tip of which pointed to the north. In the centre of the star was painted the blood-red mark of Yerzinia, its outline stencilled in black.

'We have little time, we may not even get from London before it strikes,' Abram said, taking hold of Agetta and pulling her into the light. She held up her hand to shield her face from the brightness that lit the city.

'Is this the end for us?' Blake asked.

''Tis the end for you all,' came a voice from behind them. 'We have been waiting for some time and are so glad you can join us.' Yerzinia stepped from behind a high stone chimney, her faced masked in the image of a tiger.

As Blake turned to run to the door, from the darkness stepped a figure draped in a raven's mask with long black beak and shimmering blue feathers and carrying the Nemorensis, now bound in a long red cord. He knew the figure well.

'Isaac Bonham, hiding behind the face of a blackbird,' Blake shouted. 'Not even willing to stare me eye to eye in your treachery?'

'My disguise cannot fool you, I am impressed. So this is the angel? And Agetta – so nice to see you. I shall be seeing more of you in the years to come, lots more.'

'You will see nothing if I have my way. I will gouge the eyes from your head with my own hands if I have to,' Blake shouted angrily.

'There will be no escape for you, Blake,' Yerzinia said, waving the long staff she carried in her hand.' You had your chance to join with us, but ever since that night when I pared your fingernails I knew your heart was not black enough for what we sought to achieve. Bonham, however, is my darling of darkness, and when I am free of the fetters of Lady Flamberg and her fat husband I will marry him.'

Several grey stone hands then appeared over the battlements of the chapel. The gargoyles, which had for centuries stared down upon London, had come to life and were crawling from their places.

'More demons, Yerzinia?' Abram asked.

'Friends to help me in my task. You have no place here, Raphael. Go now, and I will give you your freedom – or stay and be transformed into a Diakka.'

'Brave words, but time is running out for you. The moon is full and the comet will soon strike the earth and the time for your transformation will have passed.' Abram pulled Agetta close to him and whispered to her.

'*Who did this?*' shouted Morbus Gallicus as he stepped from the doorway clutching the severed head of Rumskin. 'Was it you, Blake, and your meddling science? Rumskin was my companion, the only thing in life that would look at me without causing me shame. Did you do this?'

'I did,' replied Abram quickly. 'Rumskin meddled in my life, so I meddled in his . . . What do you intend to do about it?'

'You're a wicked man and I will have your head as a candle-holder for what you've done,' Gallicus shouted, his voice hoarse and brash.

'Leave him, Morbus,' said Bonham as he aimed his pistol. 'I too have a score to settle with this creature and will have his blood. There is one dead angel on the steps and soon there will be another.'

'My blood is something I will freely give.'

'Leave him,' Yerzinia said anxiously. 'He tricks you, Bonham. His blood would be the death of us all and must not be spilled.' She looked at the moon and the approaching comet. 'It has begun,' she shuddered. 'I must leave this body now and take hers. Make her ready. Give her to me, Raphael, she is not yours to keep.'

Gallicus threw the head of Rumskin at Abram, hitting him in the chest, and quickly snatched Agetta, pulling her across the roof as the gargoyles leapt to surround the Archangel.

'Get her, Blake, take her from this place,' Abram shouted as he was forced back to the battlements by the swords of the encircling gargoyles, lashing out as they laughed through their sharp stone teeth.

Gallicus ran the three paces to Blake and pushed him to the ground, squashing him against the stone and holding him fast with one arm.

'Quickly!' shouted Yerzinia. 'Hold the girl and make her ready for me. It will not be long before we are together again, Isaac. This time, no one will stand in our way.'

'You cheated me, Isaac. After all these years we have been together, deeper than any friendship, is your concern only for yourself?' Blake demanded, held tight by Gallicus.

'She is my only desire, I can get more wisdom from her in one minute than from you in a lifetime,' Bonham replied. Then he unbound the Nemorensis, opening its pages and placing it in the centre of the circle. He took Agetta by the arm and held her at the north tip of the star before Yerzinia.

'Don't let your life be taken by that woman,' Blake screamed as Gallicus crushed his face into the stonework.

The Nemorensis grew larger, filling the centre of the circle and pulsating white light from the heart of its pages.

'And you wouldn't? I know what your thoughts were, your heart had been melted like mine but you didn't have the courage.'

'What when you get too old and she needs someone else and she discards you like she has Flamberg?'

'Then I will die a happy man,' Isaac replied, gazing at Yerzinia. 'Now is the time, the book is ready, the comet comes and this creature waits for you.'

'It'll destroy you all,' Abram shouted as the Nemorensis doubled in size, the pages bursting forth from the spine and spiralling into the air. 'You don't know what you are doing, Yerzinia.' He kicked out at the gargoyles that pressed him to the battlements.

'You forget – this is *my* book. I wrote every word, my heart is etched into its pages, I know what it will do. Tonight I will be transformed for the last time. No more having to jump from flesh to flesh as the centuries turn. When the stars and the Nemorensis come together in her flesh I will stay for ever.'

'And her flesh shall rot on your bones and you will never see the light of dawn,' Abram screamed.

'Curses from the mouth of an angel? Desperation brings you to me. Can't you see it's even within *your* heart to fall? There must have been some temptation, something to take your mind from blind servitude and seek a true life. No one could sit in his presence and do his will for ever. There is still time, Raphael . . .'

'Wormwood shall fall from the sky and poison the waters and bring death to many, but you – *you* will burn in an eternal fire.'

'Words, meaningless words to deceive the gullible and keep them in fear. At least what I have written has power. Look, Raphael, see for yourself how my creation takes shape and my magic fills the air.'

Abram looked up. Before him the Nemorensis stood like a glowing pillar of white marble, every page locked together and reaching skywards. Around the column a thick red cord twisted, unravelling as it span around. At its base the spine of the book had grown thicker, its gold letters twisting upwards and outwards. High above, the comet flew towards earth and the moon rose higher into the sky, as if the two would come together at any second.

From the east a howling wind lifted the water from the river, standing it like a tall spinning fountain, sucking up the dead from their watery graves and lifting the debris of crushed boats high into the air. Like a tall spectre it walked the river towards them, twisting and turning from one bank to the other, sucking up and spewing out time and again.

'One more sign,' Yerzinia shouted. 'One more sign and it will be time. The waters have given up their dead. The moon shall rise and Wormwood cometh. Hold the girl steady. I can feel the moment.'

Yerzinia clutched her stomach and writhed as if she was being ripped from the inside, birthing a spectre. Like a woman crazed she tore at her clothing and pulled the tiger mask from her head.

Blake twisted free from Gallicus and rolled across the floor, leaving his assailant to cower by the wall, hands covering his face like a frightened child. Bonham turned his head, unable to look at the transformation as he held Agetta tight with fingers that burrowed into her skin. Yerzinia staggered across the roof towards him, holding out her hands to Agetta.

'Come to me child, come to me,' she said as she drew closer. 'Let the child go, she must stand alone, there must be no compulsion.' Yerzinia stared into Agetta's eyes. 'When we first met I promised you a different life, that we could be friends. Do this for me and we will be together for ever. My life will be your life and I will show you the world and the heavens. They will be yours to keep. Open your heart to me, open your heart and I will join with you.'

Agetta remembered the first time she had seen Yerzinia smile, her face hidden by the tiger mask, her eyes sparkling like crisp jewels. The smell of Absinthium filled her mind again, stirring a deep longing . . . 'I will,' she said quietly. 'I will open my heart willingly, I became one with you in the carriage and would do anything in life or in death.'

'She plays with your mind,' Blake shouted, rushing towards her.

Bonham aimed his pistol and fired. The shot rang out across the rooftops and the ball hit Blake in the chest, knocking him to the floor.

'Then it is time.' Yerzinia smiled at Agetta. 'Give your hand to me . . . Quickly, we need to hold the moon,' she said, her face racked with pain.

Agetta held out her hand, taking hold of Yerzinia. A sudden pulse jumped through her arm, juddering every bone, rattling them in her flesh.

'Lift up your hands to the moon, welcome it to your life,' Yerzinia said as she leant against the pillar of the Nemorensis, wrapping the red cord around her wrist. 'When the comet strikes, Lady Flamberg will be no more.'

A crashing of ice crystals invaded the sky, smashing through the atmosphere and falling to earth around the city and beyond. The buildings on the bridge quaked as meteors plunged into the river, boiling the water and sending up explosions of hissing gas. Wormwood grew brighter in the eastern sky as it plunged nearer to the earth from behind the moon.

Abram shouted out: 'Lesser light, be stilled by the Hidden Name!' He kicked a way through the gargoyles that guarded him.

'It's too late for your meddling, you cannot stop the moon,' Yerzinia shouted, gripping Agetta harder and harder.

Abram shouted again: 'Lesser light, be stilled by the Hidden Name!' He held up his hand to the sky.

'Quickly, look at me, child,' Yerzinia said as she turned to face Agetta.

There was a sudden and deep groan as Yerzinia opened her mouth to release the spirit. A long vine of thick white mass issued from her body and hovered above her like some fat snake before taking shape. It blew back and forth, still attached to Yerzinia, waiting for the moment to inhabit its victim.

Then Tegatus ran from the shadowy stairway, from the darkness into the light. He was half-dead, his face was scorched with the blast from the Abaris crystal, and the last beats of his broken heart carried him across the roof. Summoning all of his strength he grabbed Yerzinia, pulling her from the girl and the Nemorensis as he tugged the red cord free from the column. The Nemorensis shrank back, the pages imploding upon themselves as the column compacted into the book. In one continuous movement, like some forgotten dance, Tegatus pressed Yerzinia towards the parapet. Bonham and Gallicus chased after him in their surprise.

As he pushed her across the roof he twisted the cord around his wrist and looped the end around her neck. The spirit was sucked swiftly within like a coiling snake as the noose quickly tightened. Yerzinia lashed out, tearing the flesh from his face as she screamed for him to stop. The spirit was stuck within her, bound by the cord, and her body erupted in huge sores that festered and rotted the flesh.

'You cannot stop me, Tegatus. Even your jealous heart will never take me in death,' she cried out as they stumbled towards the edge, high above the Thames.

Abram slammed his hand on to the sword of the final gargoyle, splattering it with his blood. The creature exploded from within into purple flames that powdered the stone with their intensity. Then Abram ran to Bonham and with one blow he dropped him to the floor, the bag of pistol shot and black powder spilling across the roof.

Tegatus pulled Yerzinia to the parapet as Gallicus ran towards him. Yerzinia screamed and grappled with Tegatus and tried to rip his eyes from their sockets as the plague blistered her skin, turning her into an old hag.

'The last flight of our hearts will be in death,' Tegatus shouted above the sound of distant explosions, and he dragged her from the roof to the surging whirlpool far below.

Yerzinia swooped to her grave like an injured bird, dragging Tegatus down and down to the black water. They crashed into the river, the spray sizzling with an otherworldly heat as Yerzinia fought to be free from the raging flood. For a brief moment wings spread from her body as she reclaimed her angelic state and tried to rise from the foam like a swan beating its wings against the crushing tide. But Tegatus still pulled on the cord, dragging her to him as he sank into the dark waters. The whirlpool that swirled through the archway sucked them quickly into the depths, and they vanished out of sight into the thick blackness.

'He took her from me,' Bonham cried as he got to his feet. 'He had no right . . . She was mine.'

'She belonged to no one, not even to you,' Abram said as he walked towards him.

'Then the girl shall join them,' Gallicus said gruffly, and he held Agetta against the wall of the battlements.

Abram looked at the blood that trickled from the sword wound in his hand. 'Remember what I whispered to you, Agetta. Now is the time to remember.'

'Perfect love casts out all fear,' she said, smiling at him.

He took a quick pace forwards and flicked a drop of blood from his finger at Gallicus. 'Blood for blood,' he said to Gallicus, and Agetta leapt away from him as he began to tremble and shake. His eyes bulged from his face, thick white smoke billowed from his nose and mouth, and flames flashed like a blue mist over his skin.

'Tares, ripe for the fire,' Abram said, and he pushed him from the battlement to the water below.

Wormwood arched towards the moon, its orbit pulled towards

the lesser light. The whole earth shuddered as the comet crashed into the moon's dark side, sending plumes of lunar dust high into space. It fractured on the surface and exploded towards the earth in a million pieces of tiny ice fragments that twisted and spun across the sky.

'What now, Yerzinia? Wormwood is caught like a moth in a web,' Abram said to the wind as he walked towards Blake. 'Don't worry, I have done this before,' he said, laughing as he plunged his hand into Blake's chest. 'See the ball I hold – and you never felt more than a twinge, my dear friend.'

Seizing his chance, Bonham grabbed the Nemorensis and ran to the stairway like a frightened dog.

Blake looked up at the sky, which was ablaze with the sparkling of ice crystals as they beat against the planet. Agetta stared at him, unsure what she had seen, as high above came a sound like the wing-beat of angels.

'You will be her keeper,' Abram said as he gave Blake her hand. 'She is a friend and not a servant, though in that she will serve you well.'

'Bonham?' Blake asked.

'He will run and hide and yes, he will trouble you again. But fear not – I am the guardian of your blood.'

Abram turned and walked to the stairway. They listened as the sound of his footsteps faded into the softening night. The brightness of the sky ebbed to darkness as the final meteors evaporated in the heavens.

'Tegatus is gone,' Agetta said as she looked down the Thames. 'He died to save me.'

'The night is not yet over and the battle not yet won. Come . . . let us go and see Mrs Malakin, she will doubtless be cowering in the cellar.' He smiled and looked at Agetta. 'I once met a man who said he would never believe in angels, perhaps that *is* the only safe thing to believe . . .'